JOSEPH CONNOLLY

S.O.S.

ff

faber and faber

First published in 2001
by Faber and Faber Limited
3 Queen Square London WC1N 3AU
This paperback edition first published in 2002

Phototypeset by Intype London Ltd
Printed in England by Mackays of Chatham plc, Chatham, Kent

© Joseph Connolly, 2002

The right of Joseph Connolly to be identified as author
of this work has been asserted in accordance with Section 77
of the Copyright, Designs and Patents Act 1988

A CIP record for this book
is available from the British Library
ISBN 0–571–20439–2

2 4 6 8 10 9 7 5 3 1

S.O.S.

Joseph Connolly is the bestselling author of six other novels: *Poor Souls* (1995), *This is it* (1996), *Stuff* (1997), *Summer Things* (1998), *Winter Breaks* (1999) and *It Can't Go On* (2000). He has also written several works of non-fiction including admired biographies of Jerome K. Jerome and P.G. Wodehouse, and the standard work on book collecting, *Modern First Editions*.

'Connolly's hyper-real stream of consciousness prose and his unique characterisation are on top form. He is a writer of supreme hilarity who also possesses an unnerving and disarming eye for human frailty.' *The Times*

'Joseph Connolly ... is horribly funny about the lives people trap themselves in. His laughter is a snarl, a hoot, a howl.' *Observer*

'This is the kind of high-octane writing that reaches into the reader and tickles the part of the brain that controls the level of excitation. Sheer stimulation in the satisfaction one derives from being so dramatically engaged. Hilarious.' *Hampstead and Highgate Express*

'Thanks to our all-seeing narrator, we're made privy to everyone's innermost thoughts ... a deliciously mischievous tale.' *Daily Mail*

'A brilliantly funny novel ... you'll love S.O.S.' *Punch*

by the same author

fiction

POOR SOULS

THIS IS IT

STUFF

SUMMER THINGS

WINTER BREAKS

IT CAN'T GO ON

non-fiction

COLLECTING MODERN FIRST EDITIONS

P.G. WODEHOUSE

JEROME K. JEROME: A CRITICAL BIOGRAPHY

MODERN FIRST EDITIONS: THEIR VALUE TO COLLECTORS

THE PENGUIN BOOK QUIZ BOOK

CHILDREN'S MODERN FIRST EDITIONS

BESIDE THE SEASIDE

ALL SHOOK UP: A FLASH OF THE FIFTIES

To Jon Riley

PART ONE

Plain Sailing

I'm in my bed, then, and blinking about in the only light I'm getting – peering here and there and in and out of corners: yeah, my room all right – know that wallpaper anywhere. It's what, now, must it be? Hey? Seven? Eight, more like, most probably. Yes. And I'm trying to make the flutter of my eyelids not too, you know – disturbing for my wife. Who, when I got in, um – not really that long ago, I suppose – seems quite recent (head doesn't hurt yet – stomach still numb: you just wait, mate) . . . mm – wife, officially declared herself dead from the neck up – was I hearing her? Only that way could she hope to continue. How could I *do* this to her, she despairingly implored (again, oh good God – yes again, again), on this bloody morning of all bloody mornings? Well, quite easy really. A sort of flair made good by practice. I'm a past master of the fuck-up, and making you quietly hate me.

Blinking – still blinking. But not actually moving my head at all, see, because I don't want to disturb in any way whatever my wife. Nicole. Is my wife's name. I don't really think she needs any more disruption, do you? Not after everything. I'm actually trying to locate my jacket . . . which, oh dear Christ (here's a nauseous feeling, but it's not the sickness, yet: here is just a convulsion – my stomach is always the first to know when I've let me down) . . . the jacket, yes, I sort of remember I sold. At some point during. For not very much. Dear oh dear. Actually . . . Nicole, I now register (my cautious toe, just barely shifting) doesn't now seem to be here. I maybe recall her declaration: a strangulated expression of determination to be elsewhere right *now*, David, because *some* of us, yes? Have things to do? *Responsibilities.* Is all this stuff going to pack itself? I think not. Is how she went. Mmm. And she's right, she's right – of *course* she's right. Always is. Can't be easy, can it? Not a bit.

Able to move about a bit more freely now, then. My watch is still on my wrist, no more scratches than usual: something. Wallet? Best not to enquire. Know soon enough. It's a bit like being a detective, this, picking over the remaining effects of someone else entirely. While trying to piece together at the scene of the crime – my crime, mine – just what sort of a person we're dealing with, here. (My crime, yes – and I seem to be the victim, too; not *exclusively*, of course – oh God no: there are many others, lots and lots.)

Just look at the state of those trousers (not the jacket: the jacket is *sold*); but Christ – just take a look at them, would you? How did they get to be so corkscrewed as that? And I'll bet you the fastenings are still tightly done; or else half ripped open. Tie's on the floor – well, you expect that. One shoe there – and the other somewhere else, we can only assume. God oh God. And on this morning of all mornings. Because I did – made a point of it: said I'd be back for dinner, you just tell me the time. Do you *mean* it, she'd gone, Nicole. Because you're always *saying* it, David, aren't you? And I never ever know what to *think*. He won't be back, asserted Rollo with confidence – and a trace, oh yes, of a smirk. Well – seventeenish now, what can you say? (Expect I was the same.) *Look*, Rollo, I'd gone (paternal authority? Don't make me laugh), I've said I'll be back, and back I'll bloody be, OK? Oh yeh? goes Rollo – *when*, exactly? Tuesday? Wednesday? Oh *leave* him, went Marianne, my little protector: God's *sake*, Rollo – you're always on and on at Dad: just *leave* him, OK? He knows we've got this trip tomorrow, doesn't he? And we're leaving early, and things. So he'll *be* here, kay? He's not *stupid*.

Ah. Got to face her, shortly. She won't *say* anything, or anything, won't quite look at me. But later, she might – a quick half-smile, eyes just tilted as her lips flatten out (yes

4

OK, Daddy, I *do* still love you, sure – but *honestly* . . .). Dear little Marianne. My own little girl.

Over there, over the chair, there's a very neat gathering of clothes. My clothes for today. Nicole will have done that, quite early last evening. She will have tipped my dinner into the bin – scraping away at the plate to be rid of all the last and tainted residue (if only life, it maybe crossed her mind, could be so simple) and then, quite without knowing why – well, in truth, in no doubt at all: *someone's* got to, haven't they? *Someone* must – she will have laid out the pre-agreed outfit for this bleeding glorified boat trip. Blazer, but of course. Linen shirt, looks like. Trousers I wear for Lord's. Ought to be so grateful. Really should be.

Got to get up. The bustle in the house is growing louder, the shifts of anticipation you can nearly feel. It's not now officially early any more, is the message I'm vaguely getting (don't ask me what time it is exactly, I simply couldn't tell you: watch has stopped, maybe broken: anyway not going – not at all giving me the information). For a while now, Nicole will have gone Oh – just let him sleep it off: everything's more or less done anyway. And Rollo will have honked out Oh – so he did actually make it home, then, did he, eventually? And Marianne, well . . . I doubt, actually, that she will have been around to witness this latest put-down of her put-upon father because any sort of outing for Marianne was ushered in by what seemed like hours – sometimes was – in one of the bathrooms, and so this Trip of a Lifetime (that's how it was billed: 'Trip of a Lifetime'. Christ. So when do we die, then? During or after?). Jesus. I really don't want to go, you know. Really not at all keen on it – wasn't, from the off. Anyway . . . now what was I . . .? Oh yeh – Marianne: she will have been doing whatever it was girls did in bathrooms for bloody ages, now, and so left to themselves, well – Nicole and Rollo will have had a field day: she resigned and capable, and he just going for the kill.

So. Best stir myself on the whole, I think. Car's booked

5

for eleven, that much I do know – and eleven has this way of inching up and confronting you. I think, you know, that last night was largely Willis's fault –

'David. Christ's sake. Get bloody up. Now. It's *today* we're leaving. *Today*.'

Jesus. Wasn't ready for that little whirlwind. She just burst in, Nicole, swiped a could-be cardigan, launched that little lot over in my direction, and now she's gone again (slammed the door). All dressed and scented, though – took that much in. And she's got a point: if we're going we're going, right? So *move* yourself, bastard.

But you see, if Willis hadn't *insisted* . . . I mean look: couple of pints after work, this sort of summer weather, where's the harm in that? But then bloody Willis had gone Hey, Dave – why don't we pop down to Terry's for just the one, what say? And I said no *way*, Willis old son – and you know why. Once we get down to Terry's . . . And you never did, ever, have to finish that sentence because everyone knew, everyone who went there, just how the ending would be. Oh come *on*, Dave mate – just a quick sharpener, and then out. And OK yes, I knew what he meant – I mean, two or so pints are all very well for knocking the corners off the thing, but then you're left in a sort of nowhere land, really, and home doesn't seem quite right. So. Famous Grouse was the nature of the sharpener – shot down flocks of them (droves, herds, however they come). Oh dear God – I'm beginning to get just a hint of the truth that I'll soon feel bad. Why do they call them that, actually? Sharpeners. When all they do is make you blunt.

So after quite a lot of that, I went round to see Trish. And did bloody Willis raise one finger to try and stop me? Like a good mate should? Did he say: Hey, Dave – steady, OK? We've had a few, right, and you're meant to be going on this bloody ship thing in the morning (Christ look at it – *is* the morning), so don't you think you ought to get Terry to call up a taxi and get yourself home? Did he say that? Well actually, thinking about it, he very well could've . . . *some-body* did, anyway . . . hard to quite recall. All the faces, voices – they blend, don't they, after a while. You end up with little save the odour of a muffed bit of lust, and maybe just the curl of a lip in anger – but quite where these pieces belong . . . well, anyone's guess, really: who can say? And the thing is, more than ever I shouldn't have gone round to Trish's. Quite apart from the real need to get home and all the rest of the gubbins staring me stark in the face, I'd *seen* Trish, hadn't I, just the night before – that was the night we'd arranged to say our, oh God, heartfelt au revoirs before I set off on this blighted cruise, or whatever they call it (oh yeh – not cruise, no: Trip of a Lifetime. Christ).

'I still don't see,' Trish had pouted – took her to that restaurant in Greek Street, funny name: likes it there – 'why you actually have to *go*. I mean you said you didn't *want* to, so why – ?'

'Been over all that, haven't we, Trish?' And by Christ hadn't we: over and over, up and down, in and out – Jesus it's wearing, tell you. '*Don't* want to go – wouldn't have crossed my mind. But it's . . . well, don't bite my head off – the *family*, isn't it?'

Bloody stupid. Worst thing to say. Took a good bit of finger-pawing, doe-eyes and chin-chucking (not to say another bleeding bottle of Lanson) to hoick my way out of that one. And all the time I was feeling resentful. I mean – why *me*? If Nicole hadn't entered the fucking competition, she never would've won the fucking prize, would she? And my whole life wouldn't now be in lumber. I don't want to go to New bloody York on the *Transylvania*, do I? (And what sort of bloody name is that for a ship?) Never would've dreamed of it in the whole of my lifetime. But something like this comes along – whole family, twelve days all in, Trip of a Lifetime – costing them a bloody fortune (cash alternative? You think I didn't check?) what actually can you do? And at the time, when the news came through –

should've seen Nicole's face, she had looked so young again: skipping about with Marianne and Rollo, all like kids at playschool – it had seemed so very far into the future as to cry out for shoving into the bulging box of admittedly dreadful things – but God, no time to dread them *yet*. And then suddenly, well – it's all over you.

Got Trish in a crème brulée with maraschino and funny little biscuits.

'*Any way* . . .' I'm oiling, 'it's only for a *bit*.'

'Not just a bit, though, is it?'

'Week. Nine days . . .'

'Twelve.'

'Twelve . . . Fine. Not that long, is it? Drop in the – '

And already the ocean was vast between us. So I'm thinking – this is the joke of it, really – I'm thinking *Yes*: yes it bloody is a long time and I don't want to *go*. Why is nobody hearing me? Hey? Don't want to *go*. Nicole started in weeks back: You don't want to *go*, do you David? *Course* I do, I hugely protest (stock reaction). You *don't* – I *know* you don't. And then I'm thinking Well if you know I don't (and you're right, you're right – you always are: I don't) why did you bloody insist that I come? In the first place? Hey? Right early on I went, Look Nicole – why don't just you and Marianne and Rollo go, hey? And maybe take your friend Annie to make up the numbers; got so much *work* on at the moment, haven't I, love? You won't *work*, she shoots back at me (razor-tipped, all this now, and steeped in something nasty) – you just want to *drink* and see your *woman*. Oh God. Walked right into it, didn't I? Like I always do. So on with the wide eyes – the hurt, white shocked-awake face: *Woman*? What *woman*? What are you going on about a *woman* now for, Godsake? I've *told* you, Nicole, there is no – Oh fuck off David! (and now she's screaming) I've just about had it with you up to *here*: you're bloody coming and that's the end of it, OK? Even this – even this big free thing, you're determined, aren't you, to fuck it up for everyone?!

8

Well no: determination doesn't enter. It's just a by-product – a gratis spin-off of what I do, and who I am. I didn't want to go simply because I just didn't want to go. Sometimes things *are* that simple – but you just try telling it to a female. I mean, sure – if I'd been allowed to (oh joy) stay in my own house and live my own life, one or two trips down Trish's way could well have been part and parcel of the general scheme of things, but it wasn't as if this was the *point*. And Annie – Nicole's friend, Annie – Christ, she would've jumped at it, Annie would: never seemed to go anywhere, poor old sod. But I well understand that if Annie had tagged along, then Nicole would have annihilated at a stroke the huge back debt of slavering envy that would soon become her eternal due, and which she no doubt intended to exact quite teasingly while levying upon each trans-atlantic anecdote a stiff and mandatory surtax (while holding interest down).

She doesn't understand me, my wife. They say that, don't they? In jokes. Half-drunk old nutters are supposed to, aren't they, say that to some thicko doxy who'll nod to just anything if there's three bloody courses in it, and then a taxi home (her home, mind, and generally alone: got to be fresh for tomorrow when she's due to spend quality time with some dough-faced, puny and penniless young loser whom she'll stroke and subsidize, coax and encourage, and then beg the bastard to fuck her blind). But me, I use this as no line: Nicole, she *thinks* she understands me – thinks she knows me inside out like all wives do, but she doesn't, she doesn't – and nor will she ever, at this rate of progress (nineteen years, and counting). Example: one night I come home, decent hour – eleven, thereabouts – and OK, I'd had a fair time with Trish, cards on the table, but on the way home I got to thinking You know what, old lad, it's not right, this: it's with *Nicole* I should be up to all this malarkey – Nicole, my wife – as well as (and here is maybe the point, why I ever started to stray) mother of my children. So anyway, I'm looking at her just sitting there, Nicole, watching some or other film on Channel could it be 4 (*sh*! she'd hissed at me, it's just coming up to the finish) and I blurted out – *Nicole*! Listen! Make me the happiest man alive! And she turned and she looked at me – and for just one crazy instant something within me leapt up from somewhere deep and I thought: Result! And then she said: I'm not divorcing you, if that's what you mean. And then she said: I've missed the bloody ending now – well, you certainly managed to fuck *that* up, didn't you David?

Or words to that effect. So I'm getting it in the neck from Nicole because, you see, I'm going on the *Transylvania* to New York when I don't *want* to (she hates me for not wanting to – so why can't I stay? No, not an option, I'm afraid) and I'm getting it too from Trish for precisely the same bloody reason – except, of course, that she's convinced that I can't bloody *wait* (all this interlarded with the usual corollary that I never, do I, take her *anywhere*). Not true! I once tried that – attempted to be, oh God, *amusing*: slumped back in her pillows and roared up to the ceiling 'I take you, Trish, all the way to heaven and back!' Did she laugh? Did she? Well what do *you* think? Yeh – you're right. She just wagged her head a bit and went, she said, to run a bath. I sometimes think: what am I doing all this for? Why do I, you know – go *on* with it? Because I sometimes think I'd be all right, me, all on my own.

⚓

Heaven and back: yes sure, David – very funny. Ho ho. God – lately, it's got to be that even the sex with you (and that's all there's really been between us for too long, now) is hardly more than just barely *achieved*. Trish, you go: I'm just so *tired*, you know . . .? Well no, David, I *don't* know, frankly. You *may* be tired – you may well be, I'm not saying you're not. But *primarily*, David, what you are is pissed on a pretty much permanent basis. You seem to leave the office later and later – and always, no matter what you've promised, you always have to go to some bloody *pub* with one of your ghastly so-called friends and by the time you get here the candles I lit for you are guttered and the bubbles and oils in the big, hot bath I drew for us both have dissipated, and long ago I sat there and cried as I watched the whole chilled mess of it drain away. The food I've cooked you don't want – I've *eaten* is what you always say to me, but you haven't, David, you haven't: what you've done is *drink*. And so just about all you are up to and good for is tugging like an ape – no *grace*, David: there's no *art* in what you do – at whatever quite delicious silk and lacy thing I'm in for you, and then when I've shown you how it ought to be done, you focus first and feast your eyes and then just fall across me, David – thunder down on me like a newly slit open sack of tumbling potatoes, and I am no more than the floor beneath you. And even then, if I left you to, oh God – *please* get on with it, all you'd do is fall asleep. How many times, David? How many times has that happened? How many times have I whispered to you, shouted at you, cursed you to hell and then squirmed my bloody way out from under the sheer and reeking rat-arsed weight of you? Only if I bite you repeatedly and make like a milkmaid with all of my fingers – only then are you likely to make it. And me? I experience little more than a jerked-out shudder and an immediate subsidence, followed by damp. So why do I want you? Why do I want you so terribly much? Why is it that I want you to leave your bloody *wife* and come and stay with me? And *talking* of your bloody wife – just *don't*: OK? Let's just not. And don't please talk to me about, Christ – family *holidays* – don't even mention one single thing about your life together, all right? Because I simply can't bear it. I'm thirty-six years old now, David: next stop forty. I want, I need – a man of my *own*; but more than that – someone to take care

11

of me: you, David, you. Don't ask me why you – maybe simply because it's you who's here, and there's no one else.

And then you leave. As soon as you wake up, you drink some of the wine I chose and uncorked and left there to breathe: it must be exhausted by now. Sometimes you don't even pour it into a glass. Would you, could you think of doing that anywhere else but here? Could you? At a party? In one of your horrible pubs? God – at *home*, would you? When you're with your family and your bloody *wife*? Just pick up a bottle of burgundy and upend it to your lips and down your throat? No. I don't think so. But you do with me. And maybe because here, with me, is the only time you can really let go: be yourself? Because I couldn't really say – can't, no, in all honesty recall, how on earth you behave when you're out. Because never – and I don't care *what* you say, David – never, ever do you take me anywhere: nowhere at all. Oh yes: you're going to mention, aren't you, those three days away – aren't you, David? Those precious and distant three days away, when your bloody kids and your bloody wife were staying with, who was it? Her mother? Not her mother? Anyway – staying somewhere with someone, doesn't matter. And you took me away to that little hotel just outside of Oxford – and *yes*, David, it was bliss. Yes it was – it was divine, totally – but it was, oh God oh God, so very long *ago*, David: so very long ago. And even then you stole from me the final afternoon because you had to get back – go back home, you said, so that you could prepare. *Prepare*, I remember going (and already, although you hadn't even left me, I was missing you terribly). *Prepare*, I said – prepare for *what*, in God's name? And at first you would not say – and then, in time and eventually, you slowly told me. You had to rumple up and thump down upon the marital bed (because she, your bloody *wife*, would never expect you to have made it) and also you had to pour away four, maybe five big bottles of Evian (because she, your bloody *wife*, knew that you would have drunk that

12

much at least to slake your permanent alcoholic dehydration – and of course you would never have thought of buying more). Pans had to be greased, plates and cups and glasses sullied and smeared and stacked up in piles by the sink. And then later you told me you had twice choked up the lavatory, feeding it sheet after sheet of virgin Andrex (the empty roll destined to garnish the bags of household rubbish that somehow had to be cobbled together, and of course just left there to rot); on the second occasion the plunger, you said, just wasn't up to coping and so you had to call out an emergency plumber and that, you told me – to my face and deadpan – was forty-five quid down the drain.

So why do I want you? Why do I want you so terribly much? Why is it that I want you to leave your bloody *wife* and come and stay with me? I don't know. I don't know. I just know I want, need – *someone* to take care of me: a man of my own. And do I think this can ever happen? I don't know. I don't know. I just don't know.

⚓

'David!'

Jesus Jesus.

'David! Now this, now, is the absolute *limit* – !'

'I'm getting up I'm getting up I'm getting up – look, I'm getting – see? I'm up I'm up I'm up.'

Nicole's fists were thumped into her hips: nice hips, oh yes – still quite trim, Nicole, as David saw with such mixed feelings.

'You disgust me,' she said – and quietly, which was rather scary, actually.

David nodded, when she'd gone. Disgust her, yes: he knew he did, he knew it, and he more or less understood why.

Felt a bit better once he'd splashed his face and fooled around with a toothbrush; gave up flossing – made him gag

13

(and that blue-green Listerine he couldn't help but swallow). This linen shirt feels nice, he was thinking now – and *then* he thought Oh by Christ yes: the *other* reason (how could I have forgotten?) I don't want to go: what the doctor said. The other day.

'Think on balance we ought to take a closer little look, Mister Arm. Could be nothing at all to worry about, but . . .'

'Uh-huh. Uh-huh. How soon do you think we ought to, um . . .?'

'Well – no *crashing* hurry, of course, but I don't really think we ought to leave it *that* long. Just a probe – see what's going on, yes?'

'Mm. Right. It's just that I'm going away . . . short while . . .'

'No problem at all, Mister Arm. Don't let it spoil your holiday. Where going? Somewhere nice? You don't have BUPA, do you? Something of that order?'

'Used to, but I . . . No. Don't.'

'It's just that we don't want to hang around *too* long, do we? Want to have it done privately?'

Well, thought David – I don't want a fucking audience.

'Will it, um . . .?'

'Cost much? Well – these things *do*, of course . . .'

David nodded: yes they do. These things, and others.

Still. Back to the present: never mind all that now. That's in the 'Pending Dread' box. Slip on the blazer, that's what to do. Ah – wallet *is* on the side, here: that is good. Sod all in it, mind, but one thing at a time, hey? Wait up – what's all this on the dressing table? A tenner, a fiver, and one, two, three pounds and what? Forty pence or so. Hm. I think that's what old what's-his-face beat me down to for the jacket. (My head, you know, is just beginning to cloud.)

Marianne didn't quite look at him as he ventured down the stairs – but then she just couldn't resist:

'Hello, Daddy!' she sang to him. 'Happy holiday!'

14

'Oh!' scoffed Rollo. 'So you did actually make it home then, did you, eventually?'

'Quiet, Rollo,' said Nicole, though sounding really quite encouraging. 'Now is everyone sure they've *got* everything, yes? I'll keep all the passports together with the tickets so we know where we are. Rollo, do you *have* to wear that awful MiniDisc thing all the time?'

Marianne sidled over to David and rubbed her shoulder up against his.

'It's going to be *great*,' she whispered.

David looked down at the light in her sweet, bright eyes.

'I know,' he said. 'I know it is.'

The cab-driver and Rollo were loading up the cases, and David looked back inside into the now dead hall. No point checking everything's off – Nicole will have seen to all that. His eye fell upon a wooden wine crate lodged under the table, now chock-full of all their wellingtons. Ah yes – the petit château, the cru bourgeois: one of his more recent attempts to wean himself away from the all-engulfing wings of the Famous Grouse. This will drink well until 2008, the wine bloke had told him – a judgement that had proved to be quite wide of the mark on account he'd necked the lot in the space of a weekend.

I wonder, thought David (on this morning of all mornings) as he clanged shut the front door ('Here,' said Nicole, jostling him aside, 'let me make sure the deadlocks are done') . . . I wonder, on the ship, whether I'll be sick or not. And how, more generally, the thing will go. This Trip of a Lifetime. Or, in rounder terms, quite in which way and how thoroughly I'll fuck it all up.

⚓

'Bloody hell – just look at you, Stewart. What's wrong? Never seen you look so down,' sort of laughed Jilly, holding out a mug.

'Ah Jilly,' sighed Stewart.

He had now just about lifted up his eyes, this is true, but his head still hung low from the scaffold of his fingers. One hand now detached itself, leaving dimpled white puckers on a seemingly quite cooked and very closely-razored cheek. It pointedly picked up papers from his small cramped desk wedged into a corner of the small cramped berth that was all the unseeing fools on high had seen fit to allocate to the administration of, oh – only every single *vestige* of round-the-clock entertainment that was so huge a part of the dazzling and ever upbeat deal offered to all our cherished passengers, and sucked up greedily by practically the lot of them. The stiffened fingers released their hold on the papers – pink, blue, green and flimsy – and one by one they fluttered back down where they would (some slipped over the edge to the floor, and there they can bloody well stay).

'They think – you know what they think, Jilly? They think it's *easy*. Everyone does. Not just the bosses but the passengers – oh God *they* do, I can see it every trip. They look at me and they think, God – what a wanker. Free trip, they think. They think – '

'What are you *talking* about, Stewart? They love you, the passengers – they all do, all the time.'

'Love me? *Love* me? Oh God, Jilly, don't be so bloody ridiculous. They're simply – well-*disposed*, is all they are. One of these crossings, everyone likes *everyone*, don't they? All part of getting your money's worth. And that's our *job*.'

'Bloody hell, Stewart. Leave this coffee here, will I? Never *seen* you like this.'

Stewart was making some sort of hissing sound through his teeth as he leant back heavily in his chair, which creaked beneath him. His plaited fingers were forming a hammock for the back of his head, and now the low, bright white and riveted ceiling seemed to have claimed his attention.

'No, Jilly, no – the reason, mm ... *why* you have never

16

before seen me 'like this', as you so kindly put it, is I think because you have never maybe encountered me before we set sail. *After* . . . ah! Different thing. Different me. Of course I'm not like this *then*. We set sail – I, as it were, take off. Follow? What I'm for. I tell you this, though, Jilly.' He leant forward now with energy and started jabbing at her a brown and tapered finger. 'There's only one job harder, more gruelling – shall I tell you? On this bloody ship, there's just one job that's tougher than Cruise Director. Know what it is? No? Guesses?'

Jilly just stood there and slapped on her simpleton look. She could be guessing all night, wouldn't matter: Stewart was going to *tell* her, wasn't he? Just you try and stop him.

'Captain, you think? The Master?' Stewart suggested airily, as if plucking idle possibilities from out of the blue beyond his porthole. 'No no. Piece of cake. Chief Engineer? Born to it: no prob. Or maybe you think it's chambermaids who have drawn the short straw on this transatlantic miracle of ours, do you? Wrong – all wrong. Chambermaids, well – no picnic, I grant you – but if they weren't chambermaiding on board they'd only be doing it somewhere else, wouldn't they? And at least the food they get's OK. No – tell you, shall I? The only job worse – '

'Coffee's getting cold, Stewart.'

'The only thing, job worse – don't want coffee, sick of coffee, been drinking the bloody stuff all night – the only job worse than Cruise Director is, yes – hole in one: *Assistant* Cruise Director: *that's* the bloody bastard.'

Jilly nodded, and sort of grinned a bit.

'Uh-huh. You, in other words.'

Stewart nodded too, and God so grimly.

'No other words for it, are there? *Me*, yes me – me, in a bloody nutshell. Don't ever get to organise anything from the *start*, oh no – commissioning and hiring and booking are deemed, oh Christ – way beyond me. I just have to see it all *happens* – and God help me if there's a hitch or a clash or

17

some other bloody cock-up because then it's all down to Stewart, isn't it? *My* bloody fault then, isn't it? Ay?'

Jilly was shifting uneasily. This was becoming rather, what? Unsettling? Bit. Over the, you know – top, kind of? Kind of, yeh. But mainly dull, the way people's griping always is (like – boring?).

'Stewart . . .' she regretted, raising her eyebrows and backing towards the door (her feet instinctively detecting the step and deftly overcoming it) ' . . . things to do, yeh? Sailing in less than three hours, now . . .'

'Mm. Don't I know it. Two hours and fifty-eight minutes, if we're searching for accuracy. Which means that everything that isn't on board for the next six days' and nights' entertainment, well – anything I've forgotten, we've all just *had* it, haven't we?'

'I'll leave you to get on with it. Poor Stewart.'

And she quickly decided Right – now or never (and she hopped it). Yeh – poor Stewart, I suppose, thought Jilly, walking the vast and deserted length of the covered Upper Deck, the thick new carpet smelling more thick and new and quite a bit sick-makingly carpety with each hushed-up step (still, though: bit of a wanker).

Stewart went back to filleting his stacks of duplicated paper, and exhaling with force, he flicked back on his PowerBook while scratching quite wildly at his scalp, and it wasn't even itchy. Have to see Margo for a wash and highlights, very soon. Half an hour. Got to be spruce: got to be ready to meet and greet.

'*And*,' he suddenly boomed out into the empty office. 'If I *do* . . . if I *do* actually, oh Christ – get it right, who gets all the bloody praise? The *Assistant* Cruise Director? I should bleeding cocoa: bloody *no*.'

No indeed: too right. Any form of credit is very much the fiefdom of the *actual* bloody Cruise Director, who never even shows his fucking face. Too busy schmoozing with the bloody Press – happens every trip. Telling you – every single trip, this is how it goes. PR boys lay on a party of journalists, whereupon His Highness the Cruise Director settles down to killing himself over all their crap jokes and even crappier anecdotes and then floats them on their own and alternative Atlantic comprised wholly of alcohol – as meanwhile the *Assistant* bloody Cruise Director, well . . . that particular poor bugger, he's left to just bloody buckle down and get on with the work in hand. Yes indeed: the work in hand.

Stewart swivelled around and was confronted again by the life-size coloured cut-outs of Marilyn Monroe – skirt up round her hips and admonishing him with just one finger and a pout – a slyly smiling and whip-thin Jimmy Dean, and who was that bastard from Gone With The Thing? And there's Elvis. Love Elvis. Wish I was Elvis, dead or not. Yes – so *they're* here, anyway, ready for the Viva America Ball on what night was it? Got it here on my trusty wallchart . . . Wednesday, yeh. Red, white and blue balloons and buckets of popcorn: mercy. Gable, isn't it? Clark Gable. Not a patch on Elvis. And Marilyn – still looking at me, she is, with that wotsname sort of thing in her eye. Doesn't do it for me, not one bit. Can't actually see what everyone raves about, with Marilyn, really. Or any of them, in truth. I maybe ought to, you know – where women are concerned – a bit sort of force myself, possibly. All part of the job, after all: part of what I'm bloody paid to do.

⚓

'Stowed all the doings, Nobby?'

The stationary train sighed just then, shrugged and stuttered forward once to thump and clatteringly connect with the buffers in front, as ringing chains were hooked and secured. Aggie was straddling the tinny footplates between two carriages – legs well astride, deck shoes planted firmly – and each time she leant forward to check on how well her husband was coping with luggage, the thick glass door hissed open. This made her feel guilty (silly, I know, she acknowledged while blushing) in some rather God how embarrassing, stupid kind of a way – and also horribly self-conscious because each time, you see, she and the door did this, all the other passengers (each of them at various stages of being ready for the off: fooling with magazines, contending with children, fiddling with mobiles, or heaving aloft macs and haversacks) glanced up and towards her, all faces simultaneously registering this mixture of expectancy and a vague irritation and then – seeing that all that had arrived was that bloody woman's head again – briskly reverting their attention to getting things sorted. Which boiled down to the truth that Aggie Simson always and immediately retreated with a true sense of shame and a rapidly hurtled two-tone glance of apology and plea for forgiveness before her Nobby's answer could have even a ghost's chance of reaching her (she could see him straining with the big case – the one they got cheap in America last time – face all mauve and seemingly miming, but the words quite lost, you see, through the now-shut thickness of the door). So maybe just pop her head round one more time (please don't hate me – I know, I know that after all these trips down all the years I'm really not so hot at this, but I just must make sure – please understand – that all is well with Nobby, and he's not in danger of straining himself anywhere, you know – *important*. I needn't worry, really – not in truth: I'm actually a bit of a silly goose, just like he says I am. Nobby is a trouper – he knows the ropes, all right: always plain sailing with Nobby. Someone once asked me where on earth I'd be without him, and I still can't begin to imagine: Nobby's my life – Nobby's my guiding light).

And here he was now – face aglow and eyes alight: the flush that came over him with a well done good job firmly under his belt.

'All cargo shipshape and Bristol fashion, Captain Honeybunch!' he reported quite impishly – and *ohhhh* . . . look at him, look: saluting her like that, and standing to attention. 'Come on, Aggie – let's get sat.'

'Oh Nobby – I'm so excited.'

'Gets better, doesn't it? Every single time it gets better and better. Listen up, Aggie: where will we be? Two hours' time?'

Aggie squeezed his fingers, and her face was taut and shiny.

'On our ship, Nobby – on our ship.'

'You're right, Captain Honeybunch – you're dead on the money. Here – you take the window seat, love.'

'Oh no, Nobby – I don't mind.'

'Don't be silly, love – here, get yourself in. Here's your *Woman's Realm*. And tell me, Captain – what'll it be when we get to cabin number four-oh-two-oh, Six Deck?'

Aggie just held his hand and felt her eyes prick with the spike of tears as they glittered with happiness and the wash of peace at being with Nobby, and going to their ship.

'All plain sailing, Nobby. From there on in.'

Nobby slumped down on to the seat beside her, just as the train began to inch forward. He patted her hand.

'You're not wrong, Aggie. You're not wrong, lass.'

⚓

Dwight was finding it pretty hard to get his mind around this here – hard, you know, to believe that these two dumb carrot juices, my one tuh-mayto juice and some kinda take on a non-alco bullshot could be costing me, sheesh, pretty much twenny of your British pounds sterling. That's what're we talking? Thirty bucks? Maybe more. On board the ship, everything's in dollars, yeah? You're hip to the deal. But in London – and I ain't been here since when? Not since Suki was born, that's for goddam sure – you gotta get used to their pounds, and plus you gotta say stuff like ten *peas* and not crack up, you know what I'm saying? OK – so we're in Harrods? Big deal: I know, sure, Harrods ain't known to be nobody's patsy when it comes down to stacking up the chips time: we ain't talking thrift shop – but hey, get real! Thirty bucks for a buncha liquidized salad? Hell, I didn't even *want* no damned tuh-mayto juice – but it's Charlene and the kids, they dragged me here. Charlene says it's good for my bowels, the tuh-mayto (and easy on the War-sister-shire soss) – she says it all the time; it's like my bowels are getting to be a kinda *thing* with her? She's talking innards so darn much I guess I ain't even hearing the half of it – and then you see the face on some guy, like right now, sitting around this crazy juice bar, and you're going inside Ay Caramba! – she's doing it again. Me, I said to them – hey guys, they got here this Green *Man*? Like – old traditional London pub? Mo was telling me, back home one time. Maybe we could grab us a couple glasses of their bitter beer? *Enough*, already (Charlene, right?): last night you're making with the Jack Daniel's like there ain't no dawn about to rise. What you're needing, Dwight – you hear me? – is fresh-squeezed fruit. You gotta be kind to your bowels, Dwight: your time of life, you gotta be thinking of your bowels, boy. Yeah right – and like, Charlene, maybe you should try and get your head around some other damn thing once in a while, OK? But hey: Charlene's Charlene – what can I tell ya?

'Hey, Dad?'

'What's on your mind, Earl? You wannanother juice you can just forget about it, kay? These prices I could buy me up a ranch – mash up my own damn carrots.'

'Naw – I was just kinda wondering, now we're in the *Harrods* store? Can we take in, like, the *sportswear*? Like I need these real neat – '

'You don't need nothing, Earl.'

'That's right,' said Suki. 'Damn right.'

'Hey!' gasped out a deep-affronted Earl, clutching his

chest as if he'd just met with a soft-nosed slug from a Magnum .45. 'Give me a *break*, here, OK?'

'Your sister's right – listen to your father,' said Charlene (Gee, thought Dwight – she's agreeing with me: what is this? Thanksgiving?). 'What about all that buncha stuff from *Hong* Kong?'

'*Yehhhh*,' sneered Suki. 'What are we, Earl? Some kind of a *catwalk* model? You wanna get a *facial*?'

The edges of Earl's mouth turned down flat, and his eyes went dull.

'Suki – listen, OK? Like – take a *hike*?'

'And Capetown,' went on Charlene. 'Miss? Miss? Excuse me? Can I get a *tooth*pick? I thank you. In Capetown too, Earl, you recall? Whole pie-la stuff. So enough, already – kay? Just cool it.'

'Aw *c'mon*, Mom . . .!'

'You heard your mother,' concluded Dwight. 'C'mon, guys – we got maybe, what? Couple hours before the train. What say we take in some sights? One week we're back in New York – last chance saloon, guys.'

'We're in Harrods, right?' checked Suki. 'Like – I thought this *was* the sight? Like – this is *it*, no?'

'C'mon! Hey, Suki!' And Dwight was really looking deep at her, you know? Like, really needing an *answer*, here? 'You gotta be kidding me, right? There's . . . jeez, what is there? There's London Castle and Big Ben's clock and Her Majesty's Palace and some kinda other thing – oh no, that's maybe in Edinborrow, that thing I'm thinking. Anyways, all I'm saying is there's like two thousand years of *heredity* here.'

'Yeh well,' said Suki. 'We ain't about to do two thousand years in a couple hours, right?'

'Yeh – right,' agreed Earl. 'So why don't we just check out the sportswear, man? Why you guys giving me such a hard time?'

'Enough, already, with the sportswear, Earl,' said Charlene, with emphasis. 'One thing I do want, though, Dwight sweetie – I gotta just take in the paddery.'

And both Suki and Earl hurled up their eyes and heads to the gorgeously decorated ceiling above them and groaned out loud, and with real true feeling – Suki branching out on her own towards the close of it, and tacking on a selection of retching noises, as her eyes were crossing and her cheeks billowed out. Dwight was silent, but he was tapping an impatient finger on the edge of his billfold (I'm waiting for change, here, and I don't believe I'm in the mood for leaving no gratooity).

'Aw God*sake*, Mom!' roared out Earl.

'*Earl*! Keep it down,' cautioned Charlene. 'Like – people are *looking*?'

'Dad – *you* tell her,' Earl went on – I suppose, yeah, a couple decibels down. 'Everyplace we've been, right, Mom's with the paddery. Every time we got offa that ship it's, like – *paddery* time? We got – in *Hong* Kong, right? How much goddam paddery we get in *Hong* Kong? And *Bang*kok? It's like the ship is gonna sink with all the paddery we got.'

'They're lovely pieces,' put in Charlene.

'Yeh but *Mom*,' Suki eagerly interjected – her eyes wide with *What*-is-she? *Nuts*? And flipping all her fingers, as if to cool them down or dry them off. 'How many – oh my God I'm gonna, like, *barf* – lovely *pieces* can one home stand? You know? Like – that *vace*, yeah? From Thailand? It's taller than *I* am, Mom! Be *real*, here.'

'Maybe, Charlene,' said Dwight, quietly, 'enough with the paddery, huh?'

'Oh but *Dwight*, honey – it's Harrods we're in now, yeah? It's a whole different ball game – like, *major* league? I mean, England – they're into real high-class paddery big time. There's the Wedgwood and the Royal War-sister-shire – '

'What?' queried Suki. 'Like in what? Kinda *soss* bowls?'

Charlene was maybe thrown just a tad. 'Kinda,' she

24

briskly agreed, before resuming the barrage of must-haves. 'And Doolton – that's *Royal* Doolton, guys, like in the *Queen*? And is it *Spood*?'

'I reckon,' reckoned Dwight,'it's Spade, no?'

'Maybe,' growled Earl with mischief, 'we're talking *Speed* here, yeh?'

'Earl!' was all Charlene was going to say. 'Don't laugh, Suki. It ain't funny. So what say, gang? Just, like, we look it over real fast, yeah? Kay?'

'Waaaaal ... OK ...' agreed Dwight; well of *course* Dwight agreed – what was he gonna do? Like, maybe – *disagree*? Sure – he could go down that route, but look at it – any which way, baby, and they were due to take in the English paddery, and you better depend on it. 'OK – quiet, Earl; quit with the pukey noises, Suki. OK, Charlene – we check it out . . .' but God*sake*, huh? Keep it small, OK? Like – *eggcups*? Believe me, honey – read my lips: we gadda ladda paddery.'

'Sure. I can pre-shate that. Hey, kids – let's hit it. You got the check, Dwight?'

Dwight nodded. 'Waiting for my change.'

'Oh God*sake*, Dwight? Leave the girl the few cents! What're we? *Poor* all of a sudden?'

'We will be,' grunted Dwight, 'once it's you with the English paddery.'

'Naw!' guffawed Earl. 'Like, Mom's getting just this one real cool little eggcup – right, Mom?'

'We'll see,' rejoined Charlene, quite primly. 'Dwight – you didn't drink your tuh-mayto.'

'The tuh-mayto I don't need.'

'Your *bowels* are needing it, Dwight – you gotta treat 'em real good.'

'I'll treat you real good instead, Charlene. OK, people – c'mon: let's do this thing. We make with the paddery, and then we hit the road.'

(And it ain't, Charlene, just a few cents: we're talking one pound and toward ninety of your lousy goddam British *peas*.)

⚓

Sammy was hunkered down, squaring his shoulders and bracing his knees, ready to hoist up and stow another case of Gevrey-Chambertin 1997; it's on the list as '96, but God – all that vanished in no time: I don't think too many people will notice (query it, anyway). The '97's good too, though maybe not so forward.

'I like a lot about this job,' he muttered, swinging aloft the case and shelving it – leaving it to Jilly to neaten things up and nudge it over to meet its neighbour. 'But by this stage, you know – I've really had enough of the *heaving*.'

'Last leg,' smiled Jilly. 'Well – till Jamaica, anyway.'

Sammy smiled as he leant across to kiss her.

'OK – let's start in on the champagne. It's amazing, isn't it? Amazes me, anyway – amount of booze these people put away.'

'They're on holiday. Off the leash.'

'I suppose it's that. But Christ – every time I think I've got the bar packed solid, I turn around and the bloody thing's empty again. And this week's always the worst. It's the English contingent.'

'Well it's a kind of a trip of a lifetime, isn't it? They don't want it to end. It's all farewells and toasts and 'let's have another bottle' stuff, isn't it? And remember, some of these people have been here right from the very beginning – must be like home, in some weird way. I think they're crazy, quite frankly. I mean, OK – so have *we*, but we're *paid* to, aren't we? It's our job. But why do you want to spend nearly four months stuck on a ship? It's *crazy*, isn't it? And the funny thing is – have you noticed, Sammy? The funny thing is that the posher the, you know – cabin, and everything, the less likely they ever are to leave. That, what are they? Egyptian family up in the King's Suite – '

'Oh them. Apparently they own half the country, or something.'

'Yeh – I heard that. Anyway – *them*. They haven't disembarked once, pretty sure. That's what Jaffa told me. All these amazing places we've docked in and all they do is just sit there, ordering up room service. I mean – they can do that in *Egypt*, can't they? I think they must be mad. Is there any more Heidsieck, Sammy? Only we've got room for, don't know – five, maybe half a dozen more.'

'We've got Red Label, yeah. Well – no danger of all that ever happening to us, is there Jilly? Not on what we earn.'

'Money's not *bad*, Sammy. Best thing is, when you're cooped up on board all the time, there's nowhere to spend it. We'll have just zillions by the end.'

'Yeh but look – we *agreed*, didn't we?'

'Oh Sammy – don't be a drag.'

'We *agreed*. Didn't we, Jilly? Agree?'

'Yesssss . . .'

'Well then. If we don't save – '

'I know, I know, I know – we'll never get our foot on the first rung of the property ladder. I know, Sammy – I know. What I don't get is why it's so bloody *important*: why can't we just rent? In *France* – '

'Because if you just rent – oh God, Jilly: you *know* all this. If you just rent, well – you're throwing away good money, aren't you? End up with nothing.'

'Except maybe a bloody good time instead of a thirty-year mortgage.'

Sammy shoved across a case of Heidsieck, and grinned at her as he laid one flat hand across his heart.

'One day, sweet damsel, when you are my wife of forty summers – you, our ten children and frankly countless and *teeming* grandchildren – '

'Oh Sammy!' shrieked Jilly, her eyes glistening – two fingers just touching the tip of her nose.

'*Then*, my dear – as you survey the moated castle and its extensive and landscaped grounds, you will thank me, most humbly.'

'Uh-huh. Right. That's a date. And in the meantime?'

'In the meantime? In the meantime we hump these bloody cases of wine and store up our pennies like squirrels.'

'Squirrels are cleverer – they don't *care* about pennies. Live in trees.'

'Nuts. Think of your pennies as nuts.'

'*You're* nuts, Sammy. You know that? You're completely barking crazy.'

'That's why you love me. I've got one more case down here and then that's the end of it. Then we do the gin and vodka.'

'You know what Jaffa was telling me?' piped up Jilly, quite brightly.

'No – what? Actually, Jilly – why do you always call him that?'

'Stewart? Because he's always got that orange face on. His dopey fake suntan. You know, I think he actually believes that people see him as some sort of, I don't know – Bondi Beach Adonis, or something. All bronzed and sun-bleached blond. Looks more like a *poodle*, I think.'

'Stewart's all right. Or at least he will be if he makes it. I think sometimes, you know, he's headed for some kind of breakdown, or something. Have you ever seen him when he's grinning like mad with the punters and giving out balloons and dancing away with all those ancient women – and then he suddenly turns away and, Christ – the look on his face, it's so . . . don't really know how to describe it . . .'

'Dark? Sort of scowling? Yeh – I've seen that.'

'Murderous, more like . . . Real sort of Jekyll and Hyde do.'

'Jesus, Sammy – you're scaring me, now. I have to work with him, remember.'

'Oh – he's safe enough. Anyway – not long now. If he can survive over three months of this, another couple of weeks won't kill him.'

'So long as he doesn't take it into his head to go around killing anyone else. Like *me*, for instance.'

'Nah,' joshed Sammy. 'I'd kill him if he did.'

'Oh gee shucks *thanks*. How much gin is there?'

'Bout . . . twenty cases, looks like.'

'Oh yeh – *that's* what I was going to say. Old Jaffa-face Stewart was giving me the rundown on how much of all this stuff we actually *go* through on one of these cruises. It's just unbelievable!'

'Nothing would amaze me. I seem to be pouring drinks non-stop all day and all night. It's almost as if they feel it's all got to be used up, or something. And it's not exactly cheap, is it? I mean the mark-up's just wicked. And it's not like the food – I mean I know they never stop stuffing themselves with food, but that's all in with the ticket, isn't it? Drink isn't, that's for sure. God, you know – apart from the meals . . . John in cabin service was telling me, one time – you know John?'

'Oh yeah – tall guy? Goofy ears?'

'No no – my height. Ginger hair. Think you're thinking of *Cyril*, pretty sure his name is. Anyway – John was saying that there is just no such thing as a quiet time, down there. Twenty-four hours a day, that phone is ringing – tea, sandwiches, steaks, pasta . . . one bloke orders a whole bloody lobster at three a.m., every single night, if you can believe it. And José – José, yes? Duchess Grill? Anyway, according to José, that's *exactly* what the guy has for his dinner! I'm telling you, we're afloat with a shipful of loonies.'

'It does sometimes seem like that. But that's exactly what I mean about all the *booze*. Jaffa says the whole ship gets through about two hundred bottles of champagne every single *day*.'

'That doesn't actually seem that much, to me. Sixteen hundred passengers, after all. How much beer?'

'Oh God – something like three *thousand* bottles of that, pretty sure. You wonder where they put it all. *And* a thousand packets of fags. We're talking every *day*, Sammy – can you believe it? Bloody expensive route to suicide, these cruises.'

'Mm. The cost of dying. But tastefully *done*,' smiled Sammy. 'Right. Let's do the vodka – about eight million gallons of that and then, God – I'd really love a cuppa.'

Jilly was thoughtful. 'Oh yes – ever so tastefully *done* . . .' she agreed. 'Here – that's another thing Jaffa was telling me: do you know what we go through most of? Over two *million*, every single year?'

'Two *million*? Blimey. Dunno. Tea bags?'

'Not close. Nowhere near.'

'Assistant Cruise Directors?'

'Silly! Be serious.'

'OK. Eggs?'

'Eggs are far less – quarter of a million, tops. Give up?'

'Yeh – go on, then: stun me.'

Jilly leaned forward and held on to Sammy's forearms: her eyes were urging him to listen and learn.

'Doilies,' she said.

Sammy just looked at her. 'Doilies? Two million *doilies*?'

Jilly nodded. 'Amazing, or what?'

And Sammy nodded too. 'Truly,' he whispered. And then, after a pause: 'I just can't think of anything at all to say about that.'

⚓

Every single time I come to Southampton, I always get stuck in a traffic jam, just like this one. And usually about here –

just as all the roads converge towards the docks and you have to cross this sort of bridge affair, is it? Just as well I allowed plenty of time. Which is all, really, I've been doing, if I'm honest. Since . . . it happened. Allowing for time – apologizing, in one sense (and to whom? Who on earth is listening?), for the continued existence of time, when really it ought to have stopped, along with Mary.

I say *every* time I come to Southampton, but goodness – do you know in all honesty I can't even remember the last occasion. Could've been as long as maybe seven, eight years back. Mary and me, we went on a sort of a two-day, well – not much more than a pleasure trip, really: can't for the life of me recall the name of the boat, ship – whatever it was; Isle of Wight came into it somewhere. We did things like that: free agents, did what we liked. Friends of ours, of course – Paul and Joan, Ed and Fanny (God – those two: they never ever stopped going on and on about it) – yes, all these friends with youngish children (*four* of the things in Ed and Fanny's case, God help us: well – whatever did they expect?) – they were forever going on about the loss of spontaneity, impulse – the spur of the moment thing. *Honestly*, they'd go – once you've worked out all the dates of the school holidays, which never ever coincide (you'd think, wouldn't you, the powers that be could at least get their heads together and coordinate that much: can't be that difficult – and it's not as if we're the only ones to suffer) and then by the time you've seen that all their beastly *projects* are under way, or at least that they've bought the scrapbooks (they seem to have more work to do in the holidays than in termtime, these days) – which means *muggins* here has to keep on going down to the travel agents and casually half-inching all these brochures about the Loire Valley and the bloody *Alps* and all the rest of it and then spend oh God just *days* knee-deep in encyclopaedias and Cow Gum putting the whole damn mess together – their job, I know – but what are you going to do? The *kids*, of course – oh Jesus:

31

you sit them in front of the Net and give them a perfectly straightforward list of nonsense to dig out – Epernay's annual yield of champagne, or something (God I could do with a glass or two right now), and hours later they're still just *sitting* there transfixed by some complete and very often pornographic irrelevance and then I just *scream* at Ed to for God's sake pull his finger out and get all these ghastly channels locked *out*, or whatever they say, and he says like he always does, I will I will – but I don't know why this sort of thing isn't tackled at *government* level – and I go Yeh, totally agree, but *until* they get around to it it's our kids, right? And it's our bloody job to protect them. And then one of them will be *ill*, or something – chicken pox last summer, don't please *remind* me – and we have to get a housesitter for the dogs (kennels are just ruinous) and God, you have to book so many *rooms*, now, because Neil – he's just twelve: can't take it in – he absolutely refuses to share any more, and quite frankly the whole thing just isn't cost-effective, when all's said and done – and *exhaustion* just doesn't come into it: I'm completely bloody knackered, I don't mind telling you, even contemplating the *idea* of a holiday, these days. Mmm. So we just go off for odd days, now.

And then Mary and me, we'd brace ourselves – secretly holding hands, sometimes we were, under the folds of the tablecloth – for here now would come the inevitable exhalation: the rounding up and rounding off of all their frustrations and passion spent. 'You two,' they'd go: 'you're just so lucky not *having* any of that.'

Yes. Well. It's not at all, I can tell you now, not at all what Mary felt she was: lucky. No, not a bit of it. Oh yes – we had a good life, admittedly – my rather dull job in insurance took good care of most things, and Mary's little florist's was something of a goldmine. So no real worries on that score – but once you've cleared the mortgage and sorted out the pensions and repapered the lounge and tacked on a modest conservatory and seen to the first-floor window frames, well . . . you're hunting about, quite frankly. Holidays are the natural thing: it takes time to discuss them, plan them, budget for them; and then there's the shopping beforehand (I left that to Mary: wasn't all that long ago she picked out for me the very smart black suit that I'm wearing right now – she had an eye, Mary: an eye for things like that). Packing, of course – that could be coaxed out into a couple of days: fresh-ironed stacklets of this and that always adding to the anticipatory feel.

We went all over: Capri and Sorrento, I recall, was a particularly successful little package. We were very partial to pasta and we'd never tasted peaches quite like that before: fresh off the tree. Crete, Dordogne – Tuscany, of course: got her to try some wine on that trip – always made me laugh, she was never a drinker, Mary. But it's all so *sour* – it's just not *sweet*, Tom, she'd go – I just don't know how you can stomach it. Fellow at the hotel – nice sort of chap, sort of courier, or something – must've overheard, I assume; anyway – sent over a bottle of Asti Spumante, and that did the trick. That's the only wine, Mary went, that has ever passed my lips that I can truly say I've *enjoyed*: one thing, though, Tom, she giggled at me then – it's gone straight to my head, just that one little glass. The giggle made me feel so fond, so warm – warm, yes, and so very protective. I'll never again hear it, now.

So yes – I took the point when Ed and Fanny went on like they did: in their terms we were – of course we were – lucky, very. But I know that Mary, deep down (she never said so, not in so many words, but you get to hear such a lot of unspoken things when you're that close to someone, you know – day and night, for years and years) . . . Mary, yes, she would eagerly have traded in all the holidays and new three-piece suites under the sun, just for a baby of her own, to love and care for. She would have liked lots – but one, I know, would have been more than enough. But, well . . . it was not to be (which is what you say when you really can't

33

bear to think about it any more). So we buckled down to the double glazing and the laying of patios – we baulked at a roof conversion, though, because look: the house already was accusingly large, so where's the sense in more?

So we continued to go hither and thither under the scathing eyes of our nailed-down friends who roared at us repeatedly how appallingly *lucky* we were. Well – we weren't complaining (were we Mary, my love?); and, as we kept on saying, we had each other. And now – except for this stopped-up bulk of bits of our lives that sticks out clumsily from deep within me – the link has now been broken.

I'm still in first gear. The cars ahead have been grudgingly astir for fifteen minutes or more, and in that time I've covered maybe just fifty yards, or so. I can see a part of the ship now, though. God. I mean – you know it's *big* (we read the brochure again and again, Mary and me) but nothing really quite prepares you. The red and black funnel, tall as any building I'm aware of. Just the one funnel, then? Oh yes – it was the old *Queen Mary* that had a pair, fairly sure (and *Titanic* had *four* of the things, much good they turned out to be). It's a shame, I said, that the *Queen Mary* doesn't exist any more – we could have pretended it was built for you. Well Tom – I could always change my name to *Transylvania*, Mary had said. Ho ho, I went – a little extreme, I think. Yes. Doesn't matter what she's called, now.

This was to have been our trip of a lifetime. Well: correction – it was to have been our very luxurious and self-indulgent trial-run for what maybe next year (and there will, won't there, be a next year? And one after that and one after that?) could have become the real thing, the big thing, the ultimate. We'd never ever been on a liner – we'd talked about it often enough, oh heavens yes (we talked about anything that would use up time), but this year we decided to go for it (and you should have heard Ed and Fanny on *that* one) – six days and nights to New York . . . a double first for us, really, because neither one of us had even been to America, let alone New York. We didn't care for long-haul flights, that's the truth of the matter (what it really boiled down to), and here was the perfect solution: plus, of course, a week was eaten up just in the getting there. And then, you see – and this is how our thinking went – if we both liked it (and why would we not?) then next year we could book up for the fully-fledged World Cruise, see just everywhere we've ever read about, or glimpsed on the telly. Australia, Hong Kong, Barbados, you name it. Expensive, oh yes very – or it is, anyway, if you want to do it in any way *properly*: no point travelling the world, is there, on some mighty ship if you're going to be stuck six decks down, cheek by jowl with the boiler room? Also, this one would be taking care of four clear months: you can see the attraction.

And then . . . it happened. And among the very many (endless) things that hurtled into me and laid siege to my thoughts – and how quiet now the house is, in which to think them – was the question of what to do about the booking. I could have cancelled – could easily have done that (there's a clause in my insurance: my cover, as you will appreciate, is always both in order and more than adequate) and I suppose this was my initial inclination. And then I thought, well . . . the time looms larger than ever, now – and maybe, because dear Mary is with me always, I can still (why not?) take her with me. Because where Tom goes, Mary goes – yes? So why not do this one last thing together? See? So here, in this car, in a sense we both are.

We're moving again. Making a fair bit of progress, now. The ship's so close, I can't honestly see any of it at all: it's just like a wall, with us in our cars so small and crouching, maybe awed by the darkness of its shadow.

⚓

'Oh ... my ... *God* ...' came young Rollo's look-at-me descant – but his mother was certainly far too preoccupied to pay any heed whatever to *that* sort of thing.

They had all, the four of them, been standing in line in this vast and rather loweringly spartan embarkation hall for, yes, just a teeny weeny bit longer than Nicole thought was fitting for the family that had, after all, won through to be the sole captors of the fabulous no-expense-spared Trip of a Lifetime (thanks in no little way, I like to think, to my tiebreaking seventeen words which I'll happily tell you about later but not just now because I want us to be *settled*).

Nicole had rather supposed that they might have been, well – piped aboard, maybe, and warmly welcomed by one or two of the shipping line's senior directors, or possibly even the Captain himself, or something, but so far not even so much as a paid-by-the-grin meeter and greeter had seen fit to show his face – but OK, yes, she was certainly gratified to discover that the very queue in which they were standing conferred on them at least a *modicum* of status. The whole elaborate checking-in system, it rather oddly seemed, was organized according to the class of onboard *restaurant*, of all things, to which your ticket entitled you; the longest queues all down the other end, then, must be for the rather lowlier eating places and bars, Nicole could only assume – *some* comfort, anyway – and presumably all these poor people (didn't, admittedly, *look* terribly poor) were going to be, what, stuck in with the cargo, or something, were they? Dangling from hammocks.

'Check ... it ... *out*,' persisted Rollo. 'Mar? Get *this* ...'

Marianne glanced across in the direction – Rollo was energetically and sideways jerking his head – but actually, frankly, couldn't quite focus on much because she hadn't got her *contacts* in, right, but she wasn't about to tell Rollo that because then he'd start in on his blind-as-a-bat routine and it's hell, quite honestly: you just can't win with Rollo because if I ever wear my *glasses* (and they're really cool, I think – designer frames, the lot) he calls me ('four-eyes') and it's no good me saying Oh *God*, Rollo, if you're going to be insulting at least you could be a bit *original* about it, couldn't you, hm? I mean honestly – 'four-eyes': bit *prep* school, isn't it, dear heart?

'Can't you see him?' hissed an irritated Rollo. '*There* . . . over *there*. Prat in black.'

'Rollo,' said Nicole – absently in a way, though still with the edge of urgency lurking beneath what she liked to think was a maternal overtone. 'Don't just *kick* your bag along like that. Lift it – it won't kill you.'

'Oh yeh . . .' said Marianne. 'I see him. God – how odd. Dad? Dad? See this guy?'

David had quite rightly judged it only a matter of time before someone – most likely Marianne, if it wasn't to be outright abuse – addressed to him some or other comment on some or other topic, and so he now breathed in sharply and put all he could muster into chivvying along the not-yet-dead muscles in his lower face and around the chin (and oh God yes – don't forget, will you, to open your bloody eyes) – urging them to rally round (come on, lads) into a semblance of animation and a passably fair simulation of ready-for-it eagerness.

'See what, love?'

Didn't sound too odd, he was reasonably sure: *felt* it, though, by God: it was as if he was using someone else's lips. And the pressure, now, at the base of my skull is coming very close to shutting me down. The war in my stomach I can just about subdue – but if I don't get down a very swift couple of (oh God) sharpeners in double-quick time, then we're booked for a bout of horizontal groaning (curtains firmly closed and a bucket of Nurofen) and I don't think, do you, in these rather singular circumstances (on this bloody day of all bloody days) that such behaviour would altogether endear me to my doting wife and helpmeet? (Or, let's put it another way: make her loathe me less?)

'Oh God – Dad never sees *anything*,' spat out Rollo, with true impatience, as well as what struck David as open disgust. '*There*! *There*! Christ what's *wrong* with you? The bloke in *black* . . .!'

'We're next, now,' said Nicole, quite hurriedly (hadn't been hearing any of all this: over the years, you are vaguely aware of so much background pointless droning, but God – you don't waste time by paying attention, no: it passes soon enough). 'Pick *up* your bag, Rollo. How many times?'

'See him, Dad?' urged Marianne. 'Three queues down.'

'Oh yes,' said David. 'I do see him now. Hm. God – once you've actually focused, he really does stand out, doesn't he?'

'That's what I've bloody been *saying*,' growled Rollo.

David, Marianne and Rollo continued to gaze in silence at Tom. Other people too were not quite casually taking in his singular appearance (if you're stuck in a queue – and this ship *will* eventually, won't it, sail? – then any sort of diversion can only be a good thing). Tom himself seemed quite unaware. *Was* unaware – had been, in truth, over every night and day he could recently recall. He had said nothing to the girl in the office over there, when he handed back the keys of the hire car. Had maybe nodded briefly at the, what was he? (and in another time, he might have registered it) – big and chummy porter as he wheeled away to somewhere Tom's one small suitcase (possibly I didn't even do that – nod at him, briefly. Certainly didn't *utter*: perfectly sure on that score). And now he just stood in line, as instructed, staring intently at the back of the mid-blue cotton hat worn by the person in front (could be a man, could be a woman – really couldn't tell you, really haven't looked).

'He must,' judged David, 'be awfully *hot* . . .'

'*Right*,' said Nicole, with finality. 'It's us, we're here.

Hello.' And she slid over four passports, along with all the rest of it.

'Good after*noon*, Madam,' said the quite extraordinarily happy-sounding woman behind the quite high and boxy check-in booth. 'Four of you travelling, yes?'

'Yes,' agreed Nicole, very readily, rapidly pointing a finger at her husband, each of her two children and finally herself – as if to check, or maybe prove it.

'I think,' considered Rollo, 'he must be some kind of a nutter. I bet the whole bloody boat's going to be full of bloody nutters.'

'*Ship*,' said Marianne. 'It's a ship.'

'Oh fuck off, Mar,' was Rollo's take on that.

'I'd be stifling,' said David – more to himself than anyone (second nature, now). 'I'm pretty warm in just this seer-sucker thing.'

'*Right*,' said Nicole – and she's said that a good deal, now, and forcibly too. The extraordinarily happy-sounding woman blinked once only, every time she did it, and her lips just momentarily froze up in tune with the temporary breakdown; less than a second later, though, a big and immediate thaw had set in, and once more she was up there with a chance of bringing back for England a Gold in the Happiness Olympics. 'Now listen, everyone – we've got to put our faces in front of this funny little thing and then it takes a *picture*, apparently. Oh not all at *once*, Rollo, Godsake – wait your turn, can't you? And David – they need your credit card.'

'And all in black . . .' mused David. 'Maybe he's the ship's undertaker.'

'Oh *Daddy*!' deplored Marianne. 'You're awful.'

'Well *someone's* got to tip them over the side, haven't they?' Loved it when Marianne laughed, like that.

'*Credit* card, David. Lady's waiting.'

'Credit card?' he came back. 'What for? What's this for, now?'

'Good after*noon*, Sir,' was launched at him then – and David flinched just a bit before being duly dazzled by this truly professional and five-star greeting, courtesy of the Delighted One. (God it just goes to show, though, doesn't it? The benefit of a proper training scheme and back-up refresher courses: you leave all this business of politeness and welcome to the hicks and amateurs and what you end up with is hardly more than varnished scorn.) 'The registration of any major credit card, Sir, frees you up to charge at any point during the crossing all purchases, services or beverages to your on-board account whereupon an itemized tally will be presented for your authorization on the morning of disembarkation.'

David had been sliding across his Mastercard long before any of this was vouchsafed unto him (he didn't know her name, this woman, but she was surely one of life's great little vouchsafers – born to it, you could tell). And look – when people want a credit card, *request* doesn't really come into it, does it? It's just what's expected, so you do it: without a credit card, these days – Christ, let's face it – you barely get to touch base. The sight of cash in the twenty-first century, and all your credibility is, just like that, shot to bits.

'Oh my *God*!' exclaimed Nicole – sort of laughing, but not really very much. 'I look absolutely *ghastly* – oh God *look*, Marianne – look at this simply ghastly picture!'

Marianne took the laminated plastic card from her mother's pinch of fingers.

'Hm. Looks like the camera was pointed up your nostrils.'

'Oh *God* . . .' Nicole was moaning, truly miserable – and none the less so when Rollo snatched the card from Marianne's hand and started snorting like he did, and said she looked like that puppet, what is it? Miss Piggy, yeh.

David, Marianne and Rollo in turn hung their heads over this counter affair and subjected themselves to the strange little camera (looked like a mouse) – David asking idly Has it clicked? Is it done? Marianne had taken heed of her mother's ill-judged attitude and ducked down her nose while giving her eyes everything she had; Rollo hammered it up without mercy – came out looking like a drivelling fool; but then look – Rollo would. As they moved off in the allocated direction – a distant escalator was looming – Nicole was still very shaken by the awfulness of her photo.

'I mean – what's it actually in aid of, this card? We don't have to *show* it, or anything, do we? It's like a sort of a child's ID or a *bus* pass, or something. Not very *civilized* . . .'

They emerged now into what looked like an immense but not remotely nice airport departure lounge: could have been acres, there, of bright green seating but not, very evidently, nearly enough. Most people were standing – quite a few, Marianne noticed, intentionally or otherwise catching the eye of other people standing, and then they smiled quite shyly. Maybe, she thought, poor Rollo should learn the art of that: God, it would help a bit if he smiled at all. Look at him now – staring at those two girls over there as if he's in a *trance*, or something. Been doing it for ages. Blonde one looks quite nice – reminds me a bit of my old schoolfriend, Sally. They seem quite young to be going on a trip like this – the Sally-type one looks only about a year or two older than me – nineteen, maybe (even a bit less, could be). Other one's more – mid-twenties, should think. Oh Rollo! God you're so hopeless – don't keep *goggling* like that; they'll never look back if you do – or *if* they do, it'll only be to . . . oh God yeh, one of them's just done it, now: held his eye just long enough to then turn away and dismiss all thought of him. As if he was just a passing fly. And look at Rollo now – gone all red, and hurting, probably. I wish I could help him, sometimes, but I never really know what to say. How to get going. He's terribly difficult to just talk to, Rollo. But all he has to do is *ask* me: that's all he has to do.

The sea of travellers and tingle of anticipation put David in mind of a documentary he had seen, one time, when all the wartime children were taken to railway stations with a cardboard box strung about their tucked-in school scarves with rough white twine: the start of a big adventure, but with everything to come – and therefore, though charged with hope, so far unknown.

Nicole was extremely gratified that – as 'Duchess Grill' ticketholders – they were free to embark immediately (isn't it lovely? This sort of thing? Sweeping past all of those people who *can't*?) but very miffed indeed that the first things the official had requested from each of them were these blasted little laminated cards.

'That is the *last*,' she quietly fumed, as they walked on through (and she meant it, you know, as David most certainly could have assured you). 'That is positively the very last time I am showing that thing. Maybe on board they could take another one, a better one, do you think so? David? Hm?'

David thought *No*, you silly vain and idle cow, of course they bloody couldn't – and what the hell does it matter anyway? It's only a bloody *card*: not going on the cover of *Vogue*, is it?

'Maybe,' he said.

God: she was just the same when she put on all that weight, that time. Nicole blamed the pills, which had completely thrown David altogether because most of the pills she put down her throat – and don't ask me, please, what the *others* were for – were meant to be all about *slimming*.

'Does this dress make me look sort of – big?' How many times a day did he have to counter that one? 'David: tell me honestly. Because I can't see me, can I? From certain angles. So does it, hm? This dress? Make me look, you know – on the big side?'

'No,' he said.

And he had meant it. The *dress* didn't make her look anything at all. I mean, let's be perfectly plain: the dress was entirely innocent, here. Jesus Christ Almighty, woman – why shove blame on the bloody *dress*?

Jennifer and Stacy sipped their Cokes and eyed with quasi-irritation (more of a sense of Hoi – what's this, then?) the thickening trickle of would-be voyagers being eagerly ushered away into yet another corridor, at the very end of which, maybe – unless all this boarding malarkey was in truth no more than a sadly misplaced and elongated gag – the bloody *Transylvania* might actually be docked and waiting, who knew?

'How come they get to go and we don't?'

'It's bloody annoying. I should imagine, Stacy, they're posher than we are. We have to wait for . . . what did she tell us? Bat at the door? Till they announce Five, was it? That's the downside of going steerage, I suppose.'

'Six, I think. What's it say on the tickets? I think she said Six.'

'No – it was Five, I remember. Anyway – they're only on Two, so God alone knows . . .'

'*Sure* she said Six . . .'

'You looking forward? God – look at that boy: he's still looking, you know. He must have a number Two ticket – his lot's going through. Rich dad, I expect.'

'What boy?'

'Oh God just listen to you! Honestly, Stacy! What *boy*! You know very well he was looking – I watched you.'

'Don't know what boy you're talking about.'

'Well if you don't want him, I wouldn't mind. He looks quite sweet. Do you know . . . I think you could be right.'

'What about? And don't start on about *boys*. Do you want another Coke? We could be here for days.'

'She *did* say Six, I'm pretty sure. Yeh – could be weeks, this rate. Well he *was* quite sweet. Looked sort of lost.'

'He was only a kid.'

'How do you know, Stacy? You didn't see him, did you? Don't even know what boy I'm *talking* about . . .'

'Look – do you want a Coke or not? I'm getting one, anyway.'

'Don't sulk.'

'I'm not sul – oh God, are you going to be like this for the whole of the bloody trip, or what? It's a real drag, when you start like this.'

'Don't think we're *going* on a trip. I think we're going to spend the whole of the week cooped up in this bloody great hangar, or whatever they call it. OK – let's get another Coke. Least they're free. Maybe we should try and nick a whole bagful – take them on the boat.'

'Why? They'll have Coke on the boat, won't they? Thought they had everything.'

'Oh yeh they'll *have* it. They'll *have* it all right. It's just Christ knows what they're going to *cost*, yeh? It's only the grub that's all in, remember, and I told you, God, how totally bloody broke we are. I think that all I'm going to do till we get to New York is eat. I've decided. I'm going to eat and eat and eat until I bloody well explode. Maybe then I won't have to buy food for the rest of the year.'

'We could've saved money by *flying* ... They've got Tango as well. Want a Tango?'

'Yeh well. I don't fly. As well you know. Anyway – flying, you don't get all the food, yeh? Tango's fine. No, actually – think I'll stick with Coke.'

'Worried about mixing your drinks?'

'Oh *don't*! I'd just bloody kill for a huge gin and tonic right *now*. We'll just have to work bloody hard tonight and find some nice rich gentleman to buy them for us. You giggle – I'll wiggle: that should do it. You know – I don't know if I've really brought the right *things* for the – you know, for the evenings.'

Stacy shrugged, and ripped her ring-pull. 'What we've got is short and black. Don't really see the problem. Bloody hell – it's really gassy, this stuff. Don't much like.'

'Oh God – look! Hally-bloody-loolia! They've just

44

changed the Two to a Three. Christ. How long is it going to be before they get to bloody Six? I should think that *Five* is probably the cargo and the livestock and the cars. Then they'll get to bloody *us*. Oh look, Stacy – those seats are empty, now – let's get them. I'm knackered, all this bloody hanging about.'

'You take my bag – I'll get the drinks.'

'Anyway,' resumed Jennifer – more or less as soon as the two of them were pretty much settled into a pair of bright green plastic bucket seats (they should, she had muttered – while her face went Oh Yuck as she shoved the last people's coffee cups well under the table – have laid on four-bloody-poster beds, they keep you waiting about so long). 'I hope the general level of men on the boat is higher than this lot round here. Think, Stacy, we ought to concentrate on the number Twos. Hey – what do you think the number *Ones* are going to be like? We didn't even *see* any of those, did we? They were probably carried on earlier in those chairs, what are they? Sedan chair things. Or lowered from a helicopter.'

'The way you go on, you know, people might think that you're looking for a husband. Isn't that what old women are meant to do on cruises and stuff? How very cute.'

'Less of the bloody *old*, bloody Stacy. Thirty-nine – that's hardly decrepit, is it? Not exactly *ancient*. We can't *all* be sweet and fresh and young like *you*, bloody Stacy. Anyway – don't *feel* thirty-nine. Feel like some dopey kid, most of the time.'

'Look like a dopey kid. It's weird you don't age. What're you on?'

'Mm. I sometimes think that everything's put on hold to get me nice and used to it, yeh? And then the minute I hit forty I'll just simply self-destruct – quite literally fall to pieces. Just hope I'm not in Tesco when it happens.'

'You're totally *nuts* – you do know that?'

'And God – don't please talk to me about *husbands*. The

45

last two, thank you, were quite enough for one little life-time, I think. I just – if I'm honest, you know, I just don't understand why on earth people still do go and get married. Don't you do it, Stace – it messes up your life, telling you.'

'Never *stop* telling me, do you? Yeh but look – your last so-called marriage is hardly *typical*, is it? How long were you actually together?'

Jennifer held her lips briefly ajar and wagged her head quite slowly.

'Seemed like a century. Thing was, though – oh Christ look! Four! They've got up to Four! telling you – might get on that boat before I'm forty. If not, *they* can pick up the bloody bits. What was I . . .?'

'Your blissful second marriage.'

'Oh yeh. Roger. Thing is, though, Stacy – I really did love that guy when I, you know – married him. Or I *thought* I did, anyway. Maybe I didn't. But when I actually, you know – the actual day of the wedding – well *you* remember: it was really great, wasn't it? Sun shining, and everything . . .'

'You looked fab.'

'*Felt* fab – felt it. Quite possibly the happiest day of my life, if I'm honest. Just like it's meant to be – like it is in the movies. But then, oh God – it all seemed to go downhill more or less immediately. Even before the honeymoon ended, it all began. Staying out late, at first – and then not coming back at all till the next bloody day. Drink, of course . . . violence – quite a lot of violence, actually.'

'God . . .'

Jennifer grinned widely, now: quite her most roguish.

'Yeh,' she agreed. 'I was really *awful*: don't know how he stood it.'

'*You*,' smiled Stacy, 'should be shot.'

'That's more or less what Roger said, poor sod. Anyway, he did, give him his due – he did put up with me for as long as he could, and we sort of, God knows how – jogged along together. But the *boredom*! Well – I've told you all this. Know it backwards. There was all the doubt and anger, you see, Stacy. Roger's. Which are a killer, of course. And then the, well – betrayal. Mine. Yes, OK. But mostly I just remember the awful awful eternal *boredom*!'

'Poor little you.'

'You're right. Telling you – ooh! Ooh look – they're up to *Five*. Oh look – bugger this. We're Five – I've decided. Can't hang around this bloody dump any longer. We're Five – let's go. What was I . . .?'

'Still with the blissful marriage.'

'Oh yeh – my bloody awful marriage. Don't forget your jacket. Coming? Got everything, yeh? Yeh, that marriage. Telling you – longest bloody month of my life.'

Stacy laughed, and reached across to kiss Jennifer hard on the lips.

'You know what?' she said. 'You're the craziest mother on earth. *None* of my friends have got a mother like you. You're utterly, totally *nuts*.'

'Poor friends,' smiled Jennifer. 'Lucky you. Come on, sweet child of mine – Christ's sake let's get on this fucking *boat*, OK?'

⚓

'Oh God I don't *believe* it,' was all Jennifer frankly could manage. 'It's *another* bloody queue up another bloody ramp that leads to bloody nowhere. God Almighty – it would have been quicker to *walk* to America.'

A smallish man with a damn big smile wheeled around to face her from just in front, managing to bash his olive green rucksack into Stacy's face as he did so.

'Always chock-a-block at this stage, dear lady. Is that not correct, Captain Honeybunch?'

As Aggie grinned her practically ga-ga complicity, Jennifer and Stacy gazed at Nobby wide-eyed, each of them willing the other to be still, not quite yet dissolve or explode

47

– Stacy praying the while that her mother would not please unleash on this silly little man one of her torrents (because well, just look at her – patience was shot, you could see that); he maybe meant well, yes? Only, after all, trying to be *nice* . . .

'Chock-a-*block*,' continued Nobby, quite chattily, 'is actually a nautical term, I don't know if you're aware? Oh yes. 'Block', you know, is a seaman's term for a pulley – a pulley, yes? Up and down? While 'chock', you see, is the term employed when, as it were, rendering it solid. So when two, so to say, pulley blocks have been hoisted right up to the point where no further purchase may be directly obtained, we reach a stage where we are in a very literal sense, full to capacity, if you follow. Chock-a-block. Interesting.'

Aggie nodded wildly. 'Nobby knows all the terms,' she assured them. 'Ask him anything. Really knows the ropes. I'm Aggie, by the way, and this is my husband Nobby.' And then she snapped to attention and saluted. 'Safe passage, shipmates!'

'Nobby . . .' repeated Jennifer, very slowly – and she could have been either held, or drifting. 'I'm, er – Jennifer – this is Stacy.'

'Charmed,' said Nobby. 'And a little while back there when my trusty Captain advised you that I 'know the ropes', yes? You recall? This term in fact dates back to the days when the rigging on one of the larger sailing vessels could comprise, oh – quite literally miles of rope, you know.'

'Really?' put in Stacy, quickly (Jennifer had that look in her eye).

'Quite literally *miles* of rope,' Nobby assured her. 'Well of course it was often vital that each and every one should be identified correctly and at considerable speed, this much is plain, and therefore an old 'hand' – crewman, yes? An old 'salt' – same thing – was said to, and here it comes: know the *ropes*. Fascinating, isn't it?'

'It's . . .' Jennifer managed. Maybe she was going to say more – possibly here was just the sum total. Either way, Aggie was talking, now:

'That's what *we* are, really, at this game, now. Old hands. We just love this ship, don't we Nobby?'

'Love her.'

'How many times we've sailed on her, Nobby?'

'This crossing will comprise our seventeenth voyage on this particular liner – which is, in my humble opinion, the very finest. *QE2* also, of course – very fine ship. They're building a new *Queen Mary*, you know, and needless to say we've booked up for the maiden voyage, have we not, love? About two years, they reckon. But there'll never be anything quite like the *Transylvania*. Very special place in our affections.'

'Really?' threw in Stacy, again.

The queue was edging forward, which was something. Jennifer could be about to laugh in the man's face, or possibly occasion him physical damage (Nobby's sort of language, I can only think – thought Stacy – is catching, maybe?).

Aggie chortled conspiratorially. 'We've got a nickname for her, haven't we, Nobby?'

Nobby smiled his secret smile, while nodding with pride. 'Our own little nickname, yes. Know what it is?'

'Well of *course* we don't . . .' snapped Jennifer.

'What is it?' put in Stacy – but she needn't, apparently, have worried: both Nobby and Aggie seemed quite unperturbed – were beaming, indeed, in tandem, as if newly beatified.

'You tell them, love,' offered Nobby, with great magnanimity.

'Oh no *you*, Nobby – *you*. Your invention, after all.' And she trained her struck-wide-open eyes on Jennifer and Stacy in turn. 'It is, you know: all his own invention.'

Nobby cast down his eyes, as if to deflect the wilder

applause. 'Just came to me one day on Quarter Deck, as I gazed at her aft. *Sylvie*, I said. Just like that. And she's been Sylvie to us ever since – isn't that so, Captain Honeybunch?'

'He calls me that,' said Aggie, quite shyly. 'But isn't it a simply perfect name for her? You see it's a sort of play on Tran-*sylv*-ania, isn't it Nobby?'

'A sort of play, yes: a sort of play – yes indeed.'

'Sort of taking out the middle bit, sort of thing,' clarified Aggie. 'Ooh – stand by, Nobby – it's nearly photo time. You don't maybe know, Jennifer and . . . *Stacy*, is it? Yes – Stacy. First-timers, are you?'

As Jennifer and Stacy numbly nodded, Nobby was nodding too – his face full to bursting with indulgence and understanding.

'Always got to be a first time, hasn't there? *We* were virgins, once.'

'Nobby!' said Aggie, quite sharply.

'Sorry,' whispered Nobby. 'No offence, I'm sure.'

'It's just that they take a 'Welcome Aboard' photo of everyone just before you board,' Aggie rattled on. 'We've got quite a collection, as well you might imagine. Always try to wear something a little bit different, don't we Nobby? For the photo.'

'Always try,' agreed Nobby, rather airily. 'Always do, yes we do – we always do try to do that, yes.'

Aggie simpered at him. 'So we can tell them apart.'

Jennifer was casting her eyes wildly behind her, now (there must be escape!), but the narrow corridor was jammed with people as far as she could see: the only way was forward.

'I need a drink,' she said.

'There's generally a welcome beverage laid on of a teatime,' allowed Nobby. 'Nice hot potful – and Sylvie can usually be relied upon not to let us down in the way of a selection of peerless scones and dainties. *Embark*, you know – that's another little word with an interesting origin.'

'Look!' gasped Jennifer. 'They want you to have your picture taken. It's your turn. *Look*!'

'Do you know you're right? Best foot forward, Aggie! Yes – *embark*. 'Barco', you see, is the Spanish word meaning ship – you go on the left of me, Captain Honeybunch . . . while 'embarcar' – are you with me? Means to actually, so to say, *go on board the ship*. Follow? Well – doesn't take a great leap, does it, to see where we obtain the word 'embark' from, no? Tell you what – what say you two join us for the photo? Hey?'

'Ooh *yes*,' enthused Aggie. 'We'd certainly have no problem identifying *that* snap, would we? Nobby and me – with our two new little friends? Oh – it's going to be a *wonderful* summer!'

The picture was pinned up later that very day outside the photo shop, on board ship, alongside hundreds of bright and glossy others. To the right of the vast and flowery wreath, Aggie and Nobby seemed to be in a state approaching rapture, their arms locked tightly around Stacy on the one side, and Jennifer on the other. And neither Aggie nor Nobby appeared to notice that Stacy looked quite pallid and thoughtful, as if gauging whether or not she could maybe just hold on for a few moments longer, or if in fact a bucket was urgently needed *now* – and nor that Jennifer (maybe due to the fact that both rigid lips were pulled so well back as to reveal practically all of her teeth, as her eyes glowed dark) radiated murderous intent. Certainly one for the album, was Aggie's view – and she cheerfully paid out thirteen dollars for a pair of prints – one of them destined to be a small token of welcome, slipped beneath the door of the cabin on Six Deck registered under the names of their two new little friends (I think they must be sisters) together with a notelet inviting them both to meet up at six-thirtyish in the Piano Bar, for maybe a sherry before a three-course slap-up dinner in the Gondola restaurant. (Aggie had scribbled as a PS: Nobby is eager to 'chew the fat' –

another of those nautical terms, as it happens – but I'm sure he'll tell you all about it himself).

⚓

'Ahhhhh . . .!' was the deeply appreciative and faintly bovine lowing sound that accompanied the spreading of Stewart's arms wide as Dwight, Charlene, Earl and Suki emerged from the covered gangway and into the softly carpeted Midships reception. 'My very most *favourite* passengers, the Johnsons. Welcome *back*, I must say. Very, very, very good to see you all again, all you Johnsons. How was London? Weather nice and bright?'

'Oh *hiiii*, Stoo,' cooed Charlene. 'How you been?'

'*Good*,' responded Stewart, with emphasis. 'Doing good, Mrs Johnson – doing great.'

A little vernacular – a touch of home – went a very long way, Stewart had found in the past: you should see him with the Japanese – bowing away like one of those little plastic ostriches (or could they be emus?) one used to see around really quite a lot, one time, eager for their sip of water. A few bruised temples in the early days, yes, before he quite got the hang of the thing – but no dishonour, he would rush to assure you, was incurred or bestowed: I haven't yet, he would intimate with a twinkle, been threatened with a Samurai sword! (We're all friends here.)

As Charlene kicked things around with Stewart, Earl was bending down to murmur into his father's ear, Hey – what's with this jerk? Like it's maybe what? Ten whole *hours* since he saw us? And Dwight just shrugged and said Beats me: these English guys, I guess it's what they do, how they maybe really are.

'Dee-aaad?' whined Suki. 'I'm kinda bushed, you know? I split – grabba couple hours, maybe. See you guys – kay?'

'Sure, honey,' approved Dwight. 'Only don't go forgetting this goddam drill they put us through every single goddam time. What's with the – jeez, that mother of yours: she ever gonna quit with this guy, or what? ... yeah – what's with the alarm and all the drill anyways? Ship goes down, ship goes *down* – am I right?'

Earl was smirking his agreement; he touched his father's shoulder. 'Catch up with you guys.'

Dwight was nodding glumly.

'Yeh sure. Your mother ever quits yapping to Stoo, then maybe I can get some shut-eye too. All we did all day is nothing and I tell you, boy: I'm pooped. Hey – *Charlene*, already – enough, yeah? Leave the guy alone.'

Charlene allowed herself to be led away, her eyes and fingers still fluttering their farewells to Stewart, who was winking hard and mouthing, while still his arms were spread so wide that anyone passing could easily assume him to be the sole custodian of prior knowledge of the truth that at any moment now something very large indeed was due to be hurled right at him, his role on earth to field it deftly. He turned then to face the next batch of (marked on his clipboard 'I' for Important) upper deck cruisers, and seemed close to passing out with the pleasure this gave him.

'All I *was*,' explained Charlene, as she and Dwight climbed the broad staircase, 'was trying for him to tell me what the *toon* was?'

'Toon? What toon is this now? What's this with *toons*, Charlene?'

'Jeez, Dwight – sometimes I think you see nothing and you hear nothing and maybe you don't even *think* nothing. You didn't catch the *band* on the quayside? You didn't hear them?'

'I heard sump'n. So what?'

'So *what*? All it was was, like – the Queen's *guard* band or some goddam thing? With, like – the big fur hats?'

'Yeh yeh ...'

'So anyways, there was this *toon*, right? They were playing? It was so *familiar* ... you ever get that? When you

53

hear this toon and you know you know it but you just can't seem to . . .?' Charlene paused at the landing on One Deck and turned to search the shut-down mask that often now was all she saw where once her husband's face had shone so brightly, filled with wit and love. 'No, Dwight . . . I guess you just don't, huh?'

But soon her eyes were dancing again as they fell upon *Julie* – and Julie was already locked on and coming right on towards them (and *shee*-ut, thought Dwight – now of all times, now when all I wanna do is lie me down with a Jack on the rocks – now it's *Julie* we gotta do).

'*Julie*, sweetie!' was Charlene's vast and dazzling greeting – and the wrists of both of them clanked and jangled as they clasped each other's hands as their eyelids closed up and their lips went off and sought out the heat of their respective cheeks or jowls. (Hey look, was Dwight's take – since *morning* they ain't seen each other: what *is* this?) 'You didn't get off, sweetie? You been here all the *time*?'

Julie had on a cocked and sneering lip (rather like, you know – real late Elvis? When he was hamming it up? Yeh OK – but on Julie, this was for real).

'London I know,' was her clipped and dismissive response. 'London I been to.'

'I got the most *darling* pieces of paddery in the *Harrods* store? You'll just love 'em, Julie sweetie. Catch ya in the Zip Bar, huh? Benny OK? Still with the stummick?'

Julie just shrugged, some.

'Benny's OK. Benny's doing fine. What can I tell you, Charlene? Benny's Benny.'

And as she peeled away, Dwight just exhaled his relief.

'Maybe now we can get to our cabin? Soon it'll be with the alarm bell schtick and I don't even got off my shoes.' And as he heaved himself up the final flight of stairs (and each tread – hey, he had thought this how many times? Each tread is real shallow, you know? So how come under me they always feel so steep?): 'Benny's *OK* . . . Benny's doing *fine*. Huh. Benny ain't neither thing, I'm telling you, Charlene. Benny's one sick guy. So what's noo? I lived with Julie, all day long I'd be gnaw-shuss.'

'God*sake*, Dwight: leave it already, huh?'

Dwight turned the key in the door of their cabin.

'So,' he sighed, 'what was it? You find out?'

'What hell talking bout *now*, Dwight? I find out what?'

'Toon. The toon. You find out what toon it was, or what?'

'Oh *yeah*,' smiled Charlene, as she slipped inside. 'It's like all these great pieces, you know? They're, like – part of your life and nobody knows what they're called? You gonna take a shower? Guess I'll take a shower.'

'Yeah. So?'

'*So*? So what's with all the *so*, Dwight?'

'The *toon*, goddam it, Charlene. Jeez.'

'Why suddenly you're so eager to know the toon, now, Dwight? Before you was saying you didn't even *hear* no toon.'

Dwight sat down heavily on one of the twin beds, and sank back his head with gratitude into the pillows.

'Time to time, Charlene,' he barely whispered, 'you drive me crazy. You know that?'

Charlene stopped stock-still.

'I drive *you* crazy? I drive *you*? Oh that's *neat*, Dwight, you know? I mean, crazy from you – that's real *neat*. I'm gonna take a shower – I'm, like, *outta* here, Dwight – and maybe when I come back you've remembered some *manners*?'

Dwight closed his eyes and opened them and stared at the riveted ceiling. And then he roared up at it:

'What's the name of the goddam *toon*?!'

'Dwight God*sake*: next *door* they'll hear you!'

He turned on her weak and watery, imploring eyes, and said so softly:

'The toon . . .? Hm . . .?'

Charlene flounced away towards the bathroom, tossing back over her shoulder:

'Flintstones.'

Dwight blinked. 'Ex*cuse* me?'

'Flintstones, Dwight. Wassamadder – you ain't hearing so good? *Flintstones*. Da-da-*da*-da-da-da-fam-i-*lee* . . .?'

Dwight listened for a while to the gushing water from behind the bathroom door, and then he closed his eyes again. OK – so now I know. All she had to do was to *tell* me, yeah? For why I wanted to know, I can't even say. But now I *do* know, so I'm cool with it. Now I can rest easy. The toon was the toon from the toon. And that, dear Lord above us, is what I learned today.

I wanna sleep, is all. Is all I wanna do. But I gotta do this drill again, yeah? And then I gotta bathe and dress and then it's, jeez – *cack*tails with Julie and Benny and then I got dinner with Charlene and Earl and Suki and all she's letting me eat, now, is goddam *chicken*, on account of my bowels. And what's in my head? Tell you all that's in my head right now? It's yours for a nickel: *Da*-da-*da*-da-da-da-fam-i-*lee* . . . Cute, or what? Any which ways, I'm kinda stuck with it.

I check the icebox: we're outta Jack and we're outta beer.

And now with the bell. You hear that? The bell? I'm thinking, you don't hear that mother, then I'm telling you, boy: like, you're dead. The bell means I gotta half-hour. Then I put on some dumb kid's water-wings and we all go troop up to the restaurant and then we get to stand around like a buncha jerks and they tell us what to do if one of the biggest goddam ships in the world starts to sink in the middle of the goddam sea. You know what you do? Tell you what you do: you toot on a whistle. Yup. More'n two thousand of us up to our fuckin' eyeballs in the Atlantic Ocean like a loada rubber ducks and every goddam one of us, we're all like, blowing on *whistles*. Maybe to the toon of The Flintstones.

Again I check the icebox (why I do that?). Yeah and guess what? We're still outta Jack and we're still outta beer.

David was sitting on the bed (his side – nearest the door and away from the portholes, as Nicole had decreed) – and was doing so as unobtrusively, he would quite humbly assure you, as he possibly could manage (because you always knew, with Nicole – there was never even the shadow of a doubt – when you were very much meant to feel in the *way*: she'd cross and recross you with a pile of whatever, destined, she rather thought, for this upper drawer just here, and then a couple of suit carriers for hanging over there, behind the curtain affair, and each and every time she'd stop dead for maybe even less than a millisecond and glance down and tut just once at the sight of David's feet just, oh God – sticking out like that, and very annoyingly attached to not just his ankles and then those protruding knees of his, but all the bloody rest of him too, and then she would make quite a fair miming show of circumventing this truly irksome obstacle – not easy, simply increases my workload – before she turned and Christ, had to suffer it again).

'Look, I'll . . .' volunteered David – trying to catch just one of Nicole's busy busy eyes, while at the same time jerking away both of his in the direction of the door, as if to make clear that his fundamental intention, here, was – for the good of all – to sling his hook.

'The champagne,' said Nicole, 'I thought was a very nice gesture. And the fruit: the fruit looks lovely. Do you know which shirt you'll be wearing tonight?'

The short answer to that would of course have to be, um – no, very much no; an extended version (though here was hardly the moment – on this day of all days) would involve the eyes in a good deal of startle, while the voice would be called on to assure Nicole in a heavy tone as flat as a bat (and rubbed in well with nose-twitching oil) that in fact No, hadn't if you want the whole truth of it, actually subjected the bulk of his mind to wrestling with that one – hadn't, you know, actually got so far down the road as to have ear-marked with pinpoint precision the one and only shirt that was to be plucked from the colour-coded ranks of its chums to proudly be on display tonight (though if you press me, sweet Nicole, I should have to confess to feeling myself strongly inclining to opt in the direction of this one I'm already bloody well wearing).

'Maybe the blue . . .? You decide, Nicole. Look – why don't I just . . .?'

'We can *order* a drink, if you want a drink. Open the champagne. And there's all sorts of – here, did you see this? Menu thing? Order all sorts of sandwiches and tea and so on. What do you mean – the *blue*? You've got loads of *blue*, haven't you? Anyway. Wasn't it odd, David, when we were leaving? You know – actually setting sail, or whatever they say.'

Well yes – David just had to concur on that one. It *had* been odd, very – and not just because by this time of day all the terrible and separate both crushing and pinprick hurts and winces booting and scurrying their way around him generally tended to congregate somewhere between the base of his skull and the tip of his spine to maybe join hands for yet one more raucous end-of-term get-together till we all meet again the next time for a rousing dressing down and knees-up (which won't be long in coming). At such moments, any sort of behaviour and the majority of percep-tions appear distorted, in that they are at once both dulled and heightened – and certainly in a state of flagrant agi-tation. But if you add to this the very singular sensation of standing on the deck of this truly extraordinarily vast liner (you don't get it, really, till you're on it) with many hundreds of eager and wind-whipped strangers to the left and right of you while almost imperceptibly this mighty thing with little you inside it inches at first and then coolly slips away from the dockside, as even more hundreds of nearly hysterical and very rum sods on shore wave at you flags and scarves as if you're going to war (and we're not, are we? Doing that?) and then when you lob on top of this the thought that from now on in it is to be the sea, the sea, the sea and then more sea – until in about a whole week's time, this gives way as dawn comes up to the looming mass and sparkle of New York City, then I think it is fair to say that *Yes*, on the whole – yes: leaving (actually setting sail, or whatever they say) was, if you like – as Nicole would anyway have it – odd, decidedly odd (not to say outright astonishing – as well as, and I'm thinking this now, just a little bit scary, in a way I have yet to nail down).

'Was,' said David. 'Was.'

'One good thing,' said Nicole, quite absently – her mind gone from setting sail by now (she'd long ago departed from that) – 'there's certainly plenty of drawerspace . . .'

And David knew (of course he knew) that you just didn't comment on that sort of comment – a low and indecipherable murmur, maybe (for what other sort of noise, in the face of such an observation, could actually and with profit be made?).

'Look,' said David, by way of a stab at direction – and standing up now, maybe, would add to the general air of shifting, here. 'I think I'll – I'll maybe just go and have a *wander*, yes? Check out the lie of the . . . well, not *land*, obviously, but you know what I . . . And then I'll, what – meet you somewhere, will I? Or shall I just come back and change and – ?'

'*Two* things,' said Nicole with emphasis; and then she was dreaming again: 'I think I'm OK for *shoes* . . . but I'm not sure I've brought enough tights, now . . . Still, I expect they've – you can probably get, I should think.' But soon she's back: '*Two* things, David, we have to do tonight –

'Cruise Director', whatever that means, wants to welcome us, which is sweet, and then we're having a quite little sort of private-ish partyette with the Captain – rather exciting. His main thing for everyone else is *tomorrow* night, apparently.'

'Really?' put in David, edging across to the door. The Cruise Director. *And* a quite little sort of private-ish partyette with the Captain: oh what joy. Probably need about four shirts in total, for that little lot.

'Which is,' continued Nicole, 'a bit more like it. I mean I'd *heard* that competition winners get treated like, you know – film stars and things, but so far I haven't seen very much sign of it, I must say.'

There was a knock on the door when David was just about on this side of it – and that made him jump, while at the same time it served to encourage one or two venomous membranes that lurked just above his left eye to nip in and give him a swift kicking and remind him who's boss. David opened the door and there was a very small and smiling brown and broad-faced young woman, peering gamely through the basketed drama of exotic flowers she was holding out before her.

'Captain and crew – he say welcome,' she said.

Nicole was at once enchanted.

'Oh how perfectly – ! David – aren't they – ?'

David nodded (would've tipped the woman, but she'd scuttled away). 'So – later then, yes? Hour? Bit less?'

'Orchids – and *lilies*, I think these are – oh and *freesias*, they'll make the room smell lovely. Not too sure about the maidenhair *fern*, though – spoils it, I think. What do you think, David? I might just remove that, I reckon. What do you think, David? Oh God – no good asking you anything, is it? Oh God *go*, if you're going, David – why do you always keep on hanging *about*?'

David nodded, once and shortly, and left the cabin. The corridor was hushed and maybe a bit too warm and so incredibly long and unchanging that David was again feeling this slight but salty prick of fear. It was a bit like, maybe . . . but then anything big, anything on this huge sort of scale would *always* seem, wouldn't it, a bit like a film set? But David felt sure that there could in truth be maybe four or six cabin doors to either side of him, and if he tried to venture further in either direction he'd be sure to slam face first into flush-fitting mirrors cunningly mounted to perpetuate the illusion.

He was barely aware of the undersides of his feet softly trudging the eternal length of the rich and royal blue carpet (he had an arm out in front of him, but no mirrors so far). From time to time, a young man in a neat white jacket and bits of gold about his shoulders would appear and grin at him really quite manically and then disappear, David wasn't sure where. A very old lady then hove into view – everything about her face and unwisely bare arms was yearning to be allowed to slump on down to the ground, and rest there; her head was bowed so low that her sole view of life, David was surprised to find himself thinking, would have to be limited to the slow and deliberate placing of her trainer-clad feet, as each of them in turn moved inexorably towards whatever was coming to her. Earrings alone must have weighed a ton. In fact, looking at her again – and now she and David were practically crossing, her softly white and crinolined face had set up a great slash of a smile that in any other context would have scared you half to death – if she could only bear to part company with even half of all that jewellery, she might well find people saying to her Oh *my* how you've *grown* (and by way of a bonus, she could then raise her sights and get a broader perspective on life).

Now then. Let's have a look at these signs . . . (And another thing – I'm not actually aware of any real *movement*, you know, although we've been at sea now for what must it be? Couple of hours? Couple of hours at least, I should say:

there's a sort of booming other-worldliness about me, yes, there is that – that slightly airless and pressurized atmosphere, but no more so than you get in the bowels of those sorts of hotels that do functions, and so on – when you emerge slain and parched from some bloody conference or workshop or Christ knows, and those cups and plates and beakers are all lined up for you on grey-topped limed-oak tables).

Black Horse Pub. Upper Deck. That's, where is it . . .? Two floors up. Right. That sounds favourite. Hm. Wonder what Rollo and Marianne are up to? They each got a cabin to themselves, you know. Because they are both young single people of opposing gender. My wife Nicole and me – we're of opposing gender too (well let's face it: opposing bloody everything, really) but we got lumped in together. Which is cosy. Not young, you see: and nor are we single.

And no, since you ask, Nicole: I don't *know* why it is (honestly couldn't tell you) that I always keep on hanging *about*. I get asked this too by Trish – but with her, I think, this means Why don't you ever just *come* to me. Think so, yes. Could be wrong. But with you, Nicole – it's different.

↓

'It's not, is it . . .?' enquired Marianne doubtfully, as if not wishing to *offend*, or anything, but at the same time earnestly seeking some big reassurance, here. 'I mean – very *grand*, is it? Do you know what I mean, Rollo? Is it what you – ? I don't think it's quite what I *expected*, I think I mean. I mean – it's very sort of big and impressive and all the rest of it . . . it's just that I don't think it's – '

'What in Christ's name are you *on* about?' zapped in Rollo.

He had been swiveling this way and that on his bar stool, glancing from time to time at the massed ranks of bottles, lit up and set against a mosaic of coloured mirrors (thinking

Mmm – Southern Comfort: like that. And mmm – Bacardi: can quite go for that with cranberry). But you couldn't really blank out Marianne for all that long; like a lot of girls, Rollo supposed (don't have much, do I? To go on) she'd only maunder on in that dorky wet girly dweeb little way of hers – not actually *saying* anything, you will of course observe: never actually concluding a *thought*, oh Christ no. Just rambling on and on and on about sod bugger all until you're just forced to bloody ask her what in Christ's name she's *on* about – and then she'd have some half-arsed and interminable go at actually starting it all up again and *telling* you (as if I gave a shit).

'The *ship*, of course,' snapped back Marianne – trying again to wriggle herself into a degree more comfort on the too-high stool (I keep on feeling it's going to tip right over). 'What on earth do you *think* I'm talking about? *Transylvania*, yes? We're on it? You've noticed?'

'OK, mm, yes – very bloody amusing. *Transylvania* – yes: we're on it – so bloody what? Stupid bloody way of getting anywhere, I think. Christ – we could be in New York by dinner time if only we'd done what *normal* people do and taken a bloody *plane*. Check out the club scene – rave till dawn: yeh! Instead of that we're stuck in this bloody stupid so-called 'pub' with phony pumps and phony glass and phony bloody everything else – and Christ, look around you, Mar – it's bloody *empty*: where the hell *is* everybody? Do you think they all saw sense and got off at the last moment? Bloody wish *I* had . . .'

'*Daft*, Rollo . . .'

'Oh no they *didn't*, though, did they? Cos we saw them all at the poxy little safety drill with orange great plastic things stuck up around their bloody ears. I didn't wear mine.'

'You did when that steward person or whatever he was *told* you to, though, didn't you? You went all red.'

'Oh shuttup, Mar, can't you? Took it off again after, though.'

'It was pretty funny, actually – all that. Everyone standing around with a lifejacket and listening to what to do if the ship went down . . . God, we'd only just got *on* it . . .' And here Marianne let out a brief and snorting half-laugh which she sort of covered up with three of her fingers, as another aspect struck her. 'And *then* – do you remember? Did you hear him, Rollo? After they'd told us all what to do if faced with *drowning*, right – he then said, all po-faced – ' and at this point Marianne had to sit up straight and drag down the corners of her mouth into an approximation of a humourless official, and her voice husked up and clouded over in tune with it all: ' 'And now – a word about *fire* . . .' Jesus! Fire and water – one of them'll get us, that's for sure. What do you prefer, Rollo? You going to burn or sink?'

Rollo had the goodness to smirk.

'D'you want another of these? Barman's pushed off now.'

'I think I'll just have a Diet Coke. Where's Dad? Do you think he's got lost?'

'He'll find us. We're in a *pub*, aren't we? He could find it blindfold. Unless he's been waylaid by some *other* bar, of course, in which case we'll have to go and haul him out at midnight.'

'Oh don't be so *mean*, Rollo. You're always going on about Dad.' And in an effort to head him off at the pass (because he did, you know – go on and on about Dad, Rollo, all the time, all the time – and once he'd started he'd never stop): 'But the *ship*, Rollo – that's what I was saying. It's not like in all those old movies, is it? When you see all the ballrooms and chandeliers and columns and stuff on those world cruises and things. Maybe I'm just thinking of *Titanic*.'

'Oh Christ don't mention the word *Titanic*. Did you hear all those little kids on the stairs just after the drill thing? Oh look, Mar – bloke's back: Coke, yeah? Yeah, um – nother Budweiser and a Diet Coke, please.'

'Ice in the Coke?' asked Sammy. 'Can I get you some nuts, or something?'

'Yeh, ice,' said Marianne. 'That Diet? Yeh? Great. I don't want nuts – you want nuts, Rollo?'

'I'm bloody *starving* – if I start in on the nuts I'll never stop. When's dinner round here? Yeh – let's have some nuts.'

Sammy smiled as he poured the beer deftly into the glass – just slanted at the angle he had been told and told to slant the damn thing.

'It's *always* dinner time on the *Transylvania*. People only stop eating to come in places like this and start drinking.'

'Oh *God* . . .' groaned Rollo. 'Is that *really* all there is to do? I mean Jesus, Mar – that's a thought, you know. It's nearly a *week* we're on this thing. What in hell are we supposed to *do*?'

'There's a kind of nightclub,' volunteered Sammy. 'Regatta Club, it's called – other end of this deck: down there, and keep going.'

'*Regatta* Club!' burst out Rollo, with true deep loathing. 'Regatta Club – *Christ*. What sort of crap happens there?'

'Some people like it. There's a band on in the early part of the evening, pretty sure. I've never actually been, if I'm honest – I'm always stuck here. And there's a deejay. Strobe lights. Not too bad.'

'*Yeah* . . .' intoned Rollo, with real and heartfelt scorn. 'A groovy popster deejay spinning all our fab and fave, oh Christ – *platters* by Abba and Ricky Martin and the Spice Girls – and that Doo-Wah-bloody-*Diddy* thing . . .!'

Sammy laughed at that out loud. 'That's pretty much exactly what Jilly said! She works here – behind the bar. She hates all that stuff.'

'Oh look!' said Marianne suddenly. 'There's Dad. Can he see us? I don't think he can see us. Dad! Dad! Oh God look at him – he's going the wrong way. Dad! *Dad*! Over here!'

Rollo said to Sammy, 'Who's this Jilly, then?'

'She's due on in five minutes. She's actually my, sort of – you know: girlfriend sort of thing.'

65

'Oh,' said Rollo. 'Right.'

Marianne touched his arm. 'It's OK – he's seen us. He's coming over. Come on, Dad! What took you so long? What *kids*, Rollo? What kids were you talking about?'

'*Christ*,' growled David, as he yanked out a stool and dumped himself up on to it. 'Don't ask. Like a bloody maze, this place.'

'Didn't you hear them?' piped up Rollo. 'All those kids running up and down the staircase.'

'Like a bloody *warren* . . .' huffed David. 'Grouse, please – large one, touch of water, no ice. Good.'

'They kept on going – ' and Rollo opened wide his eyes and constricted his throat and forced it now to cope with the coming falsetto – 'It's like the *Titanic*! It's just like the *Titanic*! Christ – you should've seen everyone's *faces* . . .'

'But that's just my *point*,' pouted out Marianne. 'It's *not*, is it? Do *you* see what I mean, Dad? It just *isn't*, is it?'

'Oh Christ,' moaned Rollo. 'Here we bloody go again.'

'It's not what, love?' asked David – rather more kindly now that the first hit of Grouse had warmed his mouth and then rushed down him.

'Oh, sort of . . .' And Marianne rolled her eyes and flipped her fingers as her lips were left to flutter around what might well prove to be the mot juste. No: didn't. '*Grand*, if you see what I mean . . .?'

'*Pretty* bloody grand . . .' grunted David.

And Rollo glanced round as a new voice now jumped in:

'Hi, everyone. My name is Jilly, and I shall be your barmaid for the evening. Happy for the moment? Get you something?'

'OK for now,' said Rollo (and I maybe did, did I, come out with it just a touch too quickly? Yeh – and I think I must've sounded like a nerd).

'*No*, Daddy – you don't see what I *mean*,' Marianne was persisting. 'I mean it's *big*, of course it is. Yes? It's *big*?'

'Well spotted,' said Rollo, drily.

'Shuttup, Rollo – I'm not talking to you. But look, Dad – look around you: it's not at all in any way *grand* . . .'

'Mm,' nodded David. 'I sort of see.' Yes – I *sort* of see: I *sort* of see a lot of things, and I so don't care about practically bloody all of them. 'Another large Grouse, please, Jilly. You kids all right? Yup? OK. Just the Grouse, then.'

'When do we *eat*?' went Rollo – smiling briefly in Jilly's direction because he thought he maybe half caught a glimpse, there, of her briefly smiling at him – but of *course* (he now saw) it wasn't that at all, was it? Oh God how *embarrassing*. All it was was a polite and simple acknowledgement of Dad having ordered a drink – that she had taken in the words and their meaning and would now turn around and jam the glass against the optic (as, indeed, she now was doing. Mm. She's got a lovely arse on her, look at it. Mm).

'Up to your mother,' sighed David. 'She's changing. I said to her where we'd be. Yeh – pretty hungry, actually.'

Yes indeed: up to your mother. I don't, you know, say this with any regret or sense of belittlement, not any more I don't. There was once a time, of course – way back – when I would breed and then feed deep resentment for anything at all that could be up to your mother because, yes, that's partly me – but also my generation, you see: I'm the man, is how the thinking goes, and so it's very much up to me. But that was then – oh, so much *then*. Now, well – now I'm all for anything whatever being up to your mother or, failing that, anyone else at all who's passing. Which maybe, at work, is beginning to show: never ever put myself forward, you see – don't want to be responsible for anything, do I, because then what it is, what it becomes is my responsibility, doesn't it? And that is not at all what I want, because in truth – if I really am about to come clean, here – I'm not actually a responsible person. Not any longer. I am responsible for nothing, and that is the way I need it to be. All it really is, I suppose, is that sometimes when one thing or another fairly naturally occurs and I just happen to be around, yes? Well, if that thing, that thing – whatever – that has just occurred, is generally perceived to be *good*, to be *positive*, and if such a result is attributed (almost always misguidedly – all I do is nothing, now) to, um – *me*, well – well then, fine (oh good). But if people are pointing the finger – if what they are actually saying is Oh Dear Me: here is a *bad* thing . . . and further, if such a result is attributed (almost always misguidedly – all I do is nothing, now) to, um – *me*, well – well then, shame (too bad).

Anyway, anyway . . . as soon as your mother, as I say, has got changed (not changed out of the outfit she finally elected to wear for the travelling down here, you understand – oh good Lord no. That particular outfit was discarded within minutes of entering the cabin in favour of some sort of wide-legged and not unshiny trousers, maybe pantaloon sort of efforts – suitable, she said, for lounging in one's berth; yes really – she truly did say that). But now that berth-lounging is out and Captain-meeting followed by Duchess Grill dining are next on the agenda, so does Nicole, your mother, find herself hanging up with care the Pierrot or Harlequin number, and easing herself with yet more of that very idiosyncratic care of hers (she has care to spare, Nicole – she is concealed from view from behind a scaffolding of care, it sometimes seems, though there's none of it there for me) . . . easing herself, as I say, into whatever svelte and chic and just-so thing she deludedly imagines to be eye-catchingly correct for shaking hands with a glorified bloody sailor (who will smile, incline his head, and fail to catch her name). This is, of course, always assuming – and it is seldom wise, with Nicole, to even contemplate assumptions – that she has not by now got firmly in her mind that Captain-meeting and Duchess Grill-dining are not two events so easily encompassed by just the one single costume. In which case – and it seems, as I mull it over, increasingly likely – she will be back down again to number

One Deck, changing the whole ensemble just one more time (maybe, in the interim for thought, slipping back on the, now I think of it, outright glossy and clownish apparel that she very determinedly deems so fit for these singular if plenteous berth-lounging moments).

So, Rollo, in answer to your question – simply put and deeply felt – When Do We Eat, the honest answer is Christ alone knows, right? An answer neatly dodged but at the same time well summed up by my telling you straight that it's up to your mother. I said to her where we'd be. But, when we encounter, she will quite surely not agree with this. She will be unshakeable in her absolute knowledge that where I said, in fact, we'd be was somewhere else entirely, and to any suggestion that there is maybe here the merest shadow of a case for arguing that this can't – can it, actually, Nicole? – be wholly true as Rollo, you see, as well as Marianne and myself have somehow managed to congregate in the precise and purported bloody fucking spot where I said we'd be, well . . . in response to any of that Nicole will merely, I fear, dismiss the two children's limited understanding on the grounds that they are, the both of them, no more than children, while my own woodenly put and futile protestations will be swept away, and then ritually atomized. Why? On account of I'm not *responsible*. And here, of course, she has a point.

'What are you thinking about, Daddy? Have you seen? Rollo seems to have made a new *friend*. How terribly *fond*.'

David heard these words from his little girl (who, going by the tone, was less than pleased about this *friend*, did she say, of Rollo's: siblings, he had observed, could be like that) and by way of reply he smiled quite distantly and touched her hand. And then he said:

'I was just thinking, as I said, that I'm actually pretty, you know – hungry, sort of. Yes – they do seem to be getting on rather well, don't they?'

Yes they do. Just take one look at him. Chatting away and

laughing with that very pretty bargirl. And what do I feel about that? Do I feel like a proud father – one who has raised his son to man's estate, and now gazes fondly at these early and crackling first steps in the endless dance? No I fucking well don't. I feel envy. Raw and mean and bloody *envy* (pure and simple – not, of course, that it could ever be either).

'Daddy – can we wait for Mummy at a table? These stools are just murder.' And as David lowered his eyes in acquiescence to that (along with just anything else that might later occur to her) and prepared to move away from the bar, Marianne suddenly clutched his arm just above the elbow, and was whispering earnestly into his ear: 'Look – see him? Just there, Daddy. That's the weird bloke from when we were boarding. I think he must be terribly lonely, or something, poor sod.'

David clocked him, and nodded. 'The man in black,' he said. 'Rollo – when you decide to put down our delightful barmaid, do you think you could ask her to pilot across a large Grouse to that table over there? Good of you.'

Rollo was caught mid-bray, but still managed to turn on to his father a look of extraordinary sourness.

'Oh *Christ* . . .' sighed Rollo, as David and Marianne moved away.

'What did he say?' asked Jilly. 'He's your father, right?'

'Oh *right*, yes. That's him. That's my father all right, yes. He said to ask you for another vat of Scotch. Christ Almighty, he'll be falling over and it's not even *dinner* time, yet. God, I'm starving. Anyway, Jilly – I got the message about the Regatta Club: shit-hole, right?'

Jilly wrinkled her nose, and one of her eyes might even nearly have winked at him before she turned away to attend to the Grouse.

'It's not,' she said airily over her shoulder, 'all *that* bad. Provided,' she tacked on with a smile as she crossed the bar with David's drink, 'you don't mind listening to Mambo Number Five about ten times a night.'

'Oh *Christ* . . .'

'*And*,' went on Jilly – who now was back – 'Voulez-Vous Coucher Avec Moi Ce Soir?'

Rollo looked down into the scummy swirl of the last of his Bud.

'*That*,' he said slowly – and now he risked a roguish glance – 'is not such a bad idea . . .'

'Ha *ha*,' said Jilly, flatly. But she didn't seem *upset*, or anything, don't think. Was she upset? Oh Christ – so hard to tell. This sort of job, she's paid to be *nice*, isn't she? So how do you tell? 'But they do stay open late, there – which is good. Cocktails are cool. And even if the music's crap, at least it's *loud*. What sort of stuff are you into, then, Rollo?'

'You want a drink, or something?'

Jilly shook her head. 'Maybe have one later. I like electronic.'

And Rollo's eyes were instantly ablaze. 'Me too! *I* do! That's what I – ! Techno, yeh? You ever go to raves?'

And Jilly's eyes were dreamy. '*Love* going to raves. Love them. Moby's my man.'

'Moby! Moby! I think Moby's just fantastic. Jesus, Jilly!'

'Trouble is, I don't go bloody anywhere, now. Been stuck on this ship for months. Seems like *years*. Only get a day – less than a day, just get a poxy few hours in New York and then we're – '

'Oh no – really? You mean you can't check out the scene?'

'Can't check out *anything*, can I? We're off to Jamaica after that. Won't see that place either. And even back in England, my bloke – Sammy, yeh? At the bar?'

'Oh yeh. Sammy. Right.'

'Right. Well he's really into *saving*, you know? Everything I spend it's, like – a sin? Getting to be a real drag.'

'What – saving like in . . . what, you getting married, or something?'

Jilly spread her fingers on the bar, and looked down. And then she really startled Rollo by suddenly looking up again, and then right at him.

'Yeah – I suppose . . . *he* thinks we are, anyway.'

'And you?'

'Yeah – I *suppose*. Dunno. Not sure. Haven't really *done* anything yet, you know? And Sammy, he says that's the whole point: we get married and we do everything together. But I don't know. On this cruise, right? You see so many couples that just bloody *hate* each other, you know? I mean, they seem to be married to the only person in the world they can't even stand to *be* with . . .'

'Mm. Mum and Dad are a bit like that.'

Jilly nodded slowly. 'So . . . I don't know. Really. I think you're wanted, Rollo – they're calling you, looks like.'

Rollo chucked his eyes skywards – for Jilly's sake, mainly – before reluctantly rolling them round to focus on whatever (he just could guess). Yeh – Mum has finally and about bloody time rolled up, and now she's making all these impatient gestures as if *she's* been stuck here waiting for *us*. Christ. Not that I've minded waiting.

'Yeh,' he said, with drawn-out resentment. 'Gotta go. So look, Jilly – what about I maybe meet up with you in the shit-hole, later?'

Jilly smiled. 'Mambo Number Five?'

'Better than nothing. Better than *this*. And the cocktails are cool, you said.'

'I'm here till eleven-thirty . . .'

'So, what . . .? Twelve, then?'

'Mm. Maybe round twelve. Yeh – why not?'

'Cool.'

'Great. See you there, then, Rollo.'

And Rollo turned away and all he thought was *Yeeee-esssss*! And then she was calling him back again:

'What's your cabin number?'

Is what Rollo could swear that she said. Possible? Jesus.

'Jesus,' he said.

'I *mean*,' clarified Jilly, with heavy and – even to Rollo – unmistakeable put-down, 'so I can charge for the *drinks*.'

And Rollo, oh God, was only doing it again: going all red, like when that manky ponce had told him to put on his bloody lifejacket thing. Oh Christ, oh Christ.

He dangled his key fob before her, signed the tab, and was hugely irritated when he realized that Marianne was fizzing at his side, and tugging at his sleeve.

'Oh God come *on*, can't you, Rollo? Mummy's going *mad*.'

Rollo brushed her away and inhaled very deeply, the better to be equipped for the pantomime sigh that now accompanied the weighty droop of his leaden eyelids.

'Here's to Techno,' he said to Jilly.

She smiled. 'It beats my heart. Midnight.'

And Rollo barely heard his mother berating just anyone for getting in her way, as she repeated again and again full into a series of increasingly startled faces, 'Signal Deck. Captain. Where is it? Signal Deck. Captain. Where *is* it? Oh God nobody knows *anything*!' But he was brought back to earth by that bloody odd bloke they had gaped at while boarding. As David, Nicole, Marianne and finally Rollo were bustling by him, he held up a pen as if to bestow upon them the Sign of the Cross. His eyes as he sat there, thought Marianne suddenly, seemed so terribly mournful.

'Most interesting article,' came his light and wistful voice, as his pen started tapping at the magazine before him. 'According to this,' he went on quite ponderously – seemingly impervious to the fact that his reluctant audience had crashed and thudded into the backs of one another, so abrupt was this curtailment of their headlong dash for the Signal Deck – 'it surely would seem that the best-selling bra in the United Kingdom goes under the name of 'Doreen'. Revels in it, one might say.'

Nicole – now practically exploding with impatience – had failed to register a word Tom had said, but bestowed upon him anyway her smile that said And Aren't You A Perfectly *Sweet* Little Idiot? – while almost punching David into forward motion. Marianne had caught her father's eye and the gleam there warned her not to erupt just yet, while promising that he too would do his utmost to keep down the worst of it. And Rollo was just thinking Jesus, listen to this: It Beats My *Heart*. And his next thought was *Midnight* (whereupon his mind took life and spun off wildly).

⚓

They didn't, mused Tom, seem at all eager to stop and chat – which must, I quite see, wholly be my fault, yes, but for the life of me I couldn't in honesty tell either of us why – quite what foot I put wrong. I'm out of the way of it, is the truth of the matter – striking up a conversation with someone quite unknown to me. Even with Mary, over all those years – did we talk? Did we? Were we really talking? There were sounds with meanings that passed between us, so yes – communication, certainly . . . but could such muted mutterings in all frankness be construed by the outsider to be general, everyday talk? Not, of course, that any of it was destined for the outsider – which is maybe where we started to come unstuck. We lived together, Mary and me – ate together, listened to the wireless together (even used to, yes, sleep together, one time, in the same quite cramped bed – but you get so scared of moving, I used to find, when another body's that close to you: you daren't even clear your throat). And if we were ever out – restaurant, say, or on one of our little jaunts – we'd address to a third party only those comments absolutely essential to the smooth running of the event itself. We would order our food, and thank the waitress when it was set before us. At the meal's closure, I would ask for the bill (and, more often than not, request it again – they could be so lax). We certainly would have expressed our appreciation had someone helped us on with our coats, but you so rarely get that, these days – like porters at stations and chairs in shops: gone, all gone.

The point, I suppose, I am making, is that even when Mary and I were out in the world and people were about us, we still felt quite secluded. And now she's gone, the only one left to talk to is myself, which is why now I am given, I can only suppose, to such protracted ponderings as these. I have tried to talk to Mary – tried that, yes – but you see, I can't actually recall quite what words I used to form, and nor her mode of response. There were just soft sounds between us, warmly undulating, launched and fielded, and somehow unerringly finding their nebulous target.

I think, now that I have finished my coffee, I shall take a short stroll. See a little bit more of the ship. Because if I have dinner this early, it'll be over so soon, and what, pray, am I meant to do then?

So I did try, you see, to talk to those people. I gave to them one of the facts I have carefully garnered and gleaned over the weeks and months: I thought they might have helped to break the ice. I had not *really* just read about 'Doreen' in a magazine, no (a little white lie, which I thought acceptable). I had in fact hoarded it (with others) for ages. I judged it to be slightly amusing, in maybe a rather endearing and British sort of a way – conceivably engaging. Apparently not. I thought that Mary might rather approve – of my talking, I mean: she would be sad for me, I felt, knowing I was sitting all alone – which is all I really did with Mary beside me, but then she would quite regularly glance across to me, you know, and smilingly encourage the continuance of my musings; whereupon it felt quite all right to do so. It is possible, I feel now – and not just now (towards the end I felt it too) – that maybe all that seemed so right between us was not that at all: in the larger sense, it could be, could it – *wrong*? A thing I hate to be. It's a difficult thought, but I have to think it: could be our togetherness drove us apart.

75

God knows, thought Stacy, where Mum's got to now. We'd gone up in the lift to some deck or other – not this one, pretty sure – heading we thought at least vaguely in the direction of the restaurant (not one of the *posh* ones, as Mum kept on pointing out: we're down the slummy end, girl) and then she discovered she'd laddered her tights.

'Oh *shit*! How the hell did that happen? Oh God – I'll have to go and change them, I suppose. Should have kept on the trousers. Where the hell are we, Stacy?'

'Says Two Deck, here. Oh come on, Mum – no one'll see your tights, will they? Let's go – I'm starving.'

'*Correction*, sweet child. My legs, I shall have you know, are one of my most attractive features.'

'You have others?'

'Cheek. All eyes, I promise, will be focused upon my legs – and although I am not wholly against the *existence* of ladders, they should really be seen only in the context of fishnet stockings whose tops are just showing beneath something short and rather slutty. You have to pick your moment, of course.'

'Oh Mum – you're quite insane. Well look – go back if you have to. I'll meet you, yes? Where shall I meet you? Restaurant?'

'Need a *drink*,' said Jennifer, with emphasis. 'I'll find you at – I don't know . . . I mean, presumably there's a bar attached to the restaurant, yes? I'll see you there. I mean – God's sake, Stacy, if you're that worried you can always come with me.'

'Oh I can't be bothered dragging back down there again. I can't stand that cabin – it's so dark and poky.'

'That's because there's two of us. And there's no window thing. And, of course, because it's dark and poky. Be thankful we're not in the engine room.'

'OK well look – I'll sit somewhere close to the aisle,

passage – what do they call them? Gangways? Near the restaurant.'

'Sit where you like. Just *don't*, do *not* – understand? Be anywhere near those dreadful people. OK? We want to sit with Cary Grant or James Bond, not that grinning one-man freak show *Nobby*.'

Yes. Well. That was simply *ages* ago, all that, and I'm still just sitting here waiting – and I keep on getting foody smells from somewhere and I'm absolutely *ravenous*, now. God knows what she's doing – even what deck she's on. Maybe she's run into Cary Grant.

It's odd, wandering about a boat, ship, this size. Never seen anything like it before. Sometimes you forget you're afloat at all because unless you go quite high – you know, the upper sort of open decks – you don't actually see the sea all that much: just little glimpses of bluey grey, here and there. You're aware of the motion forward, though, I think: the speed. It's a bit like the floor is strumming beneath you, and when you walk along your feet always feel as if they landed an inch or so away from where you thought they'd come down. On the staircases – the steps seem so shallow, I don't know if they are – you certainly feel you want to hold on to the railing, but still you find yourself getting up there in a sort of a crablike way – a bit sideways? I felt I looked like a gateleg table.

I went up too far. I was looking for Upper Deck, right, but somehow I came out on to what they call the Boat Deck (which is pretty nuts, isn't it? I mean – they're all *that*) and the view there, God – totally amazing. Well – that's the odd thing, really: I say *view*, but of course there's nothing actually there to look at. I think the weirdest thing is the constant horizon. I mean – we're all used to horizons at the seaside, right? There's the sea – boat or two, buoy maybe – and it touches the line of the sky. Then you turn back to the town and there's the pier and the traffic and the front and the noise. But it's not like that here: the horizon goes all around you. All you ever see is the deep flat grey of the ocean, and the slightly brighter sky coming down to meet it. And nothing else at all. I even thought I saw everything dip down at the corners of my eyes: I was sensing the actual curvature of the earth – it's like we're on a tiny, solitary island amid a liquid wasteland. I tell you – if this ship weren't so bloody big and solid, it's quite a scary thought. The distance – that's what makes you realize. I mean, we've been at sea for what, now? About three, four hours, I reckon – and here we are apparently in the middle of this vast world of nothingness; but we're *not* in the middle, are we? We haven't even started – there's another six *days* of this. Tell you: scary.

I wonder who all these people are. I can't decide if they're a real mix of types, or not. I mean, what I suppose I was absolutely dreading is that everyone around would be just, like, totally *ancient* – like you keep hearing people on these cruise things are. Maybe crossings are different from cruises; of course, this is just the tail end of a simply *eternal* cruise for a lot of them: they've spent whole *seasons* on board. And I heard the steward or whatever he is just say to that couple behind me that the more expensive, the grander the suite, the less likely they are to actually ever get off the ship at any of the amazing places they stop at. Mad or what? It's almost as if they're just waiting to die, and only feel safe in very posh places. But there seem to be youngish people too, and quite a few families, which I didn't expect. Hee – there was this little boy here earlier with his mother, looked like, and she was going, Oh *Timmy* (or whatever he was called) – just look at your *hands*! What have you been *touching*? We'll have to go down to the cabin and wash them. And then the little boy – all big eyes and really standing his ground, you know? He goes Oh *no* – and the mother says Oh *yes*, young man – right now. And the boy comes back with No *listen* – if we all sit down and wait, my hands will both come clean all by their *own*. Sweet. If you like kids, and stuff.

It's actually pretty cool, just sitting on your own and listening in. You don't want to *look* like you're listening, of course; I've been stirring and stirring the dregs of this orange for ages – looking right into it so people will think I don't have any ears; and no – I don't dare order another because Mum keeps banging on about the *money* thing – and anyway, all I really want to do is *eat* and that's meant to be free so where on earth *is* she? (Well – not on earth, of course: at sea.) Another thing I heard – that table over there (don't look now), just by the piano. See it? Well – the white-haired woman – *truly* one of the wrinklies, amazingly old, looks about a hundred plus – she said to whoever the other woman with her was in a quite restrained maybe Texas accent (I think it was Texan – not very good on American accents: Texan is the whiney one, yes?) that in all honesty – mah *dee-uh* – she had been homesick now for thirty-nine-and-one-bit days. God. It's so *weird* that Mum and me are on this ship – it's so un-*us*. But she's got this thing about flying, see – which amazes just everyone when she tells them: no one feels Mum could be afraid of *anything* – and she was just so adamant that we get to this wedding. I know, I know – you don't have to remind me: Mum is totally down on marriage, yeh I know – but this is her only sister (my Auntie Min) and well, I don't know what she's thinking . . . maybe she's going out there in a last-ditch effort to change Min's mind and carry her back to England, in triumph. (Auntie Min's only in America at all because she met a New Yorker in London and married him and went with him and then she, yeh, divorced him.) All I can think about now is *food*. Oh Lord – where *is* she?

'*God!*' Stacy could at last exhale. 'At *last* – I've been waiting for simply – '

'God Almighty, Stacy, where on God's earth have you *been*?'

And Stacy just sighed a bit and wagged her head and went on stabbing at the warm and rotten end of her long-dead orange. It's just typical, this: I've been hanging around for bloody *years*, and so of *course* it's my fault, isn't it?

'I've been here all the time. Where've *you* been – that's more to the point. Doesn't take that long to change a pair of tights. Did you run into James Bond, maybe. Mum? That it?'

'Need a drink,' huffed Jennifer, flopping down beside her. 'What's that funny music? Oh God look – there's someone on the *harp*. What an extraordinary sound. Need a gin. Where's the bloke? And for your information, Stacy – and if you had eyes in your sweet little face you would've already *seen* – I'm wearing my rather smart black trousers, yes? Bought in the Harvey Nichols sale for half their original price which was still nonetheless about four times the amount of money I currently possessed. How foolish is that? Think of it as an investment. Oh thank God – here's the bloke. Evening, yes – large G and T, please. Thanks. Stacy? You OK with that?'

Stacy shrugged. 'Whatever you want.'

'Well it's not what *I* want, is it? Do you want another orange, or what?'

'Well . . .'

'Too much orange is not at all good for you. Acid. Also, it discolours the teeth. Just the gin, thank you.'

And when the waiter had left, Jennifer leaned forward across the table and informed Stacy with huge accusation:

'I don't seem actually to have *packed* the bloody tights, which is a total and utter pain in the arse because if they *do* sell them on board they're bound to cost an absolute fortune. The odd thing is I distinctly remember putting them *in*. I got two Boots multipacks and I could have sworn I bundled them in with the Tampax and the Ambre Solaire.'

The gin arrived and it tinkled to Jennifer's profound satisfaction: she ate a good half of it quickly.

'This plinky-plonky harp actually rather gets on your *tits*, doesn't it? After a while. And no I *didn't*, since you ask, encounter anyone *remotely* similar to Mister Bond, and don't please think it was for the want of looking. All the men around seem to be short and fat and more or less bald – or else sort of papery *old*. Sometimes all three. Four. Except for the waiters, who seem quite sweet – but I've heard they're all of the homosexualistic persuasion. Anyway, they're too poor. Also – painful-looking pimples.' Jennifer slurped again, and her eyes now gleamed at the memory of the next lot: 'Talking of *Bond*, though – did I ever tell you about all that business with *Simon*? No? I did, didn't I?'

'Which one was Simon? Was he the stockbroker one?'

Jennifer looked at her daughter as if she was mad. '*Stock*broker? *Simon*? No of course he wasn't a stockbroker. How could *Simon* be a stockbroker?'

'Well *I* don't know, do I? How should I know? I don't actually *care*, do I?'

'Stephen. You're thinking of Stephen. *Stephen* was the stockbroker. In all probability, still is. No – Simon was in advertising.'

'Right. Great. So?'

'Well, it's just that he had this thing about James Bond, you see – liked to play out scenes from the films. Are you *sure* I've never told you all this?'

'No. You haven't. And I'm not sure I actually want to *know*, Mum, OK? Look – I'm starving. Why don't we go and eat?'

'I might just have another little drink . . .'

'Jesus.'

'*Anyway* – one day . . . well *night*, very probably, can't really remember . . .'

'*Please*, Mum . . .'

'We'd already done the *train* scene – Russia With Thing, pretty sure, when the woman's drugged and in a nightie. We actually embellished on that particular vignette just a little. In the film, Bond sort of slaps her about a bit to wake her up, but the way *we* did it – '

'Oh *God* . . .'

'The way *we* did it – don't keep on interrupting, Stacy. I can't quite seem to catch that waiter's eye. He *must* be of a homosexualistic tendency. We did it that I slapped *him* around, you see, and then he had to teach me a lesson I wouldn't in a hurry forget. Ah me. *Anyway* . . .'

'I just don't believe this. You are quite disgusting.'

'Child. You'll learn. *Anyway* – that's when he brought up *Goldfinger*, you see. Asked me how I'd feel about being *painted*.'

'Painted? What – you mean, when she – like in – ?'

'Yup. And naturally there wasn't anything to *worry* about because of course we both knew about leaving a patch of skin and all the rest of it. *Pores*, or whatever. And anyway, when men are painting, they always leave out bits all over the place, don't they? I was, I confess, just slightly concerned about the *sheets*, which is why I insisted we go to his place. Ah! You've come back to us. One more of these, please – G and T, yes? And Stacy? Yes? You OK?'

'Whatever.'

'Right. Just the one gin. Did I say large? Thank you so much.'

Stacy watched the waiter's retreat – and though she hated herself for doing it, now said:

'*And* . . .?'

'And what? Did you see? Did you *notice*, Stacy? That waiter? Didn't so much as glance at either one of us. And your nipples, you know, are perfectly delineated against the tug of that silken camisole in which you have elected to flaunt yourself. More likely viscose, I imagine. Top Shop, is it? *Obviously* one of the homosexualistic brethren. Which is no doubt very nice for him. If he likes that sort of thing. Which he does, presumably . . .'

'Look, Mum – either finish the story or let's for Christ's sake go and *eat*, OK?'

'Can't go now – ordered drink. Oh yes – the story. Well in the end, we didn't go through with it.'

Stacy held her gaze.

'Right,' she said. 'Great *story*, Mum . . .'

'Well I *would* have,' protested Jennifer, 'but then he talked of sanding *down*, do you see. Told me quite seriously that preparation was nine-tenths of a perfect job. And then when he produced a tub of filler and talked of making *good*, well, I just had to draw the line and say Now look I'm awfully *sorry* but enough is enough, you know? I think his eventual plan was to seal and varnish with three good coats of Ronseal and either sell me to Tate Modern or else utilize my various immobilized orifices for the storage of MiniDiscs. Finish. No pun intended. Didn't see him again. You know, just *thinking* about it, I don't actually think he *was*, you know . . .'

'Oh God I'm so bloody hungry. Was what?'

'Hm? Oh not Simon – I'm not talking about *Simon*. Stephen – yes? A stockbroker? I don't actually think now he was . . .'

'You don't really *need* gin, do you Mum? Your mind's messed up to start with.'

Jennifer's new drink arrived, most of it surviving for not very long at all.

'I think he was a rep for something to do with *toys*. Or maybe a wholesale butcher.'

The heart of Jennifer's easy amusement was now and immediately struck down dead. She glanced once and quickly at Stacy with large and fearful eyes, and these were now dragged with massive reluctance upwards and across to where the terrible noise had surely come from – rapidly blinking as if to deny or accelerate her arousal from the worst of nightmares.

'Ah so you *did* locate the Piano Bar! Well done – ho ho. I

knew you would – Aggie was just a little bit on the worried side, but I for myself was unconcerned: no qualms whatsoever.'

Nobby was beaming as he drew up two chairs and settled Aggie into one of them – all but tucking her in and slipping her a barley sugar, for sucking on the journey.

'How are you both faring, Jennifer? Stacy? Keeping well, I trust. Yes – you will already in this very short time have discovered how very *logical* and *pleasing* is the layout of this grand and beautiful vessel. The decks go as follows, starting from the top: Bridge, Signal, Sun, Boat – what's next, Aggie?'

Aggie grinned at Nobby, and then turned the full works on to both Jennifer and Stacy in turn. It was as if the four of them had then and there forged and anointed a secret pact, and soon they would be snaffling buns and cooling pies from an unsuspecting window sill.

'Upper and Quarter,' she said, with the smug pride of the school swot.

'Correct, Captain Honeybunch – you can't ever catch her out, hey Aggie? Ask her anything. Go on. Anything. Here, love – tell our two friends what is the overall breadth – *breadth*, mind, of Sylvie? Listen up, ladies.'

Aggie's face was near splitting with pleasure. Stacy's was held as if in a trance, or was maybe stranded amid the initial and irreversible stages of rigor mortis. Jennifer's face might well be imagined – but overlaid across the signals indicating the likely collapse of all internal organs, rage and a plummeting heart were each flagged up by purplish and then palish dapplings.

'One hundred and five feet and two-and-a-half inches.'

Nobby cocked his head and winked three times (one for every man jack of you ladies).

'Which *is* . . .?' And his bulbous eyes were egging her on.

'Thirty-two point oh-six metres. Precisely.'

'There you go. What a marvel. Isn't she a marvel? Be

honest. You're a living marvel, Aggie – Jennifer and Stacy think so, and I know I do. So yes, as I say – Upper and Quarter, as Aggie has informed us – and where we now in fact find ourselves situate. And from hence on down it's simply One to Seven decks, as you well might expect. We're on the same deck as yourselves, as it happens. We never pay the prices for the larger cabins, oh no – not us. We love every inch of her, so why trouble? Hey? Why trouble? Which *means*, of course, that we are down to dine in the selfsame restaurant.'

'It's very good,' simpered Aggie, as Jennifer and Stacy's eyes were drawn and fused, sensing something awful.

'It *is*,' allowed Nobby. 'It's *very* good. And better still – it's all Harry Freemans, barring the shandy to which Aggie is partial – and my glass of Guinness, of course.'

'I'm starving, actually . . .' muttered Stacy, plucking at Jennifer's sleeve.

Jennifer was immediately standing.

'Yes,' she rushed. 'We have to – '

'Ah well *yes*,' agreed Nobby. 'In fact we have arranged for you a little surprise, haven't we Aggie?'

Aggie nodded. 'Little surprise.'

'I know the head waiter quite well, obviously – we both go way back – and he's rigged us up a nice little table for four by the window: round job. Maiden voyage – don't want you two being lonely. They can't actually just shove the tables together any old how, you know. Oh no. All bolted down, you see – and let's hope you don't find out why! Although me – I don't much mind a bit of pitch and toss. More authentic. You really feel you're all at *sea*. So then – will we be off?'

Nobby and Aggie led the way: Jennifer and Stacy were clustered behind them, and clinging closely.

'I'm *not*,' husked out Jennifer – and her eyes were imploring, and nearly tearful. 'I . . . just . . . *can't* . . .!'

'*Food*, Mum – *food*. Just think of the *food*.' (It's odd, but for

85

all Mum's front, she sometimes gets like this, and when she does, you just have to take charge – look after her. I'll always look after my Mum.)

'But I'll be sick. I'll kill him. I'll be sick – and I'll kill *both* of them . . .'

Nobby was back and . . . *taking their arms*!

'Can't have you two *maidens* dawdling about on their *maiden* voyage, can we? Get it? *Maiden*, you see. We don't actually know the full origin of that particular term, if we're talking gospel. Ships of course are *ladies*, and I suppose it seemed natural to refer to an *untried* one – no offence – as a maiden, see? Here we are – lovely restaurant, you'll love it. *Arnold*, my dear old mate – are we well? Are we well? But listen, Jennifer – listen to this, Stacy, you'll be very interested in this. Harry *Freemans*, yes? You heard I said that? Short while back? Now here is a popular misconception. People generally assume it's simply a play on the word 'free' – as in 'gratis', follow? But nothing could be further from the truth. No no no – Harry Freemans was very much a real live living person, and he sounded a very nice cove, to boot.'

'He sounded lovely,' said Aggie. 'Jennifer – you have the seat by the window. See all the waves.'

'A very nice cove *indeed*,' went on Nobby. 'Stacy – you happy here? Yes? Prime. Yes – owned a warehouse out Tooley way, you know? Near Tower Bridge, yes? Any seaman who called there with his load was sure of a foaming tankard of finest ale. So free beer, you see, became known as a Harry *Freemans*.'

'It's a nice story, isn't it?' said Aggie, tucking her napkin into her neckline and scanning the menu. 'Ooh *look*, Nobby – they've got *sardines* as a starter.'

'And *then*, of course, it came to mean free *anything* . . .'

Nobby made quite a business of settling himself down at the very little table, right up close to Jennifer; and then he patted her frozen hand.

'Mm . . .' he said with appreciation. 'I like a nice sardine.'

PART TWO

All at Sea

Dwight had that feeling, you know? You ever had that feeling he's meaning? Like, when some outta-the-way and big-deal event has finally come a-knocking at the door and still after, hey – how long knowing it was coming? You just ain't in no kinda state to be taking it on. Like, back home, any of the goddam get-togethers Charlene keeps on fixing – Welcome Home parties, when the kids come on back from college; We Just Wanna Say *Hi* parties for any new guys to the neighbourhood – plus all the clambakes, cook-outs, cocktails and come-as-you-ares, or maybe just having the Reverend come call. Sometimes, Charlene she hits me with these, jeez – munce back. Sometimes I don't know nothing about it till the drive's fulla cars. Either which way, boy, I just feel it done snuck up on me and all I wanna do is high-tail outta there. Sump'n special's going down, then listen up – I wanna be someplace real plain and homey. I'm done up in a tux and we're in the rental stretch and going to some goddam five hunnerd bucks a plate benefit dinner (is there any guy in America I ain't yet benefited?) then what I want is just maybe to slip into jog-pants and a sweat and maybe shoot some pool and have a few beers down at Joey's, you know – kick around stuff with Barney and Harry and the rest of the guys.

And right now in this lousy stateroom or whatever the hell, I got this feeling all over me. Passed that kinda English pub on the way up here – like the Green Man I never got to see in the Harrods store? And I thought yeah – there I'd like to be, sat up real close to the bar, bowla pretzels, maybe (could be get the lowdown from a fellow American how the Nicks're doing back home, you know? You get outta touch: on a cruise, you get no nooze). And what am I instead? I'm jammed up against this here wall, baby: seats is all around, but we're all standing up and holding a glass and everyone's goddam mouth is open and yapping at the same goddam time. Charlene, she's talking to the Captain, and she ain't about to let him go, not for nobody. How many women I seen come up now? All with that pap they put on their eyelids, you know? In the same goddam colour as all the crazy, chi-chi, how-in-hell-much-that-cost-their-husband dresses (just like Charlene – about this I know) and they all come a-sidling up and the Captain, he makes with the glad-hand (and jeez – what kind of a life? Huh? I mean, why in hell don't he kick his ass upstairs and drive the goddam *boat*, stead of jerking around with this massa broads?) But does Charlene *give* a damn? No siree – she'll let 'em kinda slide in a whiles, and then they're back outta the circle afore they know what's hit 'em. Like that maybe is she English woman right this second – look at her go. Guy behind her – he's just *gotta* be the husband, right? Looks like he wants to up and plug just either one of 'em.

I'm sweating like a hog, and ain't no liquor in my glass. And get this – I'm wearing my Brooks Brothers buttondown, here (Charlene ain't never gonna get me into one of them British, is it *German* Street, shirts with, like, bones and French cuffs), but what I can't deny no more is that one more time, baby, I just went up a size. How many times this happen to me in the last couple years? Soon there won't be no shirt in the world that's gonna come close to buttoning around this lardy neck I got – but maybe by then, with the good Lord behind me for guidance, I'll be dead and buried.

Oh boy – now it's the tanned guy with the blond bouffant coming right at me: *Hi*, there, Mister Johnson, he's gonna go . . .

'*Hi*, there, Mister Johnson! Doing OK?'

'Hi, Stoo. Yeh yeh.'

And Stewart smiled broadly and then he turned away and his face hooded over and he thought Bloody rude and ungrateful *sods*.

And jeez! Did you get what that stoopid woman just said to the guy who could, I dunno, be the English dame's husband? Poor schmuck – he maybe dealt with it all in just about the only way a man can do:

'I really love, actually,' the youngish woman was fluttering to David, 'biblical names, you know?'

David stared at her momentarily, before behaving like an Englishman who had inadvertently glimpsed something not intended for his eyes, and immediately reverted his quite glazed gaze to the alluringly distant door: and there was longing in those eyes.

'I mean, *real* biblical names – yes? I mean, your name – *David*, yes?'

David dragged back his whole skull and distantly focused on one of her ears. Was he really now meant to say *Yes*? I mean – was he *really*? She had just a minute before asked him his name and he had replied *David*, is my name: David, yes (at least the question hadn't been tricky), and now she was requesting verification. This must, then, must it, be what he vaguely recalled as chit-chat. Party gabble. Small-talk (a thing that always had defeated David – along, of course, with big talk too).

'Yes . . .' he said.

'*Right*,' the woman approved. 'But I mean sort of – more *real*, you know? Obadiah? Yes?'

'Mm.'

'And, um – *Ezekiel*. That's biblical, isn't it?'

David felt panicked and wild. Got to leave, now. Can't think why I'm here. Got to now leave. I'll tug, will I, at Nicole? Will she kill me if I do that? Or shall I just go? No – if I do that, she'll kill me. I'll risk just touching her shoulder.

'Well *I* think,' Nicole was gushing, 'that the whole idea is ravishing – simply *enchanting* . . . ah, David. Captain – I'd like you to meet my husband. This is David. David – our Captain.'

Oh God, thought David – I'm in even deeper, now: I seem

to be about to talk to the man we came to see (which was never, I don't think, a part of my plan).

'Hello.'

'Greetings, David!' practically bellowed the Captain, most of the bits of his quite brown face eagerly cavorting all over the place in their efforts to please – to convey not just welcome and animation, David could only assume, but the sort of electrifying fascination that could easily leave one glassy-eyed and mute – a spent and burnt-out wreck. 'Many congratulations on your stupendous prize – and welcome to the *Transylvania*. I hope you won't be disappointed. As I said to your charming wife, all my staff and crew are at your disposal. And now – do you good people by any chance happen to know what day this is?'

Nicole was momentarily thrown, but her ecstatic grin was still stuck firmly in place, baring the teeth, while behind her eyes the bell rang to signal the start of a rapid bout of wrestling.

'*Tuesday*, isn't it . . .? David? Isn't it Tuesday? You so lose track . . .'

He doesn't, David was thinking, *look* much like a captain – let alone the Captain of a ship this size: his hair isn't white, and he hasn't got a beard. And nor, good God, is he gruff: I've seen more sullen people got up in a ginger fright wig and vast polyester loon pants (not, it again occurs to me, at all unlike Nicole's berth-lounging combo) twisting about squelching and sausagey balloons at a nine year-old's knees-up.

The Captain, maybe sensing that David was in a palsied or maybe even drunken state (God I wish!) rattled along with the gist of whatever this deeply tedious thing might turn out to be, while somehow even managing to notch up the delirium stakes a ratchet or two.

'Ah yes *Tuesday* – but not just *any* Tuesday!'

No, thought David with deep and gathering gloom – because we are still a part of, aren't we, this Day of All

Days? And those few large Grouses are wearing off fast, I can tell you that – and all they seem to be offering at this quite ludicrous party is all this endless champagne, and God it's gassy, that.

'Not . . .?' tried Nicole – and even she was getting a wee bit tired of it, David could tell.

'*C'mon*, Captain,' zipped in another voice. 'Don't you be cheating on your lil Charlene, now! You just know you're my *best* man . . .'

Nicole was thinking *What* a rude woman. David was thinking Good God, how is it possible that anyone on earth can actually sound like that (unless they were earnestly vying for the part of the fan-fluttering saloon bar hostess in a remake of *Gunsmoke*)?

The Captain elongated his blazingly energetic grimace of joy so as to easily encompass the whole bang shoot of them – and maybe, by way of a finale, gobble them all up.

'Well I'll *tell* you,' he finally conceded – and Dwight heard that bit (he had actually been thinking Yeah – and the waist in my pants: this too I gotta get fixed – feels like a goddam vice). So yeah – he just caught that bit, and what he muttered was Hally-fuckin-*looya*. But still this Captain of ours is taking time out for effect – or maybe waiting for another shoal of big-eyed broads to swim on under that net of his. There were two of them just alongside of Dwight who were certainly closing in (the crazy-looking one, he had only recently flinched from hearing, had been screamingly assuring the other that she had been in the world of fashion, *please* believe her, for such absolute *yonks* that she could remember not only when grey became the new brown, but even when backs had been dubbed the new *cleavage*).

'Eighty-nine years ago this very night,' announced the Captain delightedly, 'the *Titanic* went down.'

For just the beat of a heart, the bray and sizzle of the party all around them was all that was heard: for just that instant, it was as if everyone within hearing had been slammed in the mouth with the iron-shod hoof of a run-amok mustang – but almost immediately, then, there emerged a rippling succession of joshing comments and self-declamatory laughter, as glittering female eyes peeked over stiff and cradled fingers and grew large in panto-incredulity. The welcome result of this whole silly farce from David's point of view was a surge of not just pathetically agog and yes, good Christ, exceedingly infantile and tell-me-more enthusiasm – but also the press of surrounding bodies, along with quite a few more from the wider shores, which enabled him to ease himself back and out of the throng quite unobtrusively, and with a relief that came as close as anything to making him pleased. Right, then: let's survey the situation. Marianne seems quite deep in conversation over there, more or less where we left her, with someone or other . . . Rollo's chatting up yet another bird in the corner. God curse him (Christ Almighty – wasn't the bargirl enough for him, bastard?), and Nicole, well, she's just never going to be hauled away from the Captain, is she? Not that I feel consumed by any urgency at all to do the hauling. So she seems to be there for the duration – unless, of course, Calamity Jane there sees fit to draw on her a Colt, and fill her full of lead. So all in all, time I think to wander. Quick couple, and then meet them all down at dinner, I think is favourite. You know . . . just glancing across at Marianne again, it looks like that man . . . that man in black, she's talking to. Mm.

'This one hell-hole, or what?'

David turned to the sound of this, seemed to him, quite human voice, and grinned his complicity at the large and fleshy man there.

'Hate this sort of thing,' said David.

'Check. Name's Dwight. You with her, right?'

And David followed the trajectory of Dwight's sideways neck jerk, the virtual arc coming to rest on a rapturous Nicole.

'Right,' agreed David.

'Yeah. Mine's in there too, someplace. What is it with women?'

David shook his head. This was either the most insignificant or hugest question in the whole wide world – anyway unanswerable and usually best ignored (and certainly now).

'David,' he said, extending his hand – which was firmly gripped and at once released. 'Anywhere we can get a decent drink round here, do you know?'

'You reading my mind, boy. Wanna beat it?'

David caught Dwight's eye, and met a keen twinkle there. He exhaled very heavily, as if newly liberated.

'Very much,' he said.

And just at that moment – wouldn't you bloody know it – Nicole and Charlene hove jointly into view, each of them instinctively curling possessive fingers (their tips so brightly japanned) around the forearms of their two respective soulmates in the journey of life (it seemed almost as if they had been programmed to do this).

'You two boys making mischief?' demanded Charlene – archly, it maybe was: roguish, might well have been the overall intent. Either way – to David, here was nothing short of the worst sort of *pain*.

'*Tracks*,' said Dwight, 'is what we're making, hon. This here's David.'

As Charlene gabbled her unspeakable delight at that; Nicole held out her hand to Dwight, while hissing quite unkindly at David:

'You might at least *introduce* me, David. Hello, Dwight – how do you do. I'm Nicole. Charlene was telling me you don't share our enthusiasm for the Royal Navy – our boys in blue. Is that right?'

'Tain't just *your* navy – I just don't got a lotta time for navies, period. Army – that's more a man's life, far as I can see it.'

'Dwight,' smiled Charlene, 'is a Vietnam Vet. Right, Dwight?'

And Nicole's eyes were huge with approval.

'Oh I'm so terribly glad to *hear* that. Oh I think that's just *wonderful*.' And then to David: 'Did you hear that, David?' (And he had, of course.) 'I just think it's so marvellous that *somebody* takes the time to worry about all those poor little animals in that *terribly* odd little country. Do you not find it a bit inconvenient? Living there? Did that *war* thing affect it awfully?'

Dwight looked right at her – and David said very quickly (and for both their sakes):

'Drink?'

Dwight nodded briefly. 'You got it.'

⚓

Marianne was standing up on tiptoe, the better to try for some sort of view over both dark and colour-clad shoulders, as well as in between all the bobbing heads. She glimpsed her father ducking off and out with some really big-looking guy. Rollo and her mother she seemed to have lost sight of, for now.

'I think,' she said – with what to Tom came across as sincere regret, or at least a degree of reluctance, 'I'd really better be going, now. My parents . . .'

Tom nodded, quite understanding.

'Yes yes. I quite understand. I've enjoyed very much, this – our little talk. I – '

'It's just that I said I'd meet them all for dinner about now, you see – my brother's here too and – oh, I'm so sorry: what were you saying?'

'Hm? Me? Oh no, nothing – nothing at all. I was simply going to say that I hope, er – that is, if you're not too busy on this, uh – voyage, that maybe we might possibly . . .'

'Talk again? Oh yes – I'd love that. Truly.'

Tom dared to look at her.

'Really?' he said, quietly.

Marianne was looking for somewhere to lay down her glass. Yes – she was doing that, but also she was using the spliced-in sliver of time to examine her feelings: So – really? Truly? *Would* I love that?

'Yes,' she said. 'I'll see you. Bye, Tom.'

Yes, she thought, as she squeezed her way through the I suppose now slightly thinning out crowd, smiling her apologies – yes, I would love that. But I honestly – and this is funny (isn't it funny?) – can't quite explain to me why.

'*Hi*, there! My name's Stewart – Assistant Cruise Director. Doing OK?'

And shortly after, Stewart turned off the dazzle at the mains as he veered off, scowling: Bloody rude and ungrateful *sod* – all he did was just stare at me and go *mmm*.

Yes, that was all Tom did – because he was intent on not simply keeping watch on Marianne's retreat and the flurry of her hair as she continued to weave her way towards the door, but also to retain for a few more seconds the fleeting scent of her, the still mutual air their breaths had disturbed; there was a blur of her and others, and then she was lost to sight.

The very first thing I said to that girl – do you know what it was? I can barely believe it. She said to me hello (why did she do that?) and I replied Oh good evening: my wife, you know, has died – yes, quite recently. And she did not run nor even wince – she did not nod and pat me and move away, no she did not: she stayed and talked to me. No one – since – has done that. No one – since – has even touched.

⚓

'Mm,' went Nobby, eyes now closed as he viciously rubbed sideways and then back again at his mouth with a napkin, for all the world as if to thoroughly rid himself of any remaining traces of a leprous kiss. 'That was, if I'm any judge, a very fair ice cream.'

Through lips so compressed that words barely made it, Jennifer said We Have To Go. Now.

Stacy was up and eyeing her mother with concern; she had been silent for the better part of a course-and-a-half, Jennifer, and this could never be a good thing.

'*Course*,' continued Nobby, quite genially, 'because I'm so pally with the head waiter, as you maybe have divined, he can usually be relied upon to afford us three scoops each.'

'Two is standard,' put in Aggie, with quiet and glowing pride.

'Got to *go*,' said Jennifer – standing now, and dangerously looming.

'I haven't enjoyed a meal so much,' expanded Nobby, 'since – do you recall it, Aggie love? At the Round Table, must it have been Michaelmas time?'

'Ooh *yes*,' enthused Aggie. 'Very tasty indeed.'

'Indeed,' agreed Nobby. 'They laid on a very nice buffet fork supper with cash bar afterwards. Quite choice. Particularly partial to the shrimp.'

'I'm *going*,' said Jennifer – very firmly and, to Stacy's ears, a bit too loud (and yes it was true – inquisitive heads were making quite a show of refusing to quite revolve). 'I'm going just anywhere – not our poxy cabin because there's no room in there to swing a bloody *cat*, but somewhere, anywhere, in order to quickly become at the very least half *slewed*. Comprendo?'

Nobby blinked up at her.

'Nautical term, as it happens – swinging a cat. Doesn't refer to the feline of the species, naturally, but the somewhat barbaric old cat-o'-nine-tails. Very nasty. One needed five-and-a-half feet swinging clearance, we learn – '

'Stop it!' snapped Jennifer. She was eyeing him so coldly. 'Stop it, please, or else I shall kill you.'

Nobby and Aggie's wide-eyed faces were nonetheless impassive as they watched them leave.

'Well,' said Aggie – and Nobby nodded to that.

'First-night nerves, I expect,' he allowed. And then more dreamily: 'Half *slewed*, yes – shame she didn't tarry to hear the origins of that one . . .'

And Aggie was animated. 'Oh *I* know – don't tell me. When the yards that carry the sails are said to be 'half *slewed*', yes? It means they are not properly braced to catch the wind, and are hence rendered ineffective.'

'Prime, Aggie: prime. Whereupon they sway and shake, of course, and from this we derive the image of tipsiness. Quite, yes yes. Talking of which, I might just allow myself a small tot of rum – and then it's early for Bedfordshire, if I've any say.'

Aggie smiled her agreement. 'I'm all for that. Quite pooped. Pooped, Nobby – yes? The overwhelming effect of a huge wave that breaks across the stern or *poop* deck. How's that?'

Nobby gazed at her in full admiration.

'Captain Honeybunch – as I live and breathe, you're a walking marvel.'

And Aggie went pink and curled up in delight.

⚓

Stacy was really struggling to keep up with her, but she couldn't just let her go – not when she was like this. She upped the pace into a canter.

'God's sake, Mum – slow down, can't you? How much further? You don't even know where you're *going* . . !'

'Just follow – we'll find something.'

Oh yes, absolutely – on that particular point Jennifer was totally determined. She had of course rejected all thoughts of the bloody Piano Bar out of hand as that was where she had hit and then got gummed up in the terrible web relentlessly spun by Nobby and Aggie – and who was to say they would not return there to haunt and plague them and suck her even drier? Jennifer was not *pledged* to the committal of murder, not wholly, but neither was she over eager to lay herself bare to appalling temptation. The Zip Bar was briefly seen to be a possibility, but it looked both pricey and poncey and was anyway quiet and decorous and Jennifer badly needed to rip something up. The Black Horse pub would have done at a pinch, except that a band of drunkish men were larging it down the other end and horsing around with a karaoke mike – which needn't have been an altogether damning thing in *itself*, except that every single one of them was old and short and fat (and if by way of a wager they had all chipped in their collective reserves of remaining hair, it might just have run to sufficient for a halfway decent weaver to cobble up a fanny wig).

And then she glimpsed and was caught by the blue-green neon glowing in the not too far distance: Great, we've found it – at last, thank Christ.

'This is it, Stacy – Regatta Club, get ready: here we bloody come.'

'*Hi*!' boomed Stewart in welcome, just as Jennifer was veering inwards. 'My name's Stewart – Assistant Cruise Director. Doing OK?'

Jennifer barely glanced over as she told him to go and fuck himself, and Stacy skittered on into the club at her mother's heels as Stewart turned away, glowering, and stamped off muttering blackly from behind his tight shut pearly teeth.

⚓

'God – I see what you *mean*,' half-roared Rollo, 'about the *music* . . .'

Jilly raised her eyebrows, and over the brassy plinky-bonk of It's Not Unusual, smiled her concurrence with that one. They were two cocktails down (some long things with straws called Hawaiian Some-Things, can't be sure: plenty of pineapple sorted out and kept in line by generous jiggers of pure and evil vodka – and still they turned out bright pink).

Maybe an hour back, Rollo and Jilly had grinned like witches from the one coven as the distorted opening of Dancing Queen was mixed into the fag-end of Viva España; Jilly just practically dissolved when Mambo Number Five had first insinuated its jerky-shouldered and infectious self into the spotlit hubbub (Rollo had been round-eyed, at the time – braying to her about raves, the pimples of sweat on his upper lip shuddering with each enthusiasm; he was saying that if Stravinsky were alive today, right? Then he would be writing for Prodigy – and Jilly just nodded thinking Prodigy, OK, yeah, cool: the other band I don't know). But when the bloody song came round for the third time, it just wasn't so funny.

'Jesus – this mambo thing. You see,' explained Jilly, during a lull in the mush, 'this ship's so weird because in London, or somewhere, we'd stick our heads into a club like this and we'd be out of here in no time, right? But this is *it*: this ship, it's like a massive five-star hotel that nobody actually ever *leaves*, day and night, and this is like the manky little 'nite-spot' they shove in the basement. There's nothing else. And you can't check out. Why are you and your people actually *here*, Rollo?'

And so Rollo had sighed very large and loudly – theatrically, oh yes, but also so as to be sure that the big gurgle of resignation and heavily laboured rolling of the eyes were at once both clocked and caught despite the twin impedimenta of flickering, now sort of blue-ish strobes and the belted out and strutted invitation to come and stay at the *Wye-Em-Cee-Ay* (when everyone here just had to flap their arms above their heads a good beat out of time, while roaring out quite the wrong letter). Rollo explained about

Nicole always going in for all these competitions: buys stuff we don't even use so she can get all the coupons and labels and ringpulls and things. Even gets this magazine – believe it? It tells you about all these *other* comps, and then she goes out and gets all the gear. Your mother like that? And Jilly said No, as Rollo had known she would (he'd asked all his mates and anyone else he met: your mum like that, he'd go. And they all just stared at him and said No). Yeah well – mine is, he miserably concluded. So the kitchen, right? You open cupboards and there are these, like, dozens of tins and things and no one knows what in Christ's name is in them because all the labels are gone: bits clipped out and stapled together and long ago sent off to some P.O. Box in Oldham, together with Mum's list of holiday essentials in order of precedence, or why her thru-diner richly deserved a Universe of Leather Village makeover – or her suggestion of a name for some cute little sad-faced kitten (once she had actually won fifty cases of Rabbit and Chicken in Jelly Whiskas for christening just such an animal *Dimples* – which just has to be about as fucking stupid as you can actually *get*, right? Seeing as the moggy in question had more copious moustaches than a bloody cavalier: Jesus – we didn't even have a bloody *cat*). And all accompanied, of course, by her no-more-than-seventeen-word tiebreakers: 'I think This Crap Load Of Absolute Fuck-All Product Is The Very Best Thing Under God's Pure Sun *Because* . . .' And off she'd go. Dad always went, How come you never win a *car*? Hey? Most of these bloody things you go in for, top prize always seems to be a *car*, so how come – how is it – we never ever get the bloody *car*? Mum just said *Huh* – if you're so very *clever*, David, why don't *you* try going in for one of these sometime? Mm? It's not actually so *easy* as all of you seem to think. Of course if your wonderful *father* here was to do it, oh well yes – cars galore, I shouldn't wonder. Ferraris, Rolls-Royces – they'd be coming out of our bloody *ears*, wouldn't they David? Why can't you just be grateful for all the stuff I *do* win? (Yeh right: a million tins of cat food). Anyway . . . finally Mum did hit the big one, first prize: this trip (second prize was a car). But *surely*, Jilly protested, *you* didn't have to go on it if you didn't want to, did you? I mean – you would've had the house all to yourself . . .? Rollo shook his head quite mournfully, as the refrain from Doo-Wah-Diddy-Diddy again clanged all around it.

'You think I didn't *think* of that? Mum wasn't having it. No way. Said I'd burn the place down. Why do mothers always think that? I mean, I'd be like – *great*: Mum and Dad and Mar are off to America! Cool – where's the matches? First thing I'm going to do is fucking *torch* the place . . .'

'Hm. What about your dad?'

'Dad? Oh, *Dad* . . . It's not really up to Dad. No.'

Jilly groaned as another set of warped but nonetheless horribly familiar chords was segued into the mutated but mercifully fading cadence of the last load of pap. And then she said:

'My Dad's not like that. Anything he says at our house is, oh God – just *law*, you know? Don't know how Mum stands it. It's a bit why I'm here, actually, think. I used to work in a bar at home, yeh? And all the time he was, like, really on my case? You don't want to be coming home late on your own, he'd go – but if I went with some *guy*, he'd go totally ballistic. And then he was always on at me to, you know – *save*, and stuff, and I said *Look*, Dad – it's my money, right? OK? So I can do what I bloody well want with it. Yeh. Sammy – Sammy's a lot like that. Really gets to me. I mean Christ – I don't want to, do I – hook up with some guy who's' like my *Dad* . . .!'

Rollo smiled – touched her hand. She didn't flinch – wasn't sick. Slid it up her arm – and still she wasn't screaming the place down and lashing out wildly with the table between them. She seemed to be OK – her eyes were gleaming – and so when Rollo transferred his featherlike touch (poised, it was, and ready to flee at an instant's notice)

103

to the cool sheen and heavy bounce of the weight of her hair just there, at her neck, where it touched, which was warm, and so very . . . so very *soft*, he now discovered with pleasure that appalled him – he finally felt he could stick his neck out and meet that look in her eye and say to her straight:

'Well – I'*m* not like your dad, am I?'

Jilly lowered her eyelids, and a lopsided smile was on her face in no time.

'God . . .' she not much more than whispered. 'I can't believe I'm *doing* this . . .'

And Rollo missed that completely and so roared at her: '*What?*'

'Nothing,' Jilly assured him. 'How about another drink?'

'But I'm not, am I?' pursued Rollo. 'Like your dad? Am I? *Or* Sammy.'

Jilly looked right at him. 'No,' she said. 'You're not.'

'Let's get another drink. You got the time?'

'I just *said* that!' shouted Jilly – mostly in order to make her point, the slack taken up by the need to be heard, this time (Sugar Sugar or no Sugar Sugar).

'What? You said what? You *do* have time?'

'*No* – not that I've – ! I mean I *haven't* got time – shouldn't even be doing this. Got to be up at – ! And Christ – it's nearly – ! It's OK for you first class *passengers* . . .'

Rollo was standing. 'Let's have one more. At the bar, maybe. Bit quieter . . . we're right under a speaker, here.'

Jilly nodded and rose up to meet him quickly – just like a little yellow plastic duck popping delightedly to the surface of the bathwater, unfazed and blue-eyed, once some plump-fisted kid had packed in trying to crush and drown it. As they wove their way through tables and chairs, mostly jammed with red-faced folk, all damn well pleased with themselves, the clunk and then mega-beat of Voulez-Vous Coucher Avec Moi was (Ce Soir) all around them. Rollo wasn't going to look at her, no no no, wasn't – not even a rapidly nicked and sideways glance: it would be tacky, it would be naff. They got to the bar and Rollo only knew his eyes were upon her when he found himself thinking that her quickly tugged on, flat-lipped smile was looking just like his was feeling.

'I've maybe got time,' Jilly was giggling, 'for just maybe one.'

Rollo nodded as he hoisted himself up on to the bar stool, hooked his heels around the rung, and set to coping with the barman's seemingly eager but still evasive eye.

'Right,' he agreed, staring dead ahead. 'We'll make it quick, then. If you like.'

⚓

'Hey Suki,' Earl is going at her; the Coke bottle he's put down on the bar, and his eyebrows are jerking over to the couple who just up and sat alongside of them. 'You think this week's slogan is, what? Drink *Pink*?'

Suki idled over dull and heavy eyes to this really, like, annoying *brother*, you know?

'What *talking* about, Earl? I reckon I'm gonna split. Men here are just, like, *duh* and faggots. Else really, you know – *old*?'

'Those guys with the, like, real pink drinks is what I'm saying, Suki. What're you – blind? It's like it's lit up.'

'Jesus, Earl – I just so don't *care*, you know? What some buncha half-asses are about to *drink*, OK? I mean, like – get a *life*?'

Just to the left of Suki, a sleekly cool, New York-groomed and polished woman was smilingly letting in some redly flustered and half-cut London housewife on the truth about the source of her very evident money (something she maybe divined they all longed to know, and could be later would drive them wild).

'My friend, yes? Back in the States? He's really *verrry*

good to me. Generous isn't the word.' And then the disclosure: 'Furrier.'

And the Englishwoman is nodding and trying to concentrate and now she rams four fingers back through and across her crazy hair and stutters out:

'Really? Than what, exactly? Or than *whom*, I should say.' And then when all that confronts her is a startled blank: 'Oh – or maybe just more *generally*, do you mean?'

Suki closes her eyes. 'Tell you, Earl – everyone here, we're talking, like, totally *nuts*. Jeez, I'm so sick of it. We been on this tub how many *munce*, now? You gotta tab, or what?'

'Shit, Suki – you know I ain't carrying. The last we did in the Harrods store – and Mom and Dad, they were like in my face all of the time, yeah? How could I score?'

'Yeah? Well hell, I sure do need something, like, real fast, you know? Else I'm outta here.'

'Hey, you two,' said a new loud voice that had Suki turning: what else kinda nut is this here, now, is what she was thinking – but hey! These two guys, they look maybe OK, you know?

'Hi,' said Suki. 'How you guys rinsing it?'

Jennifer looked at Stacy for some kind of help, here – but none, she knew, was coming; so sod – let's go for it:

'*Great*,' she rejoined, with all of her mustered bravado. 'We're rinsing it extremely well. Thought you were looking as bored as we were feeling. Am I right? I'm Jennifer – this is Stacy. Hi. Bloody noisy in here.'

And yeah, OK – Suki was perking up, some: could be a cuppla cats she could maybe get down with. Earl was – jeez, will you look at him – kinda, what? *Stunned*, sure looked like. And Wow yeah, is how he was thinking: cool or *what*? Two, like, foxy-looking gals – how great is this? Last chick I meet in this joint, I'm going: Hey babe – how's it cookin', yeh? And she looks at me like I'm just some piece of *shit*, you know (with this stoopid English accent?), and what I get is How is *what* cooking, exactly? And maybe you think

106

we got here some kinda goofy *gag*, or sump'n? Well forget it. So I'm going Well fuck *you*, asshole, and she says to me Just fuck *off*, man, the dumb fuck. So here is maybe better.

'Hi,' says Earl. 'I'm Earl – and this here's my little sis, Suki, yeah?'

So she hates it big time when I innerdooce her that way; yeah and so what? What am I? My sister's keeper? Hell with that.

'*Suki!*' screamed Jennifer – and the sudden shrillness made even Stacy jerk with surprise: as for Suki, she was nearly off her stool. 'Sorry – sorry to be so – it's just: *Suki. Such* a cool name. So *sexy.* Hi, Earl – you OK?'

Earl nodded, and tried to look at her roguishly as the eyebrows came right into kinda quizzical, like maybe Jimmy Dean (hey look – what can I tell you?).

'Good. Doing good. *Now* I am, leastways.'

And that, so far as Stacy could see, was that: Jennifer had bonded – effortlessly captured two more willing victims (just look at Suki preening, now she knew her name was sexy). It was always like that. The two of them had, Stacy thought, been perfectly happy sitting over there – over to the back a bit, close by the big windows with maybe some sort of open deck outside, it looked like (too dark to see), and Jennifer had already and in no time sweet-talked some drunk old creep into buying them a bottle of champagne (though sweet-talk soon curdled into greengage sour when the poor old sod exhibited genuine signs of appearing to imagine that such largesse on his part in some way entitled him to actually sit down with them and maybe even share it). At least over there they could hear each other talk over the barrage of actually pretty good pop (Jennifer *adored* it – you could easily tell: lips pouting into a pantomime kiss and head swaying eagerly to the pound of the beat – well, her era mostly, after all) and in between sipping the champagne (it's the bubbles, really, I suppose, I like: could be sweeter, though) and laughing out loud at Jennifer's more outrageous avowals as to the ways in which she would happily dispose of the thing they call Nobby, if ever again she clapped eyes on the fucker (getting hold of a vat of that *gravy* he seemed so intent on mopping up every last vestige of, with the crudely crushed and bunched-up lumps of roll – how and *why*, Jennifer had demanded, does he get his bread to look like *tampons*? – and sticking right into it his bloody stupid head, and maybe, why not, Aggie's too). During the lulls in all that, Stacy had been quite content simply to sit back and let her eyes rove over the scene.

Jennifer had been sneering from the moment she entered (and it was she who walked me miles to get here!) but Stacy had been thinking it was actually pretty OK. It looked like a film set, maybe – a safe and brightly clean disco from a Mom, Dad and the Kids PG movie, where all ages and races were encouraged to (Yee-Hah!) let their hair down and mingle, guys, and strut your stuff, why don't ya – all in a very rehearsed and modulated manner. The sunken and central area was well filled with little round tables and quite good tub chairs that hugged tight the small of your back and made you feel both a part of it, and wanted. There was a smallish circular dance floor at one end, this made groovy by the eternally prowling coloured strobes, agitatedly painting the few intrepid dancers green and pink to the point of luminous, the brown arms and shoulders of the girls picked out and caressed by fat blobs of hot orange, big hair dappled and streaked by zigzags of lemon. There was a raised mini gallery running right around the room (where Jennifer and Stacy had been sitting for a bit – until the champagne was finished and Jennifer announced that this is *dull*: let's check out whoever's at the bar) and it was the long and broad windows all down that curvaceous flank that now and suddenly grabbed hold of Stacy's whole attention (Jennifer's still yapping to her two new American friends: I don't actually think I'll stay here much longer). It was really the strangest sight because, well – I don't know, I suppose you always assume, do you, that all that possibly can be beyond the windows of a ship, and even more so at night, is the encircling weight of daunting darkness, and then the sheer black plummet to the deep, lasciviously lapping and maybe luring-you sea. But beyond these windows stood a mournful and lonely man in a dripping sou'wester and whale-slick oilskins, and in both his hands he held a hose. Where Stacy stood was so hot and bright – suntanned girls are scooping up their hair in handfuls and then letting it go as they flaunt their chain-belted hips at the helplessly flailing men before them – tossing their heads, the silly sods, and shaking their arms from the elbow downwards, flicking their stiffened fingers, as if they have just scrambled to shore following an unexpected ducking. And beyond this diorama, stroked by colour and fuelled by the backbeat of the Vida Loca, stood this silent vision, rendering opaque with a mist of water each weeping window, like some slow-motion mime, glimpsed in a dream. Then his big sad face was lost to sight for just a moment or two before re-emerging again, framed exactly by the next big window, which he set to slungeing, with melancholy and deliberation.

'He comes,' quavered a tremulous but still twangy voice at Stacy's side, 'every goddam night. We don't rightly know who he is. But we call him the Fireman. Hi. My name is Debbie. Ain't seen you about before, right? Disco Debbie.'

Stacy beheld the almost literally inconceivably old and tiny woman beside her. How could so spare, blue and practically transparent a carcass actually be vertical and making sounds – and with such clear green eyes so alive in its skull?

'Disco Debbie . . .?' is all Stacy felt fit for.

The very old lady grinned and looked away, her tautened and glossy face betraying a blend of knowingness and abashed delight – as if she were an incognito superstar caught while trying to slum it, her elaborate disguise so easily penetrated by a persistent and adoring fan.

'Is what they call me,' she elucidated. 'I'm here every night. Yes sir. Every night. I bop till I drop, y'know? Stay here till the lights go down, mostly. Disco Debbie. Yup – that's what they call me.'

Her arms were bare and pitiably vulnerable: beneath the silk camisole, no form at all was discernible. Purple plastic veins seemed to have been appliquéd to her limbs some time lately, maybe by way of some misguided attempt at joky decoration; the bony wrists and surprisingly large hands beyond them hardly seemed up to bearing the weight of all those clanking bangles. Stacy really should have left maybe earlier – she didn't at all feel up to this, whatever might be coming; I think, she thought, I want to sleep – but if I do that now, then Mum will come barging in, oh, Christ knows when, and she'll be going Sorry Sorry Sorry as she crashes about, giggling and stupid – and then I'll be ruined for the night. But it was looking as if the old lady had done with Stacy, now: she simply slid into her hand some sort of *card*, was it? Smiled quite fondly and strolled away, really quite steadily, in the direction of the dance floor. Where she didn't so much bop as simply stand there, her two lazy, embalmed and ropelike arms high up in the air – and then she began to slowly revolve, her eyes yearning upwards in a face now touched by the ecstasy of some veiled and orgasmic religious icon.

Maybe, thought Stacy, I can find somewhere quieter to go – till Mum's had enough. She mouthed across to Jennifer *Lee-Ving*, and pointed towards the doors, though she really needn't have bothered because Jennifer at the time had her head thrown back and both eyes closed right down as she honked out her late-night-three-bottles-down hoarse but still glittering choir of laughter (which needn't at all mean that anything remotely funny had occurred). On Stacy's way out, she passed by a couple who were, could be, I don't know – fifty, maybe? But not a couple, it now transpired, because she was saying to him:

'My husband – that's George, my husband – I just couldn't get him to leave London. He's a criminal barrister.'

The man pursed his lips and said slowly:

'Your point being . . .?'

The woman was maybe thrown, but showing willing.

'I'm sorry, I – I don't quite – ?'

'Shall we see if we're still in time for these post-midnight snacks they were touting earlier? *Dockside* restaurant, I think they said – wherever that is. I'm still actually quite stuffed from dinner, but it is all *in*, after all.'

'Well,' confided the woman, as they trudged away (and look – she'd slipped her arm quite neatly under his), 'I must tell you now – I don't do wheat, and I don't do dairy.'

Stacy wandered off the other way, vaguely thinking that the pub thing they passed earlier (White Horse? Red Lion?) had been this way, hadn't it? Maybe sit there a bit. And as she ambled the full and thick-carpeted length of the endless and now almost completely deserted corridor, she glanced down at the pasteboard card in her hand: three addresses – one in New York, one in Florida and another in, goodness, Paris. And a Box number in London too, look. And at the card's centre, in wonky, larky purple print there writhed the legend, 'Disco Debbie – She Bops Till She Drops'.

And Stacy thought, as she glimpsed the pub (ah, *Black Horse* – that's it) what a very funny place this is.

⚓

Nicole was finally – oh God at last – in *bed*, thank the Lord. You know, it honestly seems to take me longer, these days, to actually remove all my make-up than it does to apply it. Which can't be right. And then there are all the night creams and moisturizers and so on, aren't there? To deal with. Flossing, and all the rest of it.

Where's David?

This bed, I have to say, is more than comfortable. And

proper cotton sheets and blankets, I was very pleased to see. I'm so very glad we went for twins. The thought of David thrashing around in this very little space is just too awful to contemplate. Anyway. Tired, yes – but I don't know if I'll sleep. I don't think I'll read, though. Too tired, quite frankly. I bought some books, couple of paperbacks, in South-ampton (God – seems *days* ago, now: isn't it odd?). There was a stall, what do you call them? Kiosk there. God knows what they're like – the covers were nice and they're both by *women*, which is half the battle these days, really: can't stand men's books, books by men. Are you the same? They're all so – oh, I don't know: not *nice*, if you know what I mean. I don't *quite* mean not nice, but you probably know. *Hardy*, of course – he's lovely. And that Morse man – quite good. Tired, yes – but I don't know if I'll sleep. I don't think I'll read, though. Too tired, quite frankly.

Anyway, Nicole – I think what you deserve is one great pat on the back: well *done*, girl! Here you are, on the *Transylvania*, no less, with all your family, and all for free. Thanks to you and you alone. I hope the children will *enjoy* it – it's so hard to tell, isn't it? With children now. Marianne – she's so very quiet. Never confides in me, you know – oh good God no. Not like Sophie's two: always having girly head-to-heads, Sophie is, she's always telling me. With her two. Shopping trips. But not my Marianne. Oh dear me no. Keeps to herself. Adores her *father*, of course. For some reason that is – and I don't care if this sounds . . . well I don't quite know *how* it will sound, and I really don't *mind*, to tell you the honest truth – but quite *why* she should adore him, what exactly she actually *sees* in him, I shall never understand. It could be, maybe, a phase . . .

And where *is* David?

Rollo. Well – Rollo's a boy, of course. Young man. And they're *quite* different, as we all know. God alone knows what he's going to do after A-levels, though. If he doesn't mess them up. No sort of *direction*. Probably expecting *us* to keep him until his old age. Which is *terribly* amusing. David can barely keep us *now*. I think he's not getting on well, you know, workwise. But we don't talk about it. Well look – I'm *here*, aren't I? If he wants to, you know – *say*, well – he knows how to get hold of me. He knows where I am.

But where is *he*, I'd like to know.

That *Charlene*, I have to say – bit of an odd fish. I don't know many Americans . . . well *none*, if I'm honest – so maybe they're all this way, are they? But it was a strange little chat we had in the, um – I think it was the *Zip* Bar, yes – that was it (this ship, I'm telling you – don't think I'll *ever* get the hang of it). David had gone off with *Dwight* (extraordinary name, isn't it? Dwight. Extraordinary). Anyway, yes – those two had gone off to, oh – God knows where, wherever men go, and Charlene said to me *Well* – and I can't actually remember her *words*, exactly, and God *please* don't ask me to do the accent – but the general sort of idea was that we, you know – have a drink and a chat, sort of thing, and –

Ooh gosh. I've just had a brainwave. No wait – listen. I really ought to write this down. Can I be bothered? Oh God – I know from experience that if you don't write these things down the minute they occur to you they'll be gone, you know – no matter how well you think you'll remember them, by morning they'll be gone. But I think my pen – it's still in my bag, and God I just can't *move*. But listen to this: I think it's a winner. Ready? Right: The reason Trill is Britain's number one birdseed is *because* . . . it puts the bounce into Britain's number one birds! Or maybe *keeps* the bounce . . . or puts the *b'doing* in number one birds (b'doing is maybe good . . . bit slangy? Don't know – needs work). First prize for that one is Disneyland on Concorde (although since that crash, I'm not too sure). When I told *David* about this competition (and most of them I don't, don't even trouble to mention them – it's not as if he *appreciates* it, or anything: quick to share in the prizes, though, isn't he?). Yes anyway, when I just happened to let drop that the reason there were (because he was going on and on) oh – not many, two or three packets of Trill in the cupboard (well, no more than six; it might just have been a dozen) was that I was closing in on getting us all to Disneyland on Concorde (maybe they'd make it a 747?) and I needed the tokens – all he had to say was Oh *marvellous*! And what're the runner-up prizes, may I politely enquire? No – don't tell me, let me hazard: a lifetime's supply of fucking *Trill*, conceivably? Sit well with the Whiskas, won't it? Investing in an *aviary*, are we, Nicole? Or are we collectively doomed to pecking at *millet* for the rest of our days? Here, Rollo – who's a pretty boy, then? Will you be laying down newspapers for us all to shit on? (He can, David, be awfully crude. There: I've said it.)

My seventeen tiebreaking words for *this* prize, the one we're actually on (isn't it amazing?) were – have I said? – oh, magnificent, really. *Judges* thought so, obviously. Never forget them – listen: 'The *Transylvania* to New York serves to fuse two continents with class, great luxury and sheer style.' Wonderful, isn't it? Like a poem. Just *came* to me, you know – like works of art are sometimes said to.

And *not* talking of works of art – where on earth *is* he?

Anyway. Tired, yes – but I don't know if I'll sleep. Don't think I'll read, though. Too tired, quite frankly. Now what was I . . .? Oh yes – friend *Charlene*, mm, yes. *Very* odd. *Nice* – oh yes, perfectly *pleasant* woman, oh Lord yes, don't get me wrong. Just – *odd*, you know? As maybe Americans are. I asked her all about living in that perfectly ghastly *Vietnam* place, but she didn't actually answer, or anything; understandable, I suppose. And I must say I do have the most frightful problem with the *accent*; I don't actually mean the sound of it, or anything . . . quite like the sound of it, really – feels quite homely, in a ghastly sort of a way. I suppose one is used to it from all the *films*, and so on. No – it's just that I so often find it hard to quite understand what they're *saying*. I mean to say look – if they're *going* to speak English, well then why on earth *don't* they? Hm? Anyway.

We were sitting in this Zip sort of cocktail place, as I say – quite nice there, I suppose. Rather good Steinway, though no one seemed remotely inclined to actually *play* the thing, which rather surprised me. I mean – first night at sea, you'd think they'd be all out to make some sort of *impression*, no? The place is just a teeny weeny bit of a *corridor*, though, I have to say. I mean, however tucked away one imagined oneself to be, there always seemed to be this stream of people passing *through* – all of them, I rather later divined, in quest of the loos, which were just around the corner, rather unhappily. I know this because after my second glass of champagne (when in Rome!) I felt the need myself, somewhat shamemakingly. I just *hate* it – do you? – when I have to leave someone like that because you just know, don't you, that your back is being watched, studied; worse, of course – far worse – when there's more than one of them because then they're going to *talk*, aren't they? About you. And no doubt I was walking with steely-eyed purpose, as we women tend to, don't we, when the loo is in question (quite unlike men – have you ever noticed? They wander about and beat at their jacket pockets, some reason, and tend to look up at the *ceiling*, helpless dolts). Anyway.

The first thing Charlene had to say . . . sounds so like one of those frightful whiney *songs*, doesn't it, 'Charlene'? By someone like that singer with the white hair and beard, what was he? Or one of those terribly bosomy women that men seem to like (for one reason or another). Now what was I . . .? Oh yes. Charlene. First thing she told me was that whenever she was in England, the thing she liked best of all was *card*. Well I mean honestly – what on earth is one supposed to *say*?

'Really?' I said.

'Oh absa-*lootly*. Dwight and me, we always make a point of having a bidder card in badder, y'know? So *Briddish*! We get a side order of fries on account of we don't go too big on potato chips? And then we get tripped up again because when the chips do come they, like, *are* fries, y'know? It's kinda confusing. Tell me, Nicole – you know the Apple, or what?'

'I don't think I, er – how do you mean *know*, exactly? I mean I know what they *are* . . .'

'I'm talking New York, honey. You done the sights? You, like, know what's on the corner of 25th and 3rd?'

'Oh God don't ask me anything at all like *that*. I'm just hopeless at mental arithmetic, always was. Is this anything to do with hypotenuses and all that sort of thing? Pi, is it?'

'Pie? No sir, lady. I'm talking Big Apple, here.'

'Oh right I *see*. Well yes I know it's terribly traditional with you, isn't it? 'Mom's homemade apple pie' and so on. I must say I'm terribly partial to Tarte Tatin, but it's hardly ever authentic, these days, is it?'

'Oh *yeah* – I think my Suki had one of those, good while back. They those kinda comic books with that little French guy and his dog and the sea captain and all . . .?'

'I don't quite think I . . . what did you think of him? Our Captain?'

'Pussycat.'

'*We* used to have a cat. Well it was Marianne – she insisted. But I don't think it's *fair*, do you? I *mean* – pets *die*, don't they? And then where are you? It was the same with Rollo's gerbil.'

'Ain't that a toob of your English candy? Rollo? Sump'n like that.'

'Rollo is my *son*. Seventeen, now. Time flies.'

'Tell me, sister. Same with Earl. *Mores*, I like.'

'Mores? Oh *Morse*, yes – good, isn't it? Do you get them over there, then?'

'Mores Bores? Sure. Also I'm a sucker for Snickers. Dwight, he ain't allowed nothing. All the time I gotta think of his bowels. You like that?'

'Well no, I – I mean obviously from time to time they cross one's *mind*, David's bowels, yes of course they do. But I wouldn't say one *dwelt*, exactly . . .' (A sucker for Morse's *knickers*, did she say?)

'Yeh well – with me, Dwight's bowels are a kinda full-time *jab*, you know what I'm saying? Also, right now – I hope our two boys are behaving themselves because also he gotta go light on the *soss*.'

'Soss, really? What – *sausages*, do you mean?'

'*Soss*, honey. I mean, Dwight – I don't want him downing baddle after baddle of the *soss*, you get me? With *his* bowels, it's crazy.'

'Oh *sauce*, yes I see. Well yes of course I can well understand that lots of bottles of sauce could be extremely irritating, in the long term. Particularly – ha ha – if it's *Worcester* . . .'

'Your War-sister-shire soss I *like*. With Tuh-mayto. I'm a virgin – Dwight's always bloody. You see the problem.'

'Well yes I *do*. Well well. God – it's never *easy*, is it?'

'Tell me, sister. So let's just hope our two guys are being two good boys, huh?'

Yes, thought Nicole now, as she shifted herself on to the side of the bed that was usually best for starting the night – let us hope so indeed (where can David have got to?). God – do you know, I've entirely forgotten – in this ridiculously short time I've actually managed to totally forget what I – ! Was it . . . Because it makes number one birds super *bouncy*? Wasn't that, was it? It was better than that – it was . . . I know! It was . . . no, no, can't get it. Lost it. Damn. Should've written it down. It's always like that – if you don't write it down the minute you . . . yes yes yes, well I *know* that, don't I? Bitter experience. It's just that my pen is still in my *bag* and . . . oh God, I simply can't move.

Tired, yes – but I don't know if I'll sleep. Don't think I'll read, though. Too tired, quite frankly.

'I guess in the States, now – New York for sure,' Dwight was opining, 'we got just these two sortsa guys. You getting ice with that, or what?' was the next thing he threw over, one thick finger jabbing at David's large Jack Daniel's.

David shook his head. 'Tiny splash of water, maybe.'

'Yeh – I noticed that. You English guys ain't so big on booze on the rocks. For me, iffin it don't clink, it ain't a drink – know what I'm saying?' Dwight now shifted with care a lot of his weight – tried to settle himself on to this bar stool so that most of his quite compendious buttocks were no longer pretty much bunched up but still hanging off the side of it, plenty, and heaving him away (didn't work too good). 'So yeah anyways – like I says, two sortsa guys is I reckon all we got. You got the little shits on Madison Avenue who just don't drink . . .' (Dwight let his lips absorb cold Bourbon) ' . . . and then you got the regular guys, the good ole boys – sorta guys I hang with. Who just don't stop. You, Dave – call you Dave? You, Dave – I like.'

'Dave's fine,' smiled David – at first, yes, not too sure it really was, actually, that fine – not too wild about 'Dave' – but then he thought Oh Christ what the hell: how long am I in fact going to know this man? All we're doing is passing through. Ships in the night, right? And look – people I've seen on board so far, Dwight is the best around by a long, long way. I like him.

'I know what you mean,' continued David. 'It's like that in London too. Not so bad as it was in the Nineties, but still it's, well – pretty awful. And *units* – they go on about all that sort of stuff in America? All this talk about units?'

Dwight rigidly shook his bullish neck, his bilberry cheeks going along with that.

'Units I don't know.'

'Let's get in another couple of these, yes? Christ – it's

bloody quiet in here, isn't it? Do people just go to bed early on this thing, or what do they do?'

'You're asking me? How long I been aboard her now? Three munce? Three years? Me, I don't care too much *what* people wanna do. Don't pay 'em too much mind. Me, most nights I sit here. Yeh, I thank you, Dave – and loadsa ice, kay? *Pre*-shate it.'

'Yeh but these *units*, right? They say, God – about twenty or twenty-five or something is about right, they reckon. That's maybe eight, ten large whiskies.'

'Waaall . . . guess that ain't too bad.'

'No, Dwight – I don't think you get it. This is in a *week*.'

Dwight held on to his glass and just looked at the man.

'You got to be *kidding* me. No bullshit? A goddam *week*? What're they – *nuts*?'

'That's what I'm telling you. And you're dead right about the way people – and Christ, these days it's the women who – they can be the worst. But you're absolutely spot-on there, Dwight – people either don't drink, or else they don't *stop*. Same with fags.'

'Oh *yeah*,' chortled Dwight. 'First time I heard you English come out with that, I'm going Ex*cuse* me?! Cigarettes, right? Me, I was a Camel man – sheez, how many packs I get through? Then I quit. Wanna know why I quit? Ask Charlene why I quit. Fact, boy – any time at all you wanna hunker down and get with all the juice on good old Dwight's fuckin' *entrails*, then Charlene's the doll you wanna call. Sometimes I get a stogy, you know? I got this guy who can get hold of *Cuban*? Tell Charlene, she kill me.'

'Mm. I used to smoke those small cigars – Hamlet: don't suppose they exist in the States. But I packed them in.'

Yes I did, thought David: I packed them in. Some mornings, I could barely speak – and all my clothes, they smelt like they belonged to men who had days ago died. One reason why, I distinctly seem to recall, in the course of that punishing bender (all of, Jesus, twenty-four hours ago!) I

119

decided to sell my jacket (for not very much). Plus, during my increasingly frequent broker phases, I just simply couldn't *run* to them: sixty and up a day – it wasn't peanuts.

'So tell me, Dwight – '

'You go one more of these?'

'Sure, sure. Why not? So listen, Dwight – what's your field? What is it you do, Dwight?'

Dwight exhaled quite heavily as he poured the not much Jack Daniel's into the fresh and brimming and could be triple new one.

'These days, it kinda does for itself, you know? Which is how I come to be taking this mother of all vacations. Till lately, I don't rightly recall when in hell I last took off any-place at all. Charlene and the kids I sent. Just kept on working. Kinda miss it. It's what I was good at. Real estate, mostly – downtown New York, some in New Jersey. Cuppla spreads out west. Retail – not too much. Wall Street – small-time. Some oil. You, Dave?'

'Ah!' gasped David – mugging quite happily, but still a bit smacked in the mouth by this very softly delivered and tempting assortment of just one or two dabblings in the life of Dwight. 'Me, I, uh – well, not very much of anything at all, really. To tell you the God's honest truth, Dwight –' (and why, I am dimly wondering now, am I on the strength of maybe one hour's acquaintance and three or four drinks, about to confess to this American plutocrat something from which I constantly shy away? Stowing the ice-packed truth in hard-to-reach places) . . . 'Well – the fact of the matter is, I'm actually pretty hopeless with, um – *money*. All round. Can't ever seem to keep *track* . . . which I know one isn't ever meant to say, or anything. Bit like driving, isn't it? Or sex. If you're no damn good at either, well . . . you're just not meant to say . . .'

'Mebby,' considered Dwight, 'you wanna think about changing what it is you do, you know? Ewe Ess of Ay: whole noo ball game. Mebby, just mebby, you wanna think about that. Could be I can help you out, some. So what is it, Dave, that you're actually, uh – engaged to do?'

And David's face was white with shock, as if it had newly occurred to him (or, more accurately, as if the news he was about to impart he had just this second learned). He turned to Dwight – and moon-eyed, he told him with no preamble:

'I'm a corporate financial adviser . . .!'

Dwight held his gaze, and then a slow grin was twisting – tugging hard now at the side of his mouth, and dragging the whole thing all over his face – just as David's eyes too were lit up by all the fun of the fair (the sheer and utter foolishness of just everything we do).

Dwight was wheezing with a rasped-out and reined-in sort of deep and throat-stopped gurgle, now – and he dabbed with his knuckles at eyes lost first in folds, and then these soft and fleshy creases.

'Dave – you kill me: you know that? Really break me up.'

And David accepted with a true and liberating delight the heavy clump of camaraderie across his shoulders – and now Dwight's big and somehow very comforting great paw seemed content to rest there, as the two clinked glasses and drink slopped out.

'I know what you mean,' laughed David. 'Sometimes, heh – I kill me too.'

Really, yeh – break me up . . .

⚓

'Those two seem to be enjoying themselves,' smiled Stacy – one elbow nudging at an ashtray on the bar as the hand beyond it idled around the Coke in her glass.

Sammy continued to buff up a jug as he nodded with eagerness.

'Mister Johnson – he's the American – been in practically every single night throughout the cruise. Bourbon man. Haven't seen the other one before. Must just have joined us,

I think. You're new on board too, aren't you? I'm Sammy, by the way. 'Your barman for the evening'.'

Sammy had strung up great big inverted commas around that last bit and later lit them because God – look at her: even younger than Jilly and me, could be. Quite glad she asked for just a Coke, actually, because although we're told not to be *too* – you know, officious or anything about all the sort of age thing on board, nor are we meant to actually, um – what did they say? Encourage or condone drinking by . . . not that I think she *is* a minor, not now I properly look at her. Could even be twenty, I suppose. Hard to tell, with girls. Got a lovely face. Great eyes. Can't actually see much more of her from where I'm standing (I missed her approach – just suddenly she was sitting there) and it's funny – well, *it's* not funny, no – it's me, I suppose, who's funny about, oh – this sort of thing because although I'm obviously, well – you know, *interested,* as in she's a *girl,* and everything (although she's not looking at me, or anything – hasn't even told me her name . . . but then why would she? Her barman for the evening) . . . but I'm not, if you know what I mean, *interested* interested because, well – you know perfectly well why, I expect. It's Jilly, isn't it? Yeh – it's Jilly who really consumes me now. Jilly, basically, is all I think of. That, and the future. And I know I've been a bit of a *drag* to her, lately (I hate it, actually, when I have to tell her what to do – but *someone's* got to, haven't they? Care for her?), but she'll see, she'll see one day that all this saving and stuff will be really worth it because some young couples, you know – they just sail on into a life together with absolutely *nothing* behind them – and God, every-thing's so fantastically expensive these days and rent's just a joke – I mean, completely *crazy* (anyone with half a mind can surely see that) and so if there's going to be any hope at all of scraping together a deposit on even a one-bed flat (and my Dad – he's great, my Dad – he said he'd help all he could) well then we've just got to, haven't we? Knuckle down and salt away anything we can. That's why this ship is so great I think, actually – there's nothing really here to spend money *on*: and it's piling up quite nicely, now – even the interest's not too bad. She will – Jilly will, one day, see that I'm right. Because I *am* right – I am.

She generally comes in for a drink – see how I am, before I close up the bar for the night. But she hasn't – not this evening, she hasn't, no. Still – she put in a fair old shift herself, didn't she? Just earlier. Must be tired. She's not a bad little worker, I have to give her that. Like my Mum, one way: a really great mate.

Maybe she's gone to bed.

⚓

Jilly was still wandering about the cabin, trailing her (God – just look at them, Rollo kept on thinking) long and maybe, who knows – could be – ice-cool fingers along the length of shiny maple surfaces, sometimes over the smoothness of steel. *God*, she kept on breathing, in some kind of awe – and Rollo sort of didn't mind, just loved watching her – and then came her maybe ironic variations on *God*, how the other half does live: stuff like that. I'll let her go on with it, whatever it is she's doing, for . . . well, as long as she likes, really (well how do you go about, actually, stopping girls from doing anything? They always seem to know exactly how they feel and then they just go for it – and at times like that all you really are is in the way). So yeh – for as long as it pleases her, then – or, until I can't any longer not just, oh Christ – *touch* her.

Really thought I was going to hate this trip – stuck on a boat with Mum and Dad – but so far, I got to say, it's actually not too bad. And could be maybe about to get a whole lot better – but with girls, like I say, it's bloody hard to know; I mean – I'm thinking one thing (yes I am – hotter and hotter) but Jilly, well – she could be thinking some other bloody thing altogether, couldn't she? If she's even thinking at all. On the other hand – she didn't come here, did she, just to admire the fixtures and fittings . . .? Or maybe that's *exactly* what she's done (girls maybe could?). It's just so hard to know – and they're never going to *tell* you, are they? All I *do* know is that she said that her cabin was no good (no good? No good for what?) because she shared it with two other girls, OK, both chambermaids or whatever they call these things – and it was anyway so far down the boat as to almost be scraping the bottom. And no – can you believe? – *window*, or anything, and hot as hell. She laughingly outlined what I think was meant to be this really grim image of the three of them crammed into a dark little booming cupboard – but all my mind ran to, I got to admit, was the orgy potential, here. Guys will get this – guys I hang around with, anyway (and particularly Zimbo – yeh, oh God, particularly him); you just get this vision, don't you, of three giggling girls in not much more than bras and stuff just putting on make-up and maybe occasionally (Christ) swiping each other with pillows and rolling around on each other's beds – and if the other two are looking anything near as good as Jilly (and in my mind they're already fucking ace) . . . well wow.

'Shame,' said Jilly, 'we don't have any *music*, or anything . . .' She was flicking from one TV circuit to the next, impatiently stabbing the rubber buttons. 'Same old usual crap . . . oh God, actually – *this* is amazing. Oh yeh – this is what Thing was talking about. You seen this, Rollo? That's this ship, that is – that's exactly what we look like now, right this minute. Look: amazing, isn't it?'

Rollo sat next to her on the bed and peered at the none too clear and pitifully tiny black-and-white image on the screen. (Why, was in his mind, are we watching television, now? Misread this, then, have I? It's the bloody TV she's come to watch . . .)

'What is it? Boat, is it? We should have brought back some drink.'

'Don't you see? That's the front bit – *prow*, pretty sure, of the *Transylvania*, us, right this very second. Bow, maybe. They've got this camera on the bridge – video camera, yeh? Sammy told me this – never actually seen it before. And night and day it films the progress of the ship. Pretty romantic, actually. God . . . it all looks so black . . .'

Rollo was busy now rootling around in one of the many maple cupboards.

'There's a *fridge*, here. Oh great. Now let's just have a look . . .'

'And see those white things? They're waves, massive waves – Christ, it's actually pretty frightening . . .'

'We've got, what's this . . .? Half-bottle of champagne. 'Hide-seek'. That's German, isn't it? Anyway. And vodka. Vodka OK, Jilly?' Let it be OK, Jilly, because I can't actually get into some fuzzy picture of just about bugger all. Also, I'm *tired*, if you want me to be honest – and if we're not actually going to, you know – *do* anything, well then I'd pretty much like to get a bit of sleep. 'Vodka, yeh? And there's some orange. Or tonic.'

'Oh *yeh*!' went Jilly. 'Vodka – great. Funny – I was pretty knackered just a bit back. Don't feel a bit tired, now. Let's have a *party*, Rollo, yeh? Shame about no bloody *music*, though . . .'

And Rollo thought he'd risk it (still got a bloody silly grin plastered right across his face, though – just in case it all goes wrong).

'We can make,' came his all-purpose, quasi-transatlantic and sideways drawl, 'our *own* music . . .' And he shoved at her a vodka and orange, and as she giggled (thank you, Christ) he tacked on: 'Can't we? *Baby* . . .' And nor did she seem to stop this giggling of hers, even as she glugged down vodka: her lips were smeared with orange. Rollo noticed this as he took the glass from her – and although the

125

vague intention had been to slowly incline his body down, and then bring both his lips to rest with warm insistence full square upon hers, his eagerness to get done and out of the way this now-or-never lust-charged swoop pretty much guaranteed that Jilly would – yeh, right now, bugger it – move her head just out of focus – not in any way, it surely seemed, by way of any bluff to avoid him, or anything, but simply in order to register what on earth it was, this latest shifting in the air. She came right back, though, and kissed him hard – and squeezed hard too, deep into each of his cheeks until he thought through the orangey bitterness that maybe his tongue or eyes could pop right out. His arms, of course, were still spread wide in glider formation – one drink hanging awkwardly from each of his hands, and his bent-double back was bloody well frankly killing him, here; otherwise, considered Rollo, all of this had really gone rather well. The initial and vital disengagement was eventually brought about – largely due to the increased urgency of Rollo's signallings (widening his eyes – the jiggling of lips and the waggling of his drinks) being finally taken on board by a seemingly reluctant Jilly: good sign, oh sure – but it wasn't her back, was it, on the point of breaking?

The glasses Rollo dumped just anywhere – and now he came right back next to her (her arms and eyes were so wide open). His dry-mouthed desire seemed huger than the whole of him, and although the rush of warmth on collision sent up a jerk of shock into the dull blunt booze-thick throb just right bang in there between his temples, it was his eyes that bulged the largest (he could effectively see them, rounded and protruding, jostling for space with lumps of cheek and nose) and his yard-long, flat and pink-cold hands were pawing and grabbing and then moving on fast, burnt by heat and frantic for just all of it – coming down hard on any stray flank whose curve was poised on making a break for it. This first-night performance was hardly even akin to his one thousand two hundred and sixty-seven (and rising) full undress and lone rehearsals – so many dark and damp-sheeted hot blankets of time to have fine-tuned all this to a sweet-pitched crescendo. And now as Jilly squirmed beneath him and gasped, all Rollo felt was, yes – too large and inept, but nonetheless all over and around this thing (excited to the point of stripped-down white fear – just a seed of it booming, before it was muted and large).

Jilly's whole face twitched and stirred and then climbed out from under him, panting for air and more, thin thongs of her hair whipping across the two of them, and clinging to her lips. She was scrabbling at Rollo's clothes, and so now was he.

'Get them . . .' she whispered with urgency, ' . . . *off* – get all this . . .!'

Rollo groaned as his chest coped with all this air it just wasn't getting.

'*God* yes – off, getting them . . . I'll – *Christ*, Jilly . . .'

'*Do* it, Chrissake – where's the – ?'

'Can't seem to . . . fucking *thing*. Jesus – I can't do the – '

'Fuck's *sake*, Rollo – where's the – ?'

'I think – God your tits are *fantastic* – it's gone round the bloody back – I can't seem to – !'

'*Do* it! *Do* it! Oh God – get this *done*, Rollo!'

'I'm *trying*. Oh shit. Oh there! That's got it.'

'*God*, Rollo . . . Want *fun* . . .!'

'Yeh. I'm . . . uh! Uh! Oh heaven – oh God. Uh!'

'I want – !'

'Mm. Mm. Mmmm. Oh!'

'Rollo!'

'*Eurrrrgh* . . .'

'Rollo?'

'Ah.'

Jilly shifted beneath the weight of him, skewing her head over sideways. And as his husky, deep and heartfelt breathing throbbed in her neck, Jilly unstuck some of her skin from his and closed her eyes and opened them. The black-and-white picture sizzled at her, as the great ship's prow continued to plough through the vast and silent, inky sea – and there to each side of us, spatterings of white, falling away.

⚓

'In America . . . you know,' clarified David, 'where we're going . . . well, where you *live*, of course. New York, right?'

Dwight nodded long and hard.

'Affirmative. Yes sir. Sure do. You know what I'm thinking, Dave? I maybe gotta get me some shut-eye, yeah? I ain't asleep soon, Charlene she's gonna come right up and knock me out.'

'One for the road?'

How many times, David was still just about capable of wondering, have I said that in my life? Jesus – the number of drinks I've had for the road – they'd flood the bloody M1 from London to Birmingham. (Plus, while we're counting: how many times did I make that very trip, and a good way beyond, my hands unaware of whatever it was my feet might be up to, while my head was floating free like a balloon, jauntily tied on to the wing mirror with a torn-off unravelling of streamer?) Because that was the awful thing – in the old days, a drink for the road bloody well meant just that (drive? I couldn't even *walk*). Come reeling out of the pub or whatever, jangling the car keys – drop them, but of course (tinkle, crash – vanished, gone) – fall to my hands and knees and scrabble around in the rain-filled tarmac puddles as other bloody idiots stumbled over and around me, cackling and gurgling, and suddenly I'd think Jesus, where in hell am I? And then I'd set to asking myself how it has come to pass that I am kneeling in the dark in the middle of a wet and icy could-be car park: *lost* something, have I? And if so, what exactly? Let's just lie down for a moment and mull it all over. And then maybe my head would collide with the fob of keys, and all would be bright white clarity – soon opaque and heavy as I corkscrewed to my feet and the whole world shied away from me as some bloody joker hoisted askew the car park at the edge somewhere and tried to slide me off it. Then I'd fall into the side of my car (my car? Looks like my car – same sort of colour) and stab the key all over the door and then clack it into the window a couple of times and then I'd form a sort of a funnel with one of my hands around the handle and guide the key through that while keeping just the one hot and engorged eye on the whole proceeding (the other one too busy alternating between larking about and closing down) while occasionally getting my shoulders to pull themselves together and not keep slithering down the car – maybe intent on keeping some long-standing appointment with those lead-clad ankles, there. Swing open the door after days and seasons (maybe seconds) and tumble bruisingly inside and slam the bugger shut and feebly grope about for that thing we fool around with and click into a buckle, can't even think what the bastard's called, while knowing of course that here is ambition gone wild so let's just start her up, shall we, and cruise on home. Mmm – I'm driving well tonight, very smooth, very cool. There in no time. (Christ Almighty! See that mad bastard with the flashing lights and honking his fucking horn?! Get us both killed.)

'Yeh sure,' agreed Dwight. 'One for the road. Where's the harm?'

Well, reflected David, as he tried to focus on finding Sammy, on *this* night of days, or whatever in hell it was now, precious little.

'What I was going to say,' he went on, ' – in America, New York – you ever, Dwight, go to these, what are they? Lap-dancing type places? Nude sort of bars?'

Dwight's eyes and lips tightened and flattened down into slits, black with amusement, as he jerked back his head shortly and once as if he had just delivered at speed into his mouth a neat cold shot of something harsh (which he hadn't, not yet, because David was still failing to make any sort of contact with – where was he? – Sammy. Ah. Was this Sammy now? Yes it was: same again, then, please – better make them double doubles this time round because after these, we're off).

'*Shooooor*!' Dwight was now assuring David conspiratorially, and very much man to man. 'Like when we do *conventions*, yeah? Outta town. Chicago, Atlanta, Denver – *Detroit*, oh man. The way those babies shake their booties. What – you ain't never been one of those places? You don't maybe got 'em in England?'

'Once, I went . . .' put in David.

'Tell you, boy – joints I been, ten bucks buys you a teasing taster. You flash your roll and *man* – it's feasting time. They got these booths in back. Maybe, we get to New York I can show you a real good time. Sure there's Charlene we gotta get around. Your lady wife sweet on you hitting the town?'

'Used to it,' grunted David.

Dwight turned to David, now – the light of animation stirring amid the dull and milky liquids of those just-open eyes. 'Jeez, Dave – some of those babes are so *young*, you hear what I'm saying? Fresh and flawless, boy – like they were since before when. Since before I can't hardly recall. Me . . .' – and now Dwight brought his lips to within twitching distance of David's ear – ' . . . I like 'em, you know – real *young*?'

David nodded. He pulled at whisky, and Dwight did too.

'Yes . . .' he said thoughtfully. 'Young is good. Very good. Tell you – Jesus, Dwight, you maybe won't believe this. Yeh we *do* have them in England, few – some are just sort of topless, you know? Which is OK. Others go the full, you know . . .'

'Manty?'

'Well . . . yeah. But they're *women*, of course.'

Why did I say that? And look at Dwight: he's thinking exactly the same damn thing. Never mind: charge on.

'Yeh – I was actually taking a client from the north of England. Kept on and on about it. Furniture manufacturer – rich as hell, but really *dull*, you know? Also had this export and import business – used to buy all this furniture from all over the world. Anyway – so he goes 'Aw-*cur*, David', he goes – they talk like that, don't know if you know. Oop north.'

'Beadles? Liverpool, right?'

'Well this was Sheffield, actually.'

'Sheffield I don't know.'

'Well no, you wouldn't. Knives. Anyway – when are we *going*, David, he goes. So I got this listings magazine, right?'

'You want I should refresh our drinks, Dave?'

'Ooh – I don't think so, Dwight. Yeh, OK. So anyway, I find this place in Hammersmith, right? Well no, you wouldn't. Well – forget Soho, this is miles away. Anyway – we get there, OK, and the place is covered in all the neon lights and all the rest of it: 'Totally Nude American Table Dancing' it says – and he's really keen. So we go in – usual thing, I expect – velvety, chromy – and I order champagne – bloody rip-off, but he was paying – and Jesus, bingo – over comes this most . . . Christ, the most beautiful girl you ever saw in your life – '

'Young? Young babe, yeah?'

'Oh *Christ* yes – young. Barely learned to walk. So she climbs up on to the table in front of us and Jesus, what a view! And she takes off just everything except the stockings and these amazing shoes and she's pouting down at us and her hips have gone mad and God, Dwight, I don't mind telling you – I was going a bit mad myself.'

'And your guy – he into it?'

'Well this is just *it*!' nearly shouted David – so back there and among the heat of it all did he suddenly feel. 'I glance across at him – thought he might have exploded, or something – and instead of gawping up at this jaw-dropping vision, he was staring down at her feet, click-clacking away, and he was frowning badly. Uh – Everything OK, I go – and he starts tut-tut-tutting away. I'm helping the girl down, now, because the record's ended – and there he is just passing a hand over the surface she'd just stepped away from. He looks at me and he goes: 'They should be *shot*'.'

Dwight was all his. 'He said that?'

David's wide eyes reassured Dwight that he had indeed heard him right. 'So I'm going, er – *sorry*? I don't understand – I thought you *wanted* . . .? And he goes No no *no* – not the girls, the girls are nice enough. The *management* – misleading the public. 'Totally Nude American Table Dancing', it said. (And now I'm really thinking he's crazy, right?)'

'Sure sounds like he's nuts.'

'But *look*, I said . . . she – she *was* totally nude: you just weren't, well – looking. And he says to me – you ready for this, Dwight? He says Aw Eye, Fur Enoof – but there's no way in hell that that was an *American* table!'

Dwight held David's huge-eyed incredulity, and their lips opened in unison to form an O of wonder, just before all the creamy laughter – soon turned to roaring – and then not much later, the wiping of eyes.

'Dave,' wheezed out Dwight, 'you know what? I maybe said it before: you just break me *up*.' And then – in one surprisingly agile movement – Dwight was off his stool and grinning and swaying. 'Fella – I gotta go.'

David turned (*whoa* – bit too quickly) and gazed with benevolence at the weaving bulk of Dwight, that red and sausagey inner tube stuck fatly between his collar and hairline seeming way over-inflated as well as flamingly seared. Dwight now raised an arm in the manner of a great dictator curtly acknowledging the awestruck devotion of at least a division of knife-sharp and jet-clad storm troopers – and without turning nor losing his balance, he called back over his shoulder:

'Catch ya later, Dave!'

David dumbly waved at the ever smaller and retreating form of his new and big friend Dwight and felt only affection and a freaky kind of bonding as he just about heard him calling out again (could have been Yes *sir*, yes *sir* – you really break me *up* . . .) and then Dwight turned into an archway and bashed his nose and briefly apologized and staggered off again and was lost to sight.

And Dwight's big hand was still raised in salute (was thinking he should maybe, uh – how's about I put it away now, huh?) when who should be coming right at him from way down the other end of this vast and quiet upholstered corridor but his own little girl, his own sweet Suki.

'*Hi* there, Suki my angel. You still up? How's your Mom doing?'

Suki stopped: her upper lip was sort of raised, and the stiff fingers of both her hands seemed indignant, splayed out at her hip bones. Her whole body looked *flared*.

'Gee, Dad – you're kinda, like – *loaded*, right?'

Dwight was barely undulating as he continued to look down on her with all the beaming kindness of Saint Nick hisself.

'My own sweet girl . . . Where's Earl?'

'Yeh – like *ask* me. Hit the sack, Dad – OK? What's cooking down the bar? Sump'n? Nothin'? Jeez – this whole tub is, like, in a *coma*?'

Suki ambled on – leaving her father fluttering gently amid the thick and total stillness, still head-waggingly benevolent and marvelling at having – guess what, at this one moment in time? Run plumb bang into his one sweet and darling little daughter . . . who was (and he focused upon this truth with a frisson of confusion) now gone someplace else.

So, thought Suki: let's just check this out, here – what's,

like, falling down? Yeah – like I figured: zero with a capital zee. Three grinning Chinese guys hanging round a mike which don't seem to be working – and yeh sure, they gimme that look, that look I get from guys all over; only with Orientals it don't come out too good, you know? Just seems they're having trouble big time taking a dump. Kinda the same with Hispanics, yeah? They do the eye thing on me and all they look is like they're just gonna *cry*, or something. Black guys I ain't into; dig all the cool, sure, and the muscles they most of them got, but when they're into, like, checking me out, all I feel is kinda like – *scared*? All the laughter goes right outta their eyes.

So what else? Barkeep. Looks beat, poor guy. How long he been standing there, fixing hits for jerks? And some girl fooling with her glass – she maybe trying to hit on Dopey the Barkeep? Nah: looking every which way but right at him. And the other end we got a drunk. English guy, I betcha. Jeez – just get the way *he's* eyeing me, now: same age as my *Dad*, Chrissake. Cute, though, kinda – in a beat-up sorta drunk and English kinda way. I mean – *what*? I'm back home in New York and I'm checking out some totally empty *pub*? And it's one a.m. – two, maybe – and so the whole fuckin' rest of the city is, like, shut *down*?

Suki perched up on a stool and said *Hi* to the barman, just as he was well into his *Hi* to her and only a second before – couldn't have been more – David leaned across and waved at her his glass (and Christ, I've really got to watch that – nearly arse over tip, that time) and said Well *Hello* There – and Suki might well have responded (dumb, oh yeh sure he is – but like I say, kinda cute) but she blanked him off entirely when she glanced across again at the girl at the bar and suddenly recognized her as one of the two in the lousy disco and so yeh OK, I'll go with *Hi* – real bright and right at her – and Stacy was already doing a *Hi* of realization and raising a finger as well as that eyebrow.

'OK,' said Suki, now. 'I guess I'll have a vodka rocks? *Stacy*, right? Getcha sump'n, Stace?'

'Have a *drink*,' came David's thick and (was that really me?) distant, dull and booming voice.

'Thanks, Suki,' smiled Stacy (she's nice, she was thinking – much better now she's on her own: often true). 'I'll maybe just have an orange.'

David waved his arm, now – all-encompassing and large, the gesture was intended to be (had him swaying quite badly again, though).

'Have a *drink*!' came the cry – buffeted by a crosswind as it was, and badly distorted by that dented megaphone he lately seemed to bawl through.

'So,' said Suki to Stacy – edging two stools closer, is the way she saw it, as David was plunged into the cold and could only wonder with misery: Why is she moving *away* from me, hm? All I did was offer her a *drink*. 'My goofy brother still with your friend, someplace? *Sister*, maybe?'

Stacy smiled, and sipped her orange.

'Not my sister no, Suki. She's actually my – '

'Have *drink*!' roared out David (God I did, didn't I? Really roared it out, that time round: didn't *mean* to – it's just how it worked).

'This your first night, right Stace?'

Stacy nodded. 'It's rather odd, isn't it?'

Suki laughed, quite briefly. 'Rather *odd* – yeah. Odd is good, odd I like. What it is, Stace, is like – *weird*? Like – *crazy* weird? I been here since, Jesus – seems like the whole of my life. I mean, don't get me wrong – we've had some real good times, you know? Like – Singapore? Totally arsem. But now all I feel is *great* – I'm going, like – *home*, you know? Need to chill out with my *friends*? New York – you know it? Tell ya – it's real kicking.'

'So I've heard,' said Stacy.

Why do I suddenly feel this? A hundred years old. We must be about the same sort of age, Suki and me – a year or two between us, maybe – and yet I'm just sitting here feeling like bloody Mary *Poppins*, or something, while she's just romping around and being *young*. Christ: it's even the same with my bloody own *mother*. How can it be that all I feel is like my mother's *auntie*? (And in answer to your earlier question, Suki – I really couldn't tell you. Is my mother still sodding about with your *I* think pretty horrible brother? Haven't got a clue. Look – with Jennifer, you just don't know.)

'Have a *drink*! Ooh Christ – !'

'You OK?' laughed Suki – looking down at the English guy, sprawled among the upturned stools, seeming amazed and gurgling away I'm Fine I'm Fine I'm Fine I'm Fine.

'Here – let me help you, sir,' said Sammy – darting from behind the bar, and already well on the way to getting David up and more or less on his feet. 'There, sir – all right?' I wish, he was thinking, that all of you'd go now. I'm really bloody tired: Jilly just must be asleep by this time, yes?

David was grasping the bar quite firmly, his eyes like alarmed and fleeing goldfish (his mouth poised quite like that as well). Suki looked at him with, who knows? Amusement? Anyway waiting for the next delivery of dumb and stupid; Sammy looked at him with pretty much dread – please, oh God *please* don't let him be sick. After this whole damn evening, I just couldn't face – not sick, not this late. Stacy was looking at Suki and thinking how pretty, how very *pretty* the way just that one long finger is idling gently on the rim of her glass (reminds me quite a lot of a girl I was at school with – Janet, who I don't think of now).

And then it came from David's mouth:

'Have a *drink* . . .!'

'Maybe,' said Sammy softly (thank you, God – all he came out with was crap), 'time for bed, sir?'

'You, er . . . could be right. Do you want to buy my jacket? No. No. Forget I said that. Stupid. Bed. Bed. I think you could be right.'

136

Yes, I think you could. I just have now to take my leave of all these good people and with some sort of dignity negotiate this runway, here, and the fields beyond it and get myself back to, um . . . get myself off to cabin number, er . . . got it written down, somewhere . . . and ease myself quietly into that big soft bed and say goodnight fondly to my dear wife, er . . . to my dear wife, um . . .

'You OK, sir?' checked Sammy, as David barrelled away.

'*Perfectly*,' David assured him. Nicole. Yes of course.

And Suki said to him You know what? You're real *neat*.

David remembered it, of course he did. It took him barely two hours to find his cabin (the corridors were good, though – one wall cannoned you right into the other, and the gently shuddering carpet kept your big and spongey feet both afloat and alive) and then there was all the car park stuff to be gone through when he fetched up at the door and then when he'd finally got the bloody thing to *open* (what's actually *wrong* with it, at all? It's all they're meant to do, doors, isn't it? Fucking *open*) David was thinking this and this only: mustn't wake, er . . . oh Christ: *Nicole*. Needn't have bothered. I don't even think it was my falling over the bloody raised-up doorstep thing and then careering into the wardrobe that did it: she was shouting and spitting at me before I'd even got the door ajar. She did the usual: shot her venom for ten or so years, demanded an explanation – and when I opened my mouth to say nothing (well look: what sort of explanation, one might reasonably ask, could she ever be seriously expecting? I *drank* too much, God's sake – how difficult is that?) then she screams at me to shut the hell *up* and let her get some *sleep* and we'll talk again in the bloody *morning*.

God, though. It's maybe that Suki I could properly do with. That would give Nicole something to shout about. And Trish. Good God – Trish: forgotten about her. Yes – as I say: pretty little American girl . . . my age, could be the last bloody time. And talking of age: *young* – oh God yeh: really

137

fresh and young. My friend Dwight could really go for Suki, big time. Green with envy, he'd be. You know – I signed the tab for all those drinks (well, scrawled some sort of mess right across the bill). It's not that I think Dwight's mean, oh no – I know mean men, and Dwight's not one. But he's *rich*, you see – and they don't think of it, do they? Spending money. Not the rich. They forget things *cost*. But I don't, no. Because I haven't really got any money at all, not to speak of. And after tonight, one helluva lot less, I suppose. Ah well. Sod it.

Hey but listen (God I'm so tired – thank God, thank God) – wasn't it odd that she thought me *neat*? yes it's odd, that, very – because to be perfectly frank, all I feel is a bloody shambles.

⚓

Jennifer's face was wet and cold, and the surrounding blackness thrilled and scared her. She went on fiddling with a thick and clanking padlocked gate (I do not need this: it is stopping me going to where I need to be) and Earl, Jesus – he could actually be maybe helping me *out*, here, instead of just tugging at my arms and whining his whine.

'Look, Jen, like – let's just split to my cabin, huh? What say? Christ it's so goddam *freezing* out here . . . and the sign says – '

'Oh Christ – the sign *says*, the sign *says*!' snapped back Jennifer – feeling the rush of wind in her frizzed-up hair as the muted crash of waves seemed at once to pitch down the nose of the ship while sending up into their faces not so much gentle spray as stinging hard gobbets of heavy slapping water.

Earl looked about and licked away at some of the salt; he wrapped around him this dumb and damp stupid lightweight jacket and yeh, he looked about. And all he saw was dark and fucking scary. This is crazy. This is, Jesus, just so goddam *crazy*, you know? Been getting along real fine, this foxy English babe and me – put away how many, back in the lit-up warmth (yeh – *tell* me bout it) of the Regatta Club, down there. Then she's going – *Earl*, come on, let's go, *Earl*, yeh? And I'm like Yeh *sure*, baby – going is good: let's do it. OK – one level I'm thinking *Jesus*, I drank so much I ain't too sure we got lift-off – know what I'm sane? But I'm figuring too, Hey – what the hell? This honey's so hot, she could set fire to the ocean. Yeh – and talking ocean, I'm getting beat up bad here by that very goddam thing. All the munce I been on this tub, I ain't never – not one time – come out on deck at night. I mean to tell you – what, like, *for*, you know? Inside we got heat, we got light, we got booze – and tonight, Earl baby, we got one long-legged chick who I tell ya is hot to trot. So how come suddenly I'm freezing my ass off in the middle of a night that is black like you ain't never in your goddam life even *seen* black, baby – and my feet like doing a skating act over this fucking slimy deck and here in front of me I got the English crazy who's trying to, what – pick a *lock*? And go up what looks to me like no more'n a ladder that leads to *where*, in Jesus Christ's name? And the *sign* – what's with her, you know? Ain't the sign plain enough to her, or what? 'Strictly no passengers beyond this point at any time' – red on white and swinging from the chain. Simple, huh? She don't speak English, the English crazy? I mean, *I'm* thinking – they gotta put up a *sign*? Who in their right mind wants to go trapezing and slithering around and climbing up ladders at any time at *all*, let alone in the middle of the fucking night? You wanna know who? Tell you who. Little Miss Fruitcake, newly escaped from the Ewe-Knighted Kingdom.

'Maybe,' is what Jennifer is thinking aloud now (and why don't I let this kid Earl in on it, where's the harm? It's not as if he's going to come up with anything sensible, is it? They're exciting, very young men – but they don't seem ever, do they, capable of actually *doing* anything – well *do* they? Except, of course, for the obvious – which is, if only he could see it, the stupid little boy, the whole bloody *point*, here). 'Maybe, yes – we could get *under* it, could we?'

'Oh yeah *sure*!' came back Earl (and he really had to shout it out, now: wind was booming, and his feet were having to be splayed out ever wider, just to keep him upright). '*Under* is neat. What – like make like a limbo dancer, huh Jennifer? We got what here? Six inches? Look – let's get *outta* here, man! Why you *doing* this?'

'OK, then – *over it*. We'll go over it. Give me a leg up, Earl. Oh come *on*, God's sake – just *do* it, can't you? Here – kneel . . . not *there* – oh Jesus, not there – there! There! yes – just there. Now put your hand – '

'*Soaked*, Jennifer – I'm like *soaked*, you know? My knee – it's on some kinda metal plate and I'm *hurting*, Jennifer and – '

'Oh shut *up*, God's sake, Earl. OK, now – I'm going to grab hold of this pole thing, right? And when I say so – '

'And my *balls* – my balls are freezing right off, I tell you Jennifer – !'

'When I *say* so, you *push* – OK? Push me up, right? But not till I say so.'

Earl just caught a hold of her goddam foot and wagged his head in a black despair – and with such force that he clipped the side of it on some other wet and hard bit of fucking metal *boat* sticking out at him, and this made him feel, Jesus, just *great*. OK, Jennifer – you got it your way: I'm holding this foot of yours, and I'm waiting for instructions – I'll push it, pull it, swing it around like a lariat or serve it sunny side up with southern fried onion rings on a sesame bun: any which way, you fucking crazy bitch – you *got* it.

Jennifer's hands were cold (OK yes sure: it's cold, I'm not denying – but so *what*, actually? It's not the bloody end of the *world*, is it? These young people – they make such a fuss); but the real problem here was the slippery wetness of everything she tried to brace herself against or even get a hold of. This sort of gatepost thing had looked fine from a purchase point of view, but I'm getting absolutely nowhere, frankly.

'OK, Earl – hear me, Earl? Yeh? OK – now push up as hard as you can when I say so – I think I'll have to make a sort of a jump for it.'

Yeh yeh, thought Earl – jump for it. We could be in bed, right? Fucking our brains out. Stead of that, we're turning to ice on the deck of a ship in the middle of the fucking ocean and Jennifer, she's gonna jump up and grab the steps, is she? And I'm pushing her up and over a gate and then what? I'm gonna *follow*, right? Jeez. How in hell I get into this?

'OK, Earl: *now*!'

And he pushed – he pushed, hoisted, got kicked in the face – put his other hand up to her hips as he slowly rose to take the full weight of her . . . and then the weight was gone from him and all he could see was nothing. So what is this? Somehow I don't know my own strength and I flipped her up into the sky and down into the Atlantic? While not great nooze, at least it would mean I could quit right now and recall what it is to be warm and dry and back with people who ain't gone mad.

'I'm *over*, Earl – I'm over. There's this staircase thing – I've just been up it. It goes down the other side and then we're there! The whole of the pointy bit is just *waiting* for us, Earl! It's all there and empty and waiting just for *us*!'

Earl was already, at Jennifer's urging, clambering up and over the gate. How happy does this make me? I get over this thing and guess what? There's a whole lot more wet and cold and empty boat, and I slip and slide on up there with the ditz they call Jennifer on account of she's told me to: I'm this side of crazy about it.

OK so I'm pretty much over and she's holding me up, pulling loose that final ankle. I cracked a couple bones along the way, and once I crashed right down over the top of the gate and right hard on into my crotch: I don't got one ice pack up there, it maybe couldda hurt. Up this steep and real *oily*, feels to me, pretty much ladder – and now, sweet Jesus, I'm scared: this new shiver and real bad taste is fear, baby – believe it. There's hardly a rail I can cling on to – and all I can see is one dim light, seems like miles off, and then these hissing ripples of foaming grey to the left and right of me, they remind me I'm teetering just over thousands of miles of deep black ocean – and the wind, the wind, it's sucking me off, sedoocing me into it. She's pulling me down the other side (her hand is like a small dead fish – or maybe, I dunno, that's mine) and now I'm skittering about on a like outta here and empty, slick-wet deck. Her eyes, though, I see – her eyes are alive, and hot is back there. Well OK – if going nuts turns her on, sure: I'm cool with that.

And it seemed like, now, Jennifer was dancing. This whole mess of black and oiled and gleaming deck, it sure is kinda like some nightmare and satanic ballroom (Jeez – how'd I thinka that?) so I guess sure, OK, why not? Her arms – way out again and straight to each side of her, you know? Eyes seem pretty much closed, and now she's going around and around – real slow and loving it, seems to me; almost like she's swimming, or just about to swim no more. And hey, man – I thought I, you know, knew this ship like *backward*? But I ain't never seen no expanse like this one here – it's just like, kinda *vast*? So wide – just so plain open. But she's moving too like I ain't never known before; not Jennifer – she's still spinning in her spaced-out thing, oh yeh sure, but it's the ship I'm talking, here. I'm used to she goes just side to side, yeah? But oh, this baby, she's pitching now – I'm real aware of the slow, slow rise of that sheer great nose on her, and now here's the heavy dive back down again, leaving a part of your stomach flying above (and while it's still floating, you kinda swallow it back?). Jennifer, she's – Jeez, where in hell she now? Ah there, there she is – I see her now, yeah; well what I see is that long and feathery

142

neckscarf just catching what little gleam of light there is, so I guess I'll just follow that, will I? Yeah? Follow it right on up to the – Jesus Christ, she's really going for it: she's going all the way forward to the very pointed switchblade end of this great and heaving monster. And I'm coming, I'm coming (sure I'm coming – here I don't wanna be left all *alone*), but every step I'm taking I'm, like, slipsliding two, three backward and I'm not doing too good, you know? We are talking ice rink, here, and the further I go, the nearer to catching up with that flickering and just faint yellow lick of her neckscarf, the more we're going up, way up – rearing right up into this black mother of a sky – and now like a rollercoaster, we're coming down *fast*: diving not just into the blacker sea, but maybe right under it and endlessly further on down into hell (and I ain't never before even *thought* like this).

Now it's like I'm climbing up a well-greased chute – on my hands and knees: I gotta be. My insides is all, like, outside of me – I'm clambering forward and I'm rolling around. It was just when I fell right over, there, that I saw – oh, way in back of us – a broad and just hardly glowing band of light from someways over us. What's this slimy thing I'm feeling? It's a hand, it's her hand – and I turn away and see her face and her lips are real twisted up with the strain of hollering out something right at me, and I ain't even hearing one single word: I lie here, heavy and wet and filled with booming sound and the movement all around of me. She's hauling me up and I'm right behind her; jammed up real tight she is, now, right up into the probing point of this fucking great ship and I'm rammed up tight in back of her and now her arms are splayed right out wide again and she looks back at me and all I can see in that tangle of sea-whipped hair and her drenched and glistening face is the hit of sex as bright as fire in each of her eyes and I know I can't hear her but she's screaming at me, yeah, just one word, again and again: *Titanic* – I know that for sure, and

I'm right there with her – really going for it now, I guess I truly am, and hot through the killing cold with a coiled up excitement and I'm tugging and ripping at her bunched up sodden goddam clothes but I'm numb and like useless and the flesh of hers I'm clutching, I don't even know which *part* of her it is, but it is cold, so cold – as cold as dead women maybe must be. But our spirits are fucking and refucking hard – like the crashing all around of me is making me rattle, and if brains can come, well then I guess ours have peaked and shot their load, now – and like some kinda shuddering jelly subsided back into a white hot state of shock, now all froze up.

Arsem.

⚓

'Come along, Nobby,' Aggie chided gently. 'It's so *late*. You and your Sylvie! Honestly – sometimes I wonder if you notice me at all.'

'*Daft*, love . . .' whispered Nobby – hugging his knees as he sat on the floor of their cabin, captivated as ever by the flickering vision before him.

'I know you love it, Nobby, but you can't watch it for the whole of the *night*, can you? It's what we agreed last time.'

Nobby looked over to her – all snug in bed, she was (curls pressed hard and flattened between a battery of kirby-grips, a scaled-down trawling net protecting the whole like a porous helmet and stoutly defying any stray wisp to even so much as think about breaking for the border). But even as he smiled and reassured her – 'You're right, you're dead right there, my Captain Honeybunch' – even as he said that, his eyes were very surely responding to the irresistible lure, and as they were dragged away and back to the television screen, his head and shoulders could do little but fall in with it.

Aggie sighed. He always *said* early to Bedfordshire –

144

always *said* it, yes, but just look at him. Nearly two-thirty in the morning it was, now – but what could she do? That man of mine – *honestly*! It's like one of those, what are they? Ménage, is it? When there are three of you? Him and me and Sylvie – always has been. I don't really *mind*, of course – understand completely. But we're on board, aren't we? We can hardly be closer to her than on *board*, for goodness sake ... I mean – *can* we? But my Nobby – he's just so utterly fascinated by the sight of her – us – ploughing on through the great ocean. He wants to witness each white breaking wave, and every up and down. He tried to explain it to me, one time. Said it was a bit like dancing with her, all through the night and on until dawn. Which I thought at the time was very poetic, and I told him so, and that seemed to please him. But enough is enough is what I say (you have to know where to draw the line). This time of night, you want to be all tucked up (shipshape, and Bristol fashion – Nobby'll tell you) so's to be ready for morning and another blissy day. And he *knows* this, Nobby – he understands it well; it's just that when there's no other distraction (and me, no – I don't really compete) well then all he's interested in is watching our progress: steady as she goes, and half speed ahead.

Last time we were on board, I caught him making enquiries to Stewart ... do you know Stewart? Assistant Cruise Director? Lovely man – can't do enough for you. Anyway, there was Nobby, bold as you like, saying to Stewart: The *video*, yes? The video that you make from the bridge, are you with me? And as Stewart was nodding, he goes: Any chance of buying a copy, maybe? And Stewart sort of gave him a look – and who can really blame him? But *Nobby*, he started explaining – it's about a hundred and thirty hours long ...! And Nobby (his eyes were so huge: excited, to my mind) just said Yes, So – What's Your Point, Exactly? There: that's my Nobby for you. And I must say that even if the video had been forthcoming, I would have had to put my foot down. I mean, back at home, what would be my chances of him slipping down the shops or fetching my prescription or cashing the Giro? Let alone seeing to the gate or taking the car in. No no no – all it would have been is this endless, silent film – twenty-four hours a day: because that's what it is with real-life footage, of course: twenty-four hours, each and every day.

'We haven't,' pouted Aggie now, 'even finished our quiz. Have we, Nobby, hm? We always do five questions each, Nobby, before we go to dreamland. You know that. It's a tradition. Turn it off now, Nobby – hm? Ask me another question.'

Nobby nodded; didn't stop watching, though.

'Right, then,' he said. 'Name me one great female writer who has voyaged on this great and fine ship of ours.'

Aggie smiled quite girlishly as she set about the business of encouraging her brow to go through its gamut of furrows: she *knew* this one.

'Marjorie Proops,' she eventually released.

'Correct, Captain Honeybunch.'

'Turn off the telly, Nobby. Please? Ask me another.'

'In a minute, love. In a minute. Name me a comedian who has travelled on Sylvie from Southampton to New York.' And then he added on, more softly, 'Blimey . . . that's very *funny* . . . I thought I saw . . . no. No.'

'Dickie Henderson, Nobby,' Aggie came back brightly. 'What, Nobby? What did you see?'

'Mm? Oh nothing. Reckon it was shadows. You said Dickie Henderson *last* time.'

'Did I? Oh. All right, then. Paul Daniels.'

'Is Paul Daniels classed as a comedian? Here – what's all this . . .?'

'Well he makes *me* laugh . . . what are you on about, Nobby?'

'Can't quite make it out . . . OK, Aggie: last question. Give me a prominent Royal who has made the crossing.'

'Easy,' beamed Aggie. 'Queen Mother.'

'Ah! Alas *no*, my Captain! The dear Queen Mother has *visited* the ship, toured her, yes – but never actually travelled. What a *shame*, Aggie: you nearly made a clean sweep, there.'

Aggie was biting her lip, really quite vexed with herself.

'Blow. I *knew* that. Oh blow. I *knew* that . . . but 'Clean Sweep', yes? Yes, Nobby? *Nautical* term. Do I get a point if I tell you? A 'clean sweep' is when a truly mountainous sea sweeps everything off the deck – sometimes even the masts and things. Am I right, Nobby? Nobby? I am, aren't I? Do I get a point? Nobby . . .? Why aren't you . . .? What *is* it, Nobby?'

Nobby was right up close to the screen, now, his eyes screwed narrow with concentration.

'Just as well there ain't no 'clean sweep' tonight . . . else our young friends here would have truly had it . . .'

Aggie was out of bed, and beside him.

'Goodness – it *is*, isn't it . . .? *People* – right up at the bows!'

Nobby just stared.

'But Nobby they *can't* be, can they? I mean – it's not *allowed*. Everyone knows that – it's just not *allowed*. There's a *sign*, and everything . . . what on earth do you suppose they're doing? Must be absolutely *freezing*.'

'What they are doing, looks like,' said Nobby – very slowly, and with a stab at the gravitas he judged it deserved – 'is making the beast with two backs.'

And in the silence, Aggie peered again.

'*Nautical* term, is that, Nobby?'

And Nobby, who gazed on, said No. No, Aggie. It isn't.

⚓

Jennifer, now, had found the right deck. It seemed to be about half a mile further down from the opulence of Earl's (each time she skittered quite playfully down yet another

147

broad and leather-nosed carpeted staircase, she expected to encounter a sort of service lift, maybe, or just a dumb waiter connecting her directly with the sea bed beneath them). The increasingly sullen droning of the ship as Jennifer went on down, lower and lower, served to point up and highlight the practically tangible silence: how could so vast a crock, chock-full of people, appear to be so utterly void?

I feel, thought Jennifer, as she tried to walk straight the length of this joke of a corridor (the floor is moving, fairly distinctly, but also I'm still really quite a lot drunk) . . . I feel, yes – no, I don't *feel*: feel is not what I mean. I *think*, yes – I think this looks like one of those childish essays in perspective we all did – when all your railway lines vanished to a point, and then you started in on the telegraph poles. I feel (*now* I'm feeling) . . . mmm, just fine. Totally charged, and thoroughly fine. Felt close to death, though, if I'm honest, by the time we, Christ, finally reached the door of Earl's cabin. We didn't meet a single soul along the way, which was really just as well because Jesus only *knows* what in God's name we could have looked like. Until I got into the warm, I didn't really realize how thoroughly chilled I had been; it was just like they say – right to the *bone*, you know? I really thought those bones of mine had actually turned blue, and throughout my veins were skulking just icicles, barely dripping. And Earl! Oh God – poor bloody Earl! His clothes were all soaked and with big black patches of gunk all over them, some reason or another (oh yeh – when he was rolling around on the deck, I suppose, mm, it must have been), and the first thing he did was crouch down to this really quite smart little fridge he's got there and break open a couple of those very dinky bottles of Scotch, or something – and the shock of *that* lot suddenly charging all through me was, oh God – pretty much *electrifying*, in a consequently rather sag-making sort of a way. Then he started running a really hot shower – twisting at the big chrome taps as if he truly loathed them – and just that first hit of thick fug felt good to me, very. And I adored the way that Earl was peeling off his wet and stinking clothes, neither shyly nor posing, and just stepped forward into the steam and stood there with his back towards me, letting all those blazing needles sting him, and then course on down the gleaming length of all his planes and flanks in a languid, yes, and streaming wash. And then he turned to me, full at me, and smiled his fabulous boyish and *American* smile and I took off all of my stuff and joined him there, yes – my arms just resting high up on his shoulders, my eyelids batting madly so that I could see him through the jets of warmth that were urging us back into human again – first turning us rosy, then making us hot.

The way he looked at me (he hurled back this sopping rag of his hair with one strong and impatient dash of his hand) – it was, I think, as if to say – and I can just hear him saying it – Jesus Aitch *Christ*: this dumb and crazy English broad – what is she? Like, *nuts*? But I was laughing, now – practically scalded and slitheringly so completely drenched as to be more or less made up of just rubber and liquid, and I pressed my face right up close to his totally smooth and hairless chest and my twisted mess of hair became jaggedly snagged on just that faint and glowing shadow of new dawn stubble that traced his jaw and throat – and Earl, now (look!) had on those lopsided and over-easy signs of giving way to not just it but me, and his dead straight white teeth looked unreal as he too, under the still crashing rush of powerful hits of blood-hot water, settled down to a round of comfortable comedy, now that he was safely out, and no longer part of the joke. I felt I could very soon, one way or another, pretty much drown – so I reached out for the wrong tap and half-heartedly fought with it (and so aware, now, that both of his hands held on to me and were lifting up my wet and deadweight breasts) and then latched on to another and despite the weakness in my slippery fingers, this steaming Niagara just cut right off so completely and suddenly that had we not both just been standing there, dripping loudly amid this new and sauna silence, it might never have been dashing all over us at all. Steam rose, though. And he was jutting right out at me. Which I always love.

'Do you know,' I heard myself gasping (it was like retraining in speech, for the first time in ages: a strange and novel patois), 'that tonight, this very night, God knows how long ago, the *Titanic* went down?'

Earl shook his head, and bent down to kiss me. I think the shock of all that hot fullness (four plump lips) went through both of us (I felt our jolt).

'And there we were,' I was only whispering now (his hands were moving around me, and mine had latched on tight), 'right up there, making like the way they did in the – yeah? Movie.' It sounded so stupid – so terribly juvenile, and utterly stupid. Which was just so great I, oh – can't tell you. 'Before it went down.'

And then I did. Went down. It was a kind of homage to very many things, it seemed at the time: it felt sacrificial, as well as just wonderful and also – do I actually mean fulfilling? After, all over the bed, we rolled and tussled like two kids vying for custody of some fleeting thing that was already no longer the point. I did not at all mind (it's something I miss) Earl coming so quickly and simply all over me: it's urgency, isn't it? It's that that's so very exciting.

And now, it seems years ago (although I'm wrapped, still, in its warmth and glow) and I haven't yet stopped tramping the length of this trick corridor – but I reckon if I've got the numbers right at all in my head, it must be that bay just up there, our cabin, about three up, or four, just on the left. But that slight flurry, there? Did I glimpse that? Or is this strange dull light (and now the insistent press of unignorable weariness) tripping me up? Looked like – and I know it couldn't really have been (Christ – it's practically *dawn*) – but it looked like, it did, it really did look like the toss of Stacy's hair, and Jennifer thought she was hearing that one single exhalation of hers that could signal, oh – just anything, really, from petulance to contentment.

And something made Jennifer slow, now: take it easy. She backed into one of the bays just here to the right, and she was glancing obliquely over. And look no, she hadn't been wrong – there was Stacy, head to one side, her black eyes lit with darkness. And from the thrown-aside tangle of her pale and streaky hair, there drew away briefly another head which now came back in – and this time the embrace was warm, the kiss more lingering. A sort of rustling, then, and some very low whispers. A slight flurry – and Stacy was away and letting herself into her cabin, and closing the door behind her, softly. Jennifer stood still, as if she had been told to count to a hundred – judging, now, the right time to emerge and just barely knock on the door so very very quietly as being maybe not until the retreating and really quite swaggering invader had diminished into near invisibility, silently covering the length of the corridor.

And so not until Suki had finally reached the end of the long, long passage and was stabbing at the elevator button did Jennifer break cover from her, oh dear God – *shouldn't* have been hiding place, really, should it? And Suki was thinking this: Mm, she was thinking – mm, mm. That I liked. That I could get with. This could be not just cool but, like – *different*? And as the elevator hissed her right back up to where she belonged, she was also thinking this: Gee – what am I? A *klutz*? I, like – *duh*! – thought they were *sisters*, those two? What planet am I on? I guess they're one baby of a lot closer than *that* – know what I'm saying? So I reckon what it is I got to be here is, maybe, real *careful*?

Arsem.

⚓

A ribbon of bright crimson light was quite suddenly splattered across the misty glass of the single porthole in his small and cluttered office, and it made Stewart wince and screw up his eyes and then tear them away from it.

Dawn again, then – and still I'm sat here. It's not, if I'm honest, that there's so much on my plate I can never get away, no no – I couldn't put my hand on my heart and claim that. But it's so . . . my job, it's sort of a twenty-four-hour thing, even when there's nothing on the face of it to actually, uh – do. Also, where I sleep (the shelf upon which my superiors see fit to install me) – well, it's even less attractive than being surrounded by all this party stuff, day and night, if you want the truth. And talking of parties (oh God oh God) – might as well screw back on my Assistant Cruise Director's head, and make an early start on sorting out the day.

First up, I've got to splash around all the posters for the Talent Contest, Thursday. I know. Oh God – don't *tell* me: I *know*. But what can you do? It's something the regulars demand, don't ask me why. It's all pretty much self-defeating, if you want to know my take on the matter. The reason (oh Christ – just remembered: got to get the veg-etarian orders down to the kitchens for the Ball tonight – forget that, and I'd really get it in the neck). Yes . . . now where was I . . .? Oh yeh – Talent Contest. No – see, it's totally crazy, really, because the reason all the old-timers, the *Transylvania* mafia, insist it goes on is so's that on every single bloody trip they can reprise their tried and tested (much loved? Hah!) sodding *routine* – but the mad part is that the regulars will have seen and heard it, seen and heard it a *thousand* times – and it's always someone like that Welsh thing, what is she, Mrs Williams who wins it anyway (or whoever else is mangling a Shirley Bassey number on that particular evening, stringy old arms stretched out and beseeching from within some stupid spangly dress; God – sometimes women can come so very close to disgusting me). Then there'll be some drunk old fart whose misguided and very wrong friends have assured him repeatedly that he's a *card*, a *natural* ('Tell you, son – ready wit like yours, you just can't lose'). So he'll lean on a microphone stand and come out with all these ancient bloody gags and intersperse them with stuff like Anyone in tonight from Yorkshire (and there always is)? Or Texas (and oh God yes – there always is)? And then he'll say *Pity* . . .! And everyone roars. They do. I know, I know – but they *do*, I tell you – and none more than all the bloody losers from Yorkshire and Texas. Mystery, I tell you. These cruises (and I should know) – they're weird.

Give it an hour, and then maybe get some breakfast. I love my food, you know. Love it too much. Got to watch the figure. Even as it is, I'll never have my blazer undone, you know. Ooh no – that would never do (too much stuff around the waistband). And yes, I admit it – I did have to get a slightly larger blazer, this year (just slightly – nothing dramatic) – but there: what can you do? This whole bloody ship is built around food and drink and parties and snacks and cocktails and tea and dinner and elevenses and light lunches and heavy lunches and yes, like I say – breakfast. Maybe just have the one sausage.

So what else? Balloons. Balloons, yes. About a hundred and fifty red, white and blue balloons to be blown up for the Viva America Ball tonight. But surely, you might be thinking, you have someone to do that sort of thing? Well no I *don't*, as it happens, no. The Cruise Director – *he* has someone to do this sort of thing, you see – oh yes: *me*. The Assistant – plain enough? Well never mind, you could go now – you've got a pump, so it won't be too bad. Well please allow me to correct you on that score. We *had* a pump, oh yes sure: when we first set sail in about the sixteenth bloody century we had pumps coming out of our *ears* – but now? You just try and lay your hands on one, mate. Gone, vanished – every man jack of them. And yes I know – how can you lose about half-a-dozen balloon pumps? Particularly in the light of the truth that it is in this office and this office only that bloody balloons get fucking *pumped*. But there it is – another of the mysteries that is part and parcel of life afloat: it is not for me to question why. No – but it *is* for me to get my laughing gear around the nozzles of a hundred and fifty bleeding balloons so that all can be bright and colonial for the Viva America Ball. And then I drape the drapes. And then I unfold my life-size cut-outs of Marilyn and Elvis and Chaplin and Laurel and Hardy – the Jameses Dean and Cagney, Humphrey Bogart (typical sort of crowd you might expect to run into at any sort of get-together, really), and then what with the band striking up Dixie and Gershwin and then a bit later those Beach Buggering Boys, all will be seen to be totally *authentic*.

And now Stewart was gently smoothing into his face and jowls a carefully judged top-up of his Clarins bronzing gel (I find I only have to shave, now, every other day, if that: I don't know why this is). And then he upended a packet of balloons all over his desk and fingered one gingerly before pushing them all aside (oh God in heaven *no* – not before breakfast) and then he stood up and strode the two paces which were all it took to get him to the far wall of his office, thinking Well at least I can unfold the cut-outs (make that early start). And so he bent to his task, as the still golden dawn now flooded the space and rendered his newly tanned cheeks not just tangerine, but practically radioactive. First up is, what have we here? Elvis Presley. He creaked open the fold at the waist, and then fooled around at the back, fumbling for Flap A which slotted quite neatly, all being well, into, yeh – Slot B, and then there was this sort of easel-type stand thing that you pulled out and fitted in . . . and there: hey presto. One two-dimensional guitar-toting King of Rock 'n' Roll, his lips gently sneering.

Stewart turned away – and then all of a sudden, caught up in a rush of hot flushing, he found himself taking it *personally*. He wheeled right back to Elvis, and smashed him in the face.

PART THREE

Making Waves

The sun filtered down through a vertical lattice, and the pattern it was making across the big green baize table immediately put Marianne in mind of the lawn, the lovely lawn, at the old house. A long-ago but potent memory – she could only have been, oh – six or so, maybe even a little bit younger, when they had left that place. She remembered her mother saying to her so sadly how terribly *happy* she was, and how they all now would be, because the new house, the place they were going to right this very minute (and all the familiar things which Marianne had maybe assumed had just grown out from the ground they stood on – all these bits of furniture, the ornaments and immutable pictures, even the big old clock that forever said ten to seven – they were all piled up in a van outside) – was, you see, so very much better than *this* old house in just, oh – every single way you can think of. My room smelled different, now that it was empty – and all the others did too; maybe the smells were coming with us (wrapped in corrugated, and stacked in the van?).

It was later, many years later, that Marianne had first overheard Nicole cursing her husband (my Dad, my Dad) to hell, to hell: Why in God's name didn't I leave you *then*?! *Then* is when I should have gone: when you dragged us all away from our beautiful big house and crammed us all into *this* hole. *Upwards*, David – that is the direction our lives were meant to be taking: why is it always that you're dragging us *down*? Marianne had been snipping at herbs on their little back patio at the time of the rant, and she remembered then as she remembered now the broad and fresh and deep green lawn at the old house that had stretched on for what seemed like just miles and miles – and all the wonderful masses of conker trees at the end (she used to bring to school just bagfuls of the things, and swap them for chews – and once a Parker propelling pencil which Nicole had forced her to take back, and this had saddened Marianne, although she still let the girl keep all of the mahogany conkers). And the warmth of the summer sun, now – the whole dazzle of the enormous window and the striping of the baize, switched on the light of the lawn at the old house, the good house, the gone house (and no, the smells had not come with us – but nor, oddly, did we leave them behind).

I've really had the most wonderful morning – and even now it's only just after ten. I heard someone or other last night in the restaurant saying that truly the best time if you want to go up high on deck is very first thing in the morning: the air is simply stunning (so the woman was assuring just anyone in earshot) – but don't be fooled by the blazing of the sun: you'll need a coat and if you're anything like me, a headscarf as well or your hair, oh my God, it just frizzes up like anything. So I got up about seven, I think – slept very well (super bed); had a shower, and then I thought I'd better phone Mum. *No*, dear, Nicole had sighingly assured her – I wasn't asleep: I have been simply *reposing*, and contemplating getting up soon. OK Mum – well look, I'm going up on deck, right: do you fancy that idea? Coming along? Well it rather *depends*, Marianne, ventured Nicole with caution – when exactly are you thinking of going?

'Well – sort of now, really. Just grab a coat.'

'*Now*? What – you mean now as in now this *minute*, now? Oh *no*, Marianne – don't be so silly. I couldn't possibly. I've got all my *creams* to do, haven't I? I haven't even thought about what to *wear* . . .'

Not true, thought Marianne: she will have given a huge amount of thought as to what particular outfit should kick off the day – it's just that she hadn't *decided*. And that could take hours. And sometimes – even when she *had* decided, even as she was wearing the thing and on the point of setting off, Nicole would then decide that in fact *No*, not this: this had been the wrong decision. And it would not be so simple an operation as slipping off Offending Garment One and buttoning herself into Absolutely Perfect Garment Two, oh no, because the tights wouldn't be at all right, you see, and nor the shoes – and plus I've now got to go through the business of transferring everything from this black and superbly understated shoulder bag (rather chic, I think) and into this very much smaller blue and quilted option which although I think you'll agree is terribly smart, and all the rest of it, can never quite accommodate all the bits and bobs I need (unless you cram it obscenely), and it always seems to be my reading glasses that get left out in the end and then it makes menus a total impossibility – so you do understand how much *time* it all takes, don't you my dear? You are, after all, a *woman* now, Marianne: I'm surprised you don't see it.

'Yeh OK,' went Marianne – not at all minding (she had only made the offer because, she supposed, it maybe must be in her nature to do that sort of thing). 'Dad OK?'

'Your *father* . . .' exhaled Nicole, ' . . . is unconscious. Which is a mercy. God alone knows what time he finally rolled in. Amazing he found the cabin. Oh God *Almighty*, Marianne – I *was* about to ask of the heavens above if he's going to be like this throughout the whole of the trip, but I realize now that that would be just plain *stupid* of me, wouldn't it? Of *course* he is . . . oh God of *course* he is . . .'

Marianne could never dream of colluding with any new strain of Dad-bashing, so it was time to get off the line. Rollo she didn't ring; she didn't at all care to know what Rollo had been up to, and nor of the state he was in.

Despite this little sort of fold-out map thing she'd found among, oh – all sorts of glossy stuff in a big and shiny folder on her dressing table, Marianne was finding it really rather difficult to locate a door that actually led to the great outside. And this after she'd even spent quite some time sitting there and studying the thing (up two floors, fairly sure, and then a left kind of dog-leg turn – not right, though, because right leads straight to the theatre (. . . God, they've got a theatre). Seems quite straightforward, I think. Right, then . . . oh wow look! There are postcards of the ship in here too: brilliant. And headed paper! God – does that mean you can post a letter from the ship? How's that work, then? How is the postman supposed to get to the middle of the Atlantic? And if he's already on board – well how does he get off? It's quite a puzzle, that. But then so many things *are* – I keep on getting these sort of 'Hang On' moments, you know? Like – when I ran my shower (and I had a bubble bath too – just couldn't resist) I thought: Hang On: how can there be hot water for every single cabin, all round the clock? How do they *do* that? Well – fresh water *generally*. Amazing. And don't even get me on to the *food*; last night alone I witnessed so much, oh God – *acres* of food and drink and chocolates and stuff, but presumably they've got just piles and piles of it left? It's like a floating town that you've just moved into and everyone's being perfectly *nice*, and everything, and while on the one hand you feel sure you'll settle in and be utterly happy here – with so much *plenty*, and all these pleasant people – you know that in a week (five-and-a-bit days, now) you'll be moving out and back into Realsville (well *relatively*; tell you one thing – getting *home* home, that's going to be the *real* shock, here).

She got there eventually: eventually she did. But in very slightly more than a vague sort of a way, it annoyed Marianne that she had had to resort to asking the way. Just as she was sure that the bright white light of morning was about to stunningly confront her, she had found herself stranded among a brassy clutch of still-shut-down boutiques, their windows stacked with such as sequined and strappy evening gowns (and your eyes could be knocked out by any colour you cared for) each of them sheathed in clear and heavy plastic and draped with a succession of toning pochettes, most of which were easily capable of swallowing up a dispenser of artificial sweeteners, and just maybe one's tablets (because you can, you know, amid the whirl of, oh – just all the gaiety, simply forget to take maybe the heart one, or else the little triangular pink one that aids digestion – and goodness knows if you do, there's a price to pay: up all night and jittery, very).

'I'm looking,' said Marianne to a stocky but still rather soignée smiling woman, who was clearly having trouble with the louvred shutters on her bijou jeweller's shop, 'looking for the, um – *sea* . . .'

The woman nodded brightly. 'It's outside,' she said. 'It's just outside.'

Marianne smiled uncertainly – not quite sure which of them had bagged outright the prize for being the most demonstrably stupid, here. She wandered away, hoping either to just find the *door*, God's sake, or else run into someone who could with confidence guide her there (and it would be nice if I'm not standing right bang beside it when this does actually happen, if ever it will). She paused a while to ferret out that little map thing (I just know I'm on the right floor – deck – so how hard can this *be*?). Two youngish American girls had idled along, and they sat down nearby (*think* they're American – their lips look quite like it).

'So, on and *on*, you know?' went one of them, wearily. (Yeh – American.)

Their eyes looked pouchy – make-up impacted, mascara now more like a grievous stain: I don't think, thought Marianne, they've yet made it to bed.

'Guys can be a real, like – downer?' the other assured her with sympathy, lightly touching her wrist. 'You bet they can. It's real hard to luck out.'

'But just like on and on and *on*, you know? Like it's always – Aw, c'mon, let me come into your *cabin*, come on babe – come on come on – let's get with your *cabin*, huh?

And I'm like I *told* you, John – my mother would *worry*. Why can't guys get that?'

'They're, like – *guys*, right?'

'I guess. But why can't they just *stop* already?'

'Yeh *right*. Dream on, lady. So, like – *what*?'

'Huh? Oh shit – in the end we go to *his* cabin, yeh? The way I figure it, let *his* mother do the worrying, right?'

Marianne wandered away in what just *must* be the direction. Oh look – this man will know, he'll be bound to. Got that lovely white shirt on with those black and gold, what are they, on-the-shoulder type things. Terribly smart. And he could be quite senior, too – must be about Dad's age, which I really rather like.

'Yes, miss – absolutely. This door here – just here, yes?'

Marianne simpered at him her dopey gratitude. Yes of course – this door right here: the one I'm standing right in front of. Great. So let's just pull – is it push? Terribly stiff. Ah, it's pull – God it's a weight . . . and oh *God*! Oh *God* – that first hit of the bright cold sparkle of all this outside world! The sea is all flecked – no, not flecked: *covered* with silver spangles, and the air is too much – just too much for my lungs to handle. And the sky – that light blue sky, with all those thin and wispy whitish veins – it's all around and over me. It feels so great: I'm glad to be here.

Marianne wrapped around her a PVC mac that had been slithering around all over her arm throughout the endless journey (and how many times was I thinking Oh God I so wish I hadn't *brought* the thing? Pleased I did now, though: she was right, that woman last night, whoever she was – you really do need it, no matter how bright the sun. She can keep the headscarf idea, though – I just love this wind, cuffing my face, dragging back all my hair by its roots, and making it stream).

My eyes are practically closed – these softly screaming, serious breezes and the dazzle of the sun are seeing to that – and as I put everything I've got into walking the walk, it is as if some big and gentle outstretched palm is not quite insistently squashing me back, relenting only if I pout and doggedly persist. The deck is much broader than I thought it would be – and the rail, oh God: the rail that is all that keeps me from thousands of miles of ocean (lapping and flirtatious, now, it sort of seems – winking constantly) is so low and gappy and stuck quite regularly with red and white roped-up lifebelts. I'm not quite sure I dare look down. There's a bench just a little further on – slatted sort of back-less bench thing. If I can make it there, I'll sit – sit awhile, yes. Five or so more struggled paces and yes, I'm here now – so I'll sit, like I said. Just sit for a bit. From here I can reach out and touch one of these really quite jaunty, I suppose they are, lifebelts (SS TRANSYLVANIA, it says on them – and yes I know that's where I am, what I'm on, but it's still quite a shock, somehow, to be told, like that). I'm leaning forward and peering down, now. It's then you get the speed. The water rushes by, and fans away into milk-white furrows to the side. Above my head (I've only just noticed) there's a lifeboat suspended: there are lots of them (enough?) strung the length of the deck. Think I'll, yes – think I'll walk again. Maybe work my way right up to the front.

Getting more used to it, now – the noise and the lash of the wind, all this spotlit sparkle – and I'm actually feeling quite suddenly hot. If I take off this coat, though, I think it will just roar and take flight; and if I just unbutton it, I just know it'll take right off with me inside it. Oh look . . . Couple. There's a couple, man and woman, right down there and coming this way. They've got Burberrys on and some sort of funny hats, can't quite see, and their arms are tightly linked. Togetherness, do we think? Or a cling-on safety measure? Maybe there could be here the underlying shadow of something more beastly – something on the lines of 'I'm telling you, mate – if I'm blown to kingdom come by the next great buffet, then you, my love, rest quite assured, are bloody coming with me!' No – I doubt that. How unkind. Even to think it.

And now they're near enough for me to see that they're grinning broadly, the both of them. Or maybe here is only a grimace (their mouths are caught in the teeth of a gale?). No, it's smiling, pretty sure, because they're nodding now, the two of them, because yes of course, we're all friends here – well *aren't* we? Yes we are, yes we are: that's the rule (all in the same boat). So I've got to call up and muster a good many of my features, now – change them all around until they form into a well-known phrase or saying that will speak unto any nation (because they could be from anywhere) that here is *greeting* – simple yet electric – and here is too the handclasp of *oneness*.

Our mutual and lunatic contortions of complicity have collided like rubber-tipped lances at the business end of a friendly joust (I heard the clash of amiability) and soon they are behind me and I plod on forward and now I can tell you that what they actually had on their heads were his-and-hers *deerstalkers* (one Black Watch, the other the red thing) and the flaps were down and over their ears, the connecting ribbons lost to sight among scarves and chins and things like that. Was any of that actually *good*, I wonder? What do you think? The lance and jousting thing? Lunatic contortions? It's difficult to know, isn't it, with this whole imagery thing. But I really would like to read English at Uni, if ever I'm up to it. Be a writer, one day. Because I really love reading: just love it.

Now what's this? Oh hey – that's not fair – it's a barrier, a dead end, a great full stop. 'No passengers allowed beyond this point at any time'. Well hell. How are you supposed to do all these healthy circuits of the deck, then, if you can't actually, you know – walk *round* the thing? Oh God. Better turn back, then. God oh God! Now the wind is *really* slicing me and I'm suddenly freezing, if I'm honest. Maybe I'll go back in. If I meet those raincoated loonies coming all the way back at me, then I'll go in for sure (can't do that grin all over again). *If*, of course, I can find the door . . .

Can't. Can't see any doors at all (so here we go again). And the Siamese twins seem to have blown away altogether – so let's just see what happens at the back of the thing, shall we? God, it is, you know – it's simply endless, this ship. Which is, I know, a tragic way, really, of trying to describe it: *not* endless, is it? (well no, not – I'm actually standing right at the end now, so very much not, then). But what else, really, can you say? Very *big*? Doesn't hit the mark at all. But I'll have to be getting it across *somehow* because Mum and Dad are never going to be doing all this for themselves, are they? As soon as she even smelled the *suspicion* of wind, Mum would be clutching her hair and just *gone* (or else giving way to a nervous breakdown); and Dad would just sniff it all briefly and say Hm, very nice, Marianne – very, uh – *fresh*: now what say we all go back in and have ourselves a little *drink*, hey? And Rollo? Oh *please* . . .

It seems to broaden out quite suddenly, when you get to the back (which it *doesn't*, obviously – but it really does appear to) and there are now all sorts of other decks, mini decks, a bit fanned out above and below you. Loads of lounger-type deck chair things all lined up down there – and a maybe little tennis court, could be (there's a net there, anyway). Actually, despite all the vastness, everything here seems terribly weeny, rather surprisingly. I mean – look at that swimming pool: bit pathetic. Not really much bigger than the hot tubs alongside. One of which has a – urgh – very bald man in it, bobbing up and down like a hardly boiling egg. Who of course is now smiling up at me, and soon he is raising a hand from amid the pulsating bubbles.

'Don't mind Harry!' calls out a woman, who Marianne had not even noticed standing alongside. 'It's only Harry. Don't mind *him*.'

Marianne slapped back on her usual half-baked smile; am

I meant, then, in some way to *know* this Harry? Am I? Know all about him?

'Do you think,' the woman went on – her voice made slow by the bending of the wind, and also maybe by the weight of thought that was backing it up, 'that the water – the water in the swimming pool, yes? Do you think it's *fresh* water, could it be? Or sea water? What do you think?'

Marianne glanced at the pale blue pool, its surface fluttered into fillets.

'I, uh – I don't know. I hadn't really, er – *thought* . . .'

The woman nodded with emphasis, as if to state Well I *have*.

'*Sea*, fairly sure. Yes – it *must* be sea water, if you look at it closely. Can't you see? All the *waves* . . .?'

Marianne stared at the ground, and nodded. Then she made a sort of pointing yet twitchy and frankly farewell movement with all of the fingers on one of her hands (the message being loosely that she was in fact, you see, an agent working undercover for the British Secret Service and if my tail sees me talking to you then the entire operation will be blown asunder and both our lives could well be at grave risk and I have only just now glimpsed M over there, lurking by the quoits, so you will understand if I just slide away?).

Marianne was relieved, now, to be quite alone again and standing at the rearmost point of the liner – actually holding on to the jutting-out flag pole (why no flag? Huh? Tell me that. Should be a Union Jack there, shouldn't there? So why not? Why isn't there? Huh?). But just look at this. Look at those massive and churned-up vees of foam we're leaving behind in our wake. What I'm doing now is, I'm focusing on one just-formed white and chopped-up eddy, and I'm keeping my eyes on that little one and that one only . . . and God, in just the space of eight, nine, ten . . . twelve seconds, now, and it's practically hitting the horizon.

I think, you know, that if anyone ever went over the

side . . . then one of those lifebelts would be just too little, three miles late.

⚓

And scattered across the sun-dappled baize of this taller than usual and big square table were what appeared to be just thousands of bits of jigsaw. Marianne plucked up a few, quite idly – most of the perimeter was already done – and with just one interesting reddish and white piece carefully pinioned between her thumb and forefinger, her hand hovered vaguely in circles through the air, sometimes shifting more angularly like an arbitrary gearstick, maybe trusting to magnetics to haul this thing down and let it just click with no small satisfaction into quite the right spot. (Hopeless at jigsaws, always was – even when I used to pick out all the straight-sided bits, I could never seem to fit them together). And the process wasn't helped by her having to whip off her glasses at the approach of just anyone (hadn't been back to the cabin, not yet, to deal with all the contact stuff), this new blindness rendering the whole scene before her yet again as no more than a small and fuzzy lawn – and don't, please, get her on to all the old house thing again – now romantically marred by a frittering of leaves.

'Why,' she had asked of a trim and eager steward, just a few moments earlier, 'is this jigsaw here, actually?'

And, she might have added, so oddly positioned – sort of half into a broad corridor, and hard by the smoking section of the I think it's called Piano Bar.

'Bit of a tradition,' smiled the steward.

Ah yes, thought Marianne – everything, just everything on board surely seems to be that: I'm not convinced that anyone in authority – and certainly not the regulars – could actually cope with anything occurring for the very first time.

'There's a sort of challenge,' the steward went on (he had

offered her tea – drop of coffee, maybe? – and although Marianne had politely declined, he still seemed to have all the time in the world for her), 'to – you know – get it finished off by the time we dock in New York. There are no prizes, or anything. People just fit in the odd piece as they're passing, like.'

Marianne nodded at length her complete understanding (one feels, I don't know – in some way compelled to point up, magnify, practically illuminate one's every remark and gesture) while doubting that that really was the way it went. From what she'd observed even during the short time she'd been loitering there – waiting for what, exactly? Dad and Mum and Rollo to one by one emerge and show their faces? Not really: but something, I'm waiting for something, feels like – it had been plain to her that practically everyone passing gave this table not even a glance. They had in mind a nice set of chairs clustered around maybe one of those little round tables, there (not in the glare of the sun, but not too far out of it either), and possibly an early morning little snack – would that be nice? To round off breakfast with, before they could idly contemplate just maybe a spot of elevenses, during which their minds and conversation could stray in the direction of lunch. But the few who *did* stop: oh my God – those two Japanese, there, and that extra-ordinarily large and blond and I think rather cruel-looking man (his face is set – so terribly serious) – their eyes were darting from piece to perimeter to box and back again, and occasionally a triumphant hand would swoop down from on high like a hawk in silence – and as the piece snapped unerringly home, there spread slowly across the face of the huge and unforgiving blond man a sneer of repletion, as if he had once and for all settled the hash of his implacable enemy; the Japanese would whoop briefly like seven-year-olds having been newly awarded an extra half-holiday, before all masks were resumed and the game in earnest began again.

The puzzle depicted – and Marianne could only note this and wonder – an Alpine scene: snow-capped mountains and plunging valleys, hugging into warm-lit coves, clusters of picturesque chalets that reminded Marianne of a musical box she had had so very briefly, oh just years ago (the fruit, as it happens, of yet another bumper conker-swapping jag, though this thing too, which played – don't ask – Come Back to Sorrento, soon – at the say-so of Nicole – went the way of the Parker propelling pencil). Marianne hadn't really minded, though – it was her royal blue velveteen jewel box she had loved, with the little pirouetty ballerina, all her prettiness and outstretched grace mirrored and twinkling as she slowly and only just a bit jerkily revolved in not quite time to some weird and plinky noise, which every single time had tenderly wrapped up Marianne in successive layers of softness, and delivered her somewhere safe and elsewhere (a place she badly needed to be).

Had enough of this. Maybe I'll go and chuck a bucket of water over that horrible brother of mine: even if it doesn't wake him up, it'd be quite fun to do. Oh . . . oh look who it is! Oh no – isn't him, is it? Maybe just sneak on my glasses (no one seems to be looking). Yup – is him. Why's he just hanging around like that? He's a very dark horse, this Tom, I think – much more interesting than he seems, and so so *sad*. I can probably understand why people might just dismiss him as some sort of a nutter (well *I* did, didn't I? At first I did, before we'd properly spoken) but I really think that sort of thing happens far too much, nowadays. Everything – everyone's judged on *appearances*: if I can't *relate* – if you're not wearing the right *labels* – then as far as I'm concerned you're either invisible or some old lunatic: either way of no concern. *That's* the attitude today. And it's wrong, I think: very.

There's a woman, leaning against the window and staring out to sea. Tom is behind her, just a couple of feet away, hardly more, and he's looking – what? Hesitant? Yes – I would say hesitant (but he always does, Tom, doesn't he? Look that). Still he's just standing there, one finger to his lips. But now he seems to have come to a decision – he's making his move.

The next thing came swiftly – and Marianne maybe was as shocked as the woman. Tom had approached her in silence (but not like a hawk) and in one fluid movement he inclined his head downwards and closing his eyes he buried most of his face quite deep into this (who is she?) woman's rather thick and sunlit tawny hair, as his hand closed in fast and was firmly massaging her tightly-trousered bottom. Marianne both felt and heard the woman's gasp as she spun around to meet this, her eyes and mouth struck open and held in not just bad surprise but also big enquiry, while a darkening flush fled up from her neck and was mottling her cheeks (a kind of mauve). From Tom, though, all trace of blood or even muscle had instantly dissolved: he seemed stricken by a pain, stuck with jagged confusion, and already his jaws were set to work as he stammered out now his hopeless apology:

'Oh my – oh God, goodness – I'm so terribly – !'

'What in hell you think you're *doing*?!'

'I thought you – oh my God, please *forgive* me – I thought – !'

'What *doing*, huh?! *Mister*!'

And although the woman was working hard on indignation, Marianne could see that already the mind behind her slapped-open eyes had latched on to the reality, here. Tom seemed suddenly so much older – thin and white and dressed in black, his eyes beseeching and yet darting with energy from side to side, to maybe ensure he wouldn't be *looked* at – and his fingers flipped hard at the air in a mute display of mortified exasperation.

' . . . *desperately* sorry. I thought you were – someone else entirely. I . . . I can't apologize *enough*, I'm just . . . !'

The whole of the woman's outraged face and pent-up body were calmed right down.

'Well . . . *okay* . . .' she was conceding – and even kindly.

But Tom was having none of that: it was as if he was pleading for his life.

' . . . quite *unforgivable* . . . I don't know what you must – !'

'*Hey* . . .' soothed the woman. 'It's OK – OK. Big ship, huh? Stuff happens. It's *OK* . . .'

And now, thought Marianne, the woman really needed to be done with it. This was kinda becoming a whole, like – *thing*, you know? People were looking over – and anyways, I gotta be someplace else real soon.

'Come on, Tom,' said Marianne. 'Come and sit down. Have some tea with me, yes?'

Both Tom and the woman turned to gaze at Marianne: the relief that hovered it seemed was unspeakable.

'*Marianne* . . .' breathed Tom. 'I – thank you, yes. Some tea would be so nice. I haven't yet had – oh *madam*, I really am so terribly . . . um – breakfast.'

Marianne smiled quite graciously at each of them in turn (and the woman, guys – she was just *outta* there) and then she took Tom by the hand and led him somewhere safe and elsewhere (a place he badly needed to be).

⚓

'Yeh well – all I'm saying is – ' (Charlene was doing it again, yeh? Talking at Dwight these same goddam words) ' – you'd been there, it maybe wouldna happened. Nobody gets to thinking you're someone you ain't if you're with someone you're with – right? Get just the plain potatoes, Dwight – those with the mayo are gonna kill you for sure. So it's with *me* you shouldda been. Is all I'm saying.'

Dwight was standing in front of her and sliding a tray down this sleekly ribbed and aluminium slipway – so long and snakey, the damn thing is . . . nah – *long* just don't do it:

171

like everything on this tub it goes on for just *ever*? And why they're in the Poolside restaurant doing self-service lunch, just don't ask him. Most days, he picks and chooses in the Duchess Grill (they know him down there, know what he likes – and also not to serve it when Charlene's around him and yakking). But sometimes – and this is one of those times, surely seems – Charlene, she takes it into her head to hit the Poolside for some kinda change. Do you good, Dwight – change is good, also the food I think up here is *lighter*? And with your bowels, Dwight – you listening to me, Dwight? Light is what they're needing.

'I can't be around you alla the time, Charlene. What you figure the guy was gonna *do*? All it was was some dumb klutz making a mistake. Jeez, Charlene – it's you that *told* me he made a mistake – so why we don't just *leave* it already, huh? Excuse me, sir – any how you can see your way to breaking a egg over the top of that steak, there, just easy like?'

'A egg, Dwight, you don't want. And mister – can I ask you to make real sure that steak is, like, *totally* lean? I thank you. The salad he'll take as it is.'

'Thousand Island is what I like.'

'The point I am *making*, Dwight, is that it brought on home to me that all through the vacation you ain't hardly never been by my side. I'm in the beauty parlour – you're in the casino. I take in a movie – you get wasted in a bar. I visit the coffee shop – then *you* take in a movie. It ain't *togetherness*, honey, is what I'm saying here. OK? No Thousand Island. And Dwight – what's with the *cream*?'

'You can't have no fruit salad, you don't got cream.'

'Where's Suki and Earl? You see them, Dwight? Always they get their food in so damn quick and they say they're gonna get us a table someplace and danged if I ever can see them again.'

'Over yonder. I see them. See – Earl's waving.'

'How'd all that cream get to be on your tray, Dwight? It *flew* there, maybe?'

'Jeez . . .'

'Just get it back. What is it with you, Dwight? You *wanna* die, or what is it?'

Dwight did some hissing and set to wagging his head as he followed Charlene across to the table. It's maybe my age or my eyes or sump'n, could be, but I'm finding that toting this here tray, you know? Looking down and placing my feet and weaving in and out around alla these tables . . . get kinda dizzy; got to go slow, else it's me or the tray that could lose it. And naw, Charlene – it ain't I wanna die; I mean – I'm *gonna* die, sure, just like we're all gonna, one day, this much I know. It don't fear me much, but I ain't just sitting here waiting for it, you know? Keen I ain't. But until the good Lord comes claim me for a angel (and I just hope He knows what He's doing) – well till then, I guess, Charlene, that what I wanna do is just, you know – *live* some?

'Kay, you guys' (Charlene the drill sergeant was back on duty, so sit up real straight now, soldier). 'Let's get us a bidda clear, here. Earl? You done with those dishes? And Coke cans all over I don't need.'

'I'm *clearing*, already,' responded Earl – placing a couple of cans on top of a sideplate and shifting the whole just someways to the left. 'Hey, Dad – how come you don't got the Béarnaise soss and the Southern fried chicken and the chocolate fudge cake and, what – no blueberry pie just like Mom never made?'

'Yeh yeh,' went Dwight, sitting down heavily. It ain't enough I can't get to eat what I wanna eat but I gotta put up with Mister Funny Guy, here? 'Hey, Suki – how you doing?'

'Doing good, Dad. Like – really rinsing it, you know?'

And Dwight was both pleased and surprised by this. Suki didn't look sulky, and it wasn't even her birthday. I ask her how she's doing, what I'm expecting back is Yeh *right*: like you really *care*? How many munce she's with the teenager

173

from hell bag – now she's cooking with Shirley Temple. Kids? Talk to me about it.

'Eat your food, Dwight,' said Charlene. 'It ain't getting no hotter. Also cut it real small, the steak, yeh honey?'

'Yeh,' grunted Dwight. 'Small. Real small.'

'So Mom,' struck up Suki, ' – hey, Earl – you needing those biscuits? What's shaking down today, Mom?'

'You want the biscuits?' checked Earl. 'Sure – take 'em. Listen, guys – I gotta bail, OK? Like – *places* to be?'

'What's with all the hurry?' Charlene wanted to know. 'You maybe gotta *train* to get?'

'Yeh sure, Earl,' said Dwight. 'Catch ya later.'

'Mom?' pursued Suki. 'What doing today? Anything? Nothing?'

'*Train* to get . . .' emphasized Charlene. 'I thought that was kinda funny, no?'

'Oh *yeah*!' enthused Earl. 'I gotcha – like, *train* to get – I see where you're coming from, Mom. Like, what we got us here is a *joke*, right? On account of there ain't no way I'm pitching up on no *train* cos like we're on a *boat* – am I right?'

'Leave it, Earl . . .' cautioned Dwight.

'You're just *offal*, Earl!' laughed Suki.

Charlene had put down her fork – the fork with which up until now she had been eagerly stabbing at all her little cut-up bits of meat: the fork now joined the discarded knife alongside.

'One day, Earl . . . one day . . .' she said, slowly.

Earl stood up, and flashed at his family an all-encompassing grin.

'Yeh right,' he agreed. 'Well I guess I'll take a rain check on that, Mom. See you guys!'

Charlene watched him go.

'What's gotten into Earl? Dwight? You know?'

Dwight swallowed whole a great lump of steak.

'Oh yeh *sure*. It's like he *talks* to me?'

'I gotta go too,' chimed in Suki. 'So Mom – you didn't tell me. You gonna be around later, or what?'

'Today I got bridge with the girls – and then I gotta start in on the packing. Yeh yeh – I *know* we got days and days, but I'm telling you – paddery like I got, needs real care, you know? Take me like forever to get it packed right.'

Yeh, thought Dwight – and then when we get it all back home (and where in Jesus she gonna *put* it all, huh?) then she takes another forever to *unpack* the mothers and then I'm paying the garbage guys to put all the boxes in the crusher and *then* what? I pay Melita to every day clean it, is all. What is it with you, Charlene? Why you do alla this? Why is it you don't wanna *live* some?

What I need right now is a cuppla drinks, someplace real quiet. Could be check out where's Dave: maybe we can hang one on.

⚓

Suki, yeah, was kinda early. It's maybe how it goes when you really wanna, like – *be* there? So Stacy – why don't she feel that? I mean – she feels that, she's *here* already, right? But like I say, I'm kinda early, so let's just loosen up and chill awhiles. It was me who said we meet here – this real scuzzy old Black Horse *pub*? Like – don't barf or nothing – I sort a think of it as *our* place, already? Spooky or what?

That guy – he just come over with my vadkan-Coke. You believe it? He's back behind that bar *again*, that poor guy – what is he? Sammy – yeh, Sammy. This is how he's gonna spend his whole *life*? Not sleeping nights and fixing drinks? Like – poor *guy*: know what I'm saying?

Last night – what there was – I didn't sleep too much either. This whole, like – thing with Stacy? Still kinda arsem in my mind. Ain't never been here before, you know? *Thought* about it, oh yeh sure – like, at *high* school? Some real foxy chicks there, man – you better believe it. But I was

175

hanging with this, like – superjock, you know? Carl? And OK, he was kindava meathead, yeh sure – but around school he was, like, Guy Numero Uno, you know? So what's a girl to do? But always, like, I gotta be seen in his *car* and I gotta go watch all these dumb football games on account of he's, like, team *captain*? One day I'm cruising by early, yeah? And any practising Carl was doing was on the dumbass cheerleaders. Pissed me right off. Soon it was, like – when the *prom* comes around? Carl is acting like I'm so cool and lucky on account of I get to go with *him*? Can you *believe* that? And then in the car afterward? All he wants is I should go down on him. And I'm going, C'mon Carl – I got my real pretty dress on and everything, yeh? My corsage, it's getting messed up bad. It's like he ain't hearing. *C'mon*, baby, he's going – *c'mon* baby – *do* it for me, *do* it for me. And I figured *hell* – I just don't got to *take* this, you know? I just don't need to, like – *go* there? What am I – some kinda ornament and a suck-off machine for one dumb doughbrain with a *dick*? Even when we *did* get it on, it was just like Wham, Bam – and no sir, I didn't even get no Thank You, Ma'am. So I thought, what – this is *it*? You read books, there's this thing called love. French class one semester we got to read some thing by *Colette*? You ever come by that? I guess it's pretty obscure. Anyhow, I could really relate, you know? There was . . . *tenderness*? Strength, sure – but like softness in *with* the strength? And a whole buncha movies – they taught me that too, I guess. That maybe you can lie down with someone and this someone ain't just gonna be jumping your *bones*, you know what I'm sane? So in the end I broke up with Carl (and in the stampede of lowlife tramps to get him for their own, I tell you – you couldda got yourself killed) and as a result I kinda found myself giving up on guys, period. On account of if you dump the top jock, where you gonna go? Like – *downward*? I don't think so. Oh sure, all sortsa guys kept hitting on me, but I figured, like – who *needs* it, you know? And on this here ship – aw Jesus, you would not believe the number of guys who've come on to me. But I guess I just been hanging loose. Sometimes, I get attracted to just the *weirdest*? Like last evening – the blitzed-out old English guy? Cute. Don't ask me. I guess I just like kinda weird. See – look at the bar guy. Sammy, yeh? All the time he's checking me out. All the time I see it. And he's a great-looking guy, you know? Young, and all. But what I get is zilch. I look at him and what I feel is nothing. And then some, like, real ancient loser from England falls offa his goddam stool and what I think is *neat*. I mean hey look – nuts or what?

But Stacy – that was like *literally* something else? We talked some and we laughed some and next item up I'm real deep *kissing* her? I really, really loved that. Like I say, I ain't never done it before, you know? But it kinda felt like coming home. For her, though – I guess I was just another chick. I mean – she's a professional, right? Rooming with that Jennifer, she's just gotta be. And yeh, I admit it – they make a cute couple. Shame it has to me who's maybe gonna break it up.

'Well well well well well . . . what a delightful surprise. We meet again, er . . . I'm awfully, um, sorry,' David now apologized. 'If I ever *did* know your name, I'm afraid I've, er . . .'

'Suki,' she smiled. 'Hi. And you are?'

'And I am? And I am David. David. Yes. Can I get you a – ?'

Suki raised her glass. 'Got. Get you one, David?'

'Oh good *Lord* no, wouldn't hear. No no. But *thank* you, of course. Um – what's funny? Have I said something funny?'

Why, thought David, is she *laughing* at me? I thought we were getting on really quite well. Jesus Jesus: what would it be like to have something this young, and so soft? I can't remember and I can't imagine. This Suki makes my Trish look old; she makes Nicole seem dead and buried.

Suki's eyes had been closed as she fizzed out her amusement.

'It's you English guys,' she smiled. 'You're just so *polite*, you know? I like it.'

David pulled out a chair and sat across the table from her.

'You've been in England lately? Politeness is barely more than a memory in England, now. Place is full of yobbos.'

'England I was in just two days back for maybe, like, a couple hours? We were in the *Harrods* store? Look – lemmy getcha drink, David, yeah? Scotch, is it? On the rocks?'

Suki raised up her hand, and David was both surprised and impressed by the sight and then speed of the barman scurrying towards them, for all the world as if he had forever been poised and awaiting such a summons.

'Well I, er – yes, Scotch, thanks so much. No ice – touch of water. Harrods, of course, is hardly *typical*, is it, uh – Suki? Full of foreigners, for a start. Oh God – no *offence*, of course . . . well, it's not as if you're *really* a foreigner, is it? I mean – American isn't *foreign* foreign. Not like you wear a veil, or something. And you do speak English. *Well* . . .' he qualified – cocking an eye and going for it ' . . . after a *fashion* . . .'

'Knotty knotty . . .' Suki playfully admonished – her eyes, it seemed to David, pretty much ablaze. Suki. Jesus. What a fucking sexy *name*: suits her.

His Scotch must have come, then – because either David or some passing poltergeist surely would appear to have drunk it all, anyway (all I have here in my hand is one empty glass). So let's get in another round, I can't see why not . . . where's the fellow? Has he seen me? Yes? No? Ah yes – now he has; doesn't seem to be in that much of a hurry this time round, I can hardly help but notice.

'*So*, Suki – looking forward to getting home, are you? Had enough? New York you live, yes? What – with your family, are you? Boyfriend, maybe?'

Suki looked at him, as she idled the pad of one stiff finger

178

over the rim of her glass (she knew that for some reason this always *worked*: guys, you know, would see in it something – don't ask me what. Last night, David was blind, but it sure did work on Stacy: don't you go thinking I didn't catch a sight of her watching; anyone's watching me, I know it before they do).

'That's one loada questions, David . . .'

'Hm? Oh God *sorry*, sorry – I didn't mean to, um . . .'

'See what I mean? Bout you English guys? Always with the 'sorry', 'sorry'. What you sorry about, David?' Her eyes were wide open and full on him. 'You done sump'n you should maybe be *sorry* about? Have you, David?' Her mouth was too (well, not *wide* open, no – but nor, let's face it, was it in any way shut).

'Not yet,' he blurted – and *damn*, he thought: oh bugger. Not only was it glib and trite and sleazy and (much worse) like some kid in a *film*, that bloody stupid comment, but also, I get the very strong feeling – if I'm not totally misreading this whole situation (and I'm not, am I? And it is, is it, a situation of sorts we have here? Maybe just a bit of one?) – then I simply and weakly supplied the summoned conclusion to her rather cheeky little flirtation. Cheeky, yes; though none the less arousing for having erred on the side of the somewhat obvious. More so, actually, if you want me to be honest. (And never mind *her* name being so bloody sexy – even the way she says *mine*, Jesus: goes right through me.) But would she let it lie?

'You aim to?'

Her whole body in that chair was squirming around, side to side – shoulders hunched forward, fingers now not just all around the rim of that glass but darting down into it, too (and when they'd done with tinkling the ice, weren't they up to her lips, each of them in turn? And did she suck them, one by one? Well *did* she? You tell me).

Right then, thought David. Right right right. Christ. Didn't expect this. This little lot I surely did not expect.

Whatever was or was not going to happen during this so-damn-crazy Trip of a Lifetime, I can honestly place my hand across my heart and swear to all you good people out there that this one, this thing, did not so much as cross my mind. Admittedly my mind has been more or less out of commission and practically concussed since way before I even so much as stepped aboard – but still . . . but still: this is, I assure you, a turn-up for the book. And look – how long am I actually going to be on this ship? Hm? Not long – few days. Now this is good and this is bad – but on the whole it's good, yes it's good, it's good this, yes – and I'll tell you why: *One*, there's no time at all for the leisured seduction (and OK, OK – I'm aware, of course I am, that I do not find myself cast here solely or even partially in the role of, uh – *seducer*, yes OK, all right . . . but this is for the time being, if you'll allow me, the way I choose to paint it) . . . and *Two*, even if the whole thing proves to be an out-and-out disaster (or even, God help me, if I am totally misreading this whole situation – and it is, is it, a situation of sorts we have here? Maybe just a bit of one?) well then very soon we're all of us *elsewhere*, aren't we? Won't ever have to think of it or speak of it or see each other again. I can't tell you how much that one thought warms me (if only life were always like that). Right, then. Right right right.

'Tell me, um – Suki. Lovely name, by the way . . . it's so . . .'

'Sexy? You think it's sexy? Stacy, yeh? She thought it was sexy.'

'Stacy? Who's, um – ?'

'You were out of it. You wouldn't recall. Go on, David.'

'Hm? Oh yeh – yeh, what I was going to ask you . . . and you might, when I, um – ask you, revise your opinion about my *politeness* – '

'Hey – wait up! My name – you were gonna say something – ?'

'Oh yes. Yes – your name. I think it's . . . it's really very, er
– *nice*.'

Suki beheld him.

'*Nice*? It's *nice*? Nice is, like – it?'

'Well *more* than nice, obviously,' hurried on David (oh
Christ leave your fucking *name* out of it for just two seconds,
can't you? Your name is fine, it's fine – it's not your bloody
name I need to talk about).

'That's the trouble with you English. You're all so – *understated*? If it's, like – *more* than nice, then say it, why don't ya?
Just *say* it. What is it? Sexy? Is it sexy?'

'It's . . . *yes*, Suki, it's sexy. Very.'

And Suki nodded. 'Neat. That's all you had to do. Now –
what you wanna ask?'

'I want to ask . . . that is to say . . .'

'Jeez, David – !'

'OK. All right. Suki – do you have a cabin of your own?'

'Sure. I'm a big girl now. What – you don't?'

'No I, uh – don't, I'm afraid.'

'Married, right?'

David nodded. He nodded long and hard.

'Right,' he said.

'I kinda figured. So what – you wanna come see it? My
cabin?'

David more or less goggled at her.

'Yes . . .' he breathed.

'Number one-oh-one-oh. A quarter after seven – that
good for you? We can have like a cocktail before dinner?'

Still goggling, oh Christ yes (and I think my mouth's open
too, now).

'That would be . . . lovely.'

The startled faun would surely have appeared a model of
composure if contrasted then with the convulsive nature
of David's reaction as the very cold voice of someone else
entirely sliced quite invasively into this blood-hot dream,
fallen from heaven (and I've just gone and given my shin

one hell of a crack on the underside of this table, I don't mind telling you).

'Hi,' said Stacy, briefly. 'Sorry. Bit late. Let's go, Suki – yes?'

'Hi babe!' called out Suki – apparently (what is it with women?) both thrilled and delighted by this bloody intrusion. 'What – you don't want to get a drink? This here is David.'

Stacy nodded. 'Yes I, uh – remember. No, Suki – let's go, yes?'

And David's anguished look to Suki bellowed out as loudly as silence can: *No* – don't go. Stay. What's she want to go for? *Stay*, Suki, God damn you. Who is this kid anyway? (And why do you call her 'babe'?).

'Kay,' said Suki, brightly. 'See you, David.'

And bugger me if the two of them weren't practically out of sight before I could even put my mind to standing up (my leg is bloody killing me). So I just sat there. Tell you, if good old Dwight hadn't soon hove into view, I would've felt not just let down, but pretty put out. Still, though – seven-fifteen, hey? Seven-fifteen. Cabin number . . . oh Christ – *what* was it? What *was* it?

'Hi there, Dave. How you hanging?'

'Good to see you, Dwight. Feeling a little tender . . .?'

'Too tough to be tender, boy. What made me think I'd find you here, huh?'

'Ha ha – yeah. What'll you have? Bourbon, yeah? Listen, Dwight – I've just *got* to tell you – uh, shall we go to the bar? Or are you happy here? OK here? Fine. Hey listen – you will not *believe* what has happened to me. There's this *girl*, right?'

And Dwight's eyes were already twinkling.

'You got my whole attention, boy. But hey listen – afore you start up, I gotta say this. I am very aware, Dave, that last evening you picked up the whole of the tab. No – let me finish, here. Now I just wanna say that any liquor we may be putting into us on this day, well – that's all down to me,

182

Dave. OK? Unnerstan? Good. That's great. Now – let's get us in a cuppla beauts, and then you start up. And make it *hot*, Dave – make it *hot*. You hear me?'

And so David did just that – cranked it up to boiling point. Because look – Dwight was one of the good guys, the real guys, and Jesus, there don't appear to be all that many of us left. So Dwight and me, we pulled at our man-sized drinks and I told him all about this fabulous *girl*.

'And she's . . .' Dwight was pursing his lips ' . . . *young*, you're telling me? Real young?'

'Young as young, Dwight, Jesus – I wish you could've seen her.'

'You and me both, boy. And you say you're seeing her *tonight*? I raise my glass to you, sir. That's mighty quick work. Sure envy ya, I don't mind saying. Every day I'm with Charlene I'm thinking what I'm needing, pining for, is one pink slice of lamb – you know what I'm saying? Shame there ain't two of 'em.'

And then this Stacy came into David's mind. And then she went right out again. Nah. He knew nothing at all about her, but the look she had given him had been, oh God – more than enough. Whatever game we might be getting up, here, there's no way that Stacy is a player.

'Well look . . .' said David (and he came in close) ' . . . I mean – all goes well, there's no reason why, maybe . . . in a day or two . . .'

Dwight was rapt.

'You mean – what, are you saying . . . this piece of ass might be willing to play ball? Like – play the field?'

'Seemed the type to me. What's to lose? I'll put in a word, shall I? When I'm – you know: *done*.'

'Oh sure, sure – unnerstood, Dave – yeah sure, gotcha. Well I reckon that's mighty neighbourly of you, friend.'

And David beamed. This is all going really terribly well. I've got not just this cracking little bird lined up, but also a very good mate to tell all about it. And yes – I mean it: when

I've had my fill, as it were – well why not? Hey? Dwight's a buddy – and what are buddies for if not to share with, after all? So yes, like Dwight says – it's only neighbourly. All I'm doing is the decent thing.

Number one-oh-one-oh: *that* was it. That *was* it.

⚓

'Jeez!' laughed Suki, as Stacy hustled her along. 'Are *you* ever in a hurry! What am I – under *house* arrest?' And then more softly – eyes still bright, though with lowered lids and cast sideways to maybe catch a flash in Stacy's own (evasive, at the moment, and jumpy). 'You, like . . . on *fire*?'

Stacy heard the words and sensed the way Suki was maybe looking – and then she snortingly smirked, at the same time reducing her pace – which yes, she had only just realized, was ridiculous: I mean God – what am I? On *fire* . . .?

'Sorry,' she breathed. 'It's just that place. Had enough of it. And that man. Why were you talking to him?'

And Suki stopped dead. They were hard by the photo shop, now – screens were littered with shiny coloured shots of eager, grinning passengers, all saying cheese just the afternoon before; the wreath of flowers loomed large in all of them. Suki now thought she might open up her eyes to their very widest (make them both round and inquisitive), cock an eyebrow and let her lower jaw drop down into ironic and unspoken exclamation: the hands on her hips helped along the general tableau which by now, if all was still in synch, should be fully armed and dripping with 'Ex-*cuse* me . . .?!'

'What is *this*, Stacy? Jealous?'

And Stacy was amazed to hear the words – she felt them slapping across first one cheek, then cuffing the next; certainly she was warm, now, from the heat of them. Because was I not just on the verge of demanding of myself the very same thing? What am I *now*? *Jealous*? Can I really be? This is how it *goes*, is it? I mean – I haven't even got round to explaining to myself so much as the tiniest part of whatever all this *is*, yet – so how come I can suddenly feel in me brewing a sour green stew of unease? Simply because, what – Suki chooses to chat away idly for one or two seconds with some overweight drunk from the night before? Unease. Is that what this is, then? A faint unease, just barely stirring? No – I think the broad flat swipe of Suki's more or less delighted instinct smacked it hard and came in closer: what I am is jealous. Jesus.

'Oh God don't be so *silly*, Suki. It's just that . . . hey! Suki? Are you actually *listening* to me?'

Suki had turned away and was enthusiastically scanning the racks and racks of photos.

'I'm trying to, like – find you here, Stace.'

'I always look awful in pictures. Come on, Suki – let's . . . look, all I really wanted to say was that I felt *bad* last night, OK, when – '

And now (oh sure, tell me about it!) – *now* Suki was listening to her, hell she was: she had turned, and her eyes were wider than when she had deliberately cranked them up to the limit.

'What? What – are you, like, *saying*? You felt *bad* – !'

But Stacy's head was shaking to and fro, repeatedly and with great determination – tightly gripped forearms, closed eyes and flatly compressed lips effectively reinforcing this big denial.

'No no *no* – no, Suki, no. I didn't mean I felt badly about . . . *that* . . . no. I felt so awful about just . . . leaving you in the corridor like that – and I was only thinking, well – my cabin's empty at the moment, right? And I just thought . . . well, if you'd, you know – *like* to . . .?'

Suki grinned. 'My cabin's always open house. Got some vadka, if you're innerested . . .?'

'No,' said Stacy, quite thoughtfully. 'No. I'd like you to be

185

in – *my* space. If that doesn't sound . . . I don't know – how *does* that sound, actually? Suki?'

Suki grinned more broadly, leant forward and very fleetingly, whispered a kiss.

'Sounds . . . just great! Oh *hey*, guys – looky here. Here you are, Stace! I found your pitcher. Alongside of . . . *Jennifer*, right?' Yeh, thought Suki: Jennifer. Right.

Stacy studied the snapshot (trying, and failing, to blank out Nobby and Aggie). 'Horrible. Terrible picture. I'm all teeth and gums. Jennifer looks OK, though. She always comes out well in everything.'

Suki was thoughtful, now. 'You – uh . . . you really dig her – right? Yeah? I mean I like get the feeling you're real – *close*?'

Stacy went in for a short bout of pink-faced scoffing, as she put her head on one side and made as if she was considering some novel and intriguing idea for the very first time.

'Yes of course. I mean she's *crazy*, oh yes sure. Totally nuts. But yeh – I love her, course I do. Couldn't not. Always have.'

Suki nodded. 'Uh-huh. And this, like – cabin idea, yeh? Like – she won't *mind*?'

What a terribly, thought Stacy quite dazedly, *odd* thing to say.

'No. Mind? Why on earth should she? No of *course* she won't mind. Why do you think she would?' I can't offhand, thought Stacy, think of anything much that Jennifer minds; well – Nobby and Aggie, fairly obviously.

Suki shrugged. 'Whatever's cool,' she said. And then – as she was suddenly buffeted sideways by this flurry and then whirlwind that had rushed out of nowhere and more or less right into the both of them – 'Hey hey! Slow up, man! Easy!' And now she was holding on to the skittering and still fast-moving scatter-limbed girl – if she hadn't, they all could have collided quite jarringly with the wall-to-wall and sunlit gurning that made up the photograph screens.

'Oh my God I'm so terribly *sorry*!' rushed out an appalled and practically winded Jilly. 'Oh God I'm right sorry, you two – are you OK? God – so sorry . . .' She had the flat of her hand across her chest, and was using the pause to gulp down air. 'I'm just so terribly late for my shift – at the bar, yeh? And Sammy'll just kill me. Look – I've got to go. I'm really awfully – !'

And Suki and Stacy, alternately and together, collaborated on a series of hissed-out and hushed OK-type noises, while fingers briefly touched forearms in a soft and sisterly show of warm reassurance. But they giggled as Jilly tore away and hurtled onward – and Yes oh *sure*, thought Jilly (really quite bitterly): it's all OK for *them*, isn't it? *Totally* fine. All with rich daddies and servants like bloody *me* to attend to their every sodding desire. God – if *they* had to spend twelve hours a day pouring out bloody drinks and being *nice* to people, they'd have a bloody breakdown; Daddy would have to send them to Switzerland or stick them in *therapy*. Ever *I've* been in trouble – up against it – all my Dad says is Think On, Lass: Aye – Think On.

'Sammy – Sammy don't! Don't be horrible. I'm *sorry* – OK?'

Sammy had been polishing glasses (it's one of the things I do, polish glass; but look, way I see it – means to an end, right?). Still couldn't resist, though, an extra twist of his wrist as he did it (quick look down – not too quick – take in the watch face) – and even, by way of possibly overdoing the thing, a pointedly casual glance over there and up at the clock (tricked out as a sunburst, it was, and ticking with menace and thuddingly at Jilly).

'It's OK! . . .' said Sammy – with such nonchalance, he nearly – in his laid-back ease – fell over backwards. 'Oversleep, did you? I would've buzzed down, but . . .'

'Yeh,' agreed Jilly, quite eagerly – making a big show now

of moving stacks of glasses from where they should be, and equally purposefully back again. She would have twisted slightly the necks of all the neatly ranked bottles of beer, so that their various and colourful labels were facing full-frontally, and precisely aligned – but Sammy, of course, had already seen to all that; it had been he, indeed, who had taught her the habit (Takes no time at all, he said – you can do it in your sleep, but it improves the look no end). 'Long night,' she tacked on – immediately wishing she could bite it back: damn, oh bugger – why'd I have to tack on that? 'What I mean is – early night, had an early night – so shattered – and I think that's often the way, don't you? Sometimes you sort of have *too* much sleep and then it's even harder, isn't it? Sammy? You get that ever? To – you know: get yourself going in the morning.' Don't let him think – allow him no moment to ponder all that. '*So* – anyway. I'm here now – so get yourself off, hey? Well-earned rest, yeh?'

Sammy just nodded. Seemed to be thinking, anyway: could be he was even pondering all that. Eventually – after a couple of eternities, it surely seemed to Jilly (I don't know why – can't quite pinpoint it – but with Sammy here as well as me I feel exposed, very) – he laid down his glass cloth, and passed both his flat palms down the sides of his trouser legs.

'OK,' he said. Easily? Warily? Ask her – she couldn't tell you, honestly didn't know. 'Usual, later? Four-ish?'

Jilly dearly wished she had something to do – some stupid task upon which she could firmly bolt just some of her stray and flapping hands, a point of concentration to which she could bend and apply herself. Why doesn't anyone want a bloody *drink*? Usually, this time, they're all of them clamouring – so why not bloody *today*?

'Yeh . . .' said Jilly, quite lightly. 'Well maybe. Probably – yeh. Well – one or things to . . . but yeh – don't see why not.

Four-ish, yeh. But if I'm a bit late or I don't, well – you know.'

Why actually, Sammy, don't you just go now? Hm? Your shift finished way over half an hour ago. Normally you don't, do you – linger? Hang about? So why are you bloody *today*? Ah but *now*, actually, thought Jilly (and some dull weight that had been at once so dense yet impossibly floating somewhere within her – filling her up while maybe mulling over just where and when and how suddenly to drop – was rapidly coming, she knew, to a harsh decision and right now had gone for it) . . . nothing really matters to me, Sammy – whether you go or whether you stay – because look, Jilly didn't know how convincing she had been in her lack of conviction that anything here was odd or prickly or out of the way, and nor could she have said how tinny or plangent was the peal of any alarm bells she might have unwittingly tripped – but now as Rollo continued his easy progress towards the bar, the air around all of them was set to thicken, and mists could maybe descend.

'Hi,' said Rollo, lifting himself up on to a bar stool.

And for that, at least, Jilly was truly grateful. He had said Hi, Rollo: Hi. Rollo had said Hi, just Hi, and nothing more. Good. It was a start (which could, of course, be half the trouble).

Rollo smiled at Jilly. Is that what he did? Yeh – in Jilly's admittedly somewhat fevered judgement it had come over as no more than that. And yes I'm *right*, look – because now he's smiling that smile over in Sammy's direction, and to me there's no change (a smile is just a smile, isn't it?). So maybe I'll just say, er . . . what shall I say? Must say something, and must do it now, because if I don't – say something, say something – yes, if I don't right this minute say something quickly, then someone else, well – they're *bound* to, aren't they? And what they say could be the wrong thing! So I'll charge through the possibility of that, will I now?

'Hi. Jilly. Your barmaid for the afternoon. What can I get you?'

And *please* don't put on any sort of a knowing, and please God not a lascivious expression. *Please* don't react as if here is some sly invitation to gnaw at and broaden some hint of secret suggestion – and *please* can you neutralize your beautiful eyes so that there cannot rise up even the faintest hot aroma of a hotter complicity? (If I could put it into words, both my fear and thrill-tinged yearning, then this is maybe how I would.)

'Just a halfa lager, please,' said Rollo, quite happily. 'Hell of a thirst.'

Jilly rushed to attend to that (not only can I turn my back, but there's something now to do!) – and while she was watching the more white than golden Heineken splatter down into the glass, she kept her fingers poised lightly on the tap while glancing sideways and simpering to Sammy: 'OK?' Which meant – Are You Off, Then? And not: Are You All Right With This? Which Actually Isn't A This: It's Honestly Nothing, Really. And not, most *certainly* not: How Am I Doing? Maybe Cool? Or Messing Up Badly?

Sammy may not have looked at Rollo (now hunched over the lager before him and apparently intent upon its depths). He may not even have looked at Jilly. But he did turn away – slip off his bar jacket, pick up his own. And then he wandered away, strolling as if on a country ramble the length of the pub to the very farthest tables – and then he turned and was out of it. And whether Jilly had been looked at or not could scarcely matter now (although still she was feeling drilled right through). Because quite suddenly – Rollo was staring full at her: now their eyes had locked – so nothing could matter at all, now, not a single bit. Her hands rushed to cover his – which lay there softly curved like paws – and only then did her eyes quickly dart about furtively, to check whether anyone had witnessed them doing so. And if they had, well so what? This too – even this –

could not matter less. Exciting, mm, but also – so much sudden letting go, it's scary too: scary, yes it is. And exciting, mm.

'Last night,' she whispered, 'was just the *best*.'

Rollo let his struck-open eyes do all the nodding for him. Yes it was. The best. Had to be, really. On account of, for Rollo, it was also the first. The very first, yes oh yes. I didn't tell her. Didn't say so. Maybe she would've liked it, who's to say? Certainly it might have explained away a good deal of my initial, uh – urgency, yes: urgency. But girls were funny, everyone knew that; well *men* did, anyway: somehow, always with you was at least that one small certain nugget of absolute knowledge, so terribly deeply ingrained. And maybe if I'd, you know – just looked sort of down and whispered Listen, Jilly – listen: stop ripping up my clothes for just a second and listen to me, OK? This is . . . God, I just can't *tell* you what this is, this means to me, Jilly – because this *thing*, right? Is my first. Well . . . if I had – just say I had said that, what would she have done? Taken it as a gift? Would her fingers have touched my face so gently, straying away to softly probe the weary pouch beneath one of my eyes, as maybe a full fat and ready-rounded tear welled up in her own, before it burst its banks and ran away? Or could she have maybe come close to snarling? Whole face twisted up into a Who's My Ickle Baby Boy, Then, cruel and nasty smirk, before laughing lightly and saying not to worry and promising then with quite cheap irony that, yes, she'd be oh-so gentle with me? You never know – not with girls, you don't. And further – at a tender time like this one, you don't want to be extending the boundaries of your vulnerability, already rubbed raw and nearly livid. Do you? So better, I think, I just stayed quiet and got it done. Which I did, oh God yes; and not even counting the first disaster (well – disaster for her, I had gauged by her sighing; for me, that sweet intensity and full charged rush of it made me lame and made me powerful) –

I got it done it must have been three or four times, must have been all of that – yes it was, it was, at the very least three, it really must have been. (And after her gasps and choked-out rasping, there had come from her a sighing of a different order.)

Someone at a table down there was very much requiring some service – Jilly could see this clearly (the man was contorting his upper body sideways, one finger poised if not yet flying, and the jerked-up eyebrows were practically hitting his hairline). Jilly was very aware of all of this, but she just had to do her best to ignore it for now because the thing she absolutely had to do next was lean in even closer to Rollo and whisper to him urgently:

'*Listen*, Rollo – I've got us the most fantastic *surprise*.'

And however you cut it, Rollo was thinking, this could only be pretty good news.

'Surprise? Yeah? What is it?'

'*Only* – ' and here was Jilly's cue to narrow her eyes and hush herself down until she was only just audible ' – the Transylvania Emperor Suite. Tomorrow. I can get it for us tomorrow afternoon!'

Her eyes were egging on Rollo's to join up and gel into a great and glittering part of this – and although he was eager as hell to fall in with this very palpable shiver of excitement of hers, he could only send flickering across the bar a tentative measure of his pretty much total lack of comprehension.

'Uh-huh,' he went. 'Uh-huh . . .'

Jilly tutted out her impatience.

'The Transylvania Emperor Suite, for your *information*, Rollo, just happens to be the absolutely top accommodation on the entire bloody *ship*. Do you know what people pay for the Emperor Suite for the whole of the World Cruise? Do you? Have you the smallest *idea*, Rollo?'

'Miss! Oh – Miss!' came the strained and hesitant enquiry

from the table down there. 'We maybe get a drink down here?'

Jilly raised up a hand, and slapped on a brand-new smile to help it on its way.

'Right with you, sir!' And then – hunkered down and whisperingly insistent again: 'Well, Rollo – *have* you? Do you *know*?'

'I, uh – well no. Not a clue. The very very best, is it? Well wait a minute – how come you – ?'

'Three hundred and fifty *thousand*, Rollo. Believe it?'

'Three *hundred* – !'

' – and fifty *thousand*. Yup. And tomorrow afternoon – it's all ours.'

Rollo just gazed at her.

'Well – well that's just – that's *fantastic*. Amazing. Jesus Christ, Jilly – right. Let's *go* for it! Wow. But listen – how – ?'

'Oh *Miss*? Yes – *Miss*? Excuse me? How bout we get a little service, huh?'

Jilly looked up – and naked irritation was all over her, this time – and the guy at the table was looking this side of spellbound with the way it was going.

'Tell you tomorrow. Got to go now, Rollo. Kay?'

And Jilly scooped up her notepad and bustled away to fill this guy's sodding order – and she was moving swiftly, now – not for the *guy* (fuck *him*) but because she knew, just knew that Rollo was on the point of coming right up with something on the lines of Yes well that's just *great*, Jilly, marvellous – but what about *today*, yes? Later, yes? Or tonight, maybe – yes? And Jilly would have had to say No – sorry, Rollo, but no: I've just got to see to Sammy, haven't I, later? Because I don't know how he's feeling, but I do know that he'll be turning it all over, and I've simply got to head off all sorts of thoughts before one of them actually *arrives* somewhere, see? Because I don't, do I (be fair to me, Rollo), at all know where all of whatever this is might quite soon be leading?

193

'So sorry about the delay, sir,' she was gushing keenly – beaming fondly at the now quite mollified man at the table. 'Fellow at the bar was feeling just a touch faint.'

'Oh yeah? Sorry to hear that. He OK now?'

'He will be soon, sir. He'll be totally fine. Now – what can I get you?'

⚓

I'm thinking two things, I suppose. What has mainly muscled its way to the forefront of my mind (well, it would have to have done, really: I'm selfish – yes and so what? My appetites are eating me up) is that soon, very soon – if I have not got these decks and levels all screwed up in my mind – I'll be back to pinning down beneath me this wonderfully uncomplicated (yes – I think that, on balance, is kind) young *American* boy, who is, it thrills me to know, easily of an age to be Stacy's little brother. *He* doesn't know that, of course – nobody seems to realize I'm knocking on forty, which is, I suppose, a blessing (and my disguise). Earl did actually mutter something or other at some hot damp point about having been 'sedooced' by an older woman ('I like, Jennifer', he had gone, 'your matooriddy, yeh?') but would he be quite so sweet if he knew the true extent of the internal ravages of ripeness, here? Well – doesn't matter. He doesn't have to know, does he? Ever. We're just here for each other in the very much *now* – and soon, well fuck it. He goes one way, I go another – and that, my friend, is that. It happens, doesn't it, in life all the time. It's just that maybe, on this ship, all the customary courtesies and conventions, all the rituals and encounters that form us (the collisions that send us reeling elsewhere), are somehow impacted and condensed, the pappy juice of it so unbelievably concentrated. Everything here, it seems to me, either fleetingly brushes past in a way that is airy and bland to the point of quite vaporous invisibility, or else it shoots you up – so scorching and bloody intense that it fills you in and takes you over. I mean – quite apart from my rather wet and very warm eagerness to get to Earl's cabin (let's just for now – if I can, if I can – set aside that particular cauldron: let's just have it bubblingly simmer, on that good old back burner), just consider the extraordinary anger that arose in me as a result of that merely irritating and wholly laughable tick that manifests itself in the form of Nobby. And the ferocity with which I met it, what? Head-on? Just stale air, hardly more. Things like Nobby surely cannot matter; and it's a big ship, very: all I have to do is avoid – or, failing that, gently deflect. And now – because of Earl – I can see me easily avoiding with a hungry willingness most things and most other people for days and days and nights.

Which brings me to the other thing: Stacy. I didn't know she liked girls: had no idea that's what she went for. It's not that she *does* that concerns or amazes me (whatever gets you through the night, right?) – no, it's simply the fact that I wasn't *aware*. Because look, with our relationship, I would have said . . . well, what I suppose I mean to say is that if some well-meaning friend (or even covert enemy) had one time taken me aside and said to me Well tell me, Jennifer (come clean) – what sort of a parent did you turn out to be? Reckon you're a *good* mother, do you then, Jennifer? I would have come back with Oh Good *Christ*, No – no no, poor Stacy, God knows how she survived me. Because I didn't bake. I never made her costumes for all those school plays, you know (well all right – no great shocks there). But I didn't attend the plays either. Not one. Because I didn't know about them. And Stacy would say What do you *mean* you didn't know? Mm? How can you *say* that? I brought the piece of paper home that *said*, didn't I? And it had a tear-off bit at the bottom so's you could get *tickets*, and everything, so what do you *mean* you didn't *know*? And I said . . . I just gazed at little Stacy quite implacably and said – I know it by heart (still I can hear my indignation) – *Paper*? Piece of *paper*? *I* never saw any piece of paper – what on earth are you *talking* about, Stacy? There *was* no paper: I think you are making it up. Because it was a funny thing – any sort of even semi-official communication, I simply couldn't read it (still can't, still can't). Letter from the Council . . . *bank* statements, oh my God: never read one of *those* in my entire life on earth – never even opened one. So as soon as I saw Stacy's school sort of crest thing on any bit of paper and the all sorts of, you know – *typing* going on underneath it – well . . . just couldn't. Not couldn't be *bothered* – it wasn't an idleness thing, no: I just simply, utterly, physically *couldn't*. You either get this or you don't. And so of course this forced me into defensive mode, which in my case tends to come out as attack. And so *therefore*, you see (and please understand), the school never *printed* such a piece of paper – and *if* they did (which they might have) well then Stacy most certainly never brought it home to me; and if she *did* bring it home (which is a possibility) well then she obviously forgot to show it. To me. So how can you dream of *criticizing* me, actually, for not coming to see your poxy little play when I didn't even know there *was* such a thing?!

So on that level, hopeless. And nor did I read to her stories, as she was tucked up in bed (but on the plus side, here, if ever she asked me a question, I told her no lies). I don't recall there actually was such a thing as 'bed time', per se. And nor was I great at getting her up. The odd thing is I *cleaned* quite a lot – which yes, I know, is frankly amazing, in the light of just everything else. But I've always had a bit of a thing about that – which I'm sure, oh yes, is no doubt terribly *unhealthy* and symptomatic of some or other dreadful phobia or underlying *denial* . . . or maybe it's just that I like things clean? (As that old fraud Freud once said – sometimes a cigar is just a cigar, you know?) Well I *do* like things clean – yes I do. But *making* things clean – I like that too: the operation.

So where are we so far? Well, there's poor little Stacy

cooped up with just her bloody awful mother with not much to eat and often late for school (although I do remember getting her there more or less on time on the first morning of half-*term*, on one occasion: well look – was it my fault? Why didn't they *tell* me it was bloody half-term? They could have *written* to me, or something). But everything was *clean*, right? Clean and . . . *fairly* wholesome. But the point I'm making here is that we *talked*. I could never afford to go out very much (unless some man was both on the go and solvent) and neither of us was ever too great on the television side of things – so we talked. Not dull little Tell Me Everything You Learned At School Today type talks, no no – and nothing very positively educational, or edifying in any way at all, really. I'd just, you know – *say* something, and Stacy'd react to that and then she would come up with some other bit of whatever and I'd put my tuppence worth down on the table, and so we passed the evenings and years.

And the odd boy came round. I didn't enquire. Didn't frankly think it was my place to (because God – I was quick enough to slap her down if ever *my* private life came up for any hint of schoolgirly nose-twitching and more than faintly snotty scrutiny). I didn't pry. Did say once to her Stacy – you're not being a bloody fool, I hope: I mean you are fitted up, right? In some way? And if not, let's Christ's sake get it done, OK? And she just looked at me, wide-eyed – that usual teenage sort of mix: I-cannot-believe-you-actually-*said*-that, gently mingling with a deep-seated unease at the nudged-at intrusion of grossness – all leavened with pity for one so old. So sod it, I thought: I've said my piece, so let her bloody get on with it.

And now this. Well of course it needn't *be* a this – I do understand that. I mean – it was terribly late, and girls *are* very pretty, I do of course see this (although I've never gone down that particular route myself, I have to say – unless you count threesomes). And being on this good ship Lollipop, as

I've already said – it makes one do the oddest things (and I can't, can I, be the only one who feels that?). It's just that I had no idea that any sort of inclination in that direction lay within her. And this makes me feel stupid. Which I really, really hate.

'Well good after*noon*, there!' was now the noise that grated first and then filled the air. Well, here was one more 'good afternoon', and so what? All the decks and bars and corridors and staircases rang and throbbed with greetings constantly – largely, I think, so that the felicitator could relentlessly impress upon whoever that he for one, at least, was most certainly having a whale of a time and the time of his life – and now it is up to you, please, to grandly reassure me if you will that all is truly wonderful at your end. (Did you ever see *The Prisoner*? Remember that at all? That weird and endless Sixties TV thing set in that funny little village in Wales? Well I honestly do think sometimes that it's a bit like that here, God help me: everyone seemingly suspended in a state constantly and precisely balanced between a childlike excitement and more or less total sedation: 'Lovely *day*!' 'ooh yes – *lovely* day – just another lovely *day*'). So yeh, like I say (hee! Just wait till Earl sees what I'm wearing underneath) . . . uh, like I say . . . sorry, completely lost it for just a second, back there – mind on other things. Oh yeh – all the happy-clappy stuff, yeh. Well anyway, look: this particular 'good after*noon*' – could have been launched by just anyone anywhere (odd, nonetheless, that it has not yet been met by a beatific chorus of practically gaga reciprocation – nearly a full second has already passed, after all). So what do I do? Slow down? Rush on? Or just be deaf and blind?

'Well . . .' drove on our anonymous compère, '*someone's* in a hurry! Fun, I hope! Yes? Fun and games?'

And so she did – had to – pause a bit, this time. Jennifer stalled her headlong and compulsive dash and looked about her briefly for the source of all this garish nuisance.

And now she had found it (oh – that's it, is it?) and it meant to her nothing – absolutely nothing whatever. So – *blink*, do we? Half-smirk tossed over to a passing idiot, bit more blinking and then off very swiftly and away?

'Stewart's my name,' yodelled happily the blond and orange man before her. 'Assistant Cruise Director – yeah? So. Having fun? Yes? *Aha*! Just look who's coming: more lovely people having fun!'

And well before Jennifer could even begin to put her mind to whether to curse or flee from all this, Nobby and Aggie were suddenly there, and quite horrible.

'*Who's* a stranger . . .?' cooed Aggie in mock admonishment, one finger wagging.

'We missed you at luncheon,' tacked on Nobby. 'Missed you – yes indeed.'

Jennifer gazed in wonder at these people. I have roundly insulted each one of them in turn – quite forcefully, I thought (not the *works*, admittedly – but enough, I should have said, for them to have at least received the subtext, here: but not, apparently). Oh God. It's like those horror films – it's just like those horror films, and now I am in one: when the oozing ogre is finally chopped and spattered, a claw flung over there amid signs of a clumsy decapitation, the walls hung at random and liberally with dripping portions of ghoulish giblets – and just when the quiveringly exhausted intended victim is slumping down into a wet and dress-ripped if fevered relief, all the bits start squelchingly regrouping into a we've-been-here-before coalescence and then suddenly the murderous and sag-tongued leer is back in place – and Jesus, off we bloodily go again. It's funny, and not a little annoying, thought Jennifer now, how ill-*prepared* one always finds oneself; I mean to say, had I just thought to bring with me a fucking great *bazooka*, I could blast all of them to hell and pieces (but then they would, wouldn't they? Gang up and reform).

'I've got to, um – ' she said (and made to).

'Nice jacket,' said Nobby. Quite simply. And yes – no one here could maybe quite have put their fingers on precisely *why*, but everyone turned towards him, and then just looked (and none more pointedly than Aggie).

'So *anyway*,' insisted Jennifer, 'like I say – I really must – ' (and this time she did).

'Have fun!' Stewart called after her. 'Have fun! Have fun!'

His seemingly limitless compulsion for saying and saying this could easily have eaten deeply into all their afternoons; maybe just as well, then, that Aggie now had something to say:

'You never, Nobby – say that about *my* jacket. My clothes. Do you, Nobby?'

'Don't I, love?'

Stewart had been on, hey – how many cruises, now? He well knew the time to duck and recede.

'See you good people!' was his parting shot; and quite a wave went with it. Does anyone, it suddenly struck him, actually ever hear a bloody word I say?

Aggie was maybe regarding his practised stroll. 'Not *ever*, far as I can recall . . .' she said, quite lightly.

Nobby resumed his usual and rather cocky expression: slapped her matily across the shoulders (which she normally, she supposed, quite liked, although it did tend to make her cough).

'That's all my eye and Betty *Martin*! Let's get ourselves up top, Aggie love.'

Aggie was temporarily distracted. She arrested their ambling by clutching at Nobby's sleeve: her eyes were wide as she took her lips just one more time through the final rehearsal.

'Oh Mihi *Beate* . . .?'

Nobby was nodding his encouragement, his yolky eyes egging her on.

'Good girl, good girl . . . And . . .?'

'Oh Mihi Beate . . . *Martine*!' she rounded off in triumph.

'Ay-*one*, Captain Honeybunch. Ace. Quite right – quite right. Bless me Saint Martin – in . . .?'

'*Portuguese*. Portuguese – yes Nobby? Not Spanish, is it?'

'In point of fact *Latin*, my love, though wholly the province of Portuguese mariners. And the nearest our boys in blue could get to it was, heh heh – All My Eye And Betty Martin. Dear oh Lord. Up to the boat deck – yes, Aggie? Up for it? Don't quite know how it came to mean moonshine . . .'

Aggie nodded, and they wended their way.

'But . . .' she persisted, as Nobby heaved open the heavy door that led out to all that sweet and roaring air. 'You *don't* ever – do you, Nobby?'

'I don't what, love? Ooh it's a fine, fine summer afternoon, Aggie. They should make her up to thirty-five knots today, all right. No trouble at all.'

' . . . Say I look nice, or anything. Mention something I'm wearing, or something. You never ever do, you know, Nobby. Not once ever.'

'Don't I, love? Well I'll make up for all that right this very minute. You look *corking*, my admiral. There. How's that?'

And yes – Aggie conceded: her fondly collapsed face was now all indulgence. 'Oh *Nobby* . . .' she went. And then she linked one of her arms with his, as they bent themselves into the cold rush of wind and marched together towards the prow.

And Nobby was thinking *Well*, love – I'll tell you this for Harry Freemans: *if* I don't ever rabbit on about any of your gear, well then it must be because, well – you dress exactly the same as I do, don't you love? Practical. Weatherproof. Warm. Muted colours – quite right: don't want to frighten the horses. And anyway – you asking for the truth, I wasn't really thinking that Jennifer's jacket was nice or not nice; all I was was just registering a fact: aye aye, I thought – I *know* this jacket, don't I? This jacket of hers – I've seen it before.

Well at least Charlene and I can agree on *that*: some sort of a communion, I suppose. Tea, now, is long done with (and I must say, thought Nicole, I do rather approve of the way they arrange it all: those lovely silver tiered things – I've got one at home – with nicely trimmed sandwiches and not-too-big cakes: very good) and now the chat has turned to the fact that although it was perfectly clear from reading the thing, that little sort of newspaper thing they pop under your door at, God – must be dawn, or something; what do they call it, actually? Hang on – I've actually got one here, somewhere . . . now where on earth? Oh God, don't *please* say I left it in the Fendi handbag, did I? Because I nearly, very nearly did go for the blue and white ensemble (not quite Chanel, but few would know) before thinking Hm: blue and white – suitable, yes (very sailor suit and all the rest of it), but not quite, Nicole, is it, up to your usual standards of *imagination*? The aim is always, surely, to be of *course* wearing something utterly suitable (mainly, I suppose, in order to demonstrate not just one's easy adaptability to any given social situation, but also to make it perfectly plain that one is wholly aware of just what is and isn't, well – utterly suitable, as I say) but then to go just that little bit further and invest it with just some wee something of a twist, you know? I mean, it could be anything, really: scarf, most obviously – but in a possibly Pucci print and *apparently* clashing colours, but when you look again, not. Merely (merely!) a rather unexpected and often thrilling juxtaposition – the sort of thing that women who are committed to to, oh God – *outfits* could scarcely imagine, and never achieve.

But blue and white, well – blue and white really just has to *be* blue and white (mix in something else and you run the danger of appearing as if draped in a flag like an Olympic medallist or a Magaluf drunkard) and so at the very last minute – and yes I know, I'm simply awful like that (just ask David) – I decided to be shot of the lot and instead I elected to hurriedly slip into this rather splendid just-off mustard shirt dress, which you might not *think* would team at all well with both primrose and sunflower (and yes I can well see how many might demur) but if you very cleverly but subtly pull it all together, as I have done, with no more than a delineation of black (there must be no hint of *wasp* here, you understand), then what you end up with is a very chic but at the same time quite surprising whole – and one that I can see has gone down very well indeed with not just friend Charlene (she whooped at me a selection of frankly cowboy and maybe mobster noises, but the general impression I gather is highly favourable) – but also with the two other women, here: Julie, who is some sort of New York pal of Charlene's (very old, but vaguely comprehensible), and this Pat person (English, thank the Lord – if a little heavy in the make-up department). Seems very nice, on what little I have to go on, but she is, poor thing, feeling just a teeny weeny little bit under the weather – more or less the first thing she had to say to us (which I must say I did think a little *off*). So anyway – and this is my point here, as it were – what with that eleventh-hour change of direction on the appearance front, it is perfectly possible that the *Daily Programme* (yes, that's what they call it – that sort of newspaper thing they put under your door) is still neatly folded in one of the zipped-up divisions in the *Fendi* bag, because for all my rummaging, I surely can't find a trace of it in here. *Anyway*, just before Julie and Pat rolled along, Charlene and I were agreeing (and it's rather a pleasant experience to agree with Charlene – well, let's be plain here: fond though I have become of her, it's quite rare that I even comprehend the noises her mouth is so forcefully emitting, so actual *correspondence* is highly refreshing) ... yes, we were both agreeing, Charlene and I, that although the powers that be have seen to it that something – and very often all sorts of different and clashing things, if I'm being fair to them – is happening somewhere during every single waking moment (and even later than that, if you could bring yourself to stomach a sort of *pub* affair – David country – or something called the Regatta Club, which sounds unspeakable) . . . yes, well – we were each of us agreeing, Charlene and I, that although all that is doubtless true, there never seems to be anything one actually if one is honest wants to *attend*: partake in: witness. You see? I mean look – have a glance at all the things I haven't done today (and it's quite remarkable, you know, because it's already nearly six, and then soon it will be dinner and then, oh God, it's the – how do they bill it? 'Viva America Ball', yes that's it. Well. I have nine things I could wear to that, and soon I'm just going to have to excuse myself from this little gathering because deciding quite which, as you well might imagine, is going to take me quite some time).

Now I was, I confess, fairly encouraged by the sight of one or two things when first I glanced at the *Daily Programme*. There is a crossword every morning, apparently, as well as a brain-teaser competition (love that word) available from the library, wherever the library might be – but then someone told me there aren't any proper prizes, so that was no good. So what else was on offer? Something called 'Body Sculpt' at the fitness centre (oh dear) and this could, if you had the inclination, be followed by a lecture on bridge and a lecture on computers! Not really *me*, I thought. Hm? What do you think? No – we're agreed, then: not at all *me*. 'Beginner's Backgammon' (no prizes) rather fell into a similar category, as did the 'Ladies Table Tennis Open Play' – not to say the (oh *please*) 'Golf Putting Clinic'. And did I want to attend a talk on the sinking of the *Titanic*? I did not. Didn't want Yoga *or* the dance class and I *certainly* had no wish to be even the tiniest bit involved in the 'Transylvania Heritage Trail', that was for absolute sure. Shuffleboard? Not. Whist? Uh-uh. Charlene at one point more or less opined that she'd a mind to attend the 'Firming, Toning and Inch Loss Seminar' and maybe I'd like to tag along? But then again, Charlene – maybe not, hm? And the same went for something called 'Body Fat Blues' – oh God don't even *ask*: why don't these people just stop *eating* all the time if they're so distressed by the truth that they look like pigs? (And was I silly, actually, to think that as a Competition Winner they would – I don't know . . . lay on *special* things? Maybe that's silly. I don't know. Don't see *why* . . .)

So, you might ask – *well*, Nicole, you might think of going: we've heard in great detail about all the things you *didn't* do today, so do tell us, please (we're all agog), how in fact you *have* filled in your time since early this morning? *Well*: I did try to catch up with Marianne at several points, but we haven't coincided. Rollo's phone seems to be either not working or else off the hook, some reason. And David . . . well. He said to me, I thought I might look in to the Black Horse – maybe Dwight's there: fancy it? I just looked at him. *No*, David, I eventually came out with – I don't, as you so horribly and typically put it, *fancy* it one tiny little *fraction*. Have I ever, David – have I ever in living memory *fancied* entering a pub at any point of the night or day, either in London or the country – let alone in the middle of the Atlantic Ocean? But oh God please do by all means look *in*, won't you, to the Black, Jesus – *Horse* – oh yes *please* do, David, look *in* – and keep on looking *in* until you can't bloody *see* any more, yes? As per bloody *usual*.

And after I'd given him up as a very bad job (not, I need hardly tell you, for the first time, this) I went along to the Steiner Salon on is it number One Deck and booked up hair and facials morning and evening for the whole of the trip (my second of the day is actually due pretty much now) and then I finally *did*, I'm delighted to be able to tell you, make one or two rather, well – exciting, I suppose, discoveries. There's something they call a 'Daily Tote' – it's really quite simple. All you have to do is guess the ship's mileage from sailing until noon today – and so on every day, I suppose it goes. It's only two dollars per bet, and if no one gets it right there's a rollover, you see, which is always rather thrilling. Also – a bit rather better – there's what they call 'Snowball Bonanza Bingo', and what you do is you trot along to the Great Lounge at four-thirty (and yes I *did* go, of course I did – why I was a little bit late for this tea, as it happens) and you pay twenty dollars for, um – three chances for five games, I think they said – still a bit hazy – but the main point here is that the jackpot *starts* at five hundred dollars (I know!) and it sort of snowballs every day (not quite sure exactly how this . . . you know: the nuts and bolts) and then by the time we get to New York, *some* lucky person scoops the lot! And that oily and grinning official-type person . . . Assistant something or other, he kept on saying to me (God – as if I *cared*) – anyway *he*, whoever he is, was telling me that the final payout reaches *thousands*. Well. I just have to make sure that the lucky person is *me*.

The best thing, though, was just before lunch. In the Casino. I know! I wasn't aware there would *be* such a thing – never even crossed my mind. I've never set foot in one before, I have to say (those you see in films are either, aren't they, awfully seedy or else madly glitzy and rather too plushily vulgar), so I was, I suppose, just very slightly nervous of quite what I'd find. But I needn't have been at *all*, as it turned out – it's all very easy, very friendly. But just before lunch – that's what I was saying – they were sort of *teaching* you, really: Blackjack, Poker, Roulette . . . even the *words* are terribly thrilling and naughty, don't you think so? And the tables, you know, are open at eleven every morning – go on right through the day. There are lots of those rather awful and clanking slot machines too, of course (they're not still called one-armed bandits, are they?) but I think that that side of things is just a little bit seaside pier, if you know what I mean. The sorts of things in the places David seems to like going to, yes? So I think the tables are rather more *me*.

And from what I've picked up, it's all really quite straight-forward. Roulette, well – you just bet on a number or black or red or a combination of both, is all it really seemed to be. Blackjack I can maybe get the hang of. Poker, I have to say, might be a teeny bit trickier because I think it involves a fair deal of *remembering* and adding up *numbers* and so forth – and the other thing, if I'm honest, is that I'd just be so hopeless at the famous 'poker face' – I really think I couldn't pull it off. When I'm losing, you see – when my number just won't come up – it really is for me very, uh . . . bad. Bad isn't really close to how it takes me, but I have no words. If I get a run of entering a lot of competitions at home and all I get after months and months is a terrible zero (or – almost worse – a handful of practically worthless tokens for some or other awful product that I've already got stacks and stacks of, double-banked and stripped of all identity, filling up cupboards and boxes) then what I feel is lower, far lower than even the threshold of alive, and worse – much, much worse – than if I were facing death itself. On the other hand . . .! When I'm winning . . . when all I'm doing is scooping it in . . .! When those letters arrive that kick off with the great big word *Congratulations*! printed in red . . . when those funny little people come around with their official briefcases stuffed with formal declarations of victory . . .! That is . . . oh goodness – if only I had the *words*! Some people say – well, what they *used* to say is that some-thing so great as that is the very best thing since sliced *bread* – didn't they? Or are they being funny? And now they say – I've heard it sometimes, maybe on television – that so-and-so, some great high, some great wondrous hit or another – that it is better than *sex*. Well – equally silly, to my mind. *Loads* of things are better than that – in fact, let's face it: anything on earth you care to *name*. But that is just my personal view and could, I admit, be coloured by having been married to David for all these long years (not really that many, but seemingly countless). Mm. So anyway –

Casino, yes? I think I'll probably maybe look in there. Time to time. Who knows?

And what's this now? Ah – it's the Pat girl talking. I really do think I have to make my excuses very shortly, but I don't after all wish to appear in any way rude, so I'll just hear out what it is she has to say: she is maybe going to tell us once more how she is feeling – how did she put it? 'A bit not right' – not (she might then go on to qualify yet once again) exactly *ill*, or anything, but just a bit . . . you know.

'Doesn't anyone else feel it, then? The movement? It can't *just* be me, can it?' asked Pat of the company, while lowering her cup (the tea was cold: she had tried to drink it often).

'Waaaaall . . .' drawled Charlene (Nicole felt rather sure that this could well be ushering in a further round of own-brand *opining*, here). 'Tell you truth, Patty – I been on this tub so dang long, I can't hardly remember it goes no other way. Maybe we get to New York and *then* I got trouble, huh?'

Julie was nodding, which involved a fair deal of wattle tremor, which Nicole would frankly prefer not to have to witness at quite such close quarters, thank you.

'Yeh well, Patty,' she trembled. 'My case – I can't barely stand. God's truth. Partly I'm old, partly it's dry martinis. So what do I care? Tonight at the ball, some guy who's paid to, he makes like he's dancing with me, yeh? And all I do is stand on his shoes and, like – hey, let *him* do the walking's what I'm saying.'

Pat sort of smiled at that. Nice smile, it occurred to Nicole. In fact (despite all the ghastly make-up) if she didn't look quite so palely green, this Pat person might really transform into quite an elegant creature, with a bit of work. I mean, perfectly hideous *clothes*, of course (too short, too tight, too cheap) – but her legs are good; figure generally. And I quite like what she's trying to do with her hair. What can she be? Mid-thirties?

'Well *last* night,' wavered Pat, 'after we set sail, yes? I just couldn't get used to it. I mean I know the sea's not *rough*, or anything, it's just that sort of very slight sideways see-saw movement. I mean I'm OK like now, when I'm sitting down – but as soon as I get up and start to move about, well . . . This is actually more or less the first time I've had the nerve to leave my cabin. I'm not *ill*, or anything – it's just that I feel – '

' – a *bit*,' cut in Nicole. 'Quite. Now listen, children – I really have to slip away. I'll see you all at the ball, I presume? Pat? You are coming? You're not going to be *Cinders*, I hope?'

Pat smiled bravely. 'Oh no. I'll be there. Hook or crook.'

And for that she was patted fondly on the hand by Julie, whose forearm then took a good long while to settle back down again.

'That's my *girl*,' she approved. 'And hey Patty! You might just meet yourself a husband. It ain't all old guys and faggots. Well . . .' she reflected more quietly, ''tis *mostly* . . .'

Pat looked down.

'Oh. Oh no. I've actually got one of those. A husband.'

'In that case,' said Nicole shortly – stirring herself now, and making to rise, 'you have my profound sympathy.'

'Oh hey!' went Charlene. 'I sure made a horse's neck outta that one, then, Patty. I told Julie you was all alone.'

'Well,' said Pat, 'I am. On this trip I am. At the moment, yes.'

'Well hell we can't have *that* – that right, Nicole?'

'We most certainly can't. Look, Pat – how about this? Come and have dinner with us, my family, yes? They're not *too* ghastly. Duchess Grill, say – what? Seven? Seven suit you? And then we can all go to the ball together.'

'Oh look . . .' stuttered Pat, ' . . . I really don't want to, you know – butt *in*, or anything . . .'

'Not butting *in*. Not a bit of it. So, I'll see you there at seven, then, yes?'

'Well . . .' Pat demurred. 'I'm not quite sure I'll actually want any *dinner* . . . I'm feeling just a bit – '

'So you can *pick*. I'll see you there. Girls – I have to go.'

And from amid a flurry of shivery limbs and clattering jewellery, Nicole briskly made good her word. She was strongly inclined, if you care at all to know the way she was thinking, towards the purple moiré. And yes I *know* it has been suggested that we all of us wear something in the way of red, white and blue, but you are already aware of my position on the *flag* side of things – and anyway, if the masses are inclined to follow this diktat, then purple moiré, I am thinking (and it's *so* beautiful – Caroline Charles in the sale), will surely make something of an impression, no? Although the raspberry-Beaujolais crushed velvet just-off-the-shoulder number is not to be lightly dismissed – but with *that* dress it's a question of *extremely* careful accessorizing because the nearest of misses can be absolutely *catastrophic*, obviously . . .

'Hi, Mum – going to get changed?'

'*Marianne* – Marianne, my poppet – where have you *been* all day long? Hm? *Missed* you, my darling. Did you enjoy your . . . what you were going to do? Walk – yes? And what have you been up to since?'

'Well,' said Marianne quite thoughtfully, dropping into line with her mother, and heading for the lifts. 'Talking to *Tom*, I suppose. That's what I seem mainly to have been doing . . .'

'Really? Tom? Nice young man, is he? I'm glad you're making *friends*, Marianne. You must introduce us at the ball. Decided what you're wearing? Now tell me – who is this Tom person? Hm? What's he like?'

They both stepped into the lift the moment the doors pinged open. Marianne touched a button and they slid back to and enclosed them.

'I don't know, Mummy,' she said quite lightly – as if

she had only just realized something (or nothing). 'I really honestly couldn't *say* . . .'

⚓

Which is true. Even now, as I hover at the fringes of this rather silly American ball thing (my dress is pinching me under the arms) I could not – despite ages of listening to all the often, uh – *surprising* things he had to say to me – tell you exactly who or what I think Tom really might *be*. I have his *nature*, yes (that is now within me) – but quite to what degree this has been only recently conditioned by his oh-so-solitary state, following on from so much togetherness, well: I really, honestly couldn't say . . .

I probably didn't speak much during dinner. And God, what a very odd atmosphere there had been: Dad didn't even turn up (oh Dad, oh Dad) and so you can well imagine the sort of state Mum was in – and particularly so because she'd invited someone else along called Pat – or Patty, Charlene was just calling her (whatever) – who kept on *eyeing* me throughout the meal, which I maybe would have cared about rather more if my mind had been on anything but Tom, and all the ins and outs and ups and downs of what he had and hadn't said. The last thing I asked him was *Well, Tom – will I see you, then? At the ball? Are you going?* And he had looked at me quite without expression and said to me flatly (disappointingly so, I felt at the time, after all that had been said and done): 'Well, Marianne – will *you* be?' And I had nodded yes, and to that he had just slightly inclined his head – might have been in acquiescence, might equally have been a faint for a subdued recoil from some maybe pain or memory. As he made to move away, I said to him as lightly as I could (and no, I don't know why): *Just don't forget it's black tie, OK?* And he turned again – Tom slowly revolved towards me, and with his eyes tipped down at each corner and practically liquid with what

seemed to me to be weary supplication, he said so woodenly (as if picking his way through something
extraordinarily complex and spiked with not just sensitivity,
but danger too): My Dear Marianne: I never wear anything
else. Maybe his tone hadn't been anything like that at all;
maybe he had merely been pointing up a very basic if over-
looked truism – kindly, as if to a simpleton. I liked, however,
the 'My Dear'.

Anyway. Glancing about me . . . (and just look at Mummy
over there with Pat or Patty and Charlene and I think it's
Dwight: at her hostessy best and resplendent in purple –
but I can catch the glint at the back of her eyes. She is
consumed by one thing, and one thing only: where in hell
is *David*? Where in Christ's name *is* he?). Anyway. Glancing
about me . . . (and God, there must be just hundreds and
hundreds of balloons – they're simply everywhere, hanging
up all over these huge and swagged sort of pelmet-type
things all round the stage, and quite a lot are rolling around
on the floor – no wags yet have seen fit to trample them . . .
don't envy the poor old sod who blew them all up; except I
expect they have machines to do all that sort of thing).
Anyway. Glancing about me . . . (and Rollo, he seems fairly
agitated, too. Quite jumpy all through dinner – and now he
looks like maybe I do: apparently just hanging about, but
somehow tensed and anticipating – what? His foot is
moving – up and down, up and down – but not at all in
time with this I think it could be Gershwin, Porter, one of
those). Anyway. Glancing about me . . . I see that Tom has
not yet come. I wonder if he will. Maybe (and this is likely,
isn't it?) in the light of something he said, oh – hours and
hours and hours ago, he has not even the slightest intention
of doing so.

At the beginning, Tom had said nothing at all. Which
made me feel suddenly and horribly empty. And I could
have gone away (I doubt whether at that point he really
would have noticed): but I didn't go away – I hung around.

He gravitated towards the large baize table and stared for a while at the partly complete perimeter, the illustration on the box, and then the scattering of pieces strewn across the centre. He then picked up just one of them from the thousands there and moved it unhesitatingly towards the uppermost edge, where his thumb then pressed it in and down. It fitted. He glanced at Marianne and said Smoke: I saw it at once – it's part of the smoke, do you see? Coming out of the chalet chimney. Shall we sit down now? Marianne had smiled her agreement with that, and thought it might be nice, now, if he offered her maybe a drink of some sort (a taste for something fresh and cooling had just now rushed into her – real squeezed orange, possibly, with lots and lots of ice and soda). Tom said nothing, so Marianne had casually offered him a drink.

'A drink? A drink?' And then Tom narrowed his eyes, and set to concentrating hard on getting his whole mind around this apparently new and wholly incomprehensible little word. 'A *drink*. Mm. A drink, a drink. Ah. *No* – I don't really think so, Marianne. But I thank you. But you please have a, um – *drink*, yes. If you would care to.'

Marianne smiled. 'No thanks,' she said. 'I'm fine.'

Tom was leaning towards her now; Marianne recognized this periodic spark of urgency that quite without warning pounced, and then seemingly took him over.

'Did you know,' he said in measured tones, 'that there exists a cheese called Pantysgawn? Aware of that?'

Marianne searched in vain his eyes for humour.

'Is this – ?' she checked ' – a joke . . .?' Her eyes were wide open, but already she was shaking her head.

Tom seemed confused. 'Joke? *Joke*? No – it's not a joke. It's a *cheese* . . .'

'Uh-huh. And it's called – ?'

'Pantysgawn. Mm. That's its name. Not aware of it, then.'

'No I'm, er – not. Is it – *nice*? Good cheese is it, Tom?'

Tom gazed at her now with near total amazement.

'Well how on earth should *I* know? I've not *had* it, or anything.'

Marianne nodded. 'Right. So why, um – ?'

'Mention it? Bring it up? Introduce this ludicrous non-sequitur – not that it was, in fact, following anything – into our conversation? Which we were not, in point of fact, actually having? I couldn't *tell* you, Marianne. It is quite beyond me. It is simply one of my *facts*. I have facts, you see. And I can only think that at some point someone must have told me – or maybe I read it – that *people*, yes? That people are interested in facts, and so from time to time I supply one. I have to say that I have never been aware of anyone's marked or even partial interest – not, at least, in any of the facts that are all I have at my disposal. Does all this, Marianne, sound very silly to you? Dull? Mad, conceivably?'

'Bit silly,' decided Marianne. 'Rather dull. Not mad.'

Tom nodded, and glanced through the broad and mottled window at the wink of the limitless sea.

'It comes,' he practically sighed, 'from Wales. The cheese. Pantysgawn, yes. Queer name, isn't it?'

Marianne hunched herself forward, and much to the astonishment of both of them, she clasped one of his knees with her hands. She looked dead into his eyes, and when she spoke her voice was just tinged with a maybe incongruous lightheartedness, though this hardly diminished its measured assurance.

'Tom. I don't *care*. And nor do you. Let's talk properly, yes? Or maybe you'd prefer – not at all?'

And as he flinched away from that, Marianne took back her hands and resettled herself (because when you are sitting comfortably, then you can begin).

'*So*, Tom,' said Marianne – with an easy confidence she was in truth not wholly feeling. 'You kick off. *Talk* to me. *Say* something, Tom. Something *proper*.'

Tom's lips tightened and he shook his head in what appeared to be a real heartfelt regret – even true sorrow.

'Can't. Just can't. Out of the way of it, you see. With Mary – that's my, uh – '

'Yes. I know. Your wife.'

'My, uh – yes: late wife. With her, with Mary, there was just a sort of a, oh – it was like ping-pong, really – more than anything, it was that. No one brought up a *subject*, as far as I can recall. Nothing was ever *broached*. But there seemed to exist a sort of rhythm, maybe. A background beat. Anyway – whatever it was, it got us through the day. So you see – I'm most terribly *sorry*, Marianne, but while I really am more flattered by, and yes – more grateful for your presence than I can possibly say – !'

'Oh *Tom*!'

' – Well I *mean* it. I do. I really do mean it. But . . . notwithstanding. I simply can't . . .' And his eyes – up till now hung low and intent upon the floor – swung up of a sudden, and were both full and on her ' . . . *speak*!'

Marianne nodded. Smiled, just slightly. OK, she thought: I'll try, then.

'That woman, Tom . . .' she began, quite tentatively.

'Woman? What woman? *Woman*?'

'Yup. Just earlier. When you went up to that woman – yes? You thought she was someone else?'

'Oh her. That woman.'

'Was it – Mary, Tom? Did she remind you of your wife?'

And Tom now gazed at her as if *she* was the mad one – and maybe both armed and dangerous along with it.

'*No!*' he practically roared at her. And then – far more softly: 'No. No . . . No one reminds me of her. No one. The woman – that woman I thought was just . . . someone else. That's all. Highly embarrassing. And I'll tell you something *else* embarrassing. The vicar. Have you met him? Did you know there's a vicar on the ship?'

Marianne had been just slightly thrown by a lot of all that, but already she was rallying bravely.

215

'I haven't, um – really thought . . . but yes I suppose there would have to be, wouldn't there? Priest too, I expect.'

Tom nodded. 'And a rabbi. Probably something Asian as well, I shouldn't wonder. Didn't enquire. Anyway – I got to talking to the vicar, yes? And I asked him . . .'

But Tom's voice now had suddenly trailed away into silence. His gaze seemed fixed intently upon nothing at all.

'Tom? What is it? Why have you stopped?'

'Hm? Oh – apologies, apologies. No – it just has suddenly occurred to me. I couldn't at all understand why anyone should want to actually come up and *talk* to me . . . which is why, Marianne, I am stunned by the fact that I am talking now –'

'Oh Tom *stop* all that and just *tell* me!'

'Well. It just seems plain now that of course the *reason* I was approached by the vicar is that he had been *briefed*, hadn't he? Apprised of my, uh – what is it? Is it a *situation*? I simply hadn't thought of it before. Anyway – we got to talking . . . and I didn't once, not once mention Mary. I don't know if I was meant to. So yes – we got to talking, and I suddenly asked him whether anyone had *died* during the course of the cruise. You know – actually died on board.'

'What an odd thing to think of. It wouldn't have crossed my mind . . .'

'No. Maybe not. Yours it maybe wouldn't have. But mine it did.'

'So . . . what did he say?'

'You will not, Marianne, *believe* what he said.'

'Well what? Someone *has* died? Or what?'

Tom allowed the pause to tick on for just two more beats, and then he let her have it:

'Thirteen,' he said, very solemnly.

Marianne watched him – maybe waiting for more. No more was coming, so she pitched in quite shrilly:

'Thir-*teen*? What do you mean, thirteen? You don't mean – ?!'

'Ah but I do. Yes. Incredible but true. Admittedly the entire cruise has been on for quite some months, now . . . but still. Thirteen. Which is why – '

Marianne was agog. 'Thir-*teen*?!'

Tom nodded – really quite eagerly. 'Which is why there are quite a few empty cabins on this final leg of the journey. Understandable. You come on a cruise with someone . . . they die – well, you don't like to, do you? Carry on without them. I asked if they tipped them over the side – but not, apparently.'

'Tom. This is getting ghoulish.'

'Well not *really*. You see it just set me thinking. I mean – Mary and me, we were meant to be taking this trip together, you see . . . but just think if something had happened to either one of us, like – *tonight*, for instance. Well. There's no way you can disembark now, is there? It's not like when the ship is stopping off here and there. No no – destination New York, no two ways about it. No other ships – no way a helicopter's going to get to us. So it would be just you, the sea – and the cold, dead person beside you.'

Marianne looked at him closely, before phrasing with care her response.

'That is – and particularly for you, Tom, in the light of . . . everything – that is, I think, a very strange way of looking at things.'

Tom nodded – almost happily now, it seemed to Marianne.

'You might very well be right about that. I do. I do – look at things fairly oddly. A thought came to me – just this very morning, I mapped out a scenario. I'd very much appreciate your viewpoint. You might well find it odd. Just say – imagine if you will, you have never before seen me, yes? Don't know me from Adam. And you are walking down some street or other, minding your own business, and you turn a corner and suddenly are confronted with the vision of me engaged in a violent struggle with a tall and muscular

217

black man with a shaven head and gold chains and so forth – and between us we seem to be wrestling with what could well be a cudgel of some sort or another. What *construction*, Marianne, would you put upon the scene?'

'Well – I don't see – '

'No no. I'm sure. But just *say* – just imagine that this is the scene before your eyes. What would you *think*?'

'Well . . . well I *suppose* I'd think that you were being mugged, yes? And that you were resisting . . .?'

'Correct. You would assume that. And so would anyone else. The police would, certainly. And if the tall and muscular black man protested his innocence – as in this particular scenario he would be surely bound to do – if he said Oh *no*, officer, you've got this all wrong! This man – he came on to me – was demanding my wallet and everything. Anyone believe him? No. Nobody. Which means that if ever I felt moved to attack just such a person, I could do so with impunity. See?'

'Ye-e-es . . .' agreed Marianne, with unease and a huge if unexplained reluctance. 'But Tom – one point. You are not exactly, are you – Mister Universe? The tall and muscular black man would beat you to a pulp.'

A flicker of consternation briefly made him wince.

'There is,' he conceded, '*that* . . .'

And God – he nearly smiled.

'*Weird*, Tom . . .!' laughed Marianne. 'Want that drink now?'

'Drink – yes indeed. I rather think I could go for some orange juice – had a glass this morning: it's particularly good.'

'Yes – that's what I . . . ice, maybe?'

Tom lost no time in nodding his full-blooded assent to that – even was rubbing his hands together, now, apparently relishing the thought (that just-there half-smile still in place).

'And possibly,' he added lightly, 'some soda water, yes? Thin it down.'

And as Marianne ordered two of those from the so-atten-tive steward, she had already begun her wander down the avenue of wondering as to just who and what this Tom might be. And now it was evening (and will he? Come to the ball? Will he? I doubt it. He might come, yes, but I doubt it) and still I couldn't tell you. It's just like I've been walking down some street or other, minding my own business, and I turn a corner and am suddenly confronted with the vision of Tom. And I don't know him from Adam.

⚓

So now I'm all dickied up in this goddam tuxedo just like I am every goddam night on this goddam tub, and what it was, what I was saying to Charlene – Charlene, listen up: I don't care too much that the stoopid valet's always saying he's a-sponging and a-pressing, this dang suit smells no better than a coyote's crotch. You go wash out your mouth right this *minute*, Dwight, is what she's yelling down my ear. And then I get all this about *Jeez*, Dwight – it ain't as if we're *poor*, you know? I told you – didn't I tell you, Dwight? I told you way afore we even got to booking this here: every night they dress formal – kay? So one tux over three munce just ain't gonna cut it. Yeah so – I tell Charlene what I told her then: ain't no way, honey, under God's sun and stars I'm gonna spring for no second tux, and I tell you for why – like, how many times I gonna be wearing one, back in New York? Tell ya how many – zero with one capital zee, baby: ain't *never* I'm gonna be dickied up in this dang thing ever again in whatever hell's left of my life. First thing I do we're back at home is I torch the mother; so much sweat and anti-sweat spray all over the goddam rag – listen, it's gonna go up like firecrackers on the fourth of July. And *sure* I can afford a brand-new tux – you reckon I ain't aware, Charlene? Hell – I can afford to buy up Saks Fifth Avenue, sweetheart, and the reason for that is I look after the dollars, and I don't throw 'em around: this, Charlene, I leave to you.

So anyways, I'm standing here, right – and I'm plumb alongside of Charlene and she's a-yapping and a-crapping with David's Nicole and some other goddam wimmin (one of 'em's Patty – looks OK, but she ain't no chicken) and this here's the Viva America *Ball*, they all kept on telling me – but it sure as hell feels to me like any other goddam night here, but for you gotta do a whole lotta standing up, and all around you got *balloons*: what're we – *kids*? Jeez.

I kinda figured Dave might be hanging loose, you know? And kinda eager to break out? But I ain't seen hide nor hair of the guy since we hadda couple drinks roundabout lunchtime. Nicole – she ain't too pleased this man of hers ain't shown (hoo boy! I try that on with Charlene, she's gonna kill me) – and speaking for myself, I ain't none too sweet neither, on account of there ain't no one else about this place I wanna jaw with, I bleeve. Sure over there there's Julie's Benny – near dying on the floor, sure looks like – but Benny, he don't hear too good; also he don't think too good. Let's face it, guys – Benny ain't no good for nothing no more: so what you gonna do? So – Dave don't show real soon, I lose Charlene and I'm like outta here. Also how I figure is this: Earl and Suki, they ain't around neither. Didn't even show down at the Grill for sump'n t'eat. Suki, it don't surprise me none – but Earl, Jesus, when's that boy not feeding his face? I guess he's got better stuff to do with his time than hang around his Mom and Dad, huh? His age, I sure as hell did, and that's a fact – yessir, you better bleeve it. Right now as I'm standing here with a glass of this French lemonade and a-yapping and a-crapping Charlene and all these goddam *balloons*, that boy of mine could be humping some dang sweet young piece of ass. Funny thing – when you're a boy, a young man, it seems like everyone else is young too, you know? Leastways, anyone worth hanging with. So the girls you meet at college – young, right? On account of anyone good has just *gotta* be. It ain't till you put on a few years – hair's going grey on ya, and you need around your waist one of them cowhide straps from one of Charlene's trunks, iffin you wanna keep up your pants. It's then you get to see that real young girls are kinda like a whole different *gender* from the crapped-out wimmin they grow up to be. And like a noo and fruity wine, you wanna sip 'em. Yes indeedy. You sure do wanna do that. And my man David – Jesus Aitch Christ: if that guy weren't telling me no lie, he's upped and caught hisself one of the sweet little honeys – with her, I guess, long blonde hair bouncing in the sun and her eyes lit up and all, like real foxy diamonds – you know what I'm saying? Warm, slim arms and legs and fingers, all clean and peachy and hot as hell itself. Man . . . I don't stop thinking like this I'm gonna turn right round now and kill Charlene for having growed *old* (and still she'd go on squawking).

'So *listen*, Nicole,' was the latest round of yak from Charlene that was filtering across to Dwight, each word squirming its way fitfully through a dense and humid mist that was causing Dwight to drip. 'Did I tell you how much I am *loving* your gorgeous dress? Ain't that dress just to *die* for, Patty? I can't recall ever I saw something so lovely as that.'

And as Nicole flushed hot with raw and deep-felt sheer and downright pleasure at that, she was thinking Oh *yes*, dear Charlene, you are perfectly right – it is utter heaven, this dress, and you might well have further observed that its cumulative and show-stopping effect is in no small way due to not just the way I carry it (it's all about knowing exactly how to place one's feet and hold one's stance) but also the don't you think quite *inspired* accessorization? Yes yes yes – but listen: *given* all this, could some kind person please *explain* to me (because I really would, actually, very much like to know, all right?) why all male eyes in the vicinity are upon not me but Pat? Well of course it's perfectly *obvious*, isn't it? (I don't in truth need a guided tour, here). It's because, isn't it, she's wearing six-inch heels and little more than a sort of powder puff affair and a glorified *belt* – which apart from being cheap and showy and vulgar and *far* too young for her is just so wholly and completely *wrong*: I mean to say, this is a *ball*, for Christ's sake – not a fucking pick-up joint! (God I'm angry.)

Charlene was still beaming all over Nicole, and what lingered in her head – lodged not too far behind the megawatt and starstruck dazzle – was yeah, Nicole, you look OK I guess (leastways you ain't making with the honeybee like earlier on, yeah? With all the banana and black schtick) – but hey, get real. Like, what are you – picking up a *Oscar*?

That thought, and the surrounding bubbly hubbub (as well as the electric organ chorus from Surfin' Safari) were now cut into by the tinkling of a bell that came from . . . where *was* it coming from, actually, thought Nicole distractedly, this rather tinny and irritating noise? Ah yes – over there, I think, up in front of the band on the podium. Still the murmur of conversations rumbled along over and all around her – spiked by the odd whoop and silly drizzling gale of party laughter – but the bell was still clinking away for all it was worth, and gradually the shushing and the hushing began to hold sway, and soon there prevailed the closest to silence you're ever really going to get at this sort of thing – because there must be just hundreds of people here, you know: hundreds and hundreds, I reckon. Oh look – it's that rather embarrassing little Assistant something-or-other person, isn't it? The one that now I come to think of it (oh God I *shouldn't* – it's just too cruel) rather reminds me of those bright red and shiny Peking *ducks* you see hanging up in all those windows in Chinatown; which is maybe why he chooses to carry through the theme and wear a bird's nest on his head.

'Good people! Good people!' Stewart was now braying

bravely, his – and yes it *did* look rather cooked – perspiring face only just about managing to rein in the wilder manifestations of some or other recent and tremulous ecstatic conversion. 'Little bit of hush, please, ladies and gentlemen . . . little bit of hush . . . shh . . . ssh down, please, ladies and gentlemen . . .'

Oh shut the fuck *up*, you bastards, thought Stewart, with savagery. Christ, it's not as if any of you's got anything to *say*, is it? Bloody hell – it's normally the *actual* Cruise Director who does all this (and where is he? Yeah well – you tell me. Where is he ever?). Raises his bloody finger – instant silence. I've been making like Quasimodo for the best part of ten minutes with all the bloody *bells* and here I am now practically *pleading* with all these sods to cut the *yap* for just two minutes, can't you? I've got to introduce the bloke who pretends to *drive* the thing – and the joke is I can barely talk anyway – my lips are completely fucked up from all those bloody *balloons*.

'Ladies and gentlemen! Thank you for your kind attention. Without more ado, it is with great pride and pleasure that I present to you our Captain. Captain Anthony *Scar*, ladies and gentlemen – please put your hands together for a great big round of applause for the Captain! Yay! Let's hear it!'

And people did what they could, give them their due – but it's never easy, is it? When you've got a glass in one hand (and are they coming *round*, do you suppose? Or is one meant, I don't know – to *go* somewhere for a refill?) and in the other a rather odd sort of little pastry and could-be chicken and something else a bit tricky to eat, quite frankly, *canapé* kind of thing (if I can find an ashtray or a crevice or a plant, I might quite discreetly get rid of it).

'My *Lords* . . .' announced the Captain (and did he glare at Stewart? He might have done) ' . . . Ladies and gentlemen. I won't break up this magnificent ball for terribly long, so please don't worry. Well – I hope all of you managed to get up on deck today . . .?'

A general and meaningless murmur arose, hung about a bit, and died the death.

'Those of you who *did* will have enjoyed the most wonderful calm blue sea and, I am reliably informed, plenty of warm sunshine. I wouldn't *know* . . .' went Captain Scar, now – voice down an octave, merest twinkle in the eyes and one finger pawing the side of his nose as his mouth turned downwards (something by way of a *pleasantry* was surely on its way, then, was Stewart's opinion: and if so, get on with it, you cunt). ' . . . I wouldn't know about *that*, I'm afraid, because as you all know, I am kept toiling night and day on the *bridge* . . .!'

The usual muted hoo-hah ensued – a clutch of dark and knowing chuckles *here*, a honked-out chorus of deploring and mock-sympathetic animal noises *there*: sort of enough.

'You don't believe me?' came the Captain's wide-eyed protestation. 'Well one or two of you must come up and see how the sweat just pours off me! ha ha. But *seriously* for a minute – I hope you *did* all enjoy the weather today . . . because tomorrow and the *next* day . . .!'

And a collective groan rose and fell like a Mexican wave in the last of its death throes – still speckled, though, with clumps of laughter from those who assumed or maybe hoped that here was just another joke.

'No joke, I'm afraid,' maundered on life-of-the-party Captain Scar. 'The augurs are not good. I'm not suggesting anything . . .' – and here all the nose and fingers, eyes and mouth stuff was hastily reinstated – ' . . . anything, um – *titanic* . . .!'

And wafted over to him were further gales of mirth – though several pockets of quite grim silence were detectable too, as people studied their feet, and those of others.

' . . . But nonetheless, I do advise you – and here's a little something for all you Londoners here tonight – I do advise you to, er, as the old bus conductors used to say while guiding their red double-deckers through a really bad pea-souper, ha ha – I do advise you to Hold On *Tight*! Anyway – enough of all that. We're all here to *enjoy* ourselves, yes? So – on behalf of my crew and staff, I wish you all – my *Lords* – ' (and did he glare at Stewart? He might have done) ' – Ladies and gentlemen – a wonderful Viva America Ball, and an equally wonderful crossing – weather or no weather. Music please, Maestro!'

Yes, thought Stewart, let's all face the music and dance. The bandleader, Christ help us, has just instructed everyone to take their partners for the foxtrot – which just has to be the blackest joke really, doesn't it? Most of the people here, on account of free booze, extreme age and often a wholly poleaxing combination of the two, can hardly find it within themselves to maintain the perpendicular. Just look at that ancient old mare over there – would've keeled right over if it hadn't been for one of our eagle-eyed and off-white deejayed minders; they're gigolos, really – but they double as pretty useful fielders.

At the first sight of her mother sashaying across the floor with her usual studied elegance, Marianne had thought with a rush Oh God – she's going to start grilling me about where on earth *Dad* is, and *I* don't know, do I? Haven't seen him all day long. But now it became quite clear to Marianne that Nicole was not at all intent upon tackling her daughter on this or any other subject – hadn't even noticed her, it actually looked like: swept right past and on towards the podium. Surely she wasn't going to ask the band to do a request, was she? (Possibly some romantic thing that reminded her of Dad – something maybe on the lines of Where Do You Go To, My Bastard?) That, anyway, certainly appeared to be her destination – but now Marianne was rather irritatingly distracted by someone or other, oh God – *talking* to her (and it isn't Tom, no – it's some little red-faced fellow with plenty of yellowing teeth) so I can't, damn, see where she's gone to, quite, and now I suppose I've got to turn and face this new and awful thing, then, have I?

'How do you do it?' came the man's rather jovial if guttural enquiry.

'I'm *sorry*?'

A tremor of uncertainty rippled quite palpably across the man's brow: he didn't look so happy, now.

'I am being of so *sorrow*,' he hugely regretted. 'Is that not correct saying? I am from Vienna, yes?'

'Ah!' went Marianne, as if a true dawning light had spread its glowing mantle upon not just this, but all other conundra the world had to offer.

'Do not you say, How do you do it? You isn't?'

'I think, maybe,' smiled Marianne, 'you mean How do you *do*. You don't actually need the 'it'.'

The man's whole forehead was deeply furrowed, now – it was as if he was seriously salting away and maybe filing alphabetically this new and valuable nugget.

'Ah so. To hell with 'it'. Excelling. I love the London.'

'Do you? Oh good. That's, um – ' (I glanced around, just then – God, it's getting so totally *packed* in here: completely lost sight of Mum, now: don't know where on earth she's got to) ' – *nice*.'

'Best place on vorld to wisit for suitings. I do buy there the ter-*vills* – yes?'

'Really?' I have to, thought Marianne, go now.

'Yes yes. And plus I do buy there the ter-*veeds*. Some have bones of herrings. Some have eyes of birds and tooths of dog. One is checked by Prince of Vales!'

'Really? I have to, I think, go now. *Sorry* . . .' she smiled, as she began to squirm her way back into the throng and away.

The man was beaming at her – and now as she receded, he raised up two waggling fingers in a gesture of farewell.

'How do you *do*!' he called after her. 'How do you *do*? Yes? To hell with 'it'!'

I think, thought Marianne, that could be Mum – way over there past that extraordinary ice sculpture thing (could be a dolphin, I think – but it's a bit melted, now). Needn't be her – only caught a glimpse – but I might as well make for that particular dot on the horizon: there's nobody else here I know. But '*Hi-i-i* . . .!' was crooning a big brown voice right into her ear; she turned, and there was the big brown face it had surely come from.

'Derek – hi. My name is Derek. Believe in getting all that sort of thing out of the way at the onset. I'm in property. Well – I *say* property: what I actually do is buy to sell. Yes? *Location*, of course – well, I expect you know that. Tend to go for the smaller period properties – right area, but just a leeedle bit out of the way, you know? A mews is favourite, but it's getting to be like gold dust, quite frankly. Basically, you want a couple of Cretan olive jars – big bastards. You slap one of these each side of the front door, chuck in the bay trees and already you're looking at kudos: money in the bank, you want the God's honest truth. Other thing you got to remember is *neutral*, yeh? You go neutral with your colours, else it's a bugger to shift. Plus, these days you need a kitchen that looks like a bloody operating theatre. Kraut job. Crazy, really – not one of those City boys and their tarts know how to boil a bloody kettle.'

And then the big brown face split into a huge and tongue-laden leer that was so utterly and frankly terrifying that Marianne felt herself positively flinch.

'So *tell* me,' went on Derek, with a confidence so thoroughly misplaced, it was truly awesome, 'what do they call *you*, lovely lady?'

'Excuse me . . .' whispered Marianne – so softly, he may well not have heard. 'I really have to go, now . . .'

She continued to squeeze and dodge and insinuate her continually apologizing self through the knots and swellings of yacking, laughing, drinking people – not really, now, in quest of anyone at all: just struggling to reach the perimeter of all this, and maybe breathe some air. She became stalled at one point, and had to endure the following – delivered almost without pause for breath by yet another freely perspiring and eager man in a far too tight dinner jacket:

'See, I was taught to write songs to this very arcane formula involving carefully chosen BPMs synchronized to time-tested melodic strings with predetermined rhythmic sequences – guaranteed, they told me, just never to fail. Yes. Not a fucking dicky-bird so far, though . . .'

Marianne spotted the narrowest gap between a pearl grey sequined dress (doing sterling work on the containment front) and a creamish tuxedo with a tawny and marbled stain on each of its elbows – and she made for it.

'*Yes* . . .' she heard, whether she liked it or not, 'and *then*, if you will, she turned around and said to me Well the whole *point*, Geoffrey – the reason I don't want to come with you to counselling, is that I actually sexually prefer women to men. Christ Almighty – it's the only thing now we actually agree on . . .'

Marianne passed on – and yes, a sort of space was clearing before her, yes it seemed to be – but now she found herself so terribly close to the band (who had just recently abandoned their seemingly endless rendition of New York, New York and were now well down the road to plucking up for themselves some Good Vibrations) – that it actually was quite deafening. And oh look it *is* Mum, great – so I'll just go up to her and . . . who's she talking to? Oh yes – would be: no less than the Skipper.

'Yes yes I know it's all terribly *fashionable* at the moment,' Nicole was cooing, 'but to be perfectly frank with you, Captain, I've never wanted to actually try any of the so-called Pacific *Rim* sort of food because I know it sounds silly but it's just the *phrase*, if I'm honest: Pacific *Rim*, yes? It habitually puts me in mind of *lavatories* – and I can't tell you how that just repels me. Ah – *Marianne*, my sweet. Captain

228

– my daughter, Marianne. The Captain and I are just about to have a dance – aren't we, Captain?'

Captain Scar shook Marianne lightly by the hand while saying to Nicole, I warn you now – I am, believe me, no Fred Astaire.

'Excuse us, darling,' said Nicole quite sweetly, as Captain Scar led her out on to the floor – and then (more whispered, quite darkly): 'You don't know where your – ?'

Marianne shook her head. 'No, Mummy,' she said. 'Haven't seen him all day.'

Nicole just briefly narrowed down her eyes into some sort of intimation of just what it was she'd *do* to David when and if he eventually emerged from whatever no doubt exceedingly alcoholically driven catastrophe he was currently engaged in – and then her whole face was alight and fluttering as she tucked all that out of sight as she began to sort of undulate and then jerk her hips a bit in front of the Captain as he plonked his feet first here and then there, as his arms assumed a fairly frightening life of their own and flailed about him (it's not really made for dancing, is it? Good Vibrations? Not really). And it's true, what he said: he was, believe him, no Fred Astaire.

'I must *say*, Captain . . . can you *hear* me? It's terribly loud . . .!'

'Just about! Call me Anthony.'

' . . . *Anthony* . . . I have to say I was horribly out on my guess for yesterday's *mileage*. Maybe you can give me some tips . . .?'

'What?'

'I said – *mileage*, yes? Got it wrong. Maybe you teach me?'

'*What*? Sorry . . .'

Nicole compressed her lips and shook her head mutely. And when the Captain indicated by means of raised eyebrows and a jabbing finger that maybe the spot they had recently vacated was possibly best if conversation was the goal, Nicole quite happily concurred, and followed him off the floor.

'Not too great at all the social side of this,' confessed Captain Scar, somewhat shamefacedly (which Nicole thought so utterly *charming*: he suddenly looks no more than boyish). 'I'm a professional sailor, you see. Not very good at parties. I tell you one thing, though, Nicole – I blew up a boat, once.'

Nicole stared – and she shut tight her mouth the instant she knew it was open.

'You – ? Did you say you – ?'

Captain Scar nodded. And then a roguish smile crept all over him.

'Mind you,' he qualified, 'it was a *dinghy* . . .'

'Oh yes but *still* . . .! I mean still that's . . . why are you smiling like that, Captain? Anthony? Hm? Oh wait – *I* see . . . you meant blow up as in blow *up*, yes? Because it was a *dinghy* . . .!'

The Captain joshingly accepted that his ruse had been rumbled.

'So – you naughty, naughty Captain – that was a *joke*, wasn't it? You made a *joke*. Well I think it's terribly terribly *naughty* of you to *tease* me like that.'

'Ha ha,' went the Captain. Yes yes – it may be naughty, I suppose – I wouldn't care to say. All I know is it's my *only* joke, you see, and so I use it mercilessly: usually goes down quite well, I think. But again, I wouldn't really know.

'And what you were saying about the *weather* earlier – yes? Was that another of your very naughty jokes too? You naughty Captain.'

'Alas not. Definitely brewing. Could be Force 9. Nothing to worry about, though. Just a bit rocky. I love it, myself. Reminds me I'm on a ship.' (So yes – I'm telling the truth about the weather; which is more than I did the other evening about the *Titanic* going down, oh Christ – this very *night*; say that every crossing – people like it, I think. One

230

day, I suppose, someone or other will blow the whistle – but so far, OK.)

Nicole was now aware of a pressing mass of mainly women, lip-lickingly eager for their slice of Captain. I'd better then, she thought, be quick about this:

'I was thinking of going to the Casino, later.'

'Ah,' said the Captain. 'The den of vice. Good luck.'

'I don't suppose you . . .?'

'Ah no – not for the likes of me. I'll be up on the bridge. In *fact* . . .' he tacked on, eyeing his watch, 'I very much fear I have to go now, Nicole. But it's been an immense pleasure making your acquaintance.'

Nicole blushed with pleasure. 'Mutual,' she said.

'Hey Nicole!' hailed Charlene (yeah – it's *me* here, baby. You about ready to put him down now? Or do you bleeve you'll have him gift-wrapped and shipped back to London for a *souvenir*?). 'Me and the guys is gonna, like, split to maybe the *Piano* Bar? Getting kinda noisy. You sweet with that, Julie honey?'

'Nah – I godda gedda bed. And Benny – I don't get him down soon he's gonna need major surgery.'

'I'm OK,' grunted Benny. (Why don't no one talk to me directly? Huh?)

No, thought Dwight, you ain't: you take one good long look at yourself, Benny boy – you're a dead man. And then he said:

'How bout we all get ourselves over the Black Horse? How you feel bout that, Patty?' Cos yeah – the more I'm looking at this Patty broad here, the more I'm liking what I see. I mean yeah OK – she ain't no co-ed, but the way I figure, how picky can I be? Plus my man Dave might be there, yeah? Then we can dump the dames that don't cut it and really tie one on.

'I thought,' said Nicole, ' . . . I was just saying to the Captain here . . . oh – he's gone. Where did he . . .? I didn't see him go.'

231

'Maybe,' said Charlene, 'you drove him off – huh, honey?'

Nicole immediately stiffened. 'I hardly *think* so.'

'Hey babe,' bantered Charlene. 'Just kidding around, you know?'

'Yes well. I *was* actually thinking of trying my luck at the Casino . . .'

'Casino,' put in Dwight, 'ain't even warmed up yet. Let's grab us a couple drinks, huh? Later, you want, we can hit the slots.'

'Waaall . . .' conceded Charlene. 'Kay. We'll get maybe one in the Black Horse – but Dwight I'm warning you here and now: you lay offa the pretzels, hear me? Telling you, Nicole – for him I gotta be, like, a full on *nurse*. I don't take good care of him, his bowels one day – they're gonna get to look like linguine. And I ain't making no late night of it neither: afore I get to bed I gotta wrap me up some paddery. Hey – what's with that poor little kid! You see her? I dunno who she is, but she sure do look lonesome.'

Stacy became instinctively aware that she was being actively *regarded* for some reason or other by people, some people – so she turned her back to them and picked up a satay stick from a great pile on the buffet table and lodged it between her teeth and tugged at it a bit and half the thing came away and she chewed on that a while, not liking it a bit – because she hadn't actually wanted to eat a satay stick, no she hadn't – not at all. Just to the left of her, an apparently exasperated and overweight man was hissing at the woman beside him:

'Why in hell can't you be like *Angela*?'

And the woman, with hard dark hair and eyes, shot right back at him:

'Why don't you earn Malcolm *money*?'

At least, thought Stacy, they've got each other to argue with. Where is Suki? This afternoon we were, oh God – *together*. I have never before experienced . . . I could have just lain there forever (and it was her cabin we ended up in; it's just, Jesus – so much *nicer*). And then she suddenly seemed in such a tearing hurry to, I don't know – get *rid* of me. Even now I can't quite believe or even remotely understand it. I mean – did I do something, say something wrong? I don't think I did. And it's not that Suki seemed put *out*, or anything – she just suddenly, she said, needed to be alone.

'But I'll see you later, yes? Will I, Suki? At this thing later on – yes? You'll be there? I'll see you then, then, will I? Or I can stay. Let me stay with you. Why can't I stay?'

'Hey – c'mon, Stace. Don't lay a heavy scene on me, OK? I'll catch you later – sure I will.'

'Kiss me,' said Stacy, simply – and it hurt her, yes it did, that Suki then laughed; she laughed as if here was, I don't know – some crazy idea, or something, but it hadn't seemed crazy before, not when they were lying, newly apart and languid, and Suki had gently blown away the strands of Stacy's long and sticky damp hair that criss-crossed her face and clung to her half-closed eyelids, and parted lips.

Anyway. So I plummeted down through the endless decks in the boomingly silent lift (I had to, apparently, get back to my level) and Mum, I suppose quite predictably, wasn't in the cabin. Barely seen her all day. I didn't, you know, actually think she'd *do* all this – not, at least, this soon and so very thoroughly. I had possibly very naïvely supposed that being cooped up here together would have given us a better chance than usual to – you know, really sort of *talk*, and things. I was forgetting, wasn't I, that the ship would be affording *opportunities* – and you know what Mum does with them, don't you? Plain for all to see. She *seizes* them – yes she does. And if none is there – well then without delay she sets about plotting their creation. So maybe, I thought, she's gone straight on (from wherever in God's name she was) to dinner? Maybe. Hasn't changed for the thing later, though – because look: little black dress still just hanging there, from those stupidly skinny little straps. So I quickly put on something shamingly similar and thought I'd sort of pile up my hair and twist it round at the back a bit – get a couple of very springy ringlets to maybe trail down past my ears. But it wasn't going to *work*, was it? I got one side pretty much OK, but the other just wasn't having any of it – and then from the sort of wasp's nest effect I'd more or less got bolted into place, a huge great section just suddenly flopped down in the front all over my face and I just thought oh *sod* it – I'll brush it all out and leave it hang where it bloody well likes (Suki, anyway, says she loves the way my hair . . . I think she said *floated* behind me, whenever I move. I have never known before that hair has *sensations*: when she drew her fingers through it – softly, and so lingeringly – it felt like every single fibre was dancing and electric. And maybe too the gentleness of each of Suki's fingers had had something to do with that, because whenever some *boy* starts fooling with your hair – I don't know, maybe this is just me – you're always, aren't you, bracing yourself for when he starts tugging it back and sometimes – once, this happened to me – wrenching great handfuls of it around to the front of your neck, and then just holding it there, around a balled-up fist, and touching your throat).

Well. Mum wasn't at dinner. So I ate mine alone. Took about twenty minutes. And then I came to this ball. Maybe Suki will be here. But she isn't. Well OK – maybe *Mum*, then, might show. But no. And it's hard, that – it's hard. Because when already a joy that hovered at the brink of kissing the very edges of love has already lapsed into aching . . . yes well then it would really help me a lot if there was someone around who could soothe or even explain it. Yes. So where is she? Where's my *Mum*, then?

Suddenly, the noise around her seemed close to intolerable – though Stacy felt sure that the levels hadn't *risen*, or anything. It took a dazzled glance upwards to the vast and spinning mirror ball (pink and golden spangles of light made luminous Laurel and Hardy's bowlers, leapt up in Marilyn's hair and – just for an instant – made a white-tuxedoed Bogart appear less than suicidal) to wholly convince Stacy that now was indeed and very much the time to go.

'Well *here's* a face I know. Oh yes. Oh yes. I well know *this* face, all right.'

That, emerging from the clamorous hubbub that now, increasingly, was walling her in, brokenly came across to Stacy as the most distinct – and God, then, I suppose the closest – of all the gobbed-out and bitten-off snatches of nuisance around her. She could have, she realized – just less than one second too late – smoothly applied and got away with the golden syrup of Total Party Deafness Syndrome, had she only allied the determined affectation with a resolute and dead-ahead transfixion, while striding with purpose towards those large and inviting glass double doors that bobbed up into and then ducked out of her line of vision from behind this undulating mass of improbably tinted and teased-out hairdos, interspersed with a smattering of pink and glistening skulls. But no – she had faltered. There was just that so slight but palpable blip in her otherwise seamless advance: her ears were felt to have detected a sparkle of noise specific to herself, and her traitorous eyes had flickered in sympathy.

'*Ye-e-e-es* . . .!' brayed Nobby, delightedly. 'I thought it was you. Didn't I say so, Aggie? Stewart? Isn't that just what I said? All the way over there, we were, and I said Hallo! *Hallo*, I said – '

'He *did*,' beamed Aggie. 'That's exactly what he said.'

Nobby nodded with wild-eyed eagerness – and Stewart alongside was working hard at back-up, what with his seeming determination to get the corners of his mouth to meet up and say Hi around the back of his head – whereupon, thought Stacy distractedly, his whole orange phizog and that great yellow barnet could be cranked right back like a Pez dispenser (though please spare us the lozenge of anything approaching tongue).

'It *is*, it *is*,' Nobby went on avowing. 'Those were, dear Stacy, my very words. Am I right? Do I tell no lie?'

Both Aggie and Stewart heartily vied with each other in a chorus of corroboration, this concluding raggedly with little less than a standing ovation.

'Jennifer not with you, dear?' asked Aggie, quite solicitously.

And Stacy suddenly was stung by bitterness. She very briefly contemplated an insolent charade – glancing with intent to the left and right of her, instantly detecting the clear and total absence of Jennifer and coming back dead-eyed and leadenly with Apparently *Not*. But the gall subsided within her quite as quickly as it had rushed right in and filled her up, and in its wake now she felt no more than the weight of the barely shifting sludge of misery.

'No,' she said. Just that: no.

'It's Stewart we have to thank, you know,' gabbled on Nobby.

Stacy gazed at him. 'What for?'

And Stewart did his best to maintain the expression (What *for*? Typical, that, isn't it? What bloody *for*? That sort of reaction, I just can't tell you, is so absolutely *typical* of the sort of shit I get).

'Well all *this* . . .!' elaborated Nobby expansively – spreading wide his arms to encompass the whole of the glory: he hit a waiter's tray to the left of him (no harm done, but it was late and the waiter seemed in no mood to smile at him) and some half-cut Londoner over to the right, who blushed and stammered out an instant apology. 'Tell you one thing, though, Stewart – old Elvis is looking a bit the worse for wear. Been in the wars, has he?'

Stewart glanced over at the cut-out; the twinkling mirror ball seemed to unerringly seek out and highlight the corrugations under the King's accusing eye and across that once-perfect nose. Stewart then shrugged and he went Ha ha. (When I get Elvis back to the office, this time I'll rip his bloody head off.)

'Ringo Starr,' said Aggie, quite amiably, 'has sailed on Sylvie.'

Stewart was nodding, fondly as an uncle, and Stacy thought if I could just be *sick* – right here and now – it would maybe be enough for me to just, oh God – leave (and why? Why *can't* I, actually, just *leave*?).

'As has,' enjoined Nobby, 'Mister George Harrison, of that ilk.'

'But not Paul,' said Aggie, quite sadly. 'But,' she tacked on, brightening up considerably, 'he might yet.'

'Nor John,' rounded off Nobby. 'Who now, of course, won't.'

'But never *Elvis* – that's what I was meaning,' elucidated Aggie. 'Elvis never did.'

'Well,' put in Stewart, quite as jovially as you might expect, 'Elvis, of course, never even made it to England. Except, I think, to change planes, one time.'

'*Ah*,' went Nobby, 'but this *isn't* England, is it, Stewart? Mid-Atlantic, that's what we are: mid-Atlantic.'

And Stewart thought Well Jesus, bloody *Nobby* – don't you think I *know* that, you stupid little irritating *cunt*.

'True,' he smiled. 'Quite true.'

But Stacy had been caught by that last and throwaway remark of Nobby's. She had, almost impossibly, completely *forgotten*, you see – that they were (wholly amazingly, and God knows quite why) in the middle of the Atlantic Ocean . . . and that makes me feel suddenly cold. Yes. So where is she? Where's my *Mum*, then?

⚓

'I should think,' barely whispered Jennifer (I'm actually, yes,

237

more thinking this than saying it), 'we've probably more or less missed it, now.'

Earl was lying beside her, his lazy half-open eyes semi-focused on the curved and creamy ceiling of his cabin – or maybe just nearly closed like that as a gauzy barricade against the meandering smoke as he let it drift up out of his mouth, following each deep inhalation of his Marlboro.

'I wish to God,' he muttered. 'Wish to God I had some grass.' This cigarette is damn near done, so what I'm gonna do is dump it out into this here ashtray, and light me up a fresh one. And it's now I'm looking at Jennifer for the first time since we got it on . . . and I'm smiling a smile, sure I am . . . but what I'm thinking is something I ain't never noticed before. She looks, close up, kinda older than I figured. When her face paint's all loused up like the way it is now, she looks real tired, you know? Also – I get turned on big time when she takes off her clothes; she kinda has this way, right, of just standing there and taking them off right *at* you? But I'm honest, here – I'd like she keep on the bra, yeah? Kinda keeps it into bundles, which is neat. Without the bra, things can get a little out of *control*? I ain't never had no English girl before – and if Jennifer, you know, is how they all are back in England, well then I'm telling you, boy: *hot*. But in the States, the girls are . . . what can I tell you? Kinda *cleaner*, is what I'm maybe saying here. And wait up – don't you go running off with no wrong idea, here. I ain't saying we're dealing with *dirty* (excepting maybe the way she yells out stuff when she's really, like, into it – and wow, that blows my mind) – but maybe a tad less *hair* would be good, you know? What I mean to say is – I'm the guy here, right? So I get to have all the body hair? And if it ain't hair with Jennifer, then we're talking stubble – and that too to me is a guy thing, OK? I mean – I wanna go down on some wild thing, I'll be sure and let you know, you see what I'm saying?

'You getting up? Jennifer? You getting up?'

Jennifer had swung her legs out of the bed, and over the side.

'I've just seen the time,' she said.

Yes, thought Jennifer – and also I've just seen the look on your face. And it hurt me, what I saw. And even as recently as this morning, such a hurt would have been impossible. All this meant to me was a young and cheeky American bloke: what better way to get through a few days at sea? But in the last few hours – when we both were thrashing together, and flailing in amazement – I have come too to gazing at him after, and when he was dozing: those eyelashes – those great soft curling eyelashes that are only ever given by God to young men. He looked so boyish, it was almost girl-like – and yet with all this manly apparatus and the hardness of his day-old beard breaking through a powder-soft complexion. And I felt within me something lurch – not a thoroughly new sensation, but one so barely remembered from decades ago (I never thought I would again come to discern its fluid and dimly-recalled features, receding as they have been ever deeper into shadows).

I appear to have dressed myself. One lazy and muscular arm is raised and vaguely beckoning for me, now. I needn't resist it – and maybe I shan't. It really depends upon how the rest of this goes.

'I should think,' she said – squirting on to each wrist some Paco Rabanne – 'it must be more or less finished, by now.'

'What? What's finished?'

'The ball. There was that ball thing – remember?'

Earl was grinning. 'I had me a ball right here, baby. You coming back over here, or what?'

And he meant, thought Jennifer, back again to bed (rather than anything broader). Few men older would display such confidence. But that was the thing, wasn't it, about youth and age? That was *one* of the things about them, anyway: how with the alternations of brashness and hesitance, we constantly seem to dumbfound one another.

'You're too much for me,' Jennifer lied – gazing down and wanting him badly. 'At my age – I just can't keep up.'

And was there just the tiniest flutter at the back of his maybe *not*, could be, startled but now wide-awake eyes? He rallied, and came back gamely:

'Your *age* – yeah *right*, Jennifer. Like you're – what? A hunnerd years old?'

Jennifer was sitting on a stool in front of a mirror, applying her lipstick.

'Not far off,' she said.

And then she thought: how exactly shall I do this? Because don't ask me why but I know it just has to be *done* – so how shall I finally be going about it? Shall I soft-pedal? Gently lead him by the hand to a half-truth, and while he grows accustomed to the semi-shock of that, hint at something further – until at last and forever the whole wide and cold awfulness (which is how he will see it) is stripped off and laid bare – pegged out and splayed and at the mercy of just anyone? I'm still not sure. I could go – Look, Earl: listen to me. You're just a (God) *teenager* – and me, well – I'm *much* older, so much older than that. (Late twenties? Enough to make him flinch? And why, actually, am I compelled to do this? I don't at all *want* him to flinch, because I just know that when he does, it will be away from me.) Or can I dare to hit him with the big word thirty? Or give him the lot? Do you know what? Don't, please, ask me quite why – but I'm going to, right now: I'm going to give him the lot.

'I'm not,' she said – maybe exaggerating the contortion of her voice as her mouth opened wide into an O, and she went on needlessly applying yet another thick coat of her jammy lipstick. 'I'm not, Earl, much off forty.'

And she timed the flicked and sidelong instant's glance into the mirror to utterly cruel perfection. He looked slapped – beaten up, even – before his eyes and wits reasserted themselves.

'Yeah – like *sure*, Jennifer! Forty! get *outta* here!'

Jennifer turned. 'It's true,' she said.

Earl sat up – and through his joshing, Jennifer detected the first uneasy stirrings (and however sick he soon might be feeling, she already was in a far worse state).

'Quit putting me *on*, Jennifer, huh? I ain't *stoopid*. Forty! *Shit . . .*'

Jennifer looked right at him.

'It's true,' she said.

Earl just momentarily held her gaze, before his face settled back down into so much joky *fun* (and who, here, was he protecting?).

'Like, *sure*. Yeh – right. And your roomie Stacy? She's what, now – eighty?'

'Stacy is around your age.' *Now,* she thought – let's go for it: 'And I'm her mother.'

And this time he didn't see the battering coming. He was dazed, and nearly breathless.

'Jeez, Jennifer – will you quit jerking me around? Like – *enough* already, OK? You're really, like, freaking me out here, you know?'

And Jennifer's eyes felt tender, and soon they were going to be stinging her. Her mouth she held firm, though. And then as she spoke, she discovered she'd lost that too:

'It's . . . true,' she faltered.

And Earl just stared at her, not knowing now what he should be feeling. I mean – guys back home, they'd think alla this is just such a *gas*, man! I mean, what – Mrs *Robinson*? Too much. Except they wouldn't *believe* it, would they? On account of I don't hardly believe it myself. But hey – this type of thing: it's *cool*, right? I mean – young guy's dream, right? Right. So that's how I'll play it – real cool.

'Hey Jennifer . . .' said Earl, quite softly – and now he was behind her, and vaguely fooling with her hair in a way that he thought was maybe reassuring. 'That's cool. I'm cool with that. Hey – it's cool . . .'

Jennifer smiled her appreciation of that, at least, and

twisted her head about so that her lips could find and kiss his fingers.

'Thank you,' she whispered. 'I'm glad that you think it's *cool . . .'*

But, she thought, you don't, do you? Do you, Earl? No. You don't.

And as he turned away, Earl maybe sensed that, hanging in the air. And all he could think was No. No way. Cool, Jennifer, is not what I think. What I think is, like – *gross*?

⚓

'Mum's gone,' said Marianne, quite shortly (surprised, and then not surprised by how terribly weary her voice was sounding, and straining still). 'Were you looking for her, Rollo? Cos she's gone off with the Americans.'

Rollo nodded briefly to that. Couldn't really think of anything to say. No, he hadn't been looking for Mum – or for Marianne, for that matter, and certainly not for Dad. He had simply been mooching about at the fringes of this now quite straggly and maybe finally tail-ending ball, stubborn and wilful in a hope against hope that despite the repeated and near-tearful regrets and cautions that Jilly had given him (starting off quite gentle and loving – escalating soon to really rather ratty, when he just wouldn't let it go) she might after all and despite everything just maybe look in. Because for once, you see, Jilly wasn't actually on duty in that bloody old pub (and if she were, well – where do you think Rollo would be headed for?) but nor – and here was the point, this was to Rollo the very disturbing part, here – nor was bloody Sammy. Very rare, you see, that their time off coincided. Now look – I *know* what Jilly said, I heard it all: she can't just, can she – *leave* him? Just like that? With no sort of explanation? I mean to say *look*, Rollo – I've been with Sammy for just ages and ages – he's convinced. God – we're going to get *married*. And don't – don't, Rollo, please go on and on and on at me because I simply don't *know* any more. I'm all confused. All this has happened so, oh – *quickly*, and I just don't know what I'm *doing* any more, Rollo. All the time, lately, if I haven't been behind the bar I've been with you, haven't I? Hm? I feel like I haven't *slept* for a year and my head just goes round and round and I frankly just can't handle any more *questions*, OK? Rollo? I find you, well – you know what I think of you, Rollo: you're really . . . *exciting*, yeah? And I've heard what you've said about what we both can do when we're all back in England – but Christ, Rollo . . . it's not just that we're both so terribly *young*, but – well God, we live at completely different ends of the *country*! And yeh yeh – I *know*, I *know*: I can get a job in London, fine, OK – but where am I actually going to be *living*, Rollo? I just can't afford London prices, quite frankly – not with the sort of job *I'm* going to get – and you, you still live with your *parents*, don't you? Well you *do*, Rollo – you *do*: there's no getting away from it. So unless you've got a spare million quid just hanging about . . .!

And what had maybe got to Jilly the most, during these gasped-out bouts of full-strength reasoning, was that maybe, oh God, I'm actually deep down far more sensible than I *want* to be. Because half of me is hearing Rollo loud and clear: just *come* – we can work out the details later. Yes! Just rush to London and into the arms of my lover and let the rest of the world go and hang. Yes . . . lovely. But only *half* of me was hearing – only the half of me, see, is taking it in. And although Rollo's, oh God – sheer *energy* makes Sammy look frankly like a dead man, what he seems to be after too is really just some *other* form of commitment, isn't it? And that's the very thing I just don't want to give. Anyone. It's not, I think . . . I think (and oh God I *am*, you know – I really am bloody *exhausted*) . . . I think what it is, what it must be is that I don't want to have to decide whether I'm going to go with someone loyal and plodding and dependable and, oh – I don't mean to be nasty, but *dull*

– he is dull, Sammy – or else some real fun guy that I can get totalled at raves with. I just want to flit. Hang loose. Be me. I *think* . . . oh Jesus – just leave me, leave me: I just can't *think* any more and I just don't want to get into any more *questions*. OK?

'No,' said Rollo. 'No, Mar – wasn't really looking for anyone. You? Why are you still hanging around?'

Marianne shook her head.

'I think this was a dolphin, once,' she said.

They were both sort of slouching beside the central display – a great deal of deep-cut crystal, surmounted by palms – and Marianne was picking at what prawns were still floating in a large silver bowl at the base of this huge and rounded dripping ice thing.

'Yeh . . .' supposed Rollo. 'Round the other side there's a bloody great pile of butter, if you can believe it. Someone was saying that it was a sculpture of the ship, few hours ago. Now it just looks like a bloody great pile of butter. It's weird here, isn't it Mar?'

Marianne nodded slowly, idly kicking at a wafting balloon.

'Funny things happen. I think it must be the air.'

Rollo hissed out some of the pressure from between his teeth, and slowly his puffed-out cheeks subsided.

'Or the lack of it.'

And both of them just had to glance over to the banquette just there: they had each of them individually been doing their utmost to *ignore* all of this, you just have to believe them – but there was this couple, you see, who could maybe have been honeymooners, all hands and giggling – or else just a man and a woman well high on something (could be sex) and already intent upon making every single moment of their Trip of a Lifetime truly one to remember. Their wishy-washy ardour had now become insistent: already they had repeatedly assured one another that they were, respectively, the sweetest ickle prettiest girl who walked

244

God's earth, not to say the biggest most muscliest he-man that ever was born. Rollo caught Marianne's eye, expecting the ignition of some sort of shared and knowing smirk, or anyway secret collusion, but all he saw there was nothing much; very possibly, he thought, there has come from me nothing to spark off.

'Well look . . .' sighed Marianne. 'No point in hanging round here. Is there? Any more. Fancy a – I don't know. Drink somewhere? Have you been to this Regatta Club disco thing?'

Rollo started. Yes I have: she wouldn't be *there*, would she? Would she? No. From what she's said about Sammy, I very much doubt it. Still, though – don't quite want to risk it. It's mad, really – I don't too much mind seeing them both in the pub, but elsewhere . . . no, I really couldn't hack it.

'Izzoo . . .?' squeaked out the sweetest ickle prettiest girl who walked God's earth, 'going to take your little bunny to her cot and tuck her up nicely for the night?'

And the biggest most muscliest man that ever was born was now kissing the tip of her nose and calling her his Poppet and promising that he would – he would, he would, he would . . .

'*No*,' said Rollo quite loudly (just got to somehow blank out all that crap). 'No. I think I'll just get some kip, maybe. Mar? Marianne? Are you listening to me? What the hell is it?'

Marianne was standing just maybe a foot away, and yet it was plain she was totally gone from him. Blimey, he thought – it's the undertaker, the nutter, the loony in black. What's she looking at him for? Well OK – I can understand why she's *looking*, maybe (well yeah – I'm looking myself), but why isn't she actually *laughing*? Hey?

'You came . . .' is what Rollo was now hearing her say.

And at first Tom said nothing. Just stood so rigidly as to rival for stillness and dimension the forest of Yankee cutouts that were clustered to the right and left of him: he looks bloody funny slap-bang next to James Dean – Christ Almighty, what a loser this guy is. So why isn't Marianne *laughing*? Hey?

And then Tom said:

'I exchanged my black tie for this ready-made bow. As you may see. I trust you approve. It is so very long since I experienced a sense of moment.'

And maybe Marianne did, did she? Glance back then at Rollo? Maybe she had, by the inclination of her head or the half-closure of one or both of her eyes, quite possibly, fleetingly indicated her intention of leaving with this man. Either way, the two of them were gone, now, that's for bloody sure: completely out of sight. Which leaves just me. Great. Right. OK. Well – can't hang about this dive any longer, that's for certain. Regatta Club – can't face. Black Horse? Dad. Kip, then – yes? Cabin? Well yes – cabin, maybe, but I'll never sleep. There's maybe some miniatures left in the fridge, so I'll hammer them, yeh – but sleep, no: I'll never sleep. (Mum sometimes says that: she knows she won't sleep. I've never before known how that was *possible*). Look, what I want to know is – where are Jilly and *him*? What can they both be *doing*? Hm? Oh God. Oh *God* . . . Well look – maybe she's gone to bed now, yes? Jilly? I mean – *alone*, right? Back down to the engine room with that bunch of chambermaids. Yes – I think so. That's the most likely scenario, isn't it? Isn't it? Because look – it's late, right? And Sammy – God damn him – Sammy's no night bird, is he? That's the whole point. And Jilly, well – she's totally exhausted, yes? She said so, she said so – you heard her yourself. So yeh – I'll get myself down to my cabin. Have a drink. Won't sleep, though: I'll never sleep. Because look, what I want to know is – where are Jilly and *him*? Hey? What can they both be *doing*? Oh God. Oh *God* . . .

⚓

'Sammy,' said Jilly – she was arch, now, and maybe approaching even a degree of exasperation. 'What is it, exactly, that you think you're doing?'

Sammy looked pained – but maybe here was no more than a manifestation of his rapidly mounting fear. Because look, I'll be frank with you: when we had first started chatting (and it cost me, you know, to get the cabin to ourselves – a tenner each for Phil and Nasseem, but this had to be seen as an investment of sorts, it looked to me) I thought maybe that how it would, you know – *go* is that I'd act a bit sort of hurt, and then maybe coy when Jilly smilingly attempted to worm out, I don't know – what was *up* with me, or something. Then I'd go: Oh – don't mind me, Jilly – I'm just being silly, I suppose. I just saw you – you know, *look* at that guy at the bar just earlier – maybe you didn't even look, maybe it was him, he who looked at you – and well, perhaps I got just a little bit jealous. What was his name, anyway? Guy at the bar.

Yes – something like that. And Jilly would have been looking at me first off like I was mad (Guy? At the bar? What guy at the bar? I don't remember any . . . oh *God*, Sammy, honestly: there are loads of guys at the *bar*, aren't there?) . . . and then, um – well, a lot more fondly, I suppose it might have gone then (Sammy my darling – don't you know yet? Aren't you *aware*? It's *you* I love, isn't it Sammy? Hm? Only you. And I have done for how long? And we're *saving* together, aren't we Sammy? Saving up? For a future? So how on *earth* can you imagine I was looking at a *guy*?).

Yes. On those lines. And then she might have sipped some of the vodka I'd brought down specially (and I would say 'investment' again, but it's nicked from the bar, if I'm being totally honest) and looked about this very cramped and not too cosy cabin quite sly and cheekily, the way she can, and then she might have said: Phil not coming? When's Nasseem due back? And I would've gone *Well*, Jilly – a little surprise, a kind of treat: we're all alone – and we will be right up until it's time for my shift. And Jilly, then, she would have put down her drink and come right over to me and stooped and kissed me, yes, and then touched me – right on that place where she knows it drives me crazy and then we might have rubbed noses, which she used to quite like, and she would have whispered right into my electrified ear – Well in *that* case, Sammy, let's not *waste* it, then . . . and . . .

And. Well. That's not, no, how any of it has gone. Not a bit.

'Yes . . .' Jilly had said, quite slowly. 'There was a guy at the bar. His name is Rollo. He looked at me. I looked at him.'

'Uh-huh. Right . . . Well that's . . . OK . . .?'

'No, Sammy – no. It's not OK. It's not OK at all.'

'Isn't it? Really? Not OK? Well – why, Jilly? Why not OK?'

'Because . . . because I *like* him, OK? I really *like* him, Sammy.'

'Right . . . uh-huh . . . OK . . .'

'*Not* bloody OK, is it! Stop saying it's *OK* – OK? *Not* OK, Sammy, so bloody stop saying it *is*.'

'Right, right – OK – I mean *right*, not OK: right. Well look, Jilly – I'm a bit . . . I mean – you want to *talk* about it? Do you?'

'Not really.'

'Right. Well fine.'

'It's *not* fine. It's *not*. Of *course* we've got to talk about it.'

'Right . . . well . . . oh God: I've completely run *out*, Jilly – I can't say 'fine' and it's not 'OK' . . .!'

'*Look*, Sammy – just look: I'm not saying there's anything *wrong* with you, am I?'

'Uh – no. I didn't actually think . . . well *is* there – ?'

'No. But. Well . . . oh *look*, Sammy, it's all this *saving* business and always being *sensible* all of the time – it's frankly been driving me *crazy*, you know? I mean look – we've been cooped up on this bloody ship for just ages and *ages* and we never *do* anything and – '

'But we're docking soon – aren't we, Jilly? And – '

'Yeh we're *docking* soon – sure. But it's not going to make a bloody bit of *difference*, is it? Huh? I mean, what? In New York we load on another twenty tons of booze and then we sail off to, oh God . . . we sail away to – oh *Jesus*, I can't even remember where it is we're even going to, now – !'

'Jamaica. But listen, Jilly – '

'Jamaica – right. And all the way there – what? Pouring drinks and saving money and going to bed early with a couple of chambermaids!'

'I thought you said you quite liked them – ?'

'Oh shut up and *listen* to me, Sammy, will you? You're just not *listening*. And we get to Jamaica, OK – and then what? Go on, Sammy – you tell me.'

'Well – long haul home, then.'

'You've left out bits, though, haven't you Sammy? Hm? It means *not* doing the clubs in Jamaica – just like we didn't even *see* New York – and then humping on *more* bloody crates of drink and then *pouring* the bloody things all the way back to England. And in England, Sammy – in England, right? What's going to happen to us then?'

'Well you *know* that, Jilly – we've been over all that – '

'Yeh I know – but what's *actually* going to happen is that according to *your* famous plan we're going to go to some building society and plank down all our savings and ask for a mortgage so we can buy our sodding little house with those sodding little *things*, what are they? All around the sodding door. Flowers! But do you know what he's going to say, the man in the building society? *Roses*, I mean. Well do you? I'll tell you – he's going to look at our pathetic little heap of money – and that's all it is, Sammy, despite the fact that we've been *saving* and *saving* and *saving* for just, oh God – *ever*, what we've actually got is just so *sad* . . . and he's going to say *No*. Just like that. Because unless we want a *stable*, or something, we're just not going to *get* a mortgage, are we? And do you know what you'll say to me then?

What you'll do then, Sammy, is you'll turn round to me and say Oh never *mind*, love – and then suggest we, Christ – I don't know, redouble our *efforts*, or something – and that means I'll be working at *two* bloody bars and you'll be minicabbing all through the night and even *that* could go on for years, couldn't it Sammy? And during those years, do you know what's going to happen? Two things – two things, Sammy: One – the bloody houses are going to get more and more and more expensive, and Two: we'll be getting . . . *older* . . . for no good *reason*. I don't . . . *want* to save my money, Sammy. Don't *want* to pool it with yours. Don't don't *don't* want to watch it *grow*. I want to *spend* it, Sammy – every penny, as I get it. And then I want a whole bloody fistful of credit cards so I can run up debts all over the bloody place, just like *real* people do. Yeh. That's what I want. I want nice things and I want *fun* . . . and I want them *now*. Because why *not*? I'm *young*, aren't I? Yes I am. And that's not, is it, Sammy . . . it's just not at all the sort of girl you *meant*!'

Sammy just looked at her (I am willing my eyes to stay wide, or else my sadness will glaze them over and then they'll fill up and then – oh worse – they'll empty before her).

'Jilly. We can *talk* about this – !'

And Jilly just threw up her arms, then, and really let him have it:

'What do you think in fuck's name I'm *doing*?'

Sammy plucked at the fringe of his could be bedspread.

'It's nearly,' he said softly, 'time for my shift.'

Jilly nodded. 'Well go to it.'

'Can't we . . .? Wouldn't you like to make love . . . maybe . . .?'

She tossed her head with petulance as well as irritation.

'Can't. Period.'

'Well . . . let me just hold you, then . . .?'

'You'll be late, Sammy. Just go, yes?'

'You want me to? I mean – now? I've still got, I don't know – half an hour, maybe?'

And Jilly swung over to him her brimming eyes – and even as they seemed to be begging someone to smash apart the rough-sawn and makeshift crate that has been hastily thrown up around Sammy, the flatness of her voice was nailing down the lid.

'Yes, Sammy. Please go now. I'm . . . sorry.'

He rose and nearly rushed away, shutting the cabin door firmly behind him. He continued to grasp the handle as his heaving back rested hard against the panels, and he stared the length of the strumming corridor. Right, he thought. OK, then. I'll go. I'll go and find Rollo. That's the first thing. Because only then can I bloody well *kill* the bastard.

⚓

This ship, thought David idly – ramming down into his straining waistband a stray and flapping shirt tail as he wended his way steadily up the broad main staircase, while rhythmically slapping at the banister rail – is a bit like a grown-up Toytown. Well – not *that* grown-up, really, is it? We've all just moved on to other and better toys, I suppose. But what I mean is . . . well, do you actually remember that string of kids' books at all? Noddy? First books I ever saw, probably (and not too distant in years from the last I ever glanced at – I've never been much of a reader; and no, not a doer either – but Christ, let's for Jesus sake not get into all that because I'm feeling, if you want to know, absolutely shattered – shattered, yes, but not quite shagged *out*, if you get me – and I'll tell you why in just a minute).

So anyway – those dinky little Noddy books – you *must* remember them, everyone does. They survived, I seem to recall, that inglorious period when a po-faced bunch of grey-brained losers did their best to have them banned – but all these stubborn children had the outright nerve to go on loving them (and this in the face of the fervent disapproval of the types of people they'd sooner see dead) – and bloody good too. And little Noddy's mate Big Ears, oh God yes. Not easy – can't be easy, can it, getting through life with a name like Big Ears . . . ah no, but here's my point: it wasn't, was it – *life?* No no – it was Toytown. See? Everyone had their own little house for one, there was just a single little high street with a few little shops and nothing was too far away from anything else, and nor very hard to understand. And right here and now is a for instance: back in London, following an evening such as this (and let's be honest: I have never, in all my years of lying, drinking, frittering away money I have yet to bloody earn – and always with one eye open for any chance at all of gratuitous fornication – never before have I spent an evening like this one: and I'll tell you why in just a minute) . . . well, in town, now, I'd be frantic for a cab, wouldn't I? And maybe it'd be pissing down, and I very well might have done something like, oh God – sold my jacket. There's even the danger of being mugged along the way (and bloody good luck to you, mate – you find anything left, how about we go halves?). But tonight? Well tonight I find myself safely ensconced in Toytown: I leave the young lady's flatlet . . . correction: I leave the *exceedingly* young and cheeky-sexy-drive-you-fucking-*crazy* lady's flatlet, turn to the left, up a few stairs and now just swing into the warm and brightly-lit bar, here, where I can enjoy a nightcap or so with maybe my new good friend Dwight – and the bar, inasmuch as I've gathered so far, will close its doors when and if I choose to leave. It's easy to see, isn't it, how people can become very used indeed to this sort of living? It's like those secure and custom-built estates – used to be just an American thing, but they're springing up everywhere, now (Surrey is thick with them): there are computer-operated gates and cameras and twenty-four-hour porterage and a little mall of bijou shops and a, what are they? *Fitness* centre and a restaurant and so on and . . . I don't know: people must soon, do they, imagine that this is how life has come to *be*. But just you dare step outside, mate, and you'll quickly and very decidedly find that it bloody well isn't. Which is why, after a very short while, people just don't ever step outside again. Except, maybe, in order to cross the Atlantic on a luxury liner, be met at New York by a chauffeured and air-conditioned stretch Lincoln and then on up in the elevator's vacuum to a serviced suite where the bellhops, concierges and maitre d's will with practised and apparently effortless ease assure the continued smooth running of your now unbroken stay in Toytown. Well . . . I wouldn't want to live there, but I must say this: it's a great place to visit.

So how do you think I'm feeling? A contented and conquering hero, sated if weary, and eager for a drink? Only partly. Because no – I haven't, have I – of *course* I haven't – forgotten about the detail: Nicole. (And here's one of the downsides of Toytown: when she's whole *boroughs* away, it's easier, I find, to blank her right out; here she kind of hovers, mm. Still managed it, though.) I *was* going to go to dinner. Honestly. It wasn't that I forgot all about it in the heat of the, er . . . well: you know. It was fully my intention to get back to the cabin at around, what time? Ooh – eightish, I imagine. Slip into the penguin suit – maybe even catch the tail end of Nicole discarding for the very last time the thoroughly amazing get-up in which she so recently twirled, in favour of another one – that one, maybe, four or five down in the crumpled pile that by now would be littering the room. Then dinner – why not? The food, I have to say, is really quite marvellous, you know – one of the reasons, pretty sure, my gut is frankly killing me. Doctor back in London, he said to me – get any pain, give me a call: like I say, no fantastic urgency – but better safe than sorry, yes? Yes. Well. I think it's just the food, quite honestly: gone a bit heavy on the food. Feeling a little bit peckish right this second, it's just occurred to me – which is frankly amazing, really, because I've not long eaten a lobster thermidor – whole damn thing, and it was a real big bastard, telling you. Plus an awful lot of champagne – and it does, it bloats you up, that: all the gas. So anyway – yes, as I say, it was no part of any sort of *plan* to cut all that; and the ball, yes – aware of that too. I was perfectly willing to jig about there a bit, as well – make a total prat of myself, along with everyone else: what's to lose? Because, you see – I'd be feeling *good*: with my secret inside me. I had my *girl*. I would have been fortified by that (always am – need it, need it). Plus – I go through all the motions, and Nicole is kept as sweet as you can reasonably expect, with Nicole.

But. I fell asleep. I know. And *yes*, she could've woken me, Suki, of course she bloody could. But she didn't. I asked her why she hadn't, but she just made a series of noises – you know what they're like: you get nothing out of kids. So, in consequence, I missed the lot – and I am very conscious, yes, that Nicole will be, um – how should we put this? *Displeased*, yes – that'll do for now – and that further, on this occasion she might even expect a fully-fledged *explanation*. Not unreasonable. (And as soon as I can concoct a halfway decent one, she's welcome to the bloody thing.) So I am, you see, at the moment by no means *looking* for her (understandably) but nor am I actively dodging the issue. Because it will have to be faced, won't it? Some time or another. And better, I think, if I casually, you know – *collide* with her and a group of people . . . better that, I feel sure, than if she's got me alone in the cabin, yes? Where there's no way out.

Oh looky look – there's good old Dwight, propping up the bar, as per bloody usual (I like dependable blokes). And he's alone, thank Christ – get in a couple fast, before all the yak breaks loose. And yeah – he's seen me, now: that big and fond, fleshy hand of his is raised up high and his whole great face is beaming – I can't tell you what a good warm feeling this chap gives me.

'Dave – my man! Where in hell you been? A damn big Bourbon suit you? And don't *tell* me – you ain't . . .?'

And the beam across *David's* face, now, was even bigger than Dwight's.

'I *have*, you know. All bloody evening. Bourbon's great.'

'You goddam son of a *gun*. You telling me I been doing alla the shit with a crowda *wimmin*, and you been a-humpin' that hot sweet young *fanny* . . .?'

Well, thought David: yes and no. And he'll tell you why in just a minute.

'Nicole, Dave – she is one angry lady. After your scalp. She gonna whup your ass, boy!'

'Where, um – is she? God I needed this drink . . .'

'Last I heard, they was all in the Casino, losing money. Charlene, she says she's gonna come get me afore my bowels, they drop out on the floor. Nicole is going – *Yeah*, and David, he better be there too. Hoo boy. Patty I tried to get to hang around some, but nah – says she's going with the gals and she'll catch me later.'

'Mm. Well – let's have a few more, then. Seems like I don't need to be sober. Who's this *Patty*, Dwight?'

'Patty you don't know. Come outta no place. Telling you, Dave – she I could maybe go right *through*, you know? She been round the block couple times, yeh sure – but I could get real acquainted with those titties of hers. Hubba hubba. But hey – hell with *that*. You gonna tell me bout this young kid, or I gotta beat it outta ya?'

David grinned slyly, while waving at the barman – who's looking (Jesus – clock that face) bloody *gloomy*. Bloody hell – they have some young kid behind the bar, they don't want to be looking like *that*. It's meant to be *fun* here, right?

'Er – two more large whatever-they-are, please.'

'Jack,' put in Dwight. 'It's good old Uncle Jack Daniel's.'

'Oh right. Well that, then. Large ones – did I say?'

'Right, sir,' said Sammy.

And he jammed the glasses with force against the twin

optics (we sell a lot of Jack Daniel's) and not for the first time, he was going *over* this: well of *course* he's not about, is he? This bastard Rollo. How did I expect to see him around, God's sake? *I'm* on duty – Jilly isn't. So where's Rollo? Hm? Where *is* the bastard? And what in hell's he *doing*?

'My tab,' grunted Dwight. 'OK, Dave – enough with the stalling, already: *give*.'

'You want to know . . .?'

'Quit it, David! I ain't fooling, now . . .'

David laughed. 'OK. I'll tell you. Here it is.'

But even as he now and with relish launched into the thing, David was quickly constructing amendments – attending already to pointing up the details of the one story he felt Dwight would most like to hear. Because the truth of the matter had come not even close to a raw and wanton seeing-to, but was almost eerily sexual in a way that had stirred him deeply, while still there fluttered in its wake those faint and featherweight strands of confusion. And he'll tell you why right now:

I went along to the cabin (on-oh-one-oh – yes, one-oh-one-oh: I hadn't forgotten it, of course I hadn't forgotten it) and I was thinking . . . mm, exactly *what*, I wonder? Because I really do want to get this right. I need to chart my feelings and actions just as they hit or happened to me, because although I'll be – yes I will – spinning out countless *versions* all down the years – and usually when taken and then stunned by drink, I have no doubt at all, and to some other puffed-out and teetering slump of incoherence long past the power of even *half* listening to any of it, the following day's erasure of his memory not much less than total . . . yeah, despite the fact that I'll forever for the sake of my idiot audiences be putting a devilish spin on this thing (and even right now, as I'm tailoring it for Dwight) the way I set it down here for myself has just got to be *right*, because this is what I, me (myself), will eternally be looking back on and taking apart and piecing back together again – so it's got to be (unlike the distended, lit-up and bespoke job that right now Dwight is, oh God you should just see him, lapping up like a sun-parched hound dog) totally true and utterly accurate. This, as I say, is for me – and yes, I suppose, it's for you as well.

So I'm where, now? Oh yes. At the door. At the door, yes, and my knuckles are raised and eager to make the connection. And then I go chilly . . . I don't mean I suddenly felt anything like *windy* (because I suppose I was that all along). No, it was just like a draught – a quick and icy, well . . . *chill*, it was a chill, that had come from nowhere and wrapped me up. What if – what if I'm about to be a walk-on in entirely the wrong . . . a different *film*? Hey? I mean – it's got to be addressed, this: dignity is at stake here, you know – and mine is as frail as a spat-upon tissue. So what if I'm all kitted out as the marshal in a Western, and I barge on through these swing saloon doors and find myself, I don't know – on the set of *Brief Encounter* (hissing steam and big regret)? What I'm meaning is . . . oh *look*, it's not as if I thought that behind that door there would not be just some sweet and maybe coked-up and toothy American chick hell-bent on, Jesus – whatever fun I can possibly give her – but instead some bloody-lipped pick-wielding maniac: *no*. It's not windy, I was feeling – but maybe: stupid, it could have been. Yeh – it could, it could: it could easily have been that. That would explain the chill factor earlier – I always feel cold whenever (quite often) I stand on the threshold of doing or saying or just *being* something stupid, and horribly well aware that there can, by my own warped reasoning, be no turning back. In a *word* . . . what if she hadn't meant it, hm? What if she'd just *said* it? Or what if she had, OK, meant it – meant it, anyway, to some or other degree at the time she said it, but now, well, the moment has passed? Or what if *yes*, she meant it – but had almost instantly completely forgotten having said a single word? So that not only was she not, now, expecting me but was not even on the other

side of this cabin door at all, but was off and frisky elsewhere, with someone else entirely? And the worst, the
worst . . . what if she had said it to me, as she did, with
the eye-flashing cockiness of one so young and cool, but
was all the while and deep inside her – laughing her head
off at this old and dumb and half-cut Englishman who
really did seem to believe that I could actually view him as
anything but the, like, most saddo and gross-out *joke*? Well
yes. What then? So suddenly chilled is what I was feeling.
And then I knocked the knock. And this was the first thing
Suki said to me as she (immediately) opened the door:

'You're late. David, you're late. I wondered if you'd
come.'

Yeah well, thought David – sorry: I've been standing
outside here for quite a while, just squeezing in a very quick
coronary. You know what, though – she looks, I don't know
(*can't* be, can she?) really pleased to see me! So OK, then:
step over the little doorstep thing, that's the first, uh – step,
and let's just see what happens next. (God, though – she
looks *so* young, Suki – reminds me in a way of . . . but no,
let's maybe not go down that route, hey? Jesus. I wonder
why I'm here.)

'I didn't think you'd, like – really want a cocktail, so I got
none. Come sit with me, David.'

And David did that – quite meekly, and despite the chasm
of decades between them, for all the world as if here was
the kick-off to an interview for some or other very menial
position (and would he get it or would he not?). And then
to his quite winded and considerable relief, Suki put up a
hand and got this out quite quickly:

'David – before you say anything – '

Because there was nothing, absolutely, he honestly felt he
could have – not just then.

' – I gotta, like, come clean? Kay? Just so's there's no
kinda misunderstanding, here. What I'm real into, yeh is –
experimentation?'

David nodded. Uh-huh. What, I wonder, can this mean? We're about to start downing a selection of chemicals, are we? (Because with these kids, you never do really know.)

'See – I'm young, right? And I guess I'm like real eager to know all kindsa stuff. I'm used to guys hitting on me all the time, OK? And this trip, sure – one or two guys, fine: neat. But I wanna know *all* of it, David. Like today? I got it on with a *girl* . . . does that shock you?'

'No . . .' said David slowly. 'Doesn't shock me.' (Bloody pain I missed it, though.)

'And now, David – hey, c'mere. Let's, like, lie down here, huh? Now, David – I know you're attracted to me, right?'

'Um. Right.'

'OK. That's cool. But it's gotta be totally the way I want it. Kay?'

And half of David, now, was very much inclined to leave, if you want the truth (this was becoming, he felt, faintly ridiculous: he had been cast as a summoned gadget, complete with fitted plug). But as he was repeatedly nicked by the flying flash from her deep blue eyes and set to imagining the limbs and the warmth of them beneath that whatever it was thing she was more or less wearing – just a huge T-shirt is all it looked like – well *then*, sweet child, I am thinking it can be any which way you say but loose (because however you cut it, tight is always favourite). He lay beside her on just the part of the bed she had kept on patting.

'Put your arm around me, David. See – what I'm gonna do now – you listening? Yeah? What I'm gonna do is kinda curl myself up, OK? Into a ball? And you, David, you *cherish* me. OK? All you gotta do is *cherish* me. That's what I want.'

So his arm was around her shoulders, and Suki was making like a hedgehog at the threatening approach of rude humanity, and David was doing his level best (give the man his due) to summon up any recall at all that would ease him down this particular avenue: Now let me see – *cherishing*, yes – give me anything you've got on how I should *cherish*, will you, because there's a touch of hurry up on this one, and frankly I'm just a bit rusty.

The radiating heat of her body was getting through to him now, though; that, and the sweet cold smell of her hair which coated his chin, even as he blew at it. One of her hands, now, had reached up for the side of his face, and the cool insistence of her fingers – he felt them probing the stubble just under his jaw – rasping it up one way, smoothing it down the other. David wondered whether sliding his own hand down and gently cupping, prior to getting a damn good hold of, one and then both of her really very jutting if tidy young breasts might strictly fall under the banner of cherishing – but either way, now the idea had taken some sort of root, it lost no time in spreading all through him like a molten compulsion and so it just *had* to be tried – and I'm doing that now, tentative and very gingerly, and it seems OK (think I heard a small and very childlike exhalation) so I think it's all right to be a bit more insistent on that front – and yes, sure enough, he felt her hand now, softly on his thigh, and moving so slightly. Her voice came out muffled from wherever deep down it was snuggled, but the words were Stroke, Stroke – it's cool when we stroke one another, David. Caress me, yes? Make me be *cute* and feel like I'm *cherished* . . .

And a bolt went right through him. This was like at school, in the sixth form: there were girls in the sixth form, but we were always watched – they were always watching like hawks. You had to find darkish and only ever semi-secret places: the back row in the lecture hall, the damp and faintly fetid changing room while fools were playing sport – the library, in the alcove, during bogus and cobbled-up late-night study jags. And in these places, one's mad and frightened hands would roam – true exploration, for each and every find was a real discovery. My fingers wormed their way in and out and around, and hot breaths were felt and knocked out of me. The pressure of other hands on parts of me deadened by familiarity, and now so hot they could be alight – and I was scared by how fantastically engorged. Such mutuality would make us both throb: so much of our longing desperate to merge, but squirming instead with a wanton urgency as clothes were tugged at with panted-out impatience and our very soul and guts were kneaded and urged on pitilessly into such quivering and throat-stopping convulsions of something too overwhelming and so like big pain that pleasure would have to wait until it could linger at the moment of startled subsidence. The final sigh hung around, like perfume.

And always, when David gave himself up to thoughts of the purest sex, he thought of that: the kick of snatched-at twilight touches. He didn't now know that Suki was gasping until the bouts of his own had passed away. And as he shuddered impossibly and an aching delight made him tense and then fabulously useless, Suki had moaned so low and yet thrillingly, as if from deep sleep . . . Oh *Daddy*, darling: just *cherish* me, won't you! And a bolt went right through me: shut my eyes and held her so tight, so tight – and still she clung and scrambled for me to hug her even closer. Later, we fed one another lobster and champagne. I drifted into sleep. And this, then, is our bedtime story.

⚓

And now, as I wind up another and quite alternative fable, I smile at Dwight and take a smug and manly, quite proud swig of Bourbon. And Dwight is alight – just take one look at him. The deep and fleshier parts of his face and bulging throat – usually crimson and dryish – are now quite purple with a could-be healthy (doubt it) sheen. His lips are wet, too: might be Bourbon, might be drool – most likely a late-night bar blend of both of those, with maybe spittle too.

'Hot *damn*!' he let loose, after a suitably awed and respectful silence had risen like a cloud, and gently floated back to earth. 'You done mounted that hot little pussy *how* many times, you dang mustang?'

David shrugged. 'Told you. Lost count. Let's have another one – yes, Dwight? Before the wives are upon us.'

But Dwight still wallowed in the ooze of his daze.

'Hot *damn*...! Hot *damn*...!' And then he was thoughtful: 'Hey – square with me now, Dave. You mind one time you said this little chick might be persuaded to, uh – put out elsewhere? This hold good?'

And that made David think. And what he thought was:

'No. I don't think so, now – no, Dwight. Sorry.'

And Dwight was eyeing him.

'You wouldn't be holding out on me, would you David? I mean – we're buddies, right?'

'Oh yeh – *course*, Dwight: *course*. I just ... well, now I, um – know her a little bit better, yes? I just don't think she's that kind of girl. That's all.'

Dwight grunted. 'Sure *sounded* like that kinda girl ... What's her name, anyways? This horny little cat.'

'Her name? oh yeah – you'll *love* her name, Dwight. It's so damn sexy! She's called ... oh *Christ*, Dwight – I think that's –!'

'What? What's bugging you? What is it, Dave?'

And David's eyes were narrowed into dread as he surveyed the distance. Slowly, the muscles in his face eased back into no more than their customary orange alert.

'It's OK ... sorry, Dwight: it's OK. I just thought I saw Nicole, there, that's all. Wasn't her – someone else. Not really quite ready for her, not yet. You get that, do you? With Charlene?'

'Jeez. All the fuckin' time. Mostly can't stand the sighta her, you want the plain truth here, David.'

David nodded. 'So why do we stay with them? Mm? I mean – it's surely not the *sex* any more. Is it ...?'

'*Kidding* me. Don't knows I'd even find it iffin I was looking.'

'Yeh. It's a bit like that with me.'

And Dwight is saying some other damn stuff, now, but I honestly can't be listening to that because I'm suddenly all full of these things that I've maybe been stamping down hard on for years and years and years. Could be why I'm so bloody stressed out. And that doctor of mine – he keeps on asking me, silly old sod, what can be causing all this . . . what? Hyper-something, he says. Try not to bring your work home with you, he goes. Right, I say. Which is why for over a year I never left the office till way after ten, sometimes later. Then I was so strung out I lay awake all night, just cringing away from the morning. Ah *yes*, he said when I told him that: you have built up a sleep debt, you see. And like any other debt (and this was hardly a brilliant route to be taking, was it? Reminding me of all my *other* bloody debts: Christ, if he'd taken my blood pressure at the time, the fucking machine would've blown into pieces) . . . yes, like any *other* debt, he was going, it has to be *serviced*: try to pay off a little every night. Yes, I said: yes fine, I'll do that. I reckon we'll be all square in about a hundred and thirty years time – call you then, will I? Let you know how I'm getting on?

No no – the way I reckon it (and suddenly, as I say, it's all over me, this) the reason I am the way I am is because I'm just so fucking *miserable*. Simple as that. I mean, look – Nicole: she despises me, doesn't she? It's as clear as day. And so does Rollo. Once I told him – *Look*, Rollo, I said: it's no good always *sneering*. I'm your *father* – I'm supposed to be a role model for you, here. Yeh? he goes: *yeh*? Well if you're a role model, Dad, then this is one play I just don't want a part in. Mm – very nice, isn't it? Your one and only son. Marianne? Well yes – she's my own little girl, and she loves me, I know she does . . . but it's uphill *work* for her, isn't it? Poor kid. I mean – I don't give her much to *go* on, do I? She's always in a position of having to defend me against Rollo and her mother and often, well – I'm just so *indefen-*

sible. So what I mean is – get *out*: why not? I mean – who's going to suffer? No one. And who will gain, with me out of the way? Well – *everybody*, conceivably. But failing everybody – *me*. Yeh me. And that's got to be important too, hasn't it? It's not *just* other people? And OK – say I go: *where* do I go? Hm? Well yes – up till now, there has only been one alternative: Trish. And the trouble with Trish is, she wants me so *badly* – I sometimes think she'd go to any lengths, Trish – and of course that frightens me to death, doesn't it? The thought – just the thought, it suffocates me utterly. Sex, of course (whatever she says), is good. Well *sex*, of course – is *all*, let's face it. She loves it, lately, when she, you know – suckles me: she likes that a lot. (Bloody hell. I don't quite know what's happened to sex, just lately: seems like we're all back to playing at Mummys and Daddys . . .)

'You know what someone told me one time, Dave?'

And David was back in the bar, with Dwight. Took advantage of these few waking moments to get in another order for drink.

'What's that, Dwight?'

'Guy says to me – whatever he got, a man ain't finished till he got a woman right by him for ever and ever. And you know what I told him?'

'What did you tell him, Dwight?'

Dwight wagged his head, and raised up soulful eyes to David.

'I told him you're *right*, mister. When he got a woman right by him for ever and ever – it's *then* he's fuckin' finished.'

David widened his mouth into silent mirth, as his shoulders jogged along with the thing. But now I'm thinking this: one word Suki used has stayed with me since. She asked me at some point – not long before I left, she said to me Hey, David – how are you *rinsing* it? Well – didn't know what she was *talking* about, naturally enough, so I just stumbled out lamely some sort of idiocy or other . . . but it's just that *word*, you know? Rinsing. Isn't it *fresh*? Why don't I just pull out all the tangles and matting and slunge away all of the deep-down grime and stand there clean and new and dripping and *rinsed*? New York City. I am, right now, not much more than a couple of days away. New York is *famous* for new beginnings, isn't it? They ask no questions there – and anyone can be *anybody*. And Suki, you know – she lives in New York. She was telling me. And Dwight – didn't he say? How many seasons ago? That he could maybe help me out? Well why *don't* I, then? Because look – Dwight's my *buddy* – and back in London, I don't really have any of those (just a few people I work against and fall over with). So I could be in the most exciting city in the world with not just Dwight but . . . is this too crazy? *Suki*. (No come on – don't laugh. Maybe I could get really good at cherishing her – and who knows? Could be she even comes to not too much mind about that side of things?) Which somehow put into his head the word 'suckling' again. And then he thought of breasts. And so he whistled this up:

'You know what, Dwight? You know why it is I think I like *breasts* so much?'

Dwight chortled. 'On accounta they're *there*?'

'Well *yes* – yes, there is that side of it, mm. But mainly, I'm just thinking – could it be this? Because I was bottle-fed.'

Dwight blinked into David's impassive face.

'As a baby,' he clarified.

And then he looked down and deep into the dark and tawny swirls of his latest jigger of Jack.

'Well,' he concluded, half suppressing a quasi-rueful bit drunk snort, 'still *am*, I suppose, in one way. Really.'

↧

Nicole was still just staring down at the green baize roulette table, her face set as if by plaster into this new and seemingly unbendable expression; it was as if a good many of the bones there had been hurriedly set upon by a band of brigands and efficiently broken and then with coolness even more hastily reset into this stark and alien configuration: her cheeks were hoisting her lips well clear of her teeth, and it seemed as if her eyelids would never close again. It appeared as if Nicole had been strung out to dry on a clothes line, and was suspended tautly and maybe forever between the twin poles of horror and fascination. You see, what it was . . . was that she simply could not *understand* it – but nor could she cease attempting to *crack* this; a repulsion was heading her off, but still she ducked it and cunningly wormed her way back in: she could not let it alone.

'Maybe enough already, Nicole. What say?'

This was Charlene – partly in the sorry light of the stack of chips that was so frequently being raked away from Nicole by a wholly bored and unsmiling croupier, but largely because she was heartily sick of just standing there and watching it happen. My Dwight – he has phases when he hits the tables: two, three days I don't see him. Then he storms back home yelling out stuff like *Hey*! What in hell sorta patsy they take me for, huh?! Yeh yeh – I don't mind too much, you know? Like, time to time, Dwight – he can afford it; Nicole I ain't so sure. Plus with Dwight, when he's in a casino he lays off the soss – says he don't wanna – get this – 'blunt his *edge*'? Yeh right. I'm like, what – you have to be *sober* to lose a thousand bucks on the roll of a dice? This you can't pull off so good when you're *smashed*? Jeez: *guys* – go figure. But times like that, leastways I can pre-shate the vacation he's giving to his bowels. One time I says to him Dwight, honey – come the time you're dead and gone, I mean to donate those bowels of yours to science, you hear me? He says Sweetheart – there ain't no science on the good Lord's earth is gonna wanna touch 'em. Way he's headed, he could sure have something there; what you gonna *do* with a guy like that?

'Just one more spin,' said Nicole, distractedly – in her

new and other-worldly and really rather spectral voice. 'Then we'll go.'

Where had Charlene heard that before? She turned now to Patty – her knuckles pale and rigid as she gripped the edge of the table, her eyes very wide and glassy as she compulsively stared at some given, fixed and distant spot.

'How you doing, girl? Maybe you'd best go lie down?'

'No no,' protested Patty, with a faint but gritted determination. 'I'll see this out. Got to *conquer* it, yes? Can't let it beat me. I just can't seem to forget that we're *moving* . . . and I feel so utterly foolish because I seem to be the only one on the entire *ship* . . .'

'Don't let it bug you. Maybe we drag away Legs Diamond, here, and go down the Black Horse? Get them to fix you up something for your stummick.'

The mention of the word stomach was maybe not great: Patty reclenched her fingers doubly hard on the table's rim, as if its jealous owner was bent on wrenching it from her.

'I just don't *believe* it . . .' came the now too familiar and wistful exhalation from Nicole. 'I mean it doesn't seem to have *heard* of the law of averages, this bloody table. I've bet on red, now – what? Five times in a row, and every single time it's come up black. I mean I just can't *believe* it . . .'

'So *leave* it already! C'mon, Nicole – enough, yeh? Let's go get our men and call it a day, huh?'

'Just one more spin,' said Nicole, quite measuredly. 'And then we'll go.'

To the left of Nicole, a fairly harassed-looking man – his bow tie undone, shirt collar grimy – was earnestly assuring his maybe new and possibly impressionable companion (as he laid down three thick square and redly mottled chips on 22) that he never ever, whatever the circumstances, granted an interview or sanctioned pictures.

'Oh really? Why's that then?'

The man hissed out his frustration as the croupier raked in his three thick square and redly mottled chips from 22.

'Hm? Oh, well . . .' And suddenly he was crushed. 'Never actually been asked to, basically.'

'I just don't – *believe* it!' went Nicole – who had heard not one word of that, nor of anything else around her. 'This time it's come up – did you *see* that? Red! I've been betting on red all this time and I finally change to black and now it's come up bloody red! I just don't *believe* . . . I just can't – !'

Charlene shook her head, and maybe not in sorrow. She was taking Nicole quite firmly by the arm, now – gently tugging her away (cos iffin I don't physically remove this momma, she gonna be here till *dawn*, you know?). The very bored croupier – who had a nearly moustache – eyed them with disinterest as he racked up great clacking banks of chips into brass-bound square boxes, and then – sidelong to his mate – he came out with this, from nowhere:

'Funny thing is, the first thing they say, these bimbos, right? You've laughed like a drain at all their crap jokes and they're well away to sticking the best part of a bottle of vodka down their throats and they turn round and they say *Here* – I'm not just some *bimbo*, you know! Which apart from being a right pain in the arse has just got to be a bloody *joke*, hasn't it? I mean – what's bloody *wrong* with them at all? Hey? I mean – they *are* just bimbos, aren't they? That's the whole bloody *point*. Or am I missing something subtle?'

'Yeh . . .' nodded his mate. 'Nah. Right.' And then more loudly, though with equal flatness: 'Madam Ate May Sue-Fate Vo Jew, Silvoo Play!'

'C'mon, Nicole. We split, yeah?'

Nicole just stared at the table. Still seemingly transfixed, she nodded slowly and with misery – but at least, thought Charlene, she was nodding, right? Now I got two dames I godda gedda holda by the arm and steer real careful on outta here – one because she's noshus to her stummick (and hoo boy – wait till this baby starts making like a roller-coaster: what's lil Patty about to do then, huh?) and the other one, well – on account of she's just some kinda nut, I guess.

The entourage inched its way with faintly ludicrous care past a couple of women feeding these two huge and lit up clanking slot machines as fervently as a thrush with a whole can of worms might gorge to the point of satiation and beyond the limitless cravings of its nestful of fledglings. The chrome-pillared swivel stool of one of them was just about coping, while the other woman had opted for a neighbouring pair.

'I've got thirty dollars left,' said one. 'Then it's midnight snacks, I think.'

'The trouble I think here is not the food but the *menu*. All this *pan* fried this and *oven* roasted that . . . I mean, how *else* are you supposed to fry things? Hm? And what do you think you're going to roast something in? A handbag?'

Charlene was checking the condition of her charges (here I go again – a full-on nurse): Patty had tottered to a halt, and her hand was flailing about her for something unyielding to grip and then hug for ever. Charlene wasn't about to release her hold on either one of them, though, for even so much as a second: Nicole would be back to that table at the speed of one greased and electric jackrabbit – and Patty, she could fall down and die on me.

'That *word*,' continued one of the women on the slots. 'That word 'handbag'. It's funny, but whenever I hear it, I always think of that line in some – do you know it? Some play or other – terribly famous. When somebody drawls out that word: 'a hand*baaaaag*?' Yes? Bernard Shaw or Shakespeare or something. I think it's supposed to be funny, but I've honestly never understood *why* . . .'

And as Charlene, Nicole and Patty finally made their enforcedly leisurely break for the corridor, they maybe did or didn't witness the second woman turning with some difficulty towards her companion and uttering in mystified tones:

'I honestly haven't the faintest idea what you're *on* about . . .'

And gee – Charlene couldn't barely get herself around it: Nicole, she gets outta that there casino and *zingo* – it's just like that she's Nicole again, you know?

'And *David*,' Nicole said suddenly, and with all the old determination. 'He'd just better not be – hey, Pat! We don't need the lift. Come on – we can walk down, yes? It's only . . . yes, Charlene – I'm just saying. That *husband* of mine – *if* he's seen fit to reappear at all – he'd just better for once be *sober*.'

'If he's with my Dwight – forget it, honey.'

'Oh God – David doesn't have to *be* with anyone. You could lock him in a wine cellar and years later he'd still be perfectly happy down there just *drinking* it. No willpower, men – just can't tear themselves away. You OK, Pat? Bit OK?'

'I think I might've been better,' faltered Pat – gripping with both hands the banister rail – 'in the lift, actually. But yes – if I can just not look down . . .'

'Your husband like mine, is he Pat?'

She smiled quite sadly. 'Yes. I'm afraid so. Exactly the same.'

Now the three of them were hard by the mouth of the Black Horse, and Nicole was aware of a familiar discomfort: the pubby hot breath of it.

'Well God help us all, is all I can say . . .' is frankly all she felt she could say.

⚓

Sammy was clenched by frustration at just having to *be* there – it was somewhere hard and deep within him, this balled-up resentment, like a tumour in his guts (because how could he? Well? Tell him. Go on. How could he find out for sure just what Jilly was doing if he could not leave this place? If he had to be bloody *here*?). All the other useless bits of him, though, seemed flaccid and washed over by a barely lukewarm and humdrum misery. He stood well back from the bar (his back now causing the liqueur bottles to clink and tinkle) – as far away as he could get from the increasingly drunk and lewd and stupid bloody English bloke and that fat American guy alongside of him (their capacity for drink was little short of startling – in common, therefore, with most of my loyal and faithful band of regulars, all the soaks and lushes; well – I say *capacity*: it's not as if either of these two was *holding* it, or anything). But this far away from the pair of them means that it's impossible, now, to avoid the ramblings of yet another and this time solitary loser practically collapsed across the bar, here, just to the left of me. At least the bloody Japanese have packed up croaking out into that uproarious microphone their Fab Four medley of not just Flom Me To You and Prease Prease Me, but also half-hearted (and rich with botched-up lyrics) smatterings and then more lusty choruses of Penny Rain and Paperback Lighter (and let's not of course forget the Yerrow Submaline). So what I'll do is, I'll just continue, will I, polishing and polishing this perfectly sparkling beer glass, and try to blank out at least the most repetitious and drivelling parts of it – while not imagining, not even beginning to picture (let alone frame) just what it might be that Jilly was right this second, oh Christ – *up* to. With that person. Who tomorrow, during my break, I must track down and, well – if not actually *slay* him, then certainly break and bruise serious parts of, conceivably with a view to disfigurement. This just must be done. Obviously.

'Telling you, Sammy . . . *Telling* you . . . you just mark my words . . .'

Sammy smiled, just about. The demolished loner had risen for air – air, yes, and of course a refill. He had been telling Sammy for quite some while – insisting that he mark

271

his words (most of which comprised the admonition to mark them, yes, and mark them well).

'Truth is . . . truth is . . . there's a book to be written here, you know – a book, book – yes a book. And you, Sammy – are you having a drink with me, my friend? Sammy? Yes? Drink for you? No? Sure? Well OK. Sure now? Yes? OK. Yes – you mark my . . . uh . . . you mark my . . . uh . . . and *you're* the one to write it, Sammy. The things you must see and hear, hey? *Words*. You mark them well, uh – Sammy. This ship – not kidding you. Book to be written – amazing nobody's done it before. Sure I can't twist your arm? No? Sure? Well OK.'

Oh look – a bunch of women are coming over to the bar, now. Is Jilly among them? Well what do *you* think? Oh God – I'll never get away, will I, tonight. And one of the women – oh Jesus: swaying badly. The other two more or less holding her up, seems like. Marvellous. Add her to my tally of incoherents and incapables: chuck her on the heap.

'See . . .' rambled on the rambler – making to wipe at wildly his wet and uncontrollable mouth, and missing by a long chalk – 'a writer's life must be very . . . all right. I'd do it myself, only I had the time. I'm in *paper*, Sammy – paper, me. Wholesale side. Not a bad living. I'm not saying it's a bad living. But your name on a book – that'd be something, wouldn't it? Hey? Sammy? That'd . . . wouldn't it? Be something.'

'Get you ladies anything?' enquired Sammy, braving it out in the face of their concerted and very determined approach.

'Dwight,' said Charlene. 'Shift your butt. We're outta here. You been eating those macadamias?'

Dwight nearly stirred.

'Charlene. Macadamias I ain't had.'

'Come on, David,' sighed Nicole. '*Can* you walk? Just lean here. Pat. You'll be fine. Do you want an Alka-Seltzer, or something?'

'Trouble *is*,' broke in the man of paper. 'Trouble *is* – if you're a *writer*, let's face it – well, you've got to *write*, haven't you? Stands to reason . . .'

'*So*,' put in Sammy, quite doggedly. 'Nothing I can get you?'

'Which *is*,' crashed on the relentless and jackknifed derailment of his train of something less than thought, ' . . . whichever way you look at it . . . a hell of a fucking stumbling block, isn't it? Fundamentally.'

Nicole, now, was at first squeezing, then maybe slightly pulling at, and very soon quite viciously jerking back on David's shoulder (Jesus Jesus – when he gets like this it's like, Christ, he's been cemented down. He just won't move – I'm not even sure he is aware of what I am doing to him, and it can only now be just this side of a dislocation).

'Yeh yeh,' said David darkly. 'Yeh yeh yeh . . .'

And Nicole's concentration upon her immutable husband – this awful thing in hand – was momentarily distracted by the sort of deep and underlying but still very horribly audible sound that you really never wish to hear hissingly rumble from somewhere profound and unthinkable within the rebellious organs and cavities of another.

'Oh God, Pat . . .' she stuttered with caution. 'You look just *awful* . . . here, sit here. Barman – have you got maybe an Alka-Seltzer or something, yes?'

Like hippos at the bogside, Dwight and David had begun to lazily stir, just about detectably (and the raised up eyebrows, downturned mouths and rueful glances were just between themselves).

'Here, Patty – here,' said Charlene – moving around the nearly dissolved and gushing tablets with a briskly swishing finger. 'You just get yourself around this baby, and you'll be fine, girl.'

'I'm OK . . .' Pat barely croaked out – which put the fear of God into just everyone who heard it, and none more so than Sammy. Dwight was standing – legs well apart – and

Charlene was dabbing at the corners of his mouth with the folded-in edges of a hastily licked-at handkerchief. David too was turning, now, and as he did so, he tried his best to focus. And then he focused. And then much to her own astonishment, Pat was just at that second convulsed by a huge and unstoppable assertion of no less than the whole of all her insides, and the instant eruption was not just gutturally raucous and very dreadfully copious, but of truly spectacular duration. David stared down at his obliterated shoes and well-speckled trousers. And then he looked back at the woman in front of his wide and then closed-down eyes with a gaping disbelief. Sammy (oh *God*, oh *God* – will this bloody day never *end* . . .?) and Nicole were fussing about with bar towels and cloths and rolls of paper, and neither was liking it a bit.

'This is, I know,' sighed Nicole, 'hardly the moment for *introductions* . . . but David – this is *Pat* . . .'

'Here, Patty,' clucked Charlene. 'Sip at this water, OK?'

'Or,' amended Nicole, 'Patty. Which is it. Pat? Pat or Patty? Are you feeling a little bit better? Yes? Little bit?'

'*Yes* . . .' agreed the newly rosy and bright-eyed Pat or Patty. 'I suddenly feel remarkably *OK*. As to my name – oh God, I'm so sorry, everyone. Awfully sorry! As to my name, Nicole . . .' And now she met David's blank and fearful eyes head on ' . . . well actually, most people call me *Trish* . . .'

Because *yes*, Nicole, she was wickedly thinking: I do have a husband of my own, you see – and he is, as I said, exactly the same. The only real problem here is that he happens to be – technically speaking – yours as well, at the moment, you bloody *wife*. But not, maybe now, for too much longer.

PART FOUR

Deep Waters

I'm pretty sure that Tom, thought Marianne, is the sort of person who'll be terribly punctual, so nine a.m. on the Boat Deck means, I should think, exactly that: no more and no less. Which is fine – I've got a couple of minutes in hand and I'm just about, what – half a corridor away? Not much more. And from what I can see of the weather, it looks like it's going to be another glorious day. I don't know what the Captain was going on about the other night – maybe he *was* joking, do you think? I mean, surely their . . . whatever they have – I don't know, instruments, computers, however it's done: they can't say Uh-oh – storm brewing, no question, and then it just *doesn't* . . . can they? So maybe it was just some sort of rather heavy-handed and not very witty *joke*; well if it was, he certainly got a lot of people wholly needlessly worried – which isn't really, is it, quite what a Captain should be *for*.

My God. Look at this! Wonders will never . . . no . . . no – it can't be, can it? Not at nine o'clock in the morning? Can't be. But – God – it *is*, you know, it jolly well is. God Almighty – can't believe it.

'Dad! Hey, Dad! Where are you rushing off to? How amazing to see you up so early.'

David whirled round to face whatever new and fearful thing *this* could be now, and managed to leap into the air as he did it – this the reaction to some grossly invasive though as yet unspecified terror that already was done with softening him up, and now was earnestly working him over.

'Hm? *Hm*? Oh, *Marianne* – hello, hello. Yes. Hello.'

'What *is* it, Daddy? You look *awful*. Couldn't you sleep?'

'Hm? *Hm*? Sleep? Don't know. Haven't tried. I've just, uh

– well yes, you see – I'm not so much up *early* as, um – still up from yesterday, if you see what I mean.'

Marianne nodded, quite sadly. 'Yes, Dad. I see.'

'Well you probably *don't*, actually – it's not, well . . . it's not the *usual*, if that's what you mean. It's just that I've had one or two, um – *surprises*, really . . . yes . . .'

'You haven't shaved. You sure you're OK?'

'Yes, I am. Of course. And no, you're right – I haven't.'

No. Haven't shaved. Went down to the cabin to *change*, very rapidly – and it's a, Jesus! Small old world, isn't it, really? I mean – did I for one minute imagine I'd wind up the evening not just sipping with Dwight but coated pretty much from head to toe in my mistress's vomit? That is my mistress *Trish*, you see – who is actually back in London, isn't she? Because I never ever take her *anywhere*, do I? So it can't, can it, have really been her? Can it? Well yes it *can*, actually – yes indeed: it was, oh yes – no mistake. Which means, then (doesn't it?), that she isn't, is she, as we speak back, in fact, in London? Yes yes – these are, it would seem (and not just on the surface) very much the facts of the matter. Trish is in fact a happy little tripper on the *Transylvania*, along with me and my children and of course my bloody *wife* – and on board too is a rather lovely young American girl who I just must find a moment for when I've sorted through these little local difficulties because she *craves*, do you see, to be *cherished*. OK? Good. I'm glad we've got all that in order. Oh my God. Oh my *God*. I think I'll lose my *mind* . . .

And shaving? No – didn't linger for that, because Nicole, you see (still unaware of this latest little time bomb, far as I can tell – certainly she hasn't *knifed* me yet), would have started up with her eternal commentaries interlarded with a more general and all-encompassing salvo of denigration, spiked by ridicule – and so what I had to do was peel off all these very deeply offensive and now quite crusty and gag-making clothes (and dump them where, exactly? Well –

Nicole can see to that) and then have a very rapid shower and then I'll just slip on this polo shirt, yes – this one will do – and these grey trousers, excellent, excellent, and deck shoes, yes fine, and now I'll just ram all my stuff into a jacket, jacket, jacket – um, this jacket, yes, and – *what*? What did you say, Nicole? *Not* this jacket? Why, in fact, not this jacket, actually, Nicole? Oh I see. I see – yes. Yes I *had* failed to pick up on that point – you are perfectly correct. It is quite the wrong shade of blue for the trousers – yes, of *course*, I quite see that now, how very remiss of me: it's almost as if I've got other things on my *mind*, isn't it? Oh my *God*. Oh my *God*. What? What are you saying to me now, Nicole? The grey? The mid-grey tweed with the heathery flecks? No – didn't bring that one along with me, actually. Why? Why didn't I? Well no reason, really (well *one* reason, actually – I *sold* it, didn't I? To person or persons unknown one loud and tanked-up hubbubby night in a hot and fetid *pub* just only a very few days ago, since you ask, my sweetness – but still years and years and years before I boarded this ship and found myself on Planet *Lunatic*, of course).

'Well look, Dad – I've got to go. Seeing someone, OK? Bit late.'

David nodded quite wildly at that and was off and away, just vaguely trailing a hand in farewell. He nearly bustled and was rather peculiarly crouched – stooped over, it looked like to Marianne: as if he was either intent upon snuffling out and hauling to the light some deeply hidden thing, or else maybe ducking detection, and hell-bent on his lair. Well. That was Dad: she'd seen him weird before. Not maybe this particular *variety* of weird, it was true, but then he was rather *known*, wasn't he – poor old Daddy – for not just the breadth and scope and abundant colour that his full and ample repertoire of weirdnesses afforded, but also the subtleties of nuance that blurred the fringes bordering on each of the incarnations, all of them gloriously combining to make up the whole of the selection on offer.

And no – I wasn't wrong about Tom: as soon as I heaved open this great big heavy door, I saw him at the far end of the deck, full-length on a lounger and intent upon the sea – *swaddled*, he practically seemed, in what appeared to be far more than just the one coat and hat and scarf, but presumably that's all there was. The air – the almost maddening rush of air has stung me and I love it! You really have to hunch yourself over (bit like Dad) to have any real hope of making some headway.

'Tom. Hello. Sorry – bit late. God, what a fabulous morning . . .'

And no – Marianne saw it immediately, now: she *had*, in a sense, been wrong about Tom. He wasn't just punctual: he had been here for very possibly hours. He shaded his eyes with the flat of his hand as he raised them up to meet her – a gesture that was almost a salute, thought Marianne suddenly – and she laughingly sprang to attention and clicked her heels.

'*Duce* . . .' she said.

'Alas . . .' was the whole of Tom's rejoinder. And then, as she stood there, he came up with this: 'Here – sit. Sit with me. I have something to tell you. Something I think you should know.'

So Marianne stretched herself out on the lounger alongside (well – she had been going to do that anyway) and of course was intrigued by what Tom had just murmured (and, she somehow thought, had been rehearsing and honing and paring right down since maybe dawn, who knew? And why did she actually think that?). But as well as merely a raw and justifiable curiosity, there pawed around her consciousness a need, she supposed, to be *admitted* to Tom – quite why this should be and to what end such a state might lead her, she honestly could not have told you – but it was a tolerant need that she had kept in check and certainly never allowed to blossom into anything like a hunger, because she had not once, ever, thought it might be even appeased, let alone fed. Her eagerness to hear him out, however, was tempered by the merest squeak of fear; if what he said came close to touching her, then there would be established between them a bond – and one whose potential had surely by now been frequently and loudly touting the shadow of its presence, but had not to date revealed a chance of being forged.

This new and protracted silence, then, was vexing, now – very.

'Well . . . Tom? What is it? Hm?'

Tom glanced at her and nodded, as if to say Yes, he knew it was his cue, and thank you for the prompt, but wait – just wait, can you, for only a very few seconds longer – and then I'll let you (if you want it) have it, yes, with pleasure.

The sun was at their backs, but still the light was blinding; Marianne put on her mid-blue tinted sunglasses, and settled down to wait. With Tom, it's what you did. The sea and sky are a seamless royal and dazzling blue – the dancing spatters of gleaming, like millions upon millions of little silver fish, all swimming in formation and taking it in turns to leap up for attention, before diving back down to resume their rightful place in the vast and sparkling eternal scheme of things.

'Do you see,' he said quite suddenly – and maybe a little too quickly ' – this lifeboat above our heads?' Marianne tilted back her head to trace this thing as Tom quite blithely continued. 'Have you noticed them? You see? They're strung up there the length of the deck. Same on the starboard side too, of course. I've checked.'

'What about them? They're quite pretty, aren't they, actually? I wonder why some are red and some are white . . .? Yes – I saw them the other morning. What are you thinking, Tom? You think we're going to *sink* . . .?'

'No. No no . . . I feel very safe. *Held*, if you like. No – it simply occurred to me earlier this morning to do a little sum. Can you see from where you are sitting the lettering stencilled down the side, just there?'

Marianne slipped down the glasses to the bridge of her nose (contacts can cope with this, she thought) but no amount of socket contortion could compete with all the shimmering light, so she slid them back up again.

'What does it say?'

'It says: 'Capacity – one hundred and thirty-nine persons'. Which I quite agree – seems a lot. Looks rather a *small* boat, from down here, doesn't it?'

'God – a hundred and thirty-*nine*. I wouldn't fancy that much. Especially at night.'

'You would – you would if you were in one, and other quite desperate souls were flailing in the sea, and screaming. Screaming.'

Marianne regarded him. 'What's your point, Tom?'

'Hm? Point? Oh – hardly have one. I simply multiplied the figure by the number of boats and yes, there's adequate space for both passengers and crew. Which is a comfort. But only *barely*, mind – and one wonders, of course, whether in a state of emergency all could be successfully launched. Particularly if we were listing.'

'But Tom – you said – !'

'Oh and I *meant* it. No no. I see no danger. As I told you: I feel very safe. And of course there's *extra* space, now, because there are thirteen fewer passengers, remember, since the commencement of the cruise . . . maybe that's where they keep them. The dead ones. In the lifeboats. Quite a twist, that would be.'

And Marianne checked her impulse to laugh: is he making a joke? And also – do I find it funny?

'Mary . . .' said Tom, then. And stopped.

'Yes, Tom: Mary. Your wife . . . what is it you want to say?'

'I don't suppose . . . no. No. I don't suppose so for a minute.'

'*What*, Tom? Suppose *what*? Say it. It's OK. You can say it.'

'Well, I was just wondering. I don't suppose, Marianne – that anyone ever calls *you* Mary? Do they? I don't suppose so, no.'

'Well . . . no, Tom, no. They don't. But if you *want* to . . .'

'Hm? Oh no. Oh no. No no no. Don't *want* to – oh Lord no. Should never presume. No – I was just *enquiring*, that's all – just came into my mind to wonder whether anyone *did*.'

'Well. They don't.'

'No. Well I didn't suppose they would. No. Shall we walk a bit? Getting a wee bit stiff, just sitting here. It can get quite chilly, can't it? If you don't from time to time move around.'

But despite his stiffness, it was Marianne who seemed to be having the most trouble in extricating herself from this very low lounger (there's nothing here much one can actually get a *hold* of) and Tom reached out a hand to her. When the two of them stood facing one another, he gently released it – but as they turned their faces into the padded punch of the buffeting wind, Marianne fluidly linked one of her arms into the crook of his elbow, and then crammed both her hands deep down into her pockets. They trudged quite doggedly to the very stern of the ship, the whiplash cracks and chafing of the wind making further communication impossible for now (Marianne had tried it once or twice, and no – hopeless). Soon they were leaning against the wet and oily wooden handrail, and staring wordlessly at the churned-up torrent of roaring white water that formed their perpetual wake.

'I was here the other day!' shouted Marianne – her thin little voice snatched from her mouth even before it could make its journey: it spun away from her and was screwed up and tossed with an easy contempt – over the side, and into infinity. 'Where we are . . . it so terribly quickly becomes – where we have *been* . . .!'

And Tom now glanced at her sharply, before his expression quite slowly relaxed – and he nodded in silence for so very long that Marianne had to begin to wonder why. She turned away now from the coldly boiling sea and gasped in shock as each of the hairs on her head exerted a panicked and concerted tremendous pull on her scalp in their apparently vicious desperation to take flight, and be done with her. The terrible bulk of the black and red funnel filled her total vision: it soared far higher than even buildings need to – and it was sometimes the very vastness of just everything around her, massed and looming, suspended amid all this seemingly boundless blueness that made her cold and fearful. She wished her arm was still entwined, and warm around another.

Tom was pointing at a door and mouthing at her, she thought it could be: In! Going In! And yes . . . it was probably the time to do that, now. The warmth of inside was scalding immediately and Marianne's ears were red and burning and full again now with so much *sound*.

'Thirteen,' said Tom.

'My God! My whole face is hot and freezing!' yelped out Marianne. 'Sorry, Tom – what did you say?'

'Thirteen,' he repeated, in exactly the same flat tone. 'Unlucky for some, we feel.'

And then he spun around to face her, quite alarmingly quickly, and this, Marianne realized, was the very first time he had truly beheld her.

'I just want you to know,' he said very softly. 'About Mary. You see – I *helped* her. Helped her, yes. And now I have to go.'

And Marianne was surprised – just struck by surprise and nothing else yet as Tom just walked away from her. He made no gesture – and she had hesitated, now, for just too long to fall in step.

'See you later . . .!' she called out – and not much more than feebly, and feeling foolish as she did so. And yes – several knots of track suited people, clinking their coffee cups: *they* looked round, oh yes – but Tom walked on, regardless.

Marianne wandered in the direction of the staircase, and past the big green baize table filled with jigsaw, her mind now verging on so much thought, she couldn't begin to even, oh – *think* . . . so I'll look at the jigsaw instead. Work had been done since the last time, that much was plain to see. Yes, look – the balcony on the chalet was very nearly quite whole, and so was the chimney, with that lazy curl of smoke. And now from the clumps of completed sky, you could see that snow was falling.

⚓

The thing is, the thing is, the thing is is, um . . . oh God oh God oh God *remind* me: what's the *thing*? What's the *thing*? Oh *please* just help me a little bit, God, David was silently beseeching. At least he *assumed* it was silent, all this beseeching – but it needn't have been, needn't have been: certainly his lips were moving as he bustled down corridors and cannoned off walls and careered in and out of function rooms and bars – no *not* to get a drink, hell with drink, I'll never ever, not me, drink again – but to *find* her, track her down, get to her before she has time to assail Nicole . . . oh but God, oh God – hang on, this is silly. This is mad, this – I'm doing it all wrong. I got out of our *cabin*, right, because what would I do if Trish just took it into her bloody little head to phone Nicole and spill the whole damn cassoulet and I was just standing there and affecting oblivion while happily going along with all the fun of the mix 'n' match game, this to involve my toning separates? Or even turn *up* – quite capable, she's perfectly capable, that woman, of just turning up at the cabin door and shouting her mouth off and watching me squirm and die. Because look – face it, face it: she did not book herself on to this trip – and how did she *do* that, actually? *When* did she do that? Even when she was begging me not to go, saying how much she'd miss me . . . she'd already bloody well got hold of her *ticket*, hadn't she? Christ oh Christ – there's no *man*, is there? There's not one man on God's earth who could dream of pulling a stunt like that. Women – oh God, women. Why do we do it? Hey? Why do we ever get *involved*, at all? Hey? Well – obvious, really: *sex*. Sex is why, yes – because I tell you one thing for free, amigo: all these people (and you hear it all the time, now – people are forever saying it) – all these people who go round telling you that such-and-such a thing is better than sex . . . well what exactly are they *on* about, someone please tell me? I mean – sometimes they're *joking*, right? Like when they say Ah yes – a lovely cup of tea: better than sex. Joke, presumably (hope so, at least, or else God help them). But then you also hear people say that, I don't know – pulling off some City business deal: better than sex. Driving like a fucking lunatic in a bloody Ferrari: better than sex. Eating sodding *chocolate*: better than sex. Coming up trumps in the Lottery – yep, you got it: better than sex. The phrase has completely taken over the 'best since sliced bread' thing and all I can say is they're *mad* – nuts, completely loopy – because look, just *look*: anything on *earth* is better than sliced bloody *bread*, isn't it? I mean – *unsliced* bread, for bloody starters. But sex, well – well the whole point is that there isn't *anything* better than sex, not ever. That's why sex is sex, Christ's sake – that's the whole bloody *point* of the thing. And that's why we sniff it out and gulp it down and mortgage first and then sell wholesale our entire bloody life on earth for the sake of it and then when the hint of more and different has us twitching and lustful, then we mess up, oh – everything we have and like a missile just *go* for it, like I do. Which is how I come to fuck up. As it were. And maybe women don't feel like that, I don't know. Mind you – the new breed probably do: the ones who drink pints of Sancerre and keep renewing their lipstick between fags and tankards – they probably do (frighten the life out of me, that type, quite frankly). But people like Nicole, well . . . I should think that winning a keyring in some competition that it took her twenty quidsworth of labels from, I don't know – denture sterilizer to even amass the wherewithal to even *enter* (and yes, she did that once) . . . I should think that for her, that'd be better than sex. Or sex with *me*, anyway. And whether she knows what it's like with anyone else, well . . . honestly couldn't tell you.

But it's *Trish*, all of a bloody sudden, who's very much the point here. And that's what I was saying, wasn't it? Oh – about two or three decks and several staircases ago (I seem to have apologized to just about every single passenger *twice* for having barged into them, trodden upon their feet, caused their children to scream and bolt – and still I'm not close to tracking her *down*). But what I was *saying* is that no matter how she managed to get on this bloody ship she didn't coldly plan to do so just by way of sorting out for herself a little bit of a *break*, did she? Touch of bracing ozone, few days' *rest*? I don't really think so. No – she came here because none of the players in this little drama has any chance whatever of *escape*: she's got us, Christ – exactly where she wants us. And right *now* she's elsewhere, oh yes – because she *chooses* to be. But when she thinks the time is right . . . oh God. Oh God oh God oh God – I think I'll lose my *mind*. And now Nicole is alone in the cabin – so Jesus Jesus: that's where Trish could be too. Right now. Or maybe she's sick again – maybe it's that. Because she hates boats, Trish – always has done, terrible sailor; and that alone shows the level of her determination, doesn't it, really? So maybe she's sick. Maybe she's *dead*, yes? No – I really shouldn't think like that. But I think I will anyway: maybe she's *dead*. Yes? Because this is the thing: I don't *want* her, you know. Not one thought of that nature has so much as crossed my mind for even one second. Now admittedly, it's not much of a come-on when it's late and you're pretty well completely plastered and your wife is just hanging around and then your mistress saunters over and spews up her guts all down and over you – I mean it's not exactly one of life's Romeo and Juliet moments, is it? No – granted: fair enough. (And it's not the first time something like this has happened to me, either. One time I was at a stag party – my allocated tart spent the whole of the evening cramming down eclairs. Turned out she was, what's that thing? Bulimic. Only time I ever heard of where the bloody cake came leaping out of the *girl*. Telling you.)

But even since . . . I was sort of assuming that I'd track her down, fuck her briefly and *then* set about giving her hell or pleading for my life, whatever seemed right at the time. But no. Don't want to fuck her. Not a bit. And maybe it's been brewing for a while, this, you know: not sure. But whenever I went over to her place lately she always wanted me to comment on the *music* and swoon over the *candles* (and the scent from some of them, telling you – put you in a coma); and then I was meant to eat some sort of gourmet *meal* when I was already full to bursting with peanuts and crisps and Scotch and Scotch – and then she wanted us to share a *bath*. Well I mean – God's *sake*. Look – I did it once (quiet life) and *honestly*. It's not as if she's got one of these big marble sunken Roman efforts or anything – it's only a bleeding *bath*, Christ's sake. Yeah – and guess whose bloody spine was jammed up hard against the taps? Yes indeed; with the plug and chain snuggling up quite cosily into the cleft between my buttocks. Isn't this, she sighed – *romantic*? I frankly thought she was unhinged. Anyway – what I'm really driving at here is that it got to the stage where there was just so much to be *got* through before I could even see a glimmer of the business end of things that I started thinking Oh Christ is it really bloody *worth* it? All this? I mean – just a basic blow-job would be, oh – so much more *convenient*. (Put it to her once: she said she just couldn't go through with it – not with a straight face. What are you supposed to think? I ask you. She didn't believe, she carried on – perfectly deadpan – she didn't honestly believe that she could pull it *off*. Dear Christ.)

Right. Anyway – this is the last bloody deck she can possibly be on. Unless, of course, she's been busy going downstairs as I've been going up. Or she's with Nicole. Or sick. Or dead. Oh Christ let's *face* it – she needn't at *all* be on this deck, need she? Bloody woman. How are you supposed to actually find anyone on this fucking ship, hey? I mean – how *are* you? Case in point: every single face I have stared at briefly and instantly discarded as being the wrong bloody *one* – every single one of them was entirely new to me. Amazing. I mean – even in *London*, Christ's sake, you time to time bump into *someone* you've met before. So where *is* she? Tried her cabin, of course – buzzed her four times now, so I'm sure she's not *there*, anyway (yeh yeh – unless she's sick or dead, I know, I know). She certainly can't be outside – that'd kill her for sure (maybe worth bearing in mind). So quite possibly at this very moment, Nicole is hunting for *me* – mad, and wholly set on cutting me up and out of her life. Do I want that? do I? I do, maybe – I think I very possibly do, yes, think so. But not *this* way, no. No no – *my* way (that's the way I want it).

I wish I could go and lie down. But it wouldn't be any good. It's not as if I'd get my *rest*, or anything. Just got to sort this out, you see. But hang on, hang on – how do I actually think that confronting Trish is in fact going to sort out *anything*? Hey? I mean no matter what I say or do the bottom line is she's going to spill her, oh God – *guts* out to Nicole, isn't she? Always assuming – no, I haven't forgotten – she hasn't already done so. So why do I chase the wild goose? Maybe I should instead find Suki: lie down beside her and feel her young fingers roaming and then stirring me up and have a very quick bout of mutual *cherishing*, why not? Think that's maybe what I might . . . wait . . . wait: look. Over there. Half behind that sort of pillar-type thing with the motley mirror: in that shop. Her, isn't it? Pretty sure, yes . . . hang on – get a bit closer (kick this old woman out of my way) and let's just see . . . yes. Yes. That's Trish. She's there. Shopping. Would be.

'*Look*, you – !'

'David. Morning. I'm feeling much better, thank you. Sorry about your – you know: *clothes*, and everything. I find that the higher I am in the ship, the less sort of wobbly I feel. Which is why my cabin's such a perfect *pain*, quite frankly – the lowest of the low. Which was actually quite *kind* of me, David – you should thank me. Because I charged it to your credit card and I could easily have got a much, much nicer cabin. Closer to you and your bloody wife. What do you think of this sweatshirt?'

David gazed at the blue thing she was holding out to him. There was red and gold at its centre and it said Transylvania in white.

'Too obvious, do you think, David? Maybe one of these pastel ones . . .?'

'You *charged* the – you *charged* the – ?! Oh my God *Almighty*, Trish – you *know* I'm absolutely . . . how in hell did you charge it to my – ?!'

'Oh don't be so *silly*, David. You just read out the numbers over the telephone, it's terribly easy . . . pink one's quite nice – wonder if they've got it in medium . . . oh don't look like *that* – honestly, David: I've done it *loads* of times. Things like food and wine and candles do cost *money*, you know. I think I'll maybe just get the set of shot glasses. You like? Sweet, aren't they?'

And do you know – even as I'm yammering away at Trish (I'm going: We've got to *talk* we've got to *talk* we've got to *talk*) all I'm now actually thinking about is *money*. I just haven't, oh Christ – *got* any. Why can't people see that? It's got so that the very *word* money just scares all sorts of hell out of me. And *finance* – oh my God, that's even worse. Every morning when I go into work and I see those words Corporate Financial Consultant on my desk, oh Jesus – I practically pass out. And it's not as if I know even the first thing *about* it – Christ, I've been winging it for years (and how long can it go on? Hey? How long?). I tried to mug up on all those supplements – you know, at the weekend, all those newspaper bits with names like You And Your Money (aargh!). Not the proper grown-up *business* sections, no – not them: too scary. Also – couldn't make head or tail of them. And even the *colour* of the *FT* brings me out in a rash. But it got to the stage where I'd just be feebly fumbling and groping my way through all these pictures of smug married couples (and how the budget affected them) and Dinky Toy collectors (Mint and Boxed: Cash In Now On That Fortune In Your Attic) and then some damn bitch who'd started up a, oh Christ *I* don't know – *start*-up company, or something (can that really be *possible*?) and then all those ads with Richard Branson's fucking face plastered right across them and I'd just freeze up and glaze over, quite frankly. And once – and yes yes, I freely admit this, even for me, this was one of my more frenzied moments, seriously inclining towards the deranged – I actually thought of *writing* to him: Branson. Dropping him a line. I was going to say, Dear Mister Branson . . . or is he a Sir? Or a Lord now, maybe? Possibly just jammed at demigod level. Anyway – Dear Whatever Branson: I read a piece lately in something or other that said you are worth two billion. Good show. Jolly well done. Now look – even if you gave away just one little million of your pounds, you'd still have, um . . . (and *buggered* if I could do the bloody sum) . . . oh – *lots* left, heaps and heaps – but the beauty of this, you see, is that I'm not asking for that much, no. No no – not by a long chalk. Not even *half* that. Just say – what? Ten grand? Not much, is it? To ask. Man such as yourself? Five? Settle for five? What say? How about it? Oh go on – *pleeeeease* . . .!

Awful thing is – those days, five grand would just about have seen me square. Now . . . well: haven't a *clue*, to be honest. Can't look at the bits of paper, you see. Just can't do it. I simply owe *everybody* – that's all I know. And now I owe a bloody shipping line as well, apparently. Oh God oh *God* . . . I think I'll lose my *mind* . . .

'Talk about *what*, David. I'll just pay for these.'

'Hm? Oh yeh – talk, talk. We've got to talk. And yes – *you* pay for those, yes good. Because I can't. Understand? *Jesus*, Trish – you *know* I'm absolutely – ! What on earth did you think you were – ?!'

'*Actually*, David – I seem to have left my purse . . .'

And from out of nowhere there echoed around them the high-pitched screaming of a hysterical child – and David thought Jesus *Christ*: I've never before sounded quite like *that* . . .

'What on earth's *wrong* with you, David? Are you all right?'

'No. Not. I'm not.'

'David. I think we ought to talk.'

'M'yes, Trish. I think you could be right.'

⚓

Stacy was keeping a low and steady eye on her mother, watching quite closely as she neatly sliced the teacake into four – this alone a very clear sign of Jennifer's preoccupation: normally she'd just cram the whole bloody thing into her mouth, while reaching out for another.

'Don't let it *get* to you, Mum. It's only a *bloke* . . .'

'Too late. Already got to me. Aren't you eating even *one* of these, Stacy? I do wish you would,' said Jennifer. 'Otherwise I think I might scoff the lot.'

'Not hungry. I'll wait for dinner.'

'You *see*, Stacy – it's perfectly all right for you. You're young – you're young and fresh and beautiful. It won't happen to you for, oh – just *decades*. And the point is – this is, you know, really the most awfully good *jam*. I wonder where they get it . . . no no, you see the point *is*, it'd never happened to me before. I'm so terribly used to everyone saying how fantastically *fab* I look ... I was very – unprepared. I mean admittedly I was egging him on – *goading* him, almost, into seeing quite clearly what was in front of his eyes. *And*, of course, telling him the absolute truth ... don't think *that's* ever happened to me before either ...'

'Oh *Mum* ...'

'But *seriously*, Stacy – you just can't conceive. When you actually see ... *repugnance* in the eyes of another. When they practically *shiver* in disgust – '

'Oh God's *sake*, Mum – you're making yourself sound like some shrivelled-up old crone ...'

'Well maybe that's exactly what I *am*. Maybe it's time to wear chintzy frocks and take up *bridge*, or something – and buy a paperback that'll tell me how to go about growing old *gracefully* ...'

'Not really you, though, is it Mum?'

Jennifer eyed her – and consciously jollying both of them along, she drew herself up and said really very archly:

'I very much hope *not*, no.'

No, dear Stacy, grace has no part. What I shall not tell you – you maybe sense the nature of it, though: I think you might – are the words he actually said to me: 'Look, Jennifer – see this. I ain't saying you ain't one special lady ... but well – no hard feelings or nothing, but I just ain't into screwing people's *moms* – know what I'm saying? See – puts me in minda *my* Mom, Jennifer – and jeez, all this stuff you told me ... just makes me wanna *hurl*.'

It was time, now, for Jennifer to rally again: 'But what about *you*, Stacy – hm? Why aren't you ... ooh look, there's a man there, waiter – are we having more tea? Because the pot's gone just a tiny bit *cold* ...'

'I'm OK. Really.'

'Sure? Really sure? Well all right, then – we shan't bother. I'll just stick a bit of water into what's left of it ... but no *listen* to me, Stacy – why aren't you spending any more time with your *own* little friend? Hm? I mean – you know I don't ever *pry*, but . . .?'

Stacy glanced up at her, not really surprised that Jennifer should know of the existence of what she very maddeningly chose to term her '*own* little friend'. It was always like this with Mum, somehow or other: it was true that she never pried (partly because she couldn't be bothered – largely, in fact; and also because up until very recently indeed, I don't think that she could have imagined that the ins and outs of anyone else's life could possibly rival in colour nor mayhem the often alarming vicissitudes of her own thing). Nonetheless, she always seemed to *know*. Parental intuition, do we think? Some faintly spooky hypersensitivity – or maybe just a hunch? Well *Jennifer*, of course, would have laughingly blown asunder all of those: how on *earth*, Stacy, could I have had a 'hunch' that at the very moment I was careering back to our cabin in the very small hours of the morning (having stolen my way to the prow of the ship and made like a *figurehead* and then been warmed and fucked by my so-young American boy – in the days before he came to really see me) that you, dear Stacy, would be snogging some sweet and pretty little girl in the softly booming shadows?

'Oh . . .' threw away Stacy, idly: 'that was just nothing.'

'Nothing. Yes. I see.'

'What I mean is . . . oh – look, I don't know what you *think* you know . . .'

'Me? I know nothing. Always best.'

'Yes but you clearly know *something* or otherwise you wouldn't have *said*, would you Mum? Anyway – quite new for me, I assure you. And quite nice. But it does turn out to be nothing, in fact. Yes.'

Yes. Apparently it does. Because look – I don't know exactly what I was expecting, but it was quite a – *step*, for me, all of that . . . and well – I just wasn't *prepared* (and that's what Mum said too, wasn't it? Just a little while back there.

That she just simply hadn't been *prepared*) . . . so nor was I, for what Suki had said to me next:

'C'mon – hell's *sake*, Stace. Don't lay this big number on me, kay?'

'Why do you always *say* things like that? I'm just here – asking you a perfectly simple question and you make like it's some fantastic *scene*.'

'Cool it, Stace. Just cool it – kay? Look – I never went with a girl before, right? And it was neat. You're a real hot chick, Stace – way to go. But, like – now I *been* there, and I'm kinda like: that's all she wrote, you know what I'm saying? Now I'm into this older *guy*? And next – who knows? Whatever. Look, Stace – for you it's kinda *different*?'

'Why? Why is it different for me? It isn't any – '

'It's *different*, Stace, on account of you are living with *Jennifer*?'

And Stacy just stared. Something had barged right into her, and she was knocked from her axis: all the many and clamouring things that had crowded into her brain and begged to be said were just sent sprawling all over the place in the face of this swift and unforeseen upheaval: her whole mind went white and blanked out at this impossibly irrelevant and very stupid *thing*, here.

'But . . .' was all she could do, for now. And then: ' . . . you live with Charlene . . .?'

And it was Suki's turn now to look as if some person both unknown and unseen had plucked from the ocean beneath them a very frisky and glisteningly wet and sinuous herring and set to with vigour slapping her around with it.

'Get *outta* here, Stace! What're you – *nuts*? Charlene is my *mother* . . .!'

There was only a flicker that betrayed Stacy's continued bemusement.

'Yes . . . and . . .?'

Suki narrowed her eyes and studied this Stacy before her. There was the beginning of dawning – a low glimmer of nearly light at the back of her glittering, black and just-not-*into*-this eyes – but then it was immediately damped back down. Suki now grinned at her own mad idea – she flipped her fingers and rolled up her eyes: it was as if she was subjecting herself to a mute but thorough carpeting for even so much as *going* there . . . but the suspicion returned, and was shining like a blade.

'You are not *telling* me . . .? Oh my *Gaad*, I just can't – ! You ain't saying, Stace, that Jennifer is your, God – *mother*?'

All Stacy did was nod: my mother, yes. Well of *course* she is: Jennifer's my mother – everyone knows that. What *else* could she be . . .?

'*Christ* . . .' whispered Stacy, then. 'You thought – did you think – ?'

'Sure I did. And you know what *now* I think? I think *yuck*, Stace, is what I think. I mean, *what*? Before, Earl and me, we kinda figured, like, what the hell, you know? But you are telling me that my *brother* has been balling your *mother*?' And Suki now was lightly clutching her temples, as if seeking a sign from the other side. 'Like – we are in *freaksville*, here . . .!'

The tear that Stacy had been denying quickly expanded and rolled away down, fluidly curling under her chin. She turned to go, and the last thing she heard from Suki came in the form of the sort of whine wailed out by those who feel they have been shabbily treated:

'I didn't even think you English were *like* that . . .'

'So,' resumed Jennifer. 'Tea's cold, cakes gone – what shall we do? Something exciting, yes? Let's find Nobby and Aggie, and then we can kill them.'

Stacy tried for a smile of indulgence, but her whole head was still filled with such a lot of . . . I think it's sadness.

'I have to see someone, Mum. What time dinner?'

'Hardly matters, does it? Seems one *eternal* dinner, sometimes. Seven? Later? Eight? Then we can go to the disco thing. And no more *toy* boys, I promise you. Stick to nice old men who buy us lots of champagne and then go and do what they're bloody well told.'

Stacy stood and stretched herself (I often feel, here, like I've just got up: just another part of all the strangeness, I suppose).

'Yes, eight's fine. But I'll come down earlier and change, and stuff. So see you, yes? And Mum? *Please* don't let it get to you . . . Yes? Promise?'

Jennifer was beaming. 'I won't. Promise. Now off you go. See you later.'

And she felt a surge of quite simple, well – *love*, it was, must be, as she watched little Stacy, somehow so alone, walking away from her, slowly. And already I've broken my promise, sweet daughter – because it's all just welled up and got to me again. The revulsion the boy felt for me . . . I almost feel it for myself. Maybe, once people cease to find me distasteful, I shall descend into being a figure of fun; I might end up like Disco Debbie – a marvel only in that after all this time, I linger on. Bopping till I drop.

I think, thought Jennifer – quite briskly, now, as she rose from the very low tub chair and smoothed back down her hoiked-up chinos – I had better get myself off to somewhere dark and secret – and yes, quite quickly. Because otherwise I think I just might be in danger of losing it, now. A thing I try not to do.

⚓

Yet one *more* job that has been foisted upon me. Well – no real surprises there, are there? Get *Stewart* to do it – good old Stew, he'll be up for it, yes why not? Fact that he's got, ooh – just about ten thousand *other* things to attend to just doesn't *register*, does it? And I mean to say – if only they'd give me just a bit more notice. The next two hours I had clearly designated as the final opportunity for all the limping saddos, all the croaky old-timers, all the drunken fat unfunny men and all their off-key wives to register for the, oh Christ help me – *Talent* Show (it's there for all to see – perfectly clear on each of the posters *eventually* chivvied out of those bastards in the print shop and Blu-Tacked up at all strategic points all over the bloody ship by just *who*, exactly, do you think? Yes indeed – got it in one. Yours fucking truly. And it's a – and by the way, it's a nightmare, Blu-Tack – you find that? Doesn't bloody *stick*, does it? God Almighty, how do they get away with it?) . . . yes, as I say, it's not strictly within my brief, all this, is it? Or even *loosely*, come to that – face it, Christ: it's nothing to bloody do with me at *all*, all this stuff to do with journalists, the swine. I mean – that's Cruise Director country, isn't it? And the Cruise Director? In bed. With a chill. Touch, they think, of a temperature. Oh dear I'm so terribly sorry to hear *that*. But never mind: Stew will handle it, Stew will be happy to step into the breach – because Stew isn't bothered, is he, by a touch of temperature? No no, Stew toils on with an impending bloody *brain* tumour while at the same time being covered in the sores of scorn and rebuff and raddled by the cancers of high *anxiety* . . . so why don't we all heave together and just chuck this one more thing into the dip-backed, balding donkey's panniers and sit back and watch his bloody legs just damn near buckle, as unbatted flies continue to worry those brown and trusting put-upon eyes?

Journalists: can't stand them. Lowest of the low, bloody journalists are. Not that I've actually had that much experience of them in the past, thank God (as I bloody said – not my *field*, is it? Which the powers that be would do well to remember) – but whenever I *have* been in contact, well: you say one thing, and they go and write up something else completely. I mean to say – is it because they're all so permanently pissed on someone else's booze and they simply don't hear or remember? Or are they all genetically programmed to grin with their faces and swallow with their throats and then just turn round and fuck you all up, right royally? Three of them on board, this trip. Don't know what papers – two provincial and a broadsheet national, apparently: *Times*, I think – needn't be. Nice for some, isn't it? First class cabins, endless drink (or else how could they get them here?), and now that they've taken it into their collective and empty little heads to want a guided tour of all the parts of the ship that *ordinary* people who have shelled out bloody thousands just to *be* here will never get to see in a million bloody *years* . . . well then let's not keep them waiting: get old *Stew* to do it – always a smile and a ready quip! *Bastards* . . .

Mind you, one good thing about it (and they're already due, our noble members of Her Majesty's Press: sods can't even be on time) . . . yes, the positive point here is that I can finally get away from Nobby and Aggie. I mean – *nice* souls, don't get me wrong – always a pleasure to see them on every single trip (and how do they *do* that, actually? Are they very rich? Or simply very mad?). But they do tend to get just the tiniest bit *clingy*: can just become rather wearing. Still – you know me: show willing (what I'm paid for – or so they tell me).

'*Right*, then, Nobby. That's you down for your usual little talk about nautical terms, then . . . maybe not quite so long, though, this time, hey? Keep them wanting more, hey Nobby?'

'I hear what you're saying, Stewart, but it's not that simple a topic to *condense*. I mean – anything less than an hour and you're really not getting much more than the *flavour* of the thing . . .'

'Which is exactly what we *want*, Nobby. Exactly what we're after. The very *essence*, yes? Ten minutes tops, this time, I'm afraid. Captain's orders.'

'Oh really? Orders from the *Captain*? Oh well in that case . . .'

Stewart smiled his encouragement and was nodding eagerly as he red-inked Nobby into his slot. Well of *course* it's not Captain's orders, you silly little sod: you don't honestly believe the Captain gets himself involved with all *this* crap, do you? No no no – this is all for me: my crap.

'And Aggie – tell me again. What exactly is it you are proposing to do?'

Aggie shot a glance full of first-night nerves over in Nobby's direction – her whole mouth tightly and briefly elongating to its utmost extent, as if she was preparing to fit into it for the sake of a bet an old LP, or similar.

'The *Madison* . . .' she said. And she gnawed a nervous nail.

Stewart nodded. 'Yes. That's what you said before. Um – what exactly *is* this? The Madison?'

'It's the steps to a dance. You go *left* one pace, and *back* one pace and – '

'Yes, OK – right, I see. So – duration of a single, then?'

'If I can keep it up. No, hang on – it's *right* one pace, isn't it Nobby? And *then* back one pace and – '

'Search me, Captain Honeybunch!' laughed Nobby. 'Should've stuck with your hand jive, you want my opinion.'

'Oh but Nobby I *always* do the hand jive, don't I, Stewart? Every single trip I do the hand jive, don't I?'

'Yes,' said Stewart. Yes you do indeed. Every single trip. Mm. 'And oh look – if I'm not very much mistaken, my extremely important party of journalists has arrived. Greetings, all. Welcome. My name is Stewart. Assistant Cruise Director. All well? Excellent. OK then, Nobby and Aggie – *à bientôt*, yes? *Ciao*.'

And yes it *has* crossed my mind that they both might like to stay and talk to the journalists (thought it the second I very stupidly let slip the bloody *word*) and they in their turn, highly probably, would very much like to give to Nobby especially, ooh – more than enough rope. But no – we won't make it that easy for them, shall we? We won't deliver unto them a monomaniacal sap spread out on a plate with a parsley garnish just so that they can all ritually shred the poor devil in the course of their noxious little articles, while jeeringly writing off cruises in general and this one in particular as being still very much the province of the old, the rich, the idle, or else the padded cell brigade. No – this time let's see if we can't get them to be *positive*, for once, shall we? Get them to actually write about what's in front of their bloody eyes, if only they weren't too stupid to see it. Mind you . . . if they want a *real* story, it's me, isn't it, they should actually be talking to. By Christ *I* could give them a story that would make their bloody hair stand on end . . . and not very much *of* it, in the case of what just has to be the broadsheet guy (smarmy bloody look all over his fucking superior face – and the two misshapen women from the provincials – you can see they're feeling it too: they've probably hated him for days, now). But just take one *look* at his hair, won't you? Grazed upon by a herd of starved alpacas. Why does the man appear to be a stranger to a simple backcomb and scalp tint? Has he not heard of *volumizer*? Dear oh dear. And they call themselves professionals . . .

⚓

Dwight fell in easily with his customary amble (one piece of this tub I sure do like a lot: long, straight lanes like one eternal bowlerama – see where's I'm headed, and I take it real slow – ain't no hassle to get anyplace). His eyes were quietly bright as a result of a whole heap of amusement, the odd throaty wheeze and nasal fart escaping him – and all on account of David's last call. Jeez, I am telling you – my man David, he sure did sound like one spooked critter. And here I can see the sunny upland of my situation: sure I ain't got me no filly I can call my own – no sweet thighs to make me horny, drive me wild – but nor I got alla the ice-cold fear I was sure aware of in David, when I get the call. That, or else that shit-hot baby of his is cooking so bad, she maybe reduced the man to no more'n a poola chop suey, broke down and steaming. Anyways – said I'd sure be pleased to meet with the man, share a couple drinks, see how's I can maybe help him out some. Yeah – why not? Telling ya – Dave is one of the good guys: *buddy*, right? Plus – was I ready to get out from under Charlene!

'You sure? You sure bout that, Dwight? You don't have any baxes anyplace?'

Dwight looked about him: whole damn suite was looking like a warehouse – some kinda *package* depot? Jeez – how many more baxes one lady take?

'Baxes I don't got. What I want with baxes? Call down the, what're they – stoords.'

'You don't think I *did* already? They say *Gee* we're so *sorry*, Ma'am, but cuppla days from docking, everyone they're after baxes and we're *out*. Well *sure* all these guys want baxes – it's now baxes are wanted. So why they don't thinka this? And the shaps – the shaps too – all over the world. They sellya some piece of paddery – then it should come in a *bax*, right? Jeez. Maybe I shouldda had it all *shipped* . . .'

'This here *is* a ship, Charlene.'

Charlene nodded. 'That's kinda how I figured . . . where hell you going *now*, Dwight? You ain't aiming to help me out here?'

'Had a call from *David*? Sounded kinda *jumpy*?'

'Always with this *David*! What is *David* all of a sudden, Dwight? Your *wife*? Don't I deserve a little quality time, here? I'd ask Suki, only I could gedda holda her. You seen Suki, Dwight?'

'Suki today I ain't seen. Shapping, I'd guess.'

'And *Earl*. Hell, Dwight – Earl I don't even remember what he *looks* like.'

Dwight shook his head, as he made for the door.

'Earl I ain't seen neither.' And if the boy's got any sense – if there's any of his old man in him at all – then Earl is screwing his way round the ship. The Lord knows *I* would:

what else we put here for? Wrapping up paddery in *baxes*?
Get outta here.

And that's just what I did: get me outta there – fast I
could. Charlene, she comes out with two, three more dumb
things (whole buncha stuff about I don't even so much as
thinka *looking* at green olives – I hearing her good? Plus, you
gotta drink Bourbon, you make sure there's a whole loada
soda: I got that? Yeh, Charlene – sure I do: nix with the
olives, loada soda). Then I'm gone.

And now I'm here, not too far from the old Black Horse.
Hell – I know just about every goddam incha this tub, now.
Gonna be kinda weird, being back home. But, like – *good*
weird, you know? Oh but looky looky here! Hoooo-*ee*! What
do we have ourselves here? Well well well – if it ain't my
buddy David's jailbait co-ed, looking just like they can look,
when they've a mind to: pure and holy, like the mother of
God. Hot dog. And this time there ain't nobody around.
Yep. Well – mebby's I take a shot at it: what's to lose? I saw
her not too much after sun-up this morning – talking to
David with, like, real kinda *energy*, you know? I didn't
rightly care to innerupt (although what I recall was going
through my mind was Hey, Dave! Don't be *talking* to the
broad – fuck her teenage brains out, what're you thinking
about?). Then David, he moves off (me he didn't see – kinda
looked like he had stuff on his mind?) and yeah, right there
and then I was gonna make my move – on account of, like I
say, what's to lose? Then she takes herself on deck, this
baby, and I think OK, sure – on deck, cool . . . so I'm out on
deck and whaddya know? Some other guy out there – nuts-
looking kinda English guy dressed like for a *funeral*? She lies
down nexta the dweeb and I'm just left hanging, y'know?
So I got to figuring, and the way I see it is this: *Item* – either
David had it right the first time – this babe *does* put out, and
sure looks like the older and more klutzy the guy the better
(which, my age, this here gut, is kinda warming) – or else
Item: David damn well knows it, and he *was* holding out.

303

On me, his buddy – me, Dwight, his good old buddy. Well now see here, my friend – all kinda loyalties and friendships, they end, kaput, where dames is concerned. This we all know. *So*, buddy boy – you like it or you don't, at this I gotta take me one shot. Like I say – what's to lose?

'*Hi*, there, sweetheart,' was the spur for Marianne to spin round and meet this head-on – alert, at first, and filled with relief, yes, and also even excitement at the fact that she had, at last, been found and addressed . . . but at once, yes, in the very same instant, she just knew that these words, this voice, the entire nature of the greeting . . . all were completely, yes, quite grotesquely wrong. She anyway was facing the large American man.

'You busy, little lady? What say we talk some? Drink, mebbys.' Here was Dwight at his very most sugary, all of it not too subtly cut by a hefty infusion of grimy undertone (though to his mind, real down-home and friendly, like).

'That's, um – very kind of you, but . . . I don't mean to be rude, but – I *don't* know you, do I?'

'Not yet you don't, honey. Aim to put that right. But you ·*do* know very well a great buddy of mine. David? he told me . . . well, let's just say I am aware, my sweet one, of a whole lotta, what you *do*. Read me?'

'Oh I *see* . . . I didn't know you knew . . . oh right. Well look, um – ?'

'Dwight. Name's Dwight, Princess.' And was he now bearing down on her? Leaning right into her, as he opened his mouth? Or was this just the way Marianne – even more tense, now – was suddenly perceiving it? 'But *you*, babe, can call me *Horny* . . .'

She blinked. He *did* say that, didn't he? Either way, I have to go – right *now*.

'Look. There's someone I really must . . . It's been very *nice*, um – '

'Aw *c'mon*, baby! You don't have to be like that with your ole Uncle Dwight! Let's you and me get acquainted, what say? You'll be right fine with me – I'm a real gennulman, just like David.'

'I'm sure you are, um – *Dwight* . . . but honestly, I really do have to – '

'And one more thing, honey . . .'

And Marianne – a good yard away from him, now – twisted her face up with difficulty into some sort of tolerant and maybe not too disgusted grin of forbearance: OK then – all right: *one* more thing, if you must, and then I run.

Dwight licked his lips, and brought in close his eyebrows.

'I sure do pre-shate the cut of your titties . . .'

Marianne looked, quite without seeing – actually clamped the palms of her hands hard against her ears and, yes – she ran.

'Sure upset you take that attitood!' she heard hurled after her. 'Maybe see ya round some time! No hard feelings, I sure do hope!'

Marianne stopped running only when she realized that she was being at first just looked at and then quite openly regarded by various pockets of curious people (always eager, these snuggled-together groups, for just any sort of distraction at all); and also, she thought – where am I actually *going*? Where does one actually, now, begin to even *look*, when all I've been doing is looking and looking just *everywhere*? And I've rung down to his cabin, oh – I've completely lost all track of the number of times I've done that. And Tom, I don't really think . . . he isn't the sort of person to just sit in his cabin for hours on end – he likes to be *alone*, oh yes, but not, I feel pretty sure, in his *cabin*, for some reason. Unless he's asleep, of course – but God; I've rung him now about a hundred times: you'd have to be dead, to sleep through that.

So I went up to the Boat Deck – right around, twice . . . up one deck again to the pool, and so on . . . been to all the cafés and bars. Even waited outside the cinema for the end of the film . . . and no, I didn't really expect him to be filing out of there. And of *course* he wouldn't be in the Regatta Club or the Casino . . . but I checked them both anyway. And nothing. He hadn't taken tea; or, at least, no one I asked there – waiter, couple of women knitting – none of them could recall a tall, pale, silent fellow all dressed up in black, and . . . well, you *would*, wouldn't you? Someone would. So I went to that person – can't even remember his name: Assistant Cruise . . . something or other, and he didn't of course even know who I was talking about and didn't in all honesty seem to care very much (had some people with him). He said: Have you checked in the hairdresser's? And I said No, no I haven't – and I turned away thinking Oh my God you absolute *fool*: hairdresser! You just don't know my Tom at *all*.

So you see after just hours and hours of this – and the more I did it, the more I somehow felt I was sealed up in my own big see-through and airless bubble, just bowling on down the corridors and staircases, as people looked and didn't, but mainly kept their distance – I just felt so, well – *initially* relieved and excited, yes, just that someone unseen had *spoken*. But no – not Tom. Hadn't been him. So . . . I think what I'll do is . . . maybe I'll just go round everything just one more time, comb it thoroughly . . . because all it is, probably, is that we're both just *missing* one another. Soon I'll be saying to him – breathless with relief by now, and excited beyond measure as well – Oh *Tom*: what do you mean you were in the Poolside restaurant? I *went* to the Poolside restaurant! And then you were sitting on the Sun Deck? But I searched all *over* the Sun Deck for you! And then we'll agree that Well – it doesn't matter any more, does it? Because now we've found one another, yes. Yes. And it would be nice too, very nice, if – when I find him – Tom does not say Oh, I was reading in the Library (and yes – I've checked the Library) or Oh, I was helping with the jigsaw (and of *course* I've been there: three *times* I've been there); it would be nice if his eyes dipped down and he lowered his

voice and said *Marianne*: Marianne – *there* you are! Oh thank
God – I've been looking for you *everywhere* . . .

Well. If so – if that's the case – he has yet to find me. The
only one who has sought me out is – urgh, oh God: that
monster *Dwight*. Can that awful person truly be a friend
of . . .? But then I suppose he needn't *really* be an awful
person – could be all he was was drunk, or something. Bit
like Dad gets.

⚓

Dwight was twiddling around with one thick forefinger
the big and glassy lumps of ice in his just-don't-let-on-to-
Charlene-the-size-of-this-mother (bar guy – Sammy?
Telling me one time how he made 'em, the rocks – Evian, so
they don't cloud up none). Dwight heard and then saw
David's rapid approach to the bar – and hoo boy: what in
hell's got into this guy? Recalls to my mind 'Nam, one time
– we was all sweating hard and moving fast and low and
the ground was sucking us down as we hacked and ripped
our way through all that fuckin' jungle, hoping each of us
to our God that we could maybe luck out and weave
through the crossfire and duck the sniping from all those
unseen gooks – and you just knowed in your heart that any
moment now, the next crack you hear is gonna find ya,
yeah, and tear you up good; me, I come through. Waaall –
guess I find out pretty soon what it is that's bugging this
guy. Meantime, I gotta say this:

'Hey, David. I caught your little girl. Me she didn't like.'

'Marianne? Really? Well – *odd*, Dwight. She seems to
like most people, far as I can tell. Oh God – a *drink*: thank
Christ. Listen, Dwight – I've really got to talk to you.'

'Mary Ann, huh? That her name? Well all I can tell you is
that me, she froze out big time. Maybe she don't like Americans, period.'

'Oh I doubt *that*. Now listen to me, Dwight – never mind Marianne, for now. I've got trouble. Real trouble.'

'And she ain't a part of it?'

David was toying with being confused – but oh Christ, didn't have *time* to be: let's get *on* with this, God's sake:

'No. No no – course not. Why should she be? No – listen, Dwight. I've got *woman* trouble. Serious.'

Dwight's eyes were narrow, now.

'Well that's what I'm *saying* here, Dave. So what's the score? She putting the screws on you? Gun-to-your-head time – that it?'

'*Exactly* it. Yes. Yes that's it. But there's just one good side to this – well *two*, actually. See – thing is, I don't actually *want* her any more. I said to her – *Look*, Trish – you've just got to understand – '

Dwight had his palm raised now, and his eyes were practically closed.

'Hey! Whoa! Slow up, here! Who in hell's this *Trish*, now? Huh?'

'Hm? Oh yeh – course. You don't know, do you? Well you *do* know, actually, Dwight – you just maybe don't remember. *Patty*, yes? The sick one?'

'Oh yeh yeh: Pukey Patty. Gotcha. Jeez, David – what in hell you playing about with her for when you got yourself Mary *Ann*?'

David just stared at him.

'*What*? Well – I mean . . . Marianne's all grown up now, isn't she? I mean – I don't really honestly see . . .!'

'OK. The babe's all grown up now. Cool. So – lemmy just get this right in my mind, David. This dame Patty – *Trish*, right? She shows up – she goes Technicolor all down your pants and next minute you're *banging* her?'

'No no no no *no*. *No*, Dwight: listen. I've known her for *years*. She's my, you know – '

'What? The *London* connection?'

'You could – yes, you could say that. Known her for years.'

'Well now listen here, Dave – I don't reckon to be no sorta expert on these here matters, but why in hell you bring her on the *boat*?'

'*Bring* her . . .? I didn't *bring* her! Christ, she just – oh God: *Came*. And now she's threatening to tell just bloody everything to *Nicole*, see? But here's the ray of hope . . . well, *you're* the ray of hope, Dwight, if I'm being honest. You see – I've been doing a lot of thinking, right? And what I've decided is, well – I've just outgrown *both* of them. Nicole, Trish – both of them. I just dread the sight of either one of them, to be perfectly frank with you. And now I've got this *new* girl – the really young and *new* one, well . . . I thought I could maybe – make a brand-new start, yes? New York? Remember one time you said something about . . . I don't know – helping me out? Fixing me up? And then I can, you know – *be* with this girl, yes . . . and *cherish* her, and everything. Yes. Think that's it. What do you think? Oh and yeah – something else, Dwight. Something else I forgot. See – I don't want any *unpleasantness*, if you see what I mean. For the kids' sake, more than mine. And what I don't want specifically is some great *scene* – here or in America. I just want Trish to, well – *vanish*, really . . . and Nicole and the kids, I'll just say *Look* – bit of business has been put my way by my good friend Dwight, here, yes? So you all fly back to London when our little break is over, and then I'll follow – few days later. See?'

'Uh-huh. And?'

'And? Well I *won't*, of course. I'll stay. New life. New job. New girl. God – it sounds just bloody *great*, actually.'

Dwight drained his drink – looked this way and that for the barman, and couldn't locate neither hide nor hair of the guy.

'What do we do to get service round here . . .? OK, Dave – I'm hearing you loud and clear. Kinda envy ya, boy. So sure

– OK: I can setcha up with a job, nul problemo. So what's the big deal?'

'Oh God *thanks*, Dwight! But yes – right. Well this is the rather, um – embarrassing bit, um – yes. You see – in order for Trish *not* to make a fuss . . . you know: go round upsetting people . . . she wants, um – money. Says she doesn't much care about me anymore, but she does still care about money. Money, yes. I don't know if you *know*, or anything, Dwight, but money is among the many things I haven't actually, er – *got*.'

Dwight nodded. 'I kinda figured. Money, huh? She said that?'

And David nodded too, quite like a maniac. Yes oh *yes* – she'd bloody well said *that*, all right:

'*God*, David,' she'd gone. 'I do feel a bit . . . don't *you*, at all? I really do feel a bit, urr – *queasy*. Why's it just me? I've taken *pills*, and everything, but they honestly don't seem to be doing anything. Oh by the way – I went back for those shot glasses . . . and I did get the pink sweatshirt, in the end. And also some really attractive placemats. But don't worry – they didn't cost much.'

'They didn't cost much. I see. You mean you charged them – ?'

'To your, yep – account. Well *look*, David – you take care of your bloody *wife*, don't you? So you should bloody well expect to take care of me too. It's only fair, isn't it? And God – it's only a few *pounds*. Now listen, David – when I tell her just *everything* – '

'*No*, Trish. No. You really mustn't do that. Look – I'll tell her: I will. I'll say – look, Nicole, I'm – uh . . . *leaving* you, in fact.'

'You'll say that. Uh-huh. I don't believe you, David. You won't say that. What you'll do is you'll go on and on and on saying to *me* that you'll say that – just like you've been doing for years. No, David – what we need now is *action*, see? That's why I'm here.'

'But Trish – I've given you my *word* . . .!'

Trish just shook her head. '*Action*, David,' she said. 'Unless . . .'

And of course David leapt at it – just as, he suspected, Trish had known he would.

'Unless? Unless what? What? *Christ*, Trish – how long have you been working all of this out? You don't love me at *all*, do you, Trish? You keep *saying* you do, but you don't – you can't. You just couldn't be doing all this to me, not if you loved me. *Christ*, Trish – people who love one another just don't go about plotting to fucking *destroy* them!'

'OK, then, we'll go back to the plan of action.'

'Oh – *Jeeeeesus*! OK, OK – tell me the 'unless'. Give me the 'unless', Trish, you bloody goddam bitch.'

'Language, David. Now listen – it's all so perfectly simple. I've never actually been to New York before . . . well, never been *anywhere*, really, have I David? Anyway – what just *might* persuade me to give you a bit of time – keep my mouth shut – is if I were to stay in New York for say, ooh – I don't know – three months, say . . .?'

And David wasn't sure quite how he should react, here. Three months? Sure. I'm surprised you've actually suggested that we're apart at all – but you want three months? Fine. Take six. *Year* do you?

'Mmm . . .' he tried, with caution. 'And . . .?'

'Well by *that* time even a rather pathetic little thing like *you*, David, will have plucked up courage to speak to his bloody wife – and then you can fly out and join me. See? New life. New start. Got it?'

'Yes . . .' nodded David – mind now forced screaming into overdrive – 'yes, yes. I see. Got it.'

Well what I see is this (this is what I've got): New life – new start – sounds good to me. But not with *you*, Trish – no. Because anything in any way, you see, to do with you, it – well, it just *isn't*, is it? *New*. Plus, I get the very strong feeling that what is on the table here is not simply a sweetly put

311

request for three months' hotel bills and all the other, oh – quite tear-making expenses that a woman such as yourself could just so effortlessly run up in New York City (and whatever you want to say about Nicole – my bloody *wife*, as you will insist on habitually calling her – she can't hold a bloody candle to you on that front, and she's no amateur, believe me) . . . No – what I think you want, surprise surprise, is cash in hand, pure and simple. Whereupon you could with very little difficulty be persuaded, I think, not to hang around in New York, but take firm hold of your loot and go just *anywhere*, hear me? Anywhere else on earth. Because you will not be *required* in New York, Trish: what you will be is surplus. Why? You'd like to know why? Tell you why, Trish: because *I* shall be there. Yes I shall. Me me me. *My* new life – *my* new start. Oh yes – and did I mention? With my brand-new *girl* (and she won't be the only thing I'll be cherishing, here). So I looked up at Trish and I said to her fair and square:

'OK, Trish. How much?'

'It's not *just* a question of money, David. You do understand that? I do want you as well. I want, if I'm honest – not so much to have you . . . more, really, to take you *away*. But if I'm *really* honest, what I want is . . . what I want is, yes – I want money. I do.'

'OK, Trish. How much?'

'Oh *David*! You're doing this deliberately now, aren't you? You're doing your level bloody best to make all this sound so terribly *sordid* and somehow, I don't know – as if I'm the one in the *wrong*, here! I mean – *you're* the one, David. You're the one, aren't you David? Who got us all *into* this?'

David sighed, now. God, he was – in so many ways – weary of this.

'OK, Trish. How much?'

And suddenly her eyes were small and hard like gunmetal bearings, one cold white light glinting askance out of each of them.

'Twenty thousand, I reckon should do it.'

David was shocked and faintly nauseated by not just the amount – not even the suddenness of her having finally come out with it, but the fact that either one of them could really be party to such a conversation as this. Amazing, too, that she actually believes I've *got* that sort of money. I don't have – face it – *any* kind of money. I keep on *telling* people. So why don't they hear me? Still, all this will serve to make this parting – when it comes – sweet, just sweet (and no damned sorrow about it). So, there we are: there we have it. There was just this one little matter, then, to be taken care of. And that means I have to, very soon, have a talk with my good friend Dwight. And pray that that is, in fact, what he turns out to be: a very good friend indeed.

And David, now, was watching the man's eyes, as Dwight turned it over.

'Plus . . . !' put in David, as he waited for the verdict to come through, 'she said pounds. Pounds. Not dollars. Jesus.'

Dwight pulled a grin. 'She ain't nobody's patsy, our Patty – huh? Kay, David. Sure. I can draft ya, what – forty thousand bucks against your pay check. You pay it off when you've a mind. You easy with that?'

David let go all of his breath in a coughed-out rush – as if he had finally been granted permission to do just that.

'Oh Christ *thank* you, Dwight – oh God I can't *tell* you what a – oh Dwight, Dwight. What can I say? I have to warn you, though – about this job, whatever it is you've got in mind . . . I can't actually *do* much.'

Dwight had eased his bulk away and down from the stool, and was ambling now to the hatch in the bar. He ducked under that with quite some difficulty (had fumbled with the catch, but the hell with that) and now he reached for two fresh glasses: jammed them up against the Jack Daniel's optics.

'They don't wanna come serve me – I'll goddam serve

myself. Tell you truth, Dave – all a man can do is pay his dooze. I ain't that hot at nothing, neither. As to what you *say*, Dave: you don't say nothing. What you do is you raise up your glass, you hear me? And we drink a toast: new life, new start, new girl – New *York*! How's about that?'

And David, as he stared down into the drink, was very close to tears. This was just too, too great. For just how long had people been *preaching* to him? Nicole, mainly, but Trish too, God blast her – about all the virtues attached to ambition, drive, and more than that: self-help. Well I've never been good at it. And it's overrated, isn't it, if ever there's the glowing alternative. I'm incapable of helping myself: I want someone to help me *for* me – and now, at last, someone has. And as David looked up to meet Dwight's big and red and smiling face, he found himself even nearer to those tears, and now, oh God damn it – yes, he was there. He wiped at his face with his knuckles, and smirked – and now he laughed and happily clinked his glass with Dwight's.

'Amen,' was all he said.

⚓

As soon as they were both inside the door (Jilly had very swiftly locked it again, and with an only quasi-guilty grin of complicity, put the key safely away) – the first thing Rollo did was kiss her, yes . . . but it was his hands, just lightly fingering her tiny and tight-belted waist at first, before he gave in to their pleading and let them roll away and roundly with the flow of her – Christ, women's *hips*, mmm . . . yes, oh yes, it was his hands that were creaming off all the goodness, here: his mouth, he really felt, was merely attending to its duty (girls, pretty sure, get more out of this side of things than we do, maybe).

It was when they stood back from one another – it was then, yes, that Rollo watched her (his illicit collaborator)

314

and Jilly's eyes blazed back at him with a nearly haughty and defiant challenge: Isn't this *exciting*? Isn't it? Isn't it *fun*? Isn't it . . .? And Rollo let his heavy eyelids do the nodding for him: yes it is, yes it bloody *is*. And then he looked about him.

'Christ Almighty. It's absolutely *huge*, this place . . .'

'Oh God – this isn't *all* of it. There's three other rooms through there – the bathroom looks like something out of a movie – you know, one of those old black-and-white movies. And the *main* bedroom – oh wow. You want to see it?'

A what-do-you-think smirk was Rollo's comeback to that one.

'And people really do pay . . . how much did you say? All that money just for this? I mean it's *great*, yeah . . . but Jesus . . .'

'There's a sun deck thing through there and up the stairs. But it's actually, I think, a bit too . . . even right up here, you can feel the sway, now, can't you? The waves are really quite big, now. Have you seen? But *we* don't care, do we? *I* don't, anyway . . .'

'God you are *fabulous*, Jilly,' said Rollo, quite suddenly – and it seemed to please both of them that he had. 'But are you sure it's, you know – OK, and everything? I mean – how did you get the key?'

'Oh everyone does it, time to time. See, the people who had this for the whole World Cruise – and can you *believe* it? There were only two of them. Just two people in all these rooms! We're not meant to know who, but he – the bloke – was something terribly high up in *Disney*, or something, apparently. That's what I heard, anyway. And not only that – oh God, Rollo: this you just will *never* believe. They had the first class cabin next door as *well* – it links up, see. See that door next to all the mirror? Links up.'

'Bloody hell. Why did they – ?'

Jilly's eyes were dancing. 'Get this – they said they

needed that – needed that for all the wife's *evening* clothes! God Almighty!'

'*Kidding* me! Christ – these people . . .!'

'Joke was, they we:e never ever *seen* in the restaurant. There's an awfully exclusive sort of cocktail bar type thing quite near – God, I'm not even allowed to *serve* in it . . . which is fair enough, I suppose: couldn't make a cocktail to save my life. But anyway – point is, they never went there either. Just stayed in this suite for just about ever – calling up room service, and changing their *clothes.*'

'God!' laughed Rollo. 'Sounds like my Mum's dream world. Actually no – that's not right: she'd *definitely* want to be seen. But look, Jilly – why aren't they *here*? I mean, how did you – ?'

'Well this is it: when we got to Southampton, they apparently decided they'd had enough – fancied a week or so in London. So they just went. Happens, sometimes. See – what you have to remember, Rollo, is that, I don't know – a quarter of a million or something to these people, it's – well, it's like fifty pee to us.'

'I've *got* fifty pence,' smiled Rollo. 'Can I stay?'

And Jilly went up to him.

'I *would* say for as long as you like . . . but will you settle for an hour? Then it's my shift. And there's no chance of the key being missed till then. *Kiss* me, Rollo . . .'

And Rollo did that: lip service.

Jilly took him by the hand and led him past the pair of nine-foot white leather sofas and the horrible paintings and these quite enormous picture windows (and it was right, what Jilly had said – the sea is definitely getting up: God, we're so high, though, it seems just miles down) and then through a mirrored passageway and on into a very large and low and maybe maple panelled room – and at its centre, a dusky pink and chintzy pretty much fully upholstered bed that was not, in point of fact, very much smaller than the space that held it.

'There's the most fantastic sound system,' enthused Jilly. And then, with huge regret: 'But I just don't *dare* . . . Sometimes there's a half-bottle of champagne in the fridge, though.'

Rollo was unbuttoning his shirt.

'You've done this before,' he said. Not actually *minding*, though. I mean Christ – her position, I'd be up here all the bloody time: different girl every day. So I'm not *minding*, no: just saying . . . But I like Jilly – really like her a lot. I'd love it if she was my, you know – *proper* girlfriend. That'd be great. And she could – she *could* get a job in London: easy. Then we could be together properly. Yes – I'd really love that. So although I just said to her, um – You've done this before, I maybe wasn't just *saying* it, no: could be that I mind, a bit.

'Well I *haven't*, actually,' said Jilly quite airily. 'Do you think this bra is pretty?'

'I – *yes*. I do. It's very . . . it's lovely.'

'Wore it specially. No, Rollo – I've *been* here, obviously. But only on my own. To look around. To be perfectly honest, I did *ask* him, once. Sammy. Come here and *touch* me, Rollo.'

Rollo was aching for her, now. He was so very close, he could feel her warmth already. His fingers stood poised and flexed, like those of a pianist awaiting his cue – and although they were straining to be away, they shied off at the point of contact, fearful of the sizzle, and then getting burned. He placed his two lips to the side of her throat.

'*And* . . .' sighed Jilly. 'Oh *God*, Rollo, I just love it when you do that. And *he* said . . . ah! Ah! Oh God not my *ears*! Not my *ears*! Oh Jesus I just go crazy when you do that to my *ears*! God you're – *gorgeous*, Rollo.'

They pulled away from each other, then – maybe a simultaneous impulse: standing up, here, and half dressed just wasn't going to do it. They watched one another with half-fright and hunger as the final ungainly contortions were somehow not too embarrassingly completed – reluctant and clingy bits of bloody *clothing* were tugged at, wrenched round and shrugged off – hurled away from them and kicked into distant corners.

'*What* did he say . . .?' gasped Rollo, for something to say.

'Mm? Oh – he just said it was too *dangerous*, too *risky*. See what I mean, Rollo? Just no *fun* . . .'

The sight of her naked sent him into something like a trance. Only when she had taken him near to swooning did he dare look back into her eyes: they pricked him deep, and made him boil.

'Rollo,' she breathed. '*Do* it to me. Come.'

Rollo went – just went for her. And then (her arms and mouth were open) he stopped dead right there and said *Fridge*, where's the fridge? And Jilly said *Jesus*, Rollo – please, *please* . . . and Rollo said Wait: *fridge* – where is it? And Jilly vaguely pointed – then more energetically with eyes closed and fingers flapping when Rollo stooped down to the wrong cupboard altogether – and as he seemed bent on fooling around down there, Jilly just flounced across to the bed and fell backwards down and into the sheer soft vastness of it and she let her eyelashes touch to only filter a gauze of redness, aware of just icicles of anticipation – hot jabs of tenderness. Her eyes then flew up as she yelped and hot ice – *real* hot ice, had shocked her neck and slithered all over her and stuck to her as she sat up and flailed in a frenzy of bubbled-up sex and white amazement and felt before she saw the bottle forced between her lips and the uprushing spangles of champagne quietened her down – she even heard them hushing her – but she was squealing again as the chilling gobbets of it coursed away down from her mouth and spattered her breasts and she had only just half enough time to gulp out air before all that was knocked right out of her as she took the full weight of the hard and eager man across her and opened up all of her limbs to him and then the way she bunched up when she felt him inside of her made Rollo feel safe and warm and finally *home* – so very enclasped and badly needed, that all he had to do was

318

sweep back handfuls of her hair – strew them across the tracts of milk-white pillow so that now he could concentrate hard on the sweet hot face beneath him, and the tremendous pulsations that he was forcing down drunkenly – while already the impulses within him swept all that aside as they left him gasping, and then whipped him right up.

'*Jesus*, Jilly – oh – sweet . . . *God* . . .!'

And as his limbs clamped rigid, Jilly jerked hard from deep underneath him somewhere and Rollo felt his hand let go its grip on the bottle that he had no idea that still he had been grasping and he heard it thump to the floor and fizz out what was left of it – and yes, there was uncertainty and a good amount of unease in both their eyes, now, and they could not help but listen in pain to it rolling away and leaving in its wake, oh God – just what sort of a mess . . .? And then it clunked into something, and stopped. Rollo and Jilly clung to one another in silence, and then, quite quietly, they began to stickily unpeel themselves from where their skin had bonded.

The unreal thunder, now, that made Jilly shriek and then go into spasm as Rollo roared and fell right off her and on to the floor had erupted from somewhere not quite here but hardly distant, and that one and sudden shocking implosion was immediately replaced by a silent vacuum, heavy with foreboding – but yes, yes – now there was the leaden thud of something coming this way fast. Jilly bundled sheets around her – held them close and up to her throat – while Rollo stood there, undecided . . . and then he made instinctively for his, Christ – where *are* they? Bloody *trousers*! Didn't get there, though (no, he didn't make it) – and now the bedroom door, already just ajar, was swung open so hard and wide it slammed the wall and Rollo did not know if he was rushing the man, there, or else just rampaging to and through the one way out of here – but whichever way he thought this thing might be going, it took a turn for the worse as he barged and then fell heavily into the dark red, outraged and practically palsied form of Sammy, the baseball bat he held high in the air knocked away from him now as the two staggered back and tumbled jarringly down three hard and head-clunking steps that spewed them into one more vast and ludicrous area and Sammy was crying through screwed down eyelids as he sought to hurt a sweat-wet naked Rollo who was coughing and hitting out wildly at anything looming, and often soft parts of himself. Jilly was screaming and screaming to God's name *stop – stop* it, both of you – you're *crazy, crazy*! And the sheet around her was tricking her feet and making her slither and she too toppled over and down those three bloody steps and whether or not that had been the plan, hard on top of the fiercely wrestling Sammy and Rollo and the muffled struggles of all three of them, now, were being hampered badly by the heavy and foot-snagging bedsheet which someone's maddened arm eventually threw off and away from them as Rollo, somehow, like a new-born colt, gangled to his feet – and cold and scared and calling up manliness he covered his groin with one shaky hand and even as he was conscious there of a touching softness and dried-on caking, the index finger of the other hand, now, was up and wagging, his wet eyes wild in a spinning head, and his mouth set far from firm:

'Now *look*,' he quavered. 'I'm *warning* you . . .!'

Sammy snarled and grasped then threw away both of Jilly's stiff and pleading arms and scrambled up and just hurtled his whole body into this bastard's stomach and Rollo was sent over the edge into cascades of sheer injury and he fell over backwards and utterly as if completely eviscerated by a runaway train and left there void and coping with a herd of cows stampeding into the chasm that had once held guts that saw him through. Sammy was straddling a near passed out Rollo, now (much in the way Jilly had had lined up for later), and as he raised up his fist, she screamed out and ranted and danced up and down as if imploring the gods for a deluge of rain – and neither the prone and truly now out of it Rollo and nor the driven and quite maddened Sammy, his lower face coated with furious spittle – neither was at all aware of Jilly's breasts jiggling in agitation, her hair quite lunatic – for these, as well as the fevered fighting, were the sole preserve of those at the door of the main apartment – and *No* . . . is all that got through to Stewart, as his heart leapt up and his eyes just died – this *wasn't*, was it? Not by any stretch could this be judged the best of all moments to be highlighting the peerless attractions of the Emperor – oh God help me what can be *happening*? – Suite, oh Christ – to a visiting party of fucking *journalists*. And apart from the scuffling, there was audible not even the hiss that everyone sensed – though the dark and malevolent chortle from the just had to be *broadsheet* guy had the swift and startled effect of roping back everyone into the here and now (whatever this could be). Just too late, though, had come any of anything to prevent just all of it having been so terminally displayed: Stewart turned his back – the blood-rush to the now livid orange of his face combining to form no colour known to man – and with arms thrown wide and much heavy clearing of the throat (couldn't run to a chortle like the just had to be broadsheet guy – none would come) he shepherded out and away his excited charges – and one of the women he had to physically take hold of, spin around and *propel* right out of there. Ha ha, he went. Ha ha ha.

Stewart glanced back just once, before he softly closed the door behind him: Sammy was sitting cross-legged, wagging his head cradled by stiff and pale fingers. Jilly had gathered back the sheet around her and she softly wept into a corner of it, her hair falling forward over the whole of her face; but for the pumping of his glistening chest, the naked man could well be dead. Right, then: very good. Well that's it, thought Stewart, that is it: I am finished. And yes he was

aware that other stupid bastards could be thinking this as
well.

⌁

'Just waiting for my daughter, actually. Maybe she's gone to
some other bar, I don't know. Sure she said this one, though.
One does rather a lot of waiting around on this ship. Do you
find that? *Jennifer*, by the way.'

'Hello,' smiled David. 'David. Yes well – pretty much
used to that, in my life. Hanging around. Seem to have been
doing that for just, oh Christ – years.' And then he snorted
and fooled with his glass. 'Sorry – don't mean to, ah – '

'No no – not at all. I think I know exactly what you're
saying.'

Finally I get to meet someone *sane*. Typical, isn't it? So
much wasted time. Where was David when I was making
such a bloody fool of myself with the boy-child Earl and, oh
Christ – evading the plague that is Nobby? Still: couple of
days to go (never say die, yes?).

'Get you a drink, Jennifer?'

And no: no. No – I am *not* going to find myself attracted
to this bloody woman, *actually*. Christ – I haven't got enough
on my plate? What do I imagine? A *fourth* entanglement on
board would just add the final garnish to the dog's dinner I
seem to so bloody effortlessly make of just bloody *everything*? I don't really think so.

'Well I *suppose* there's time for one more. She's actually
normally quite punctual, Stacy – *I'm* the one who just loses
all track. But I think that's another thing about this ship, you
know. You start to behave, I don't know – um . . .?'

'Uncharacteristically? Vodka you're drinking, is it?'

'Uncharacteristically – just so. Very good. No – actually
it's gin and tonic. Haven't had one in simply ages and I just
got that *taste*, you know?'

'Whisky man, myself. Scotch, I used to drink. Seem to be on Bourbon, now . . .'

'See what I mean? This ship.'

David nodded. 'I think you could be right.'

He ordered the drinks from this increasingly miserable little turd of a barman – bloody *Sammy*, he's called, is he? All smiles just a few days ago: look at him now. And that's a helluva shiner he's got. Probably deserved it. Tell you something, though – OK, Nicole is history: we know that. And Trish, yes all right – she's gone the way of all flesh. Suki, mm – gorgeous, granted . . . but Jesus, just a baby, really. Well *isn't* she? And is cherishing, actually, now what I'm praying for? It's someone like this Jennifer I should've gone for: more my speed. Too late now, though: too late now.

'So tell me, David – what is it that you actually *do*?'

'Oh heavens – you don't want to hear about all that. Terribly dull.'

'No no – I wouldn't have asked. Tell me – go on.'

David took the usual deep breath. 'Well I, uh – well what I actually am is a financial, um – consultant.'

The flat of Jennifer's hand flew to her breast.

'Man of my *dreams*,' she orated. 'I'm just hopeless about *anything* to do with money in any shape or form.'

David nodded eagerly, and his eyes were wide and sincere.

'Oh me *too*. Absolutely. Can't get a hold of it – not one bit.'

'Oh come on – you're just saying that! No – what *I* mean is – I've no idea from one day to the next whether I've actually got any money or not.'

'Well I'm exactly the *same*. It's *awful*, isn't it?'

'When a bill arrives,' pursued Jennifer (puzzled, yes OK, but pursuing it anyway), 'I simply can't bring myself to even *open* the thing.'

'No – nor me. I stick them all away in a drawer. Can't even look at them.'

'Yes! Yes! Just physically *incapable* –'

' – of even so much as *touching* the thing. Yes – I know exactly what you mean.'

And they both sort of laughed at that. What an *intriguing* man, she thought. Odd, oh yes – but intriguing, very.

'But look – did I mishear you? I thought you said you were a –'

'I did, yes. A financial consultant. It's just that . . . cheers, Jennifer, cheers . . . it's just that, well – I didn't say I was a *good* one, or anything, did I? Completely hopeless, if you want the truth. This year alone I've sent two companies to the wall single-handed. They were shocked to find themselves suddenly in receivership – me, well, I was completely astonished. Didn't see it coming. Still can't make head or tail of how it could have happened. Christ – I don't know why I'm laughing. It's all a bloody tragedy, really. Isn't it?'

But they *were* laughing, the two of them – and really enjoying it, seemed like to Jennifer. David's face was the first to cloud over: he had espied something sour from afar.

'Ah . . .!' he sighed, with real regret. 'Sorry, I have to, ah – said I'd, um . . .'

'Wife?'

David hissed like a let-down tyre: it was as if his wheeze was rumbled.

'Wife, yes. Yes indeed. Said I'd have an early dinner, for once.'

Jennifer glanced in the direction of an agitated woman standing by the door, and very reluctant, it seemed, to venture further.

'Well,' she said. 'Wives, I understand, don't at all like to be kept waiting. I was one myself, once. Well twice, actually. So I should know.'

Now look: leaving a bar for the sake of Nicole was never a very easy thing for David to do – but this time, somehow, it seemed even harder.

'Bye,' he said. God – she's very fine, you know, this

woman. Very fine indeed – the way she sits, the way she drinks: just my speed. 'It's been . . . nice.'

Jennifer smiled and raised her glass. 'Very,' she said.

And it annoyed her – watching this rather attractive and God, absolutely *normal* man bustle away with his head down, and into the maw of his wife. Mm. Maybe say die, yes? I don't think he's the type to stray. Jennifer drank her gin and tonic, and sadly shook her head. Christ. It's all a bloody tragedy, really. Isn't it?

⚓

'Outstanding! Yeah oh yeah – very nice, very nice . . .'

Earl's eyes were wide with real appreciation. This little lady I did not expect to be seeing again – but hell, now she's here (and what she said is, she come looking for me) – well, let's go for it, momma – see what's shaking down.

Stacy smiled, and ceased for now her pirouette. She was wearing the black short skirt with that peachy, clingy angora top: result wear.

'I'm glad you like it,' she said. 'You hang about this bar a lot?'

'Nah. Cuppla beers. Buy you one? *Stace*, right?'

'Stacy, yes. Well thank you, Earl. Maybe a Diet Coke.'

'Sure thing. Maybe getcha triple vodka, go with that?'

Stacy's eyes were cast down; then they rose and twinkled at him: two of her fingers alighted briefly on the knobbly bones at his wrist, just by the steel and massive chronometer. Yeh he is, she thought: he's a good-looking bloke. Never really noticed it before.

'Don't need it,' she said.

'Whatcha got in the bag, Stace? It's a kinda big bag.'

Stacy held his gaze of amused enquiry.

'Tate & Lyle's,' she giggled. And then she giggled again.

'Tatum *what*? What in hell's that?'

'It's a syrup. Got it from the kitchens. Want to taste?'

And Earl was momentarily thrown.

'Do I, er . . .? Well look – I gotta beer, here . . .'

Stacy had gently prised open the lid of the catering-size can of Golden Syrup.

'Just a taste . . .'

Earl was eyeing her extended finger, coated in gold. He then glanced nervously to the left and right of him: this was getting kinda – what? Well – just not the kinda thing people do in *bars*, right? Like – she just *got* here? But hell – way she's looking . . . and that finger, it's coming straight on tord me . . . hell, it's just on my lips now, boy – well look, way I figure, just *suck* on that mother, yeah?

Stacy's whole face was sparkling at him. 'You like . . .?'

Earl closed his eyes in acquiescence. 'Big time,' he said. 'Say, uh – you reckon maybe we go someplace a little more, uh . . .?'

Stacy was already gathering her things.

'Perfect,' she said.

Which is pretty much all that was said. Once or twice, as they silently padded their way down one more corridor of hush, Earl threw in a couple of things on the lines of 'Er – *so*, uh . . .?' or 'Well, I guess this is . . .' But there was sure no kickback, here, so hell – let's just go for it and see what's cooking.

'Nice cabin . . .' approved Stacy.

Earl glanced about, as if all this were new to him.

'Yeh. Nice. It's cool. *So*, Stace – what do we do?'

'What do you want to do, Earl?'

And this she said straight, so damn straight – all the ooze and schmooze has quit her, which is kinda freaky.

'Well hell, Stace. I mean – *duh*! Way you was coming on to me, I didn't figure we'd wind up playing *chequers*, you know?'

'OK,' smiled Stacy (and hey – I think it's OK again: sure looks foxy to me). 'Let's play a different game.'

'Yo! Way to go, Stace! C'mon over here, honey.'

Stacy was rummaging around in her bag.

'Whatcha looking for babe? Hey, c'mon – we don't need one of *them* things . . .'. And Stacy's eyes were upon him, as there rose up and around his face a slit-eyed, twisted and wholly lascivious gaping leer. 'Mean to *say*, Stace . . . it ain't as if you don't know where I *been* . . .?'

Stacy stood stock-still for barely a second.

'Lie down, Earl. Lie down on the bed.'

'More like it! Hey – what's that thing, Stace?'

'It's a blindfold – you like games, don't you, Earl?'

'I . . . *guess* . . . it's kinda like in the movie, right?'

'Right. Yes. Well lie *down*, then. Now tell me if it's too tight, OK? Is that all right? Comfy? Now Earl – taste this . . .'

And from his dark cocoon, Earl was all senses, now. He opened his mouth and received her syrupy finger.

'Now, Earl – while you're sucking me off, I want to watch you take off all your clothes. Do it, Earl. Do it now. Get the clothes off, Earl.'

Earl started to unbutton his shirt. Is this hot, or what? Well – tell you truth, I ain't too sure. All English women like this? I couldda gotten my clothes off a whole bunch easier a while back, you know? Like – when I was *standing*? So what the hay? I unbutton, I unzip – I can tug hard at these mothers: yeah sure – this I can cut. But wait up: where hell is she now? I got the syrup in my mouth, but the finger I lost.

'It's OK, Earl. I'm just getting pillows.'

'Pillows, huh? That's cool. OK, Stace – reckon I'm nekkid. Come get me, honey. Bliss me *out*.'

'Mm,' approved Stacy. 'Magnificent.'

Her fingers very lightly grazed the softness of his thighs, and then she shuddered at the sight of the hardness in between. Earl just barely whimpered – tautened briefly, and then relaxed into an easy and gloating anticipation. Which means now just has to be the moment to *do* it.

Earl felt more syrup slid into his mouth, a little bit more.

He just had time to half splutter out *Hey*, Stace – maybe enough with the goddam syrup, huh? But by then Stacy had upended this vast and heavy tin of Golden Syrup right over the centre of him – sweeping it down over his legs and then rapidly back again over his chest and arms, and still there were great and gobbety masses of the stuff to fill up his mouth to glorious gagging point, as well as just obliterating his hair with the final slick of it – and *Christ*, now: just before the concussion of shock and revulsion is swept out by sheer fury – and it's happening, yes, it's happening right now – I must just very swiftly crack the bastard hard across the jaw with my already they feel bruised and aching knuckles and fast, very fast, utterly blanket him with these slit-open pillows and catch my last sweet glimpse of him rasping and choking as the feathers that cling to him and invade are making him retch, and making him roar.

She ran to the door as the ferociously enraged and puking monster rose up like Swamp Thing and quickly slithered badly in the mess of his own goo as a dizzy cloud of feathers was sent up into his face, wiping out his eyes. Stacy stood poised at the door, just one snarl and a grapple away.

'You hurt my *Mum*, Earl. And I don't like it. Not a bloody *bit*.'

And then she was out of there and running: *yeah*, you sod – I just wish you could've gone halves with your bloody *sister*. By the time she reached the lift, Stacy was not just thrilled and laughing but also, she noticed with delight – apart from the fist that had slugged the creep – not even in the slightest bit sticky.

⚓

'I'm not saying I *won't*, Nicole. I didn't say I *wouldn't*. I merely observed that I think it's rather stupid having to dress for dinner every night, that's all. Just think it's daft.'

'It's what you *do*, David. That's why they call it a *dinner* suit, you see: you wear it to *dinner*. Not a very difficult concept, surely. Who's your new friend?'

'Yes I know but it's all so self-*conscious*, isn't it? Everyone's prancing about with a sort of 'look at me: I'm all dressed up for *dinner*' bloody fool look all over their faces. It's just so forced.'

'Well I'm terribly *sorry*, David. Next time I win a luxury all-expenses-paid cruise I shall try to persuade them to give me one of the lower class cabins and then you can probably roll up to dinner at the self-service place wearing bloody *overalls*, I shouldn't wonder. Rather like your new friend, whoever she was. *Very* casual . . .'

'Her name is, um – I can't actually remember her name, now. I thought she looked OK. Oh *God*, Nicole – you're not going to – why are you taking off your dress again? You've only just this minute put it *on* . . .'

Yes you have, you stupid woman. And if you're reaching for the goldy one – and you are, you've hoiked it down, now – that means that the red shoes are a no-no, doesn't it, Nicole? Yes it does – I've learned that much over the years. And the tights will have to go and probably your bloody underwear too, more than bloody likely. And her name is *Jennifer*, as it happens, my sweet, and I think she looked bloody wonderful in whatever it was she was wearing. I didn't actually notice what she was wearing, as a matter of fact, because I wasn't, I don't suppose, *meant* to. She was dressed like a human *being*, Nicole. And that's how she sounded, too. She was all right.

Anyway – that was earlier. We got to dinner, eventually. What have you two been *doing*, went Marianne: we were just about to order. Yes well – you of *all* people, Marianne, should know perfectly well what we've been *doing*. I've been sitting on my allocated corner of the bed, doing my level best to ignore the insistent drumbeat inside my head (it goes like this: Come *on* come *on* come *on* come *on*) while your bloody mother continues to faff about with handbags and scarves and bracelets and – oh Christ, this time she's *really* excelled herself: *gloves*. Matching gloves. I know, I know, but what can you do? Maybe later she's intending to crack a safe or so, who can say? Rather nasty bruise on Rollo's cheekbone, just there. Wonder how he got it? Let's just hope his mother doesn't notice or she'll be going on about it for the rest of the night.

'Have you noticed the *sway*?' said Marianne – to anyone, really.

'I *think* . . .' thought Nicole, 'I'll just have smoked salmon to start. Simple. Maybe just a touch of caviar with it.'

'Caesar Salad for me,' grunted David. 'Yes I *have*, Marianne. You have to walk down the corridors like, what is it? Cartoon thing. Popeye, yes. It's not so bad up here, though. What having, Rollo?'

'Steak, I think. Not specially hungry.'

'Yes, Rollo,' admonished Nicole, 'but you still have to *eat*. What are you starting with? Hm? What about the gnocchi? You like gnocchi, don't you? Oh my *God*, Rollo – how did you get that awful bruise on your cheek? Hm? Have you put anything on it?'

'I'll have the bouillon, Daddy,' said Marianne. 'Had it the other night, actually – it's wonderful. With angel hair pasta. Divine.'

'*Answer* me, Rollo,' insisted Nicole – who was still eyeing his face as if expecting it to at any moment explode into a rainbow of streamers.

'Oh it's nothing, Mum – I just . . . the wardrobe door. Stupid.'

'And *then*, maybe . . .' reckoned David, 'mmm – roast veal sounds good. You want to be more careful, Rollo.'

'Oh *yes*,' swept in Nicole – just as he might have known she would. 'And *you*, of course, David, have never walked into *anything*, have you? In your whole life. Good *God*, David – some nights you can't even walk through an open *door*. Forever slamming face-first into the *wall*. God help us.'

'*Mum . . .!*' whispered Marianne. '*Waiter . . .*'

'Ah yes. Good evening, Peter. Well this evening?'

'*Very* well, Madam, thank you. Did you all have a good day?' But there didn't seem to be a great take-up on that line of questioning, so Peter rattled on glibly, with professional ease. 'So – what may I get for you all this evening?'

Nicole was egging on David with her eyes.

'*Order*, David.'

'Yes. Right. OK, then – my wife will have the smoked salmon – that right? Yes. And with caviar? What say? Yes – a *bit*. Just a *bit* of caviar. Right. Yes – *with* caviar, thank you. Marianne – you're having the bouillon thing, yes? Yes – and with all the, you know – etcetera. Rollo? Decided? No? Sure? Right – *nothing* over there . . .'

'Oh *Rollo*,' deplored Nicole. 'Why? Why not order something?'

'Told you, Mum. Not very hungry.'

'Oh but still you must *eat*, Rollo. What's wrong with you?'

'*Am* eating, Mum. Having the steak. Told you.'

'*Right*,' resumed David (oh Christ – it could go on all bloody night, this bloody palaver). 'Right, OK – nothing there – and I'll have the Caesar Salad. OK. Then to follow . . .' (Oh sweet Lord – here we go again: the bloody waistband on these bloody trousers – telling you . . . cutting me in half) ' . . . well look, all just order what you want, yes? Easier, I think. I'll be having the roast veal, please – all the bits, what is it? Wild mushrooms, risotto – yeh, all that. Nicole?'

'That does sound very *nice* . . . oh *God*: did you feel *that* one? Heavens, Peter – the ship is really rocking around tonight, isn't it?'

'I've known it worse,' laughed Peter. 'This isn't too bad.'

'Not too good either . . .' came Nicole's quite hesitant judgment on that. 'I do hope *Pat*'s all right. Not too bad, anyway. I tried to persuade her to come to dinner, you know, but she said she wasn't at all up for it. Poor Pat.'

'Order, Nicole,' said David, quite swiftly.

'Oh yes – *sorry*, Peter. Yes – I think I'll be terribly boring and have what my husband is having: sounds wonderful. What about you, Marianne? And Rollo – are you *sure* you just want a steak? Yes? Well all right – a steak for my son, then. Fillet – medium, please. And plenty of chips. He can never get enough chips, can you Rollo?'

'Not actually that *hungry*,' tried Rollo, quite feebly.

'Oh don't be so *silly*. You're always hungry for *chips*!'

'Could I have the roast cod, please?' piped up Marianne. 'New potatoes – ooh and yes, some of that wonderful pea puree, if you've got that.'

'Certainly, Madam,' said Peter, scribbling in his pad. 'Pea puree. Absolutely no problem at all. Would you care to see the wine list, sir?'

'*Yes*,' said David, immediately. 'Well actually no – needn't bother. That burgundy I had last time: very good. The wine fellow knows – he'll tell you. Sauvigny, or something. Couple of bottles of that.'

'Well *I* won't be drinking much,' said Nicole, rather stiffly. 'A glass will do me. And Marianne only *sips* – don't you, Marianne? And some fizzy water, please, Peter.'

'I'll have a lager,' said Rollo. 'Lager, yep.'

'There you *see*, David: no one's going to be drinking the wine, are they?'

David sighed. 'Right, um – Peter. So that's one lager, one bottle of sparkling and a couple of bottles of the burgundy. Right? OK – good.' (Thank Christ that's over – and bring the wine *quickly*, will you?)

'You cold, Mum?' went Rollo.

At the departure of Peter, Nicole's face had relaxed – well down from hyperactive and quite a bit mad – but it returned to taut and plastic rather rapidly, now.

'No. Why? What do you mean?'

'I just wondered about the gloves. You can borrow my balaclava, if you like.'

Which David thought was quite hysterically *funny*, actually: didn't show it, though.

'Highly amusing,' was Nicole's conclusion to that particular avenue of surmise. 'I think you ought to put something on that *bruise*, Rollo. Savlon, or something.'

'It's fine,' said Rollo.

Yes it is fine, as it happens, because all I ended up with was a bruise. Ribs are aching a bit. Telling you, though – those people hadn't come in when they did, he was going to kill me, that bloke Sammy, you know. Wasn't fooling. Christ – he scared me half to death. I still haven't got over the shock of him just bursting *in*, like that. Got all his spit on my face, which was pretty disgusting. Don't quite know *what's* going to happen, now. Jilly wouldn't talk, afterwards. Wouldn't say a word to me. Just kept shaking her head. Anyway – try and get to her later. Right now I'd better have a go at *saying* something, I reckon: one more mention of the bruise and I might just tell them exactly how I got it. Which would be something, wouldn't it?

'How's your weirdo chum, Marianne? Still a bundle of laughs, is he?'

'Oh shut *up*, Rollo. You don't know *anything*.'

'What 'chum'?' Nicole wanted to know. 'Who, Marianne?'

'The *loony*,' laughed out Rollo. 'The vampire from the black lagoon.'

'What on earth are you *talking* about, Rollo? Marianne – what is, who is Rollo talking about?'

'Oh . . .' supplied Marianne, with deep reluctance. 'Someone I've been – talking to, that's all. Someone I met.'

'I see,' said Nicole. 'Is that this 'Tom' you mentioned to me? Well you might have introduced us. But maybe from the way Rollo was *describing* him . . . maybe not.'

'Oh he's not like that at *all*,' snapped Marianne. 'He's very – nice.'

Yes – he is. Very nice and very wise and very deep, I

think. But the point is where *is* he? Oh dear God where *is* he? I've just searched *everywhere*. I asked one of the, I don't know quite exactly what he was – steward, or something, he could have been. Anyway – in *uniform* . . . and he said Oh, not to worry, Miss – it's a big ship, this – you'll bump into him sooner or later. Yes but *look*, I was going, I've searched just everywhere and I've left dozens of messages in his cabin and I'm really very *worried*. Hm, he went: hm. Tell you what, Miss – if he still hasn't shown up by the morning, report it to one of the officers on duty, yes? They'll probably put out a Tannoy announcement, or something. But I really shouldn't *worry*, Miss, if I were you. Sometimes, tell you – there's a woman works in the Purser's office, and I don't clap eyes on her for days on end – I wouldn't mind but I'm *married* to her: can be a blessing, sometimes. Yes well, I said: *thank* you. But I'm not at all sure he was taking me seriously.

'Where's the bloke with the bloody *wine* . . .?' hissed out David, impatiently.

'Oh just *wait*, can't you, David! You and your bloody *wine* . . . Does anyone want,' continued Nicole, perfectly seamlessly, 'to come to the Casino, tonight? Terribly good fun.'

'How much have you won, Mum?' asked Rollo, quite cheekily.

'Oh Rollo that's not really the *point*, is it? It's just – fun, yes?'

'How much,' grunted David, 'have you *lost*, then?'

'Oh leave her, Dad,' put in Marianne. 'If she's *enjoying* herself . . .'

'Well *thank* you, Marianne,' gushed Nicole. 'At least *someone* in this family is on my side. So will you come? Yes, Marianne? Say yes.'

'Well . . .' doubted Marianne, 'it's not really my *thing*, Mum . . .'

No it isn't. Also – I've just got to look for Tom and this time *find* him . . .

'What about you, Rollo? No good asking *you*, is it David? You'll be getting plastered with Dwight, no doubt.'

'You can lose for both of us,' smiled David. And then he got worried. 'Actually, Nicole – you will go *easy*, won't you? I mean look – how much *have* you lost, actually?'

'Oh you have to go and *spoil* it, don't you, David? That's just you all over, isn't it? If anything good's happening, then along comes bloody *David* to fuck it all up.' And in the silence, she was contrite. 'Sorry, Marianne. I'm sorry, Rollo.'

Hm, thought David: I don't get a 'sorry', you notice. Yes well – I take that not at all spontaneous outburst to be a hastily erected smokescreen – an attempted obliteration of the fact that she has, in truth, dropped a fortune. On my credit card, of course. The one and only, general purpose, free for all, just come and *get* it, why don't you, credit card – nominally the sole liability of apparently the only man on this bloody ship who hasn't actually got any *money*. Oh God. Oh God oh God oh *God* . . . I think I could lose my *mind* . . .

'Would you,' asked Peter, 'care to taste the wine, sir?'

'No,' said David. 'Just pour it, will you?'

⚓

So Nicole ended up going to the Casino on her own. She ran into Charlene on the way, but she was in a great rush to be in her cabin and get more packing done – yet *again*: my God – how much packing can one woman do? (Not too much now, Charlene had assured her: just the stuff I got in the *Harrods* store? The Wedgwood, the War-Sister and the Spayed, Spood – I can't never recall how that one goes.) And yes, Nicole had lost again. Rather a lot. Don't actually want to *talk* about it, thank you, if that's *quite* all right with you (I think it must be rigged). And now I have changed into the crimson taffeta and asked for and received fairly

335

concise directions to the Captain's quarters, and that is where I am headed. Because there's something, I think, I just must try; I'm a trier, you see – and I need to win.

Goodness, though – the ship is really moving about tonight. I mean it always goes a bit from side to *side* (you expect that) – but now it's very discernibly going forward and back (up and down) as well. God *knows* how Pat's coping down below – God only *knows*. Poor Pat.

It was just that time of evening that Captain Scar attempted to keep aside for just himself (play a little Mozart). It didn't often *work*, of course – and so he was not at all surprised, but still bloody irritated all the same, when his Number Two had knocked on the door, stepped in briskly, coughed politely, and informed him that a first class passenger had requested a quick word, sir. And yes, thought the Captain, it's all right for *you*, man, to chuck your eyes up to heaven and pull down the corners of your mouth – but I'm the one who's got to bloody *deal* with her, aren't I? And yes, oh yes – it will be a 'her': it always bloody was.

'*Anthony . . .*' was Nicole's very fulsome greeting (it was as if she had all of a rush just remembered the word). She glided across the floor with one arm extended before her like a jouster's lance, knowing well that her determined tread would encourage the long and feather-light chiffon scarf at her throat to float on air and sail away gorgeously in her breathtaking wake. 'I know it's most *awfully* late and I do so much apologize but I'm just so terribly *worried* on behalf of my daughter, Anthony, and I felt I simply had to confide in you immediately.'

And she glanced to the left and right of her: the expression on her face suggested that she had up until this very moment been most profoundly asleep for a hundred long years and now, at the kiss of a prince, she had awoken, more beautiful than ever, and was as we speak stretching with abandon and luxuriously across a silken divan held up by glistening blackamoors at the tented and bejewelled epicentre of no less than a fabulous palace.

'What a perfectly *charming* room,' she quite effortlessly effused. 'All so terribly masculine and nautical. What pretty little boats . . .'

'Ha. Yes, I – yes. I'm very pleased you like it, Madam. *Ships,* actually . . . You are worried, you say . . .?'

'*Nicole,*' underlined Nicole. 'You remember, don't you?'

'*Nicole*. Yes of course.'

'We danced . . .'

'Yes we did. Of course we did. I remember it well, Nicole.'

'You *do* remember . . .?'

'Yes yes. Very vividly. A treasured memory. Nicole, of course. You are worried about something, Nicole? Please do sit. Can I offer you anything at all?'

The last bit of that had been somewhat rushed, because Nicole was already sitting, legs very elegantly crossed at the ankle, and she seemed to be glancing about her.

'At the ball – do you recall? You were saying how terribly hard you worked and that one or two of us should come up and see for themselves. How the sweat just *pours* off you. So I thought I would. A glass of champagne would be *divine,*' she concluded, smilingly.

'Of course,' agreed the Captain, moving away to the intercom on his desk. Might as well turn off the Mozart, while I'm over here – sorry and all that, my dear Amadeus, but believe me, I'm thinking of you: you've no chance in the face of this. Captain Scar murmured his request for champagne, and softly replaced the handset. Every other drink known to Christendom I've got in this cabinet, here – but no, this *Nicole* person (who apparently I *danced* with? Did I really? Well perfectly possible, of course – how many of these bloody women have I had to dance with, down the years?) . . . yes, this *Nicole* woman had to have champagne, yes of course. And also – did I mention? She's *worried*, yes: very worried indeed. As now, no doubt, she will tell me again. And yes I know: this very composed woman before me – Christ, it's as if she's settled herself down for the night – does not at all appear to be consumed by a single concern or care in the world, but there it is: she's worried. She said so. And yes – here it comes one more time:

'It's on my daughter's behalf, Anthony, that I'm here. As I said. At first she didn't even want to talk about it, but I managed to get it out of her eventually. A mother always knows, you know, when something is bothering one of her children. Are you a family man, Anthony?'

'Two boys,' smiled the Captain. 'Nearly grown up, now. Good lads.'

'They must miss you – at sea all the time. So must your wife . . .'

'Yes, well – isn't actually a wife any more. Usual story, I'm afraid. Goes with the job, it sometimes seems. Anyway – never mind all that. Ah! Your champagne, Nicole. Thank you, Howard.'

The steward appeared to bow from the neck in the Captain's direction (how perfectly *lovely*, thought Nicole – he did it just the way you're supposed to, if ever you meet one of the Royals). Howard was gone very swiftly – and so silently, he barely disturbed the air.

'Are you not joining me, Anthony? Terribly *rude* – making me drink on my own . . .'

'Oh, well – yes, I'll have a – I'll just mix myself a . . .'

He walked to the cabinet and poured just a tonic water into a heavy crystal glass, added lots of ice and then threw in a quarter lime.

'Tell me the problem,' he called over his shoulder.

'*Nicole* . . .'

'Nicole, yes – I haven't forgotten. Tell me the problem. Nicole.'

'Well apparently my daughter, that's Marianne – I think you met her?'

'Yes yes. Marianne. Mm. Remember her well.'

'Well she's got to know this person called *Tom*, it appears
– who's now, um, well – disappeared, she says. Quite
worrying for her.'

'I see. Mm. Well of course she is a very large ship, you
know, Nicole, and – '

'Well that's exactly what I *told* her. But she's been over it
with a fine, oh – what do they say? Tooth comb. Tooth comb
– how terribly *odd* ... And anyway, she hasn't seen him
since morning. Left messages, of course – and nothing.
Absolutely nothing. Quite *worrying* for her, you see.'

'I do see – yes of course. Well look, Nicole – you tell your
daughter this – '

'*Marianne.*'

'Hm? Yes. Of course. Now listen to me, Marianne – I
mean *Nicole*, Nicole – yes. You tell Marianne that if she still
has no luck by morning I'll institute a thorough ship search.
That'll winkle him out. We do them, time to time – and
believe me, she really mustn't worry. People always turn up
in the end.'

'Well that's very reassuring, Anthony. I shall tell her
immediately. Well ... right, then ...' she concluded –
standing now, smoothing down her dress and adjusting her
scarf. 'I mustn't take up any more of your valuable time,
Anthony. Thank you so much for the champagne.'

'The pleasure was all mine.' Nicole was advancing
towards him. 'Nicole,' he tacked on.

She placed one fingernail at the tip of his chin.

'You don't, I suppose, do you, Anthony ... want to *sleep*
with me at all, do you?'

The Captain looked down. Here we go. It's this one again.
Here we bloody go again.

'Nicole ... you are a very attractive woman ...'

'No ...' sighed Nicole, quite resignedly. 'I didn't really
think you did. Or you would have *said*, I expect. Ah well. I
suppose these prizes can't include *everything* ...'

339

And Captain Scar leapt at that: a lifebelt bobbing amid the foaming sea.

'Ah of *course* – you won the competition, didn't you? Yes yes. Well let me do this, Nicole: in two days' time? Yes? When we dock in New York? Let me invite you and your family up on to the Bridge. The view is really very spectacular, I assure you. Watch dawn break over the skyline.'

'Oh – *thank* you, Anthony. That will be *lovely*. Oh yes – *thank* you.'

And then the whole ship heaved just slightly more detectably than it had been doing for the whole of the evening, now – but not enough, surely, to have sent Nicole skittering forward and right into the Captain. She stayed there, nestled up to him – she looked up straight into his eyes. Neither moved. The swaying ship was gently croaking.

'No . . .?' she whispered, softly. 'Sure . . .? Not even just – hold me a bit . . .?'

The Captain closed his eyes. 'I'm sorry . . .' he said, so quietly.

She nodded, and moved away quickly to the door. Just before she slipped outside, she smiled over at him, quite bravely – ignoring the sting of tears that must mean, she just knew, that she was looking such a mess.

'*Nicole* . . .' she managed to say.

The Captain let the air rush out of him, the second she had closed the door. Nicole, yes indeed: I won't forget.

⚓

It was finally what could more or less be called morning, and Marianne – still unaware that she was freezing and practically welded to her seat – strained in the just-dawn to discern through aching eyes clotted with tears the hazy seaming that roughly joined the harshness of the sky to the roll of the dirt-grey sea: it was swollen like a gangrenous limb might well be – grotesquely distended, a network of veins was threaded all over the surface and at the point of bursting wide open. She had been sitting on this hard wet seat at the stern of the ship for so many hours: from very soon after she had first read the letter. Marianne had then and at once felt totally compelled to escape the breathlessness of her cabin – anywhere enclosed – and without even considering the dark and the cold, she was soon and quite blindly battling her way down slimy decks and clattering steps to the very rearmost point of the ship. She could only hear the churning of the wake – there was nothing at all to see – and her thin little jacket was damp and useless. Now, her stiff white fingers were still clamped hard to the single sheet of paper: she could not move them. There was just barely enough grudging light from amid all this crushing greyness . . . so maybe she could read it through just one more time. (She had been grimly holding on to something, and her hand now had become a part of whatever it was: the great and elaborate swells of ocean, she knew, could suddenly pitch her over.)

'Marianne. My dear. I think I should explain. When I said to you that I helped my Mary, I mean that I helped her to leave me. She was in such pain. They gave her things, of course, for the pain, but still it never seemed to leave her. Through a friend, I located something that would take the anxiety from her eyes and make her face relax again. Having eased her pain, however, I found my own increasing day by day up until the point where it has become intolerable. And so I think what I now must do is ease it, and then I can maybe find her again. I so very nearly *love* you, Marianne – but nothing can get through the pain. Goodbye. Thank you. Be safe. Tom.'

She raised her eyes and the hurt erupted from her in one great gasp of sheer disbelief. She stared at the relentless maw of this fat and greedy ocean – she was aware now too of shivering badly for the very first time. Marianne focused on just this one dark and angry wave, and so very soon it was lost to sight. Because where we are, she thought . . . it so very quickly becomes where we have *been*.

⚓

She had not wanted to show the officer on duty the letter. She had already, and as calmly as she could manage, confided to him her convictions (they had started out as her darkest forebodings, but soon she owned up to what just had to be the terrible truth, here). But you could tell that even now, no one was taking her *seriously*. Everyone she spoke to just kept telling her how big the ship was – as if she didn't *know* that, or something. The *sea*, she kept on saying, fighting back at least the worst of her tears – but the *sea*, the *sea* is so much *bigger*. And if he cannot be found anywhere on board . . . well then. Still he demurred, this rather harassed-looking officer, whoever he was. Still he hummed and hawed. So then she showed him the letter.

'Right,' he said. 'Yes. This throws a different light on it. I shall inform the Captain. We'll set up a ship search.'

Yes I *suppose* so, he was thinking: I suppose I just have to, in the face of this. But God – he won't at all be *pleased*, the Old Man. Last thing you want, isn't it? And Christ – if that bunch of *journalists* get hold of it . . . Jesus, they're already going to have a field day, aren't they? Bloody orgy going on in the Emperor Suite, far as I can make it out. I've had to sack two bar staff this morning – severely reprimand the Assistant Cruise Director . . . who led them right *to* it, stupid bloody sod – and now it surely looks as if we've got a bloody jumper on our hands. Dear God. Old Man won't be very *pleased*, I can tell you that much.

They had, at least, kept Marianne well informed about the progress of the search. This was only because, she suspected, they did not want her shouting her mouth off about anything to do with it at all. And later in the afternoon, they actually made this very plain to her: Would appreciate it *greatly*, Miss, if you wouldn't, um – mention all this to anyone. It upsets the passengers, anything of this kind, as you might understand. Marianne said she did – understand. Thirty people, apparently, had been assigned to search the whole ship – and it was very discreetly done. Even though Marianne was aware of its happening, she never saw anyone actively *searching*. After nearly eight hours, she was summoned by the Captain. He asked her to sit down.

'Well I'm sorry to have to *tell* you, Nicole . . .'

'Marianne. Nicole is my mother. I'm Marianne.'

'*Marianne* – oh God of *course*. Please forgive me. Well, um – Marianne – '

'You haven't found him.'

'We, um – no. No. The search has failed to, um . . .'

'I didn't expect him to be found. I just hoped.'

'Well quite, quite. We all did. And may I speak for the entire crew and staff when I say I really am most – '

'It's all right. I didn't really know him that well. Didn't know him at *all*, in fact. If I'd understood him, I maybe could've . . .'

'You really mustn't blame yourself, you know. When people are that determined . . . well, you just can't stop them.'

Marianne nodded. 'What happens next? Anything? Have you – dealt with this sort of thing before?'

Captain Scar looked down.

'We, um – have a policy not to actually ever talk about any of that, I'm afraid. Probably understand why. But what happens next is that we alert next of kin, of course – '

'I don't think there is any. That was the point.'

'Yes well – we go through all the motions – all the procedures. Contact the relevant authorities in New York. Before we sail to Jamaica, the ship will be swept again. Just in case. And, um – well that's *it*, really. No more we can really, um . . . Now tell me, Marianne. How are you bearing up?

343

Hm? Want the Doc to fix you up with something? Help you get a bit of sleep. Probably need it.'

Marianne had risen: just had to, she thought, go now.

'Thank you, no. I shall be . . . perfectly fine. Goodbye, Captain.'

'Goodbye. I really am so sorry. Marianne.'

Oh *Christ*, he thought, when he was alone again. Bugger bugger *bugger*. Why can't a crossing ever be *simple*? Hey? And what next? Hm? After the bloody orgy, after the bloody suicide – what bloody *next*? Because they say that, don't they? Comes in *threes*, all this sort of thing.

⚓

'Hiya, David my man! Finally I gotcha. Three times I called already.'

David cradled the phone into the crook of his shoulder, and continued to button his shirt: the last one got sweaty – sweaty, yes, and badly crumpled too.

'Yes – I've just got here. So, Dwight – we meeting, or what?'

'Sure thing, buddy boy. Unless you aiming to take in this here *Talent* Show . . .?'

'Ha! Joking. OK, Dwight – usual place, usual time. And you're *OK*, are you?'

'OK how, David? What saying?'

'Well it's just all the pitching of the ship. People are dropping like flies all over the place. Apparently the doctors have been inundated with people wanting some sort of injection they've got for all this, or something – but the joke is, someone was telling me, it won't take effect until we've docked at New York! Whereupon they'll all be poleaxed!'

'Jeez . . . kidding me. What a buncha klutzes. Naw, Dave – I'm just fine. Constitootion of an ox. Oh and hey *David* – I saw that hot babe of yours, cuppla hours back. Seemed to me like she was *crying*? What *doing* to her, Dave, you old

344

goat? Anyways – still she cut me dead. Me she don't like, *period*.'

Crying? Really? Well all David can tell you is that his little Suki had certainly not been crying earlier, when they were both entwined and wholly intent upon a fairly severe session of *cherishing*: how the shirt came to get that way, as a matter of fact.

'I'm sure you're *imagining* all this, you know, Dwight. She'd love you! Tell you what – I'll bring her along to the bar. Yes? Telling you – you'll have loads in common. Oh and *Dwight*, um – I hate to mention it, but um – the *money*, yes? Because she's been quiet so far, Trish – well, she's sick as a dog, thank Christ – but it's a bit of a time bomb, you know?'

'Relax, David. It's fixed. I spoke to her direct.'

'You did? Really? And what did she . . .? How did she . . .?'

'She's sweet with the whole thing. Nul problemo. And, uh – so am *I*, David. If you know what I mean. You're OK with that, I hope? Don't mind?'

'Mind? No. No – course I don't *mind*. Great. Best of luck. I think you'll be OK with her, actually, Dwight. It's *money* she loves, quite frankly.'

Yeah, thought Dwight: dead right. That's just the message I got from her, loud and clear. How it went was like this: first I had to get some real distance between me and Charlene, was numero uno, if you know what I'm saying. Some damn lousy piece of junk she got in the *Harrods* store? Some dumb kinda paddery broad in a big stoopid dress? Her *hand* is broke off, is the way she was going: so how come, Dwight – you care to tell me how the *hand* is broke off, huh? And I'm back with What're you – *nuts*? You think I been, what – stroking the paddery dame's hand so goddam hard I wore it clean *away*? If it's broke it's on accounta you didn't store it right, Charlene – sure as hell ain't nothing to do with me, you hear me? Maybe, she says, I can wire the Harrods store. Charlene, I says to her – you wire the Harrods store from onboard this ship and it's gonna cost me the sorta money I can *buy* the fuckin' Harrods store – I getting through to you? *Live* with it, Charlene – suck it up. From where I'm coming from, it ain't the worst thing in the whole goddam world, you know?

Sheez . . . So I call up David, and nix. So I was gonna grab me a couple drinks – beat up bad on my goddam bowels just one more time – and then I gets to thinking, hey – stead I give the cash to David and he squares it with the Patty broad, maybe I can do myself a bitta good here, huh? Cos I'm telling ya – she's OK, Patty. No kid, but real *usable*: you know what I'm sane? Plus – I like a deal. With a deal upfront, you know where you stand. So I get to her cabin, right? And Jesus what a shit-hole – make a cell in San Quentin seem real homey, you know? And what I was expecting to see, I guess, was the kinda cool dame of a cuppla nights back? What it didn't never strike me is she'd be just about as close to death as one woman can surely get herself without she just goes right on ahead and dies on ya. She was one sick lady. And the smella the cabin I didn't too much like.

'Hi, Patty. You looking good. What's cooking?'

'*Gah*! Urrrrgh . . . don't *say* that – oh God don't *say* that, Dwight . . .!'

'Say what, Patty? What's *cooking* . . .?'

'*Gaaaah* . . .!' is all I get outta her this time around. Next I know I'm a-hollering at her through the bathroom door.

'I sure can pre-shate this is maybe not the greatest time, huh? . . . But I would like to put to you one proposition, Patty. What I hear, you're one lady for a deal, honey.'

Not too sure she spoke some or she didn't; I'm getting this kinda noise like a moonsick hound dog. So maybe I go on:

'See, Patty – I talked a bit with our amigo David, yeah? We're kinda – *buddies*? Seems you want a little pocket money, I didn't get that wrong. Well could be I can help you out, is all I'm saying. You hear me in there, Patty? You still living? Ain't no deal if ya gone died on me, girl. Tap on the door, Patty, if you still alive.'

And some sorta rumble came across (she maybe fall over?) so I figure OK, Dwight my man – wrap this up quick and get your ass outta here.

'So what I'm, like, putting your way, Patty, is I maybe setcha up in a condo in New York. You like the sounda that? Somewhere midtown – real classy. And maybe you wanna do a little shopping, yeh? Well could be I can fix that. What say? Patty? What say? And time to time, I come over – see how you doing . . . That sound good to you? Or what? It's time to *talk*, now, Patty . . . don't be holding out on me, now . . .'

So I wait around some, and nothing. So OK, is how I'm figuring – if she died, she died: I did all I could. Then boom! The door's wide open and she's kinda just hanging on to the side of it and oh yeah *sure* she looks like hell – hoo boy, big time – but listen up: this wrap she's wearing – it's come all loose, you know, and from where I'm standing, the view from the neck down is mighty fine. Yessir ma'am – never give no mind to your face right now, it looks something put out in the trash following one mother of a Halloween: I do not regret one single word I just said to you, lady, on accounta hear me, sweet babe: I sure do like the cut of your titties.

'*Dwight* . . .' she gasped – and then she looked alarmed and deeply uneasy about what just this much effort had kicked off in her insides. 'I think . . . that is . . . just *marvellous* . . . if only I can, oh God – *live* that long? . . .'

Dwight grinned broadly, and patted her back encouragingly. Not, as it turned out, the best of moves on his part, he maybe saw now – because Patty looked goggle-eyed and stunned and then quite assailed and then, oh God – so pale *grey* as she lurched back into the bathroom and just about managed to hurl closed the door.

'You'll be just fine . . .!' a pretty damn pleased Dwight was yelling through the panels. 'Deal is though, honey – you don't go talking bout nothing with Nicole. OK?' As he waited, he heard a horrible noise. 'You wanna maybe come up and do some of that on the *Talent* Show, Patty? Could be you wind up Miss Twenny-First Century *Barf* you know? Naw – just kidding around, Patty honey. I'll see ya!'

What a gal. So – what I'm thinking now, just sat up at the bar and fooling with a fresh Jack Daniel's, is I sure did get me a deal. I been needing this for how long? This way, back home – I get outta the house and I got me someplace to *go*, you know? Just a shame she's so wasted tonight, my Patty. On account of if David is bringing along his red-hot momma, we could maybe have made us up a foursome. Which couldda been neat. And where *is* that boy? By my watch, he's overdo. And he can say what he likes – that girla his, she don't like me one leedle bit. A guy gets to know these things. So how the evening's gonna go down, I couldn't rightly say.

That him, way down yonder? I do bleeve so – and Jeez, my eyes ain't too good, this kinda distance, but it sure looks to me like he's *dragging* her in. What gives?

'Come *on* – come *on*,' David was urging – and yes, pretty much dragging her. (Don't know what's wrong with the girl: chattering away nineteen to the dozen – Sure, David, sure, I'll meet with this buddy of yours, why hell not? – and then we turn in here and suddenly she freezes up and starts pulling away from me.) 'Don't be shy – you'll love him, I tell you.'

And then when Dwight was able to focus just a little bit better, he got right off that stool and strutted off to meet this head-on.

'Dwight – here she is, my gorgeous little girl. Say hello, Suki.'

'Oh *Christ* . . .' moaned Suki. 'I'm *outta* here . . .!'

But David had a hold of her.

348

'Don't be *rude*, Suki. Say something to my good friend Dwight. Dwight? What's wrong? Dwight? Why are you – why are you *looking* at me like that? Dwight?'

'You . . .' said Dwight, really deep, and very slowly, ' . . . *bastard* . . .!'

David was frankly amazed.

'What?' he said. '*What* . . .? What's *wrong* with everyone? *Speak*, someone, will you? Is this some joke I'm not in on, or something?'

And as Dwight just stood there – rigid and empurpled with an unspeakable rage and beginning to teeter – Suki just rolled up her eyes and cried out OH GEE I'M JUST SO *SORRY*, DADDY . . .! I just had no *idea* . . .

David glanced at Dwight – so suddenly that it was as if his face had been slapped round in the direction. He felt his mouth drop open, as icy cold invaded the whole of him. It wasn't so much the fear of the here and now that had him tight – more he felt quite bloodless at the terrible realization that once again, one more time, a future of sorts that had been dangled before him by the gleeful gods, drunk on cruelty, had now and immediately been jerked right away from him at the very last second. Once again, one more time, he was on the dump. There could be no more.

And Dwight then knew that he had to right now, punch this guy out good – just as David got wind of it too. He twitched and ducked and ran for cover.

⚓

'Not many *people*, are there . . .?' sniffed Jennifer, glancing around the auditorium. 'Must be, what – how many seats are there here, do you think, Stacy? Four hundred? Less? Three? More? Hell of a *lot*, anyway. Practically *empty* . . .'

'Weather, I expect,' said Stacy. 'It's just an *amazing* sensation – bucking up and down like this. Don't you think? Man at the door said it was set to get even worse, later on. I can't imagine it any worse. We're not going to sink, are we, Mum? It's not going to be like the *Titanic*?'

'Well all I can say is your Auntie Min will be terribly disappointed if we *do*. I don't suppose anyone else is going to her silly little wedding.'

'I'm not sure if I like it or I don't . . .' Stacy was musing. 'The really huge lurches leave your stomach sort of up in the air. Do you get that? But it's a bit like those fairground horses, in a way. Just more so.'

'All right, everyone?' chivvied a beaming Stewart, bearing down on them both – face almost neon tonight, and a clipboard jammed under his arm. 'Everybody happy? Fun fun fun – yes?'

'Where *is* everyone?' asked Jennifer. 'Are we terribly early, or something?'

'Bit of a thin house . . .' agreed Stewart, quite ruefully.

Bit of a thin house my *arse*: never *seen* so bloody few people turn out for the Talent Show. Bloody storm, I suppose. And more than half my entrants have dropped out too. Mrs Myrtle's not going to do her Shirley Bassey – can't guarantee her dinner won't pop out; John Cummings says he can't do the conjuring because all the props will be sliding all over the place (fair point – it's all you can do to stand upright, at the moment). It's looking like the star of the show is going to be Nobby with his nautical terms and Aggie with her, oh God help us all – *Madison*. Not forgetting the redoubtable Disco Debbie, of course – she's still well up for bopping till she drops, poor old sod. Let's just hope she doesn't *literally* drop, that's all. That really would be the icing on the cake.

You know what, don't you? I mean look – I might as well come right out and say it: I am totally *fed up*. Truly pissed off with just everything, now. I mean – it was *my* fault, was it, that those bloody little yobs were screwing each other on the floor of the Emperor Suite? That's down to *me*, is it? This one they think they can lay quite fairly and squarely at *my* door? A severe reprimand, I got: it's on my record. Very nice. That'll have them all queueing up to get me, won't it? Ever I'm after another job. But *look*, I argued – if I'd *known* there was anyone in there, well then of *course* I wouldn't have led in a party of journalists, would I? I'm not *stupid*. Nonetheless, they went – nonetheless: if it hadn't been for you, no one would have known. And I was going But *listen* to me, why can't you? *I* didn't know, did I? How could I? But it was no good. Blue in the face. Made not one jot of difference. And do you know what really did it? When they were writing up my record, they had to ask me my *name*. I know. Unbelievable, isn't it? After all these years on this bloody ship – and the only time I get even *noticed* is when they slap on me an official bloody *reprimand* and they don't even know what I'm *called* . . .! I'm telling you – it's all too much, quite frankly. It's all just getting on top of me.

Anyway – ten minutes overdue already: can't delay this bloody show any longer, can I? Perfectly plain no one else is coming. Right, then – let's just go through the running order . . . cross out the names of practically everyone . . . right . . . now then: got the prizes (chocolates – *hah*! As if people don't get enough to stuff themselves with . . . and cruets and shot glasses with the name of the ship on them: lovely). And I've got my flare gun all primed and charged. They love that bit, generally. It's only a low-voltage thing – mild S.O.S. – but it makes everyone really jump when it goes off – and then this rather pretty cascade of gold sort of stars and circles fizzes right up and then floats down slowly, just like a lit-up fountain: star turn – always do this at the end. Right then – here we go.

And the very second he stepped on to the stage (Hi, everyone! Greetings and felicitations! – well, you all know me: Stewart, Assistant Cruise Director . . .) – he had no sooner got the words out of his mouth, and she was *doing* it, that bloody woman at the front. God Almighty.

'Come *on*, then!' shouted Jennifer. 'Get *on* with it! Why are we *waiting*? Why are we way-ay-*ting*?!'

'*Shh*, Mum!' giggled Stacy. 'Honestly . . .!'

'Oh shut *up*, Stacy. This is why I'm *here* – have a bit of fun. Come *on*! Come *on*! Are you the stripper? Get 'em off!'

Stewart just glowered at her – and very tersely announced the first act: Caroline, from Morecambe, who was going to sing for us that perennial old favourite – Greensleeves.

Jennifer groaned, and glanced about her in search of any sort of distraction. Oh God – a few seats away it was Nobby and Aggie! Argh! Look the other way, fast. Couple of horrible-looking businessmen on the other side. One of them was speaking quite loudly (maybe not much of a Greensleeves man).

'See, in the greeting card game, you always wanna be one jump ahead. Now wom sign? Like – we noticed the trend way back – so we don't print nuffing in 'em, nowadays. You got to listen to what the punters is *sighing*. So fundamentally, it's back to bye-sicks. Now wom sign?'

'Oh *God*, Stacy,' deplored Jennifer. 'Shall we get out of here? I thought it would be funnier than this. More of a laugh.'

'Let's just see what's up next.'

Next up was a mother and daughter duo (all the way from Texas! Anyone here tonight from Texas? No? Nobody? No one at all? Well . . . let's hear it anyway for Abigail and Trixie . . . um, what is this? *June*. No, not June – Jane. Abigail and Trixie-*Jane*, ladies and and gentlemen! Yay!). Jennifer tolerated the first few bars of Stand By Your Man, and absolutely no more.

'Boo! Boo! What man would stand by either of *you*? Rubbish! Get off!'

As Stacy just died of embarrassment and Jennifer continued to hoot with delight, Stewart was off that stage and making for them fast. His mouth was set, and he truly had the aspect of one who was lit up from within.

'*Right*! That is absolutely the *limit*!' he practically spat at Jennifer – and she was shaken, momentarily, by the sheer uncut fury and hatred she saw in his face. But she pulled herself together.

'Who the hell are *you*, anyway?' she drawled at him.

And that, really, was it. Stewart closed his eyes tight, and the muscles in his neck bunched up and bulged hard. Who am I? Who *am* I? I'll *tell* you who I am. I am now, right this second, about to teach everyone – everyone aboard this bloody, bloody ship, a lesson. After tonight, everybody will know my bloody name. No one again will ever have to *ask*.

'Right . . .' he said, quite ominously quietly. '*You*!' And he pointed an aggressive finger at Jennifer's face. 'Up. Right now. You're coming with me.' And then he stunned himself by adding: 'You're under *arrest*.'

Jennifer was shaken, yes, but was rallying round quite quickly.

'Oh just go and *fuck* yourself, whatever you're called . . .'

Stewart was white, and his forehead glistened. He drew out his flare gun and jabbed it into her ribs. The shock of it made Jennifer half rise – and she waved back a would-be calming hand to Stacy, who had just briefly squealed out her protest.

'Right. Now out. Out of here. If you do not – I will kill you.'

Stewart was learning the words long after he had formed them, it seemed: an echo from somewhere else, in another time. The ship was pitching so violently, now, that he and Jennifer were quite desperately swaying and clinging on to one another for a sort of support, the black stubby gun still stuck between them. Jennifer began to move as well as she could in the direction he indicated (I mean Jesus I cannot . . . I am not *believing* this . . . but just take one look at him, will you? I think he's mad – very).

353

The two had lumbered out to the perimeter of the room. Several times he had to bark at Stacy to stay exactly where she bloody well was . . . they were nearly out of there – and now bloody *Nobby* was hanging on to his arm.

'Stewart? What on earth do you think that you're doing?'

'Go away, Nobby. This is nothing to do with you.'

'I'm rather afraid, Stewart, it is. No – it's quite all right, Aggie – I'm perfectly capable of handling this.'

Stewart staggered back as the entire floor beneath them all bucked – regained his foothold, though, and looked about him in a fast-rising panic, approaching frenzy. He was sweating, and his lips were dry. Abigail and Trixie-Jane had warbled out the last of Stand By Your Man, and both were just hanging about, now, dangling their arms and looking rather lost. Eyes were flickering from all corners in Stewart's direction, and a growing rumble was discernible: he had to act fast, now, or else he would lose it completely.

'All right then, Nobby – have it your own way. You come too. Out. Keep walking, the both of you. If you do not – I will kill you.'

'Oh *please* no!' Jennifer was imploring. 'Mercy, mercy – *please* not Nobby too! Kill me now, Christ's sake . . .!'

And all a paralysed Aggie and very appalled Stacy could do was watch these three people – bowed legs so clumping and wide apart, as if astride their phantom horses – lurch, bump and collidingly skitter more or less and then eventually out of there, leaving behind them a bankrupt contest, and just one clattering door.

⚓

The view from the Bridge was nightmarish, quite frankly – even for a pro. Captain Scar stood peering through the thick and streaming glass – the wipers were simply not close to coping. On each precipitous and roaring descent, the bows momentarily disappeared altogether beneath the rush of the sea, before rising up again, shrugging away rivers of water to washingly obliterate the decks. (We are due later on, he was thinking, to sail within a very few miles of the icebergs that did for the *Titanic*. I mentioned this to the journalists – they said they terribly wanted to see them. I then told them that the optimum vantage point would be up on the Bridge at around four a.m. . . . whereupon they terribly didn't.)

The Captain turned at the sound of the very discreet, attention-seeking coughlet.

'Oh hullo, Alan. What're you doing up here?'

'Um – a word, if I may, sir?'

'Of course. Fire away.'

Alan glanced about him at the officers on the Bridge.

'Maybe in your quarters, sir?'

Captain Scar was uneasy. Something was wrong. Something else was *wrong*.

'Yes, of course,' he said slowly, following Alan down the stairs – both of them thrown like puppets, and hanging on grimly.

The Captain sat at his desk with his head in his hands as his Number Two apprised him of everything he knew. When he had finished, the Captain said nothing. And then he said this:

'And he won't come to the *door*, you say?'

'Absolutely not, sir. They're all in there, in his office – we know that much . . . but no matter how long we're pounding at the door, well – absolutely no response whatever, sir. Extraordinary business.'

'Indeed,' said Captain Scar. 'We don't have a key?'

'Locked *and* bolted, sir. Take explosive to break it down. Too risky.'

Captain Scar nodded like one condemned and reached for the telephone.

'I'll talk to him. What did you say his name was again?'

'Stewart, sir, apparently. But he won't answer it, sir. We've had the phone ringing pretty well constantly, now. No good at all, I'm afraid.'

'God Almighty. Well what do you think, Alan? *Mad*, is he?'

'I just can't fathom it, sir. He can't possibly hope to *gain* anything from this. Maybe he's just, I don't know – *depressed*, sir.'

The Captain looked at him. 'Depressed. Yes. Quite possibly. I don't feel terribly elated myself, Alan, just at this very moment. So OK – what's the position? What have we got?'

'Well, sir – guard at the door, obviously, and, um – well, not much more to be done, I'm afraid, sir. Sort of have to, I don't know – *starve* him out, I suppose . . .'

The Captain's expression of total bemusement was reflected in that of his Number Two.

'Good God. Right. OK, then, Alan. That will be all. Keep me informed, of course.'

'Of course, sir. Good night, sir.'

'If you say so, Alan.'

Captain Scar stood at the centre of the empty room and clenched his fists and jaw and any other part of him that could be deemed clenchable. Oh dear Christ, why this? Why this now? We're barely twenty-four hours from New York, and I have on my hands here what our American cousins refer to, I believe, as a '*situation*'. The situation *being* that my Assistant Cruise Director, whatever the bloody man's name is, has abducted two passengers . . . dear *Christ* . . . has taken two passengers against their will and has them holed up in his office, totally incommunicado. And according to next of kin – at *gunpoint*. Excellent. Quite perfect. And if our friends from the Press get hold of *this* little lot . . .? Maybe I should set course for those icebergs and keep on bloody going . . .

He moved to his drinks cabinet and poured just a tonic water into a heavy crystal glass, added lots of ice, and then threw in a quarter lime. And by way of an impassioned afterthought, filled it to the brim with gin.

⚓

It reminds me of something, all of this . . . and David was quite amazed to find himself thinking it, as he slowly ambled (well Christ – where was the fire?) the endless length of the padded and silent corridor. Amazed, I suppose, because at least it is a *thought*, yes? The result of a mental impulse which hadn't actually come about as a result of some fresh-probed and now no longer dormant anxiety (it is stirring again – flayed and tender) and nor the deep gut-shriek of stripped-back fear. It was simply the fact that the passage was piled now with trunks and packing cases bound with wire and rope: some other vast sorts of chest – looked like wardrobes on wheels . . . which, thinking about it, yes, they well could be. These all belonged, David had only just now and very slowly worked out (and God, it wasn't difficult), to the long-haulers, the globetrotters, the seen-it-all-before World Cruisers; this whole week – the duration of the entire prime time and big league crossing for us little Englanders – who maybe were more easily satisfied – would have seemed to them no more than last knockings, tail endings . . . and yes yes yes: that's it. Yes, of course – that's what all this recalls to me, now: End Of Term. In that terrible place they packed me off to, my people – far too young, I was, to have been just sent away, like that. I still, even now, remember only the cold and the clatter – the noise and the desolation. There must have *been* fun times, I suppose . . . and my mother, oh – so many years later, she kept on urging me to recall them . . . more, I think, to make her feel better about it than me. Oh come *on*, David, she'd go – there must have *been* fun times! It can't all have been as drab and fearsome as you make out, can it, David? Well – maybe there were, maybe there had been fun times, I really couldn't say. Certainly I recall no such moment – not even one single second when the chill across my heart was suddenly warmed by the realization that now, right now, I am having a real fun time. No. I just remember (because I can't forget it) being barked at and jeered and hit and gated and forever *cold* – and always starving amid the eternal *clatter*. My father and she, my mother told me sombrely – as if uttering a prayer – had gone without and worked so hard for the money to make all of this possible. I made no comment then – and now, now I very definitely have nothing at all to say on the matter. There had been just this one gleam – a faint respite – when one or two days before the end of term, the main hall and the passageways leading away from it were jammed high and haphazardly with all our trunks: *proof* that soon one would be out of there.

And here was, again, that very air. A pent-up excitement – and the barely stifled fizz of moment: the knowledge that soon there would be more, and different. And yes, during this crossing, there have *been* fun times – but now, to me, this ship seems to be simply a place I must very soon leave . . . leave, yes, and leave behind me for ever. On to the next thing. Which will be better, yes? More sound. And it will not trick me.

Christ, I feel wiped out; had a terrible night, just the worst. Didn't get a wink. Storm's blown over, anyway: I heard it die, not much before dawn. And I've heard all about poor Marianne, now. Nicole told me. It just goes to show, though, doesn't it? How right bloody royally and deep-down *hopeless* I am? In the light of all this? I mean to say – was I remotely aware that Marianne had formed some sort of attachment to someone? No. Far too busy drinking, drinking with, oh God – Dwight (my ex-best buddy) and plotting to buy off Trish (my ex-best woman) and then just cutting dinners and teas and parties because there was *cherishing* to be done with, um – as it turns out (and oh *please* don't make me go under the great hot red flush of so much *shame* – not again, not again) . . . with the girl who does, in fact, turn out to be, er . . . oh my God *you* finish it, *you* do it: I just can't.

Anyway. When I heard from Nicole (And you are *listening* to me, David, are you? Not in one of your *trances*? . . . and I wasn't actually listening much, no – *was* in a bit of a trance, in truth: well, wouldn't *you* be? Didn't really focus on paying attention until the gist of the thing became clear to me – that Marianne, my little girl, was in *pain*, here. And then I had to get Nicole to say over to me again just practically the whole of it, which pissed her right off, as you might, I suppose, expect). So when I had finally assimilated that this new friend of Marianne's had – oh God, it's just so faint-makingly terrifying to even *think* about this (have you seen this sea? Have you *seen* it?) – gone over the *side*, Christ . . . well of course my impulse was to go to her, talk to her, take care of her (but not, now – because I can't ever really use the word again – *cherish* her in any shape or form . . . Oh Dwight – oh Dwight: I really am so very *sorry*. I know you won't ever let me *tell* you that – because I've tried, of course I have, I've tried and tried – but maybe in some way you will know that I feel it). But then I thought Yes but *look* – I'm no good at this, am I? I mean *tell* me – please do tell me the last time I helped, oh – just *anyone* in any way whatever? You can't, can you? No you can't because I don't. Ever. Help. I just take hold of a thing and then I fuck it all up.

But so many times I nearly rang her. Picked up the phone, put it down again. Because what do you say to a daughter in pain? And then she rang me. *Marianne*, I went: how are you? I mean – not too, um . . .? Look – I was just going to *call* you! And she said – sounded so small and lost and impossibly distant – Yeh, Daddy, sure: I know you were. Which made me feel, oh – just *how* good? Can we, she said – my own little girl – *talk* a bit . . .? And I said Oh my God of *course* we can, *course* we can – of *course* we can, Marianne.

And so I'm now on my way to meet her. She said her cabin. But I said No – Black Horse. And she said Oh *Daddy* . . .! And I said I *know*, I *know* – but trust me, it'll be better there. And it will, it will – it won't be *great* (because face it: what do you say to a daughter in pain?) but it will be a bit better because it isn't so enclosed and when I dry up completely there might at least be other noises. Plus I can get a *drink*, which I will probably (there is no probably about it) need.

Marianne's already here: of course she is. Christ – poor little kid: she had a night like mine, by the looks of her. I'm signalling Hi. She's held up her glass – that Cola stuff she drinks, looks like – so she's sorted, at least, in that department. Get myself a, um – *Scotch*, I think: bit fed up with Bourbon, now. Which looks like it's going to take a while. God Almighty – yesterday there was no one here serving at all, and today there's the two of them over there and all they seem to want to do is huddle up at the other end and bloody *natter*. I suppose in their eyes, it's all over. Docking tomorrow, and be damned with everyone. Oh look – miracles will never . . . Yes yes I *do* want a drink, yes, since you ask. Why I'm standing at the bar and bloody *staring* at you, point of fact. Christ – tell you . . .!

'At least,' said Sammy – watching the back of David, now, as he stumped away (he had swallowed half his drink the moment Jilly had set it before him) – 'I won't have to put up with all the rude old drunks, any more.' And then he turned his wet and vanquished eyes, heavy with hurt, full on to Jilly, who was – as always, now, it seemed to Sammy – just looking down and saying nothing. 'I am trying,' uttered Sammy, 'to find a silver lining. But there isn't one.'

'You'll get a job,' said Jilly, quietly. 'Back in England.'

'Maybe. Depends on the reference. Won't be *glowing*, will it?'

'You're a good barman . . .'

Sammy nodded to that. 'But not very good for anything else, it seems . . .'

'Oh *please*, Sammy – please. Not again. Not again. I just can't go through it all again. Can't.'

'Oh *please*, Jilly – please. Please change your mind and come back to me. Won't you? We could be back in England by tomorrow night . . .'

'Yeh and *then* what, Sammy? I go back to my *parents* and try to explain why I'm not on my way to bloody *Jamaica* and you don't have anywhere to live at *all* and . . . oh, it's just *hopeless*, Sammy. It's no *good*. You'd only keep chucking it all in my face – yes you *would*, Sammy, you would – I don't care what you say *now*, I just know that you would. And I'm not – I'm just not cut out for the sort of life you're after. Am I? And I've *said* all this. I've said and said and *said* it. If we were together any more we'd just never ever talk about anything *else*. Driving me mad . . .'

'So. Well. You'll be with *him*, won't you. In New York.'

Jilly hissed out her exasperation.

'I won't be – *with* him, no Sammy. I mean – he'll be there, yes, and I'll be there too. I've never been to New York, Sammy – and I want to *see* it, OK? Which is what I've been saying all *along*. God . . .'

'What I don't understand,' said Sammy – biting on his lip, and trying to be wise and strong about this – 'is that you – *you*, Jilly, are the one who has *done* this to us – '

'*Jesus* . . .!'

'No listen – it's *you*, Jilly – it is. You're the one who's *done* all this and all you do is *shout* at me. I've lost everything, here – and all you do is *shout* at me.'

'I'm not . . . shouting. Look, Sammy – hear me. For the ten thousandth time I'm *sorry*, OK? I can't undo things, and I can't be, oh – someone I'm just *not*. So please. Let's just get through this – last day . . . and *stop* all this.'

Jilly just walked away from the bar and out of there, then – leaving Sammy to tend his wounds and batten down the wildest of his flailing grievances: come to terms with so much astonishment.

'Good God,' muttered David, as Jilly swept past their table, leaving just the after-rush of her swishing behind her. 'She's in a bloody hurry to get out of here. Jesus – if you don't *like* working in a bar, why take the job in the first place?'

Which he had said quite uncaringly – only did it to fill in a gap – gap, yes: another of those. Because all that has happened so far at this little pow-wow is that Marianne very quietly asked him (and she's been crying, you know, my own little girl – look at those sad sweet eyes: she's been crying, yes) – asked whether Mummy had told him ...? And David had said Yes, she – mm, bare bones anyway, yes she did. And Marianne had nodded quite solemnly, and said Oh – if only he'd talked to me *more*: explained to me exactly just how wretched he was feeling ... And that was followed by a gap, David really needing another drink right now, but reluctant to leave the table after such a short while (which would betoken evasion? Might well do, might well do – but all it is is I need another *drink*). Then Marianne looked at David, and the eyes of both of them dissolved at once. David had to look away – and Marianne said to him or maybe not to him at all that she had grown really quite *fond* of Tom: really very ... *fond* ... and now I have to live with him being gone from me. And David nodded (gap) and could only think I hope, Marianne, I do so hope that this is the first and only time in your life that you are left alone: me – I've lost track completely. Will you, one day – leave *me* alone, Marianne? I suppose you will. I suppose you must do.

David was agitating his empty glass, now, really quite energetically – up and down the ridges his thumbnail was click-click-clicking. Glanced with venom *how* many times at the bloody idiot kid behind the bar, but Christ – looks like he's in a bloody *coma*, or something. Oh Christ – maybe I'll just go up and get myself a refill. Not doing any bloody good hanging around Marianne, am I? Haven't even said to her a single bloody word. So maybe I'll just – oh hey look, that's – it is, just walked in – it's *Dwight*! And the leap of hot pleasure and the balm of relief at just the sight of old Dwight was immediately and hissingly extinguished as he remembered, saw again, with appalling clarity that no, no no – Dwight wasn't, was he, any more a friend of his? They could not laugh and drink, not now. They would not work, side by side.

And now Dwight had seen him: his face went sour and his mouth turned down in open disgust. He turned and walked right out of there. And . . . do you know . . . even though I have my raw and wretched daughter right here before my eyes (cowed and cold, she looked now, Marianne) this has hurt me more, so much more than just any of all of it. He's not coming back, is he? No, thought David, he's not. He's not.

Too fuckin' *right* I ain't: asshole's lucky I didn't waste him. Tries to tell me he's *sorry*, the little shit. Oh yeh *sure* – I can see only too well how he's just all broke *up*. Jeez – he's done with screwing around with Suki (and Christ have I laid into *that* little prasty-toot) what he does is he goes on back to his *other* little sweet piece of ass. Mebby – just mebby, he been alone and looking real bad, I bleeve I just might've – hell, I dunno – *talked* with the guy . . . bought him a drink, mebby. But now: forget *it*. I'll just go and take it out some more on Suki. She been trying to tell me it weren't hardly nothing between them, just kinda necking and stuff – like what we used to call heavy *petting*? Oh *yeah*, I'm going – well that sure ain't the take I got outta the bastard *David*. Who I really *liked*, you know? And hell – I'm being honest, here – I guess my little Suki done screwed her way round campus, like, three entire circuits and back again – but what else stand can I be taking, here? My *daughter*, right? Yeh right. So David gets froze out: it's the way it's gotta be. And

Charlene – Charlene I ain't even told the half of it, you know? Which is why, maybe, she's shooting at me You just leave Suki *alone*, you hear me Dwight? It's the *David* bastard's fault, your shit buddy: she ain't nothing but a baby. And Earl, he's going Yeah, cool it, Dad – just back off, kay? And I'm going What hell *you* know bout anything at all in this whole goddam world, Earl? And why hell you got yourself a *feather* sticking outta your ear, boy? You fixing to *fly* someplace? I guess, put in Suki – who needed all the friends she could get, right? – it kinda musta gotten stuck on all this kinky new *hair* gel he's taken to using? And hey – don't ask – Earl just claws out the gummy feather, closes tight his eyes and says Yeh sure: *right*.

'Shut hell up *alla* youse!' Charlene is now yelling. 'What typa vacation this turning into? Huh? Now let's just chill out, here. Dwight – getchaself over to Julie and Benny's, hear me? She can't raise up Benny offa the can and he says he don't want no stoords on accounta it's private business. That's Benny. Go figure.'

Dwight just wagged his head – and slowly across his face a smile seeped in from somewhere.

'Hey, people – we all good'n ready to get back home?'

'Sure am,' said Suki. 'And Dad? *Sorry* – kay?'

'You bet,' sighed Earl, and he was nodding quite briskly.

And Charlene too – she was nodding, and maybe turning it over.

'Yeah – yeah I guess . . . like maybe it's enough already?'

And Dwight just suddenly thought of David.

'Amen,' he said, so quietly.

⚓

Aggie and Stacy just stood there, now – Aggie so grey and exhausted following the ragged expiry of her first night within living memory without Nobby by her side: as she had groaned in her creaking cabin, knocked this way and that – and not just by the toss of the sea – she had attempted to cope with her amazement at knowing that he, her Nobby, was being *held* somewhere – and by *Stewart*, of all people in the world. And he hadn't got his pills, you know – that alone was worrying enough: but could he be *eating* properly? That was just one of the points on which she craved really any sort of reassurance from this frustratingly calm and methodical Captain seated before her. What, she had repeatedly pleaded, was actually being *done* at all? But before the Captain could answer (or at least deflect the worst of the thrust) a jabber-lipped Stacy – hardly less frantic – had broken in with the first anxiety to force its way up through all the others and break and splatter to the surface.

'And how in God's name did he get that, oh my God – *gun*? I mean – *how*, for Christ's sake? How is that *possible*?'

Aggie quailed: she had tried not to think of the gun. Tried and failed. The very *word*, it made her tremble.

'It is not, I can assure you of *this*,' responded the Captain (thank Christ – sure ground here, at least), 'one of ours. We have very few firearms aboard and all are registered, locked away and very closely monitored. None has been signed for by authorized personnel and none, repeat none, is missing. I can only assume if there *is* a gun – '

'What do you – ?! What are you – ?!' Stacy was near apoplectic, now, and cursing her lips for just not pulling themselves together and helping her *out*, here. 'Are you suggesting we both *imagined* it? How on earth else do you – '

'I am not suggesting anything. I merely – '

'*Listen*. How do you think he's keeping my Mum in that bloody room? Force of *personality*? *Card* tricks? Look – I'm telling you. I know my Mum. If there was no gun, Christ – she would've killed him with her two bare hands, by now.'

'Or,' put in Aggie, 'Nobby would have overcome him and tied him up.'

'Look, ladies . . .' sighed the Captain. 'I understand your distress. All I can repeat is – '

And suddenly Aggie was sobbing unnaturally – and she nearly screamed at the Captain:

'Because he *is*, you know – he's very good at *knots* . . .!'

Stacy put her arm around her – she felt so frail, and her bones were leaping.

'It's OK, Aggie – it'll be OK. They'll be safe. Promise.'

'I'm sure this is true,' said the Captain. 'The New York police have been alerted, as I said. If this situation is not resolved, they will board the moment we dock. I have insisted there will be no violence. At the very latest you will all be reunited by tomorrow, soon after dawn. Look . . . it's a terrible thing that's happened, but there's really nothing more we can do. We were hoping that food, or something, would be requested, whereupon my men could have rushed him, but . . . well, no call has been received.'

And the Captain very much regretted saying just any small part of all that. The silence was sobering, as people retired to within themselves and thought their thoughts. Stacy was feeling across her shoulder the spreading warmth of Aggie's seeping tears, as she clung to her so tightly. Is my Mum being hurt? Is she? Because he looked mad, that bastard, you know. If only there was just some small form of communication . . . if only she could know just what in God's name was going on in that bloody little *room* . . .

⚓

'Does anyone,' asked Stewart, quite mildly, 'want this last cream cracker, at all? Or there's still some Quality Street there, pretty sure. Maybe only the hard ones, now.'

'Oh God *Almighty*, Stewart!' bellowed Jennifer. 'I'm absolutely *starving*. Can't you for Christ's sake at least get us something decent to *eat*?'

'No . . .' said Nobby, quite thoughtfully. 'He really

couldn't do that, Jennifer, if you stop and think about it for a minute. You see – '

'Oh my *God* . . .!' wailed out Jennifer. 'This has to be all my bloody worst nightmares come together to drive me *crazy*! We're stuck in this airless bloody storeroom with our smile-a-minute Assistant Cruise Director waving around a, Jesus – bloody *gun* – and then I've got *you*, Nobby, haven't I? Haven't I? Hm? How *many*, Nobby – can you recall? I mean, we've been in here how long, now? Sixteen hours? Eighteen hours? Something like that?'

'Nineteen hours and forty-six minutes,' replied Nobby promptly, and with a fair degree of delight. 'If we're counting. But I fail to *see*, dear Jennifer – '

'Shut up! Shut up! Hear me? I am *not* your dear Jennifer, you see Nobby – I can't be, can I? Because I hate you. I've always hated you. I hated you from the very first moment I ever set *eyes* on you, bloody Nobby. And see if you can answer me: how many *terms* have you come up with now, Nobby? Hm? How many nautical bloody *terms* – ?!'

'Well,' mused Stewart, 'if nobody wants the last cracker, I think I might have it myself.'

'But Jennifer,' protested Nobby, 'we've got to talk about *something*, haven't we? Keep our spirits up. Like being down a bomb shelter, many ways.'

'I'd prefer the bloody *bomb*. Jeeeesus! *Look*, Stewart – enough is enough, OK? Why are you *doing* this? I mean you've had your bit of *fun*, yes? Now God's sake just open the door and let's get out of here, hm? Yes? *Pleeeease*?'

Stewart unstuck a cracker crumb from the corner of his lower lip, and shook his head.

'Can't be done, I'm afraid. And Nobby's quite right about the food, you know. If I opened the door, they rush me. Open a porthole, they might use gas. No . . . stuck here, I'm afraid. But to answer your question – I don't *know*, Jennifer, why I'm doing this. I don't even remember how it all came into being . . .'

And at that point, Stewart looked glummer than anyone.

'Got us over a barrel . . .' said Nobby, quite idly.

Jennifer eyed him sharply.

'*Don't*!' she warned. 'Even if it is one – just *don't*!'

'But it's very interesting, this one, Jennifer. In the old Royal Navy – '

Jennifer had rammed her palms over her ears and was drumming a tight tattoo with the heels of her feet, not at all in time with the frenzied and nasal succession of discords that now were warbling out from her lips.

'Not listening! Can't hear you! Not listening! Doo-bee-doo-bee-doo-bee-*doo* . . .!'

'Why don't you,' suggested Stewart, quite kindly, 'lie down for a while, maybe?'

And Jennifer heard *that* all right, over the tail end of this throwaway and impromptu bout of busking.

'Oh yes very *funny*, Stewart! Lie down! What – like we all did last night, do you mean? All snug and cosy? There's no bloody room to stand *up* in here, is there Stewart? Never mind lie *down*. Hm? Last night I was slumped against a cut-out of Clint bloody *Eastwood* with a packet of balloons for a pillow. Every pitch of the ship, my head bashed into that *mirror* ball, there. Nobby was on the *ironing* board – '

'Wasn't great,' muttered Nobby. 'But it's like a bicycle – you learn to adapt . . .'

' – and *you*, Stewart, where were you? Remember? Yes, that's right – you were sitting on the lavatory in that horrible bit at the back – all bloody *night*, weren't you? And who had to hear it? Who had to bloody *smell* it?'

'Yes, I – um: sorry about that. I think it was the Boeuf Stroganoff . . .'

'Well you're bloody *lucky*, aren't you? I didn't have time for any dinner because I was bloody *kidnapped*, you see . . .!'

Jennifer blinked once and just looked at the man. Her voice became softer (oh God look – I've done my best with shrill, so let's just see where softer gets us):

'Stewart. Listen to me. Listen – yes? Why are you going *on* with this? Hm? Tomorrow morning we're in New York – right? What can you gain? You've *got* to let us out tomorrow, haven't you? So why not just put down the gun and do it now? Hm? What's . . . what's wrong, Stewart? Do you not feel well?'

Stewart was screwing up his eyes and touching one temple.

'I . . . suddenly . . . feel a bit . . . be OK: get this, sometimes.'

'I've got some Rennies,' volunteered Nobby.

'No – it's my . . . oh God, I don't know what it is. Could be a brain tumour.'

'Ah *no* . . .' came back Nobby, brightly. 'You don't want to worry about *that*. Very fashionable, isn't it nowadays? Worrying about all that sort of thing at the slightest twinge. Friend of mine, not long ago – we share a half at the Legion, most Wednesdays – *he* said that to me: convinced, he was, he had a brain tumour.'

Stewart was nodding with care, maybe needing more.

'Yes . . .?' he ventured. 'And . . .?'

'Well *telling* you,' insisted Nobby. 'Nothing to worry about at all. Turned out it was all in his head, see?'

Jennifer's eyes turned up to the ceiling.

'Any straitjackets among your boxes of tricks, Stewart? That gun of yours – it is *loaded*, I presume? Why don't you just shoot me? Hm? It would be *kind*. Kinder still – shoot fucking *Nobby*, let me go and then as soon as we're in America you can sling your hook. How's that sound?'

'Ah!' interjected Nobby, with energy. 'Now that's a good one – 'sling your hook'. This goes back to the days of *hammocks*, when – '

'*Stewart!*' screamed Jennifer. 'Please have mercy on my *soul*. Give me the gun – *I'll* kill him – I'll do it *now* . . .!'

But Stewart didn't seem to be listening. He peered with not much curiosity through the misty porthole.

369

'Sea's fairly calm again,' he said without expression. 'Be dark quite soon.'

⚓

Nobby had, in his stockinged feet, softly padded the very few paces it took to get to her. He was about to apply the very lightest pressure to her shoulder, and hope to rouse her – but he was momentarily arrested by the pale-lit vision of the soft plains and hills of her upturned face – the darker valleys – touched as they were by moonlight. He had never before seen her in repose; usually, I find with this woman, she seems to be constantly snarling. Pity she hates me. I think she's lovely. Sorry, Aggie, but I do. Shame to disturb, but I really am wanting a quick word – and Stewart, he was ages nodding off (and lying on a palette in front of the doorway, there – that gun across his stomach – who can really blame him?).

There were brief and uncertain flickerings about Jennifer's nose and eyelids, as Nobby with reluctance continued to stir her – and then more discernible signs of a growing realization, and the sick despair that came with that. Nobby's face just hung before her. She moaned and closed tight her eyes and opened them again of a sudden, but no, no no – it was no good at all: Nobby's face just hung before her.

'I just wanted to *say*,' he launched in quite hurriedly, and whispering darkly (if I pause for breath, she'll only abuse me), 'that when I said to you that time I *liked* it, yes? When I said –'

'Oh Nobby . . .' sighed Jennifer, 'why is it you just can't *die*? Hm? Christ my back is – ah! – bloody killing me . . .'

'No listen – hear me out. When I said I liked your *jacket*, yes? You must recall. I didn't so much mean I *liked* it – although I am sure it is in itself a very fine *garment* –'

'Oh God oh God oh God oh *God* . . .'

' – but what I really hoped to convey – didn't, obviously – is that I *recognized* it, yes? Because I saw you, you see. On the video. That night. Late that night when you and someone went right up to the bows.'

'Oh,' said Jennifer. 'That. *Video*? What video?'

'Doesn't really matter. Suffice it to say that I would have given *anything* to have been that man . . . the man who was with you. You are a very handsome woman, Jennifer, and – no no, please, please just let me finish – and I have never ever been to the bows of this wonderful ship – not once, ever. Always wanted to – asked to do it, oh – so many times, but no. Stewart would tell you that, if he was awake. It's my great ambition. But they always said no.'

Jennifer shrugged. 'Should've just gone. Like I did. What's the bloody time? Oh God my *legs* . . . I can't move. I'm so *starving* . . . and don't bloody call me 'handsome'.'

And both Jennifer and Nobby started quite badly when a new voice, now, cut through the just-grey light, and into the hush.

'Well *this* time, Nobby,' said Stewart with care, 'the answer is *yes*. As soon as I'm sure it's safe, I'll show you both the quickest way down. I am all,' he concluded, 'in favour of ambition.'

'*Me*?' piped up Jennifer, scrambling to her feet – rubbing at some bits of her, twisting back into shape one or two more. '*I* don't want to go. Bloody freezing up there, telling you. But listen – does that mean you're finally letting us *out*, then? Seen sense? Yes, Stewart? The game's now over, is it? Oh God I'm so bloody *hungry* . . .'

Nobby was checking his watch. 'About two hours now, my reckoning. And then we should be docking. Always a golden moment.'

'No you *must* go, Jennifer,' said Stewart, with gentle insistence. 'I have to know where you both *are*, you see. There are two more caramels left, if you're interested . . .'

Jennifer was just about coping with the nearly half-light.

She glanced at the now quite girlishly excited Nobby, and then quickly over to the near-maniacal Stewart ... and whatever form her latest howl of protest might have taken, she simply let it die. No point, was there? It was time, now, to humour the loonies.

⚓

Captain Scar was uneasy, if you want him to be honest. It wasn't simply the presence of civilians on the Bridge – no no, this sort of time there were always those (VIPs and so on). No, what is quite frankly, I think, putting the fear of God into me – and no matter that we've all been through this a thousand times before, docking a ship of this size is anyway constantly just that little bit anxious – no, what is rather getting to me is the nature of the *mix* of this par-ticular straggling band of gawpers and hopefuls. It's still dark – just about five a.m. – and out on the uncovered wings, still bloody cold. So far all was well: little knots of disparate people all with scarves and macs and so forth wrapped about them (the first-timers already wide-eyed and excitedly fingering their tiny silver cameras). A volun-tary more or less silence prevailed – not much of anything for anyone to do, and absolutely zero in terms of visibility; except for that clutch of Japanese men, way over to star-board. All chattering at the same time and laughing their bloody heads off, for some damn reason or another: been doing it non-stop from the moment they arrived. Something high up in Sony or one of those, I think they are, Alan was telling me: I try not to get involved, all that side of things. Leaves me cold.

To be perfectly blunt about it, it's these bloody *journalists* who are worrying all sorts of hell out of me. What's-her-name's family is up here, of course – what was she called? Nicole (yes – I haven't forgotten). Well – I couldn't change my *mind*, could I? Not simply because it did, in fact, oh God

– turn out that that friend of her daughter's really bloody
has done a jumper. Oh Christ. So far we've kept an airtight
lid on that one – so let's just pray it stays that way. And then
there's . . . oh Christ – and this one is really my fault, you
know. Maybe I shouldn't have gone along with this one at
all, but God – they were so damn shrill and insistent, those
two . . . what're they called? *Stacy*, yes – whose mother is,
well – you know . . . and Nobby's wife, Aggie. Still not a
whistle out of our little locked-room mystery. Cut off the
phone now, it appears (and where in Christ's name did that
bastard get a *gun*?). Anyway – they were going on and on
about the police, when we docked. NYPD, yes? And how
they didn't want them just charging on board with their
bombs and machine guns like they did in the films. Well –
you can imagine: I felt sick at the very *thought*. What – they
think I *do* want that? End of my career, I'm telling you, if
there's anything of that nature. So . . . I tried to reassure the
both of them, didn't I? *Honestly*, I begged them, you really
must *believe* me. I have received confirmation that two strike
vehicles will be positioned precisely on the quay awaiting
our approach. They have strict instructions to report to me
personally up on the Bridge the minute they board – only
then will some plan of action be agreed upon and
implemented. Well – walked right into it, I suppose. Stacy
seemed to be the official spokesperson, now (and poor old
Aggie, poor old thing – she's practically gone to pieces over
all of this, you know . . . and let's be frank: who can bloody
blame her?). Anyway, this Stacy person was going on and
on about Well if that's really the *case*, then we want to see
them – we want to be with you when they actually arrive.
And all my I Do Assure Yous just weren't going to make it,
were they? In the face of this. So *yes*, I said: fine, OK – if
that's the way you want it: fine. Yes. So. They're here too.
Not actually in anyone's *way*, thank God – but here all the
bloody same. Yes. Anyway. The fine upstanding members
of Her Majesty's Freeloaders are over on the port wing,

passing around a hip flask, looks like: wouldn't mind a couple of swigs out of it myself. So. Play it by ear, shall we? Nothing else I can really do. Get myself back inside now, I think. Be a sailor again.

'So, Alan. Everything all right?'

'Steady as she goes, sir. Glimpse of dawn through the glasses.'

'Uh-huh. Tugs in place?'

'All in place, sir. And, um – police also confirmed, sir.'

'Good,' said Captain Scar. Oh yes, he thought: *great*.

'Get you something, sir? Cup of something?'

The Captain was quite seriously mulling this over (I've got a sudden yen – isn't it unbelievable? – for some bloody pea *soup*, of all things on earth) but Alan was forced to break abruptly into his thoughts, now, as he held the binoculars steady and said quite urgently out of the side of his mouth:

'Sir? Sir – I think I just saw something.'

'Saw? Saw something? How do you mean, Alan? Well? *What* . . .?'

'Sorry, sir . . . gone, whatever it was. Can't see a thing, now. Sorry, sir. Shadows, maybe.'

'*Christ*, Alan. This is all quite tense enough without you bloody *seeing* things. I mean – *God*.'

Alan was abashed: not often the Old Man got like this. Things on his mind.

'Sorry, sir,' he said, hushed and truly contrite.

But the Captain had waved away all of that, and wandered out now to the port wing (say something nice to someone, I suppose I'd better had). But oh. Oh: what's this now? It's Nicole, that's what it is.

'Oh do *listen*, David – this young man's from *The Times*. How terribly exciting. Well yes we *have*, since you ask – had a perfectly *lovely* crossing, haven't we, David? Rollo?'

They both of them shifted a bit, and shuffled around. Rollo managed a *Yeh*; David (Christ my head is splitting)

374

just peered away into the mist that was around him, and wrapping him up.

And the Captain was moving quite quickly, now, because this little shit from *The Times* had rapidly turned his attention towards, oh Christ – what's her bloody name? Daughter of the other one: *Nicole*, blast it . . .

'And you?' the reporter wanted to know. 'Pleasant trip? No complaints?'

'No,' said Marianne, quite flatly.

'No . . . what?' checked the *Times* man. 'No it *wasn't* pleasant? Or no you haven't got any, um – complaints?'

'*Well*, ladies and gentlemen!' boomed the Captain, at his most cocktail party affable – rubbing together his hands as if a feast was in store. 'Everything all right? Any moment now, I think, and we'll get a bit of light. Everyone got their cameras ready? Some unbelievable views. Promise you.'

'What I meant was,' said Marianne, simply, 'no I didn't *like* it at all because my friend committed *suicide* by, oh – jumping off the *ship* . . .!'

And as yet more hot tears were somehow wrung from her, Nicole was already clucking, and rushing to enfold her. And all Captain Scar could do was groan so softly as his stomach hit the deck – watching quite helplessly as all the journalists suddenly were clustered and eager to every side of Marianne (rather like, he just about thought, flies to a cowpat). It was then that he was aware of his sleeve being plucked – and just that one thing, now, was driving him mad.

'Oh what *is* it?' he hissed, as he turned to find out. 'Oh it's *you*, Alan . . .'

Alan was not much more than whispering.

'Needed on Bridge, sir. Immediately.'

And the Captain didn't even have time, now, to wish he was dead; he hustled away in the wake of Alan, smiling like an idiot into any face he met along the way.

Back in the hushed and comforting sanctity of the Bridge,

all seemed blissfully ordered. Capped and blazered officers all at their posts, their faces only barely lit by glowing green and amber lights, winking out from the dials and screens. But before Captain Scar could ask someone here if they wouldn't mind telling him what in hell is going *on*, Alan had passed over to him the binoculars and was energetically pointing through the still opaque windshield down to the deck below, and onwards towards the bows. The Captain snatched up the glasses, and peered. Soon he was lowering them again – and he found himself uttering in total disbelief:

'What in God's name . . .?'

'See to it, will we sir?'

And the Captain snapped out of it.

'Absolutely. Right *now*, Alan, Christ's sake. Before anyone else – '

But it was too late, clearly, for any of that. Suddenly this Stacy was right by his side: she let out one yelp, and flew right out of there.

⚓

'You'd better be quick,' Stewart was urging, 'if you're still really up for this, Nobby. Light's getting up. Bound to spot us soon.'

Nobby didn't answer. His heart and throat were stopped up with excitement as he carefully and with grim-set determination groped his way forward amid all this dark, uncharted space. Jennifer had more than once now tried on with Stewart all sorts of variations of stuff on the lines of *Look*, you guys – I'll just wait around for you here, OK? Or – Tell you *what*: you two go on and I'll keep a look-out, yes? But he wasn't having any of it. Kept on jabbing the barrel of his gun into the small of her back and pressing her onward. And tell you – if Jennifer was actually destined to get out of all this more or less in one piece (because OK, Stewart was

acting a *bit* more sanely now, yes OK, but what does it take
to make one twitching nutter jerk back on a trigger?) – well
if she came out a survivor, then she was quite decided that
the first thing she would do was bust his jaw, just for starters. Oh Christ – what am I *doing* here? Oh God I'm so
cold . . . can't even remember if I'm hungry any more.
Getting faintly lighter now, at least. That's something.
Surely they'll see us, won't they? Soon? God I bloody hope
so. But maybe they won't – because people often only see
what they *expect* to, don't they? They're all intent on looking
out for the first signs of New York, or whatever it is they do.
Not combing the decks for a frozen woman and a luminous
crazy with a gun in his hand – not to say the fucking little
gibbering idiot that is *Nobby*.

Now that they were practically there (he could just make
out the very apex of the bows) Stewart was really loving all
this. He was with Nobby on this one – never ventured this
far forward: never even remotely occurred to him to do so.
But what was so terribly liberating about, oh – just *all* of
this, really, was the fact that the three of them were here on
his, Stewart's, say-so. Yes indeed – Stewart, your Assistant
Cruise Director, is calling the shots for the first bloody time
in his entire life on earth: this – understand it – is my *design*.
(But for how much longer will they let it stand?)

'Quick, Nobby – be quick. Do what you have to do!'

And Nobby knew exactly what: how many times in his
hot and untamed imagination had he magicked into being
this breathtaking scene? He bundled Jennifer forward –
didn't even hear her yelling at him to take his fucking little
greasy hands *off* her – and then he lifted out her arms. And
here she was! The spreadeagled and awesome figurehead at
the bows of Sylvie, his wonderful ship! And Nobby was
aware of a clattering, now – a still distant but worryingly
insistent drumbeat, rapidly closing in, and intent on closing
him down. He feverishly gripped hold of Jennifer around
the waist and pressed himself against her – she could hear

his panting, and now – much to her unspeakably profound disgust – she could feel him bucking himself into her – ah ah ah! – like a slack-tongued dog on heat. Almost immediately they were surrounded by sounds – rough, strong hands were pulling harshly at Nobby and Jennifer squirmed around and away from him and with a rush of amazement fell right into the arms of, oh God – *Stacy*, my baby, my angel, oh *sweetheart*!

'Are you OK, Mum?' Stacy was gasping – tears were dashing all over her face.

Jennifer just nodded and held her as she dumbly gazed upon the extraordinary things taking place all around her. The light had suddenly come up and swept over them – the sailors glowed incandescent in the gleam of a broad and horizontal searing orange band that was striping the vast and steely sky, just touched now by blue. Three of the men were circling with caution a moon-faced Stewart, his wide and frightened eyes as well as his gun darting to each of them in turn, and away again. Jennifer and Stacy just clung to one another, unable or unwilling to move.

'Come on, mate!' shouted out one of the sailors. 'Put the bloody gun down, you arse. You're not going to *escape*, are you? Hey?'

Jennifer saw, almost dazedly, a sudden and massive splattering of tiny glittering lights to the right and left of her: a huge and slender skyline was silently emerging from where before had been only so much empty distance. She looked at Stewart, and saw there only tiredness and resignation.

'My *name* . . .' he sighed out, so yieldingly, 'is Stewart. I'm not your 'mate'. I'm *Stewart* . . .'

And then – as if all his bones had suddenly walked out on him – he crumpled down to the deck. Just before the sailors were wading in to pinion him down, he looked up once and howled like a stricken creature – this so startling as to jerk the breath out of everyone. He pointed the gun towards the sky, and let it have it: (it's only a low-voltage thing – mild

S.O.S. – but it makes everyone really jump when it goes off – and then this rather pretty cascade of gold sort of stars and circles fizzes right up and then floats down slowly, just like a lit-up fountain: star turn – always do this at the end). For an instant, everyone on deck was transformed into an excited huddle of open-mouthed children, awed and bedazzled before a sparkling bonfire. The three men moved in fast, and then they had him.

'*Doc!*' bawled out a voice from somewhere close to Jennifer. She turned abruptly and gasped when she saw Aggie and a ship's officer crouched over Nobby, who was just lying there. 'Get the Doc – *pronto!*'

Jennifer could only be astonished as the vast great hulk of the ship was gently gliding beneath the quite colossal arch of a suspension bridge – the lights of cars were zipping like fireflies: she could almost smell the hum of the city. Another man, now, was running towards them fast – skidded to a clumsy halt, and now was kneeling over Nobby. He carelessly brushed aside Aggie's rigid and imploring hands, and urgently pressed his fingers into Nobby's wrist. Then he started pumping down hard on his birdlike chest – pausing to listen – pumping down again. He pinched closed Nobby's two cold nostrils – blew with force into his gaping mouth. Once more the man thumped hard Nobby's uncomplaining chest – listened intently – thumped him yet again. And then he relapsed into stillness and silence: his face looked old and weary in the stark and bright morning light. He bowed his head briefly, glanced to his side at a stricken Aggie, and softly he muttered to her that he was sorry, very sorry: I'm afraid it's all over.

⚓

'I don't think,' sighed out Jennifer – grinning broadly and hugely replete – 'that I've ever in my life eaten so much breakfast. Three eggs – '

'Four!' laughed Stacy.

'Was it four? OK, then – *four* eggs, bacon, sausages, toast – '

'Tomatoes. Mushrooms – '

'Yeh – didn't really too much *go* for the mushrooms, actually. Bit bitter.'

'Why did you eat them, then?'

'Oh God because they were *there*. I'm telling you, Stacy – I've just never *been* so hungry. Nearly drove me crazy. Christ – nearly two bloody days on crackers and fucking Quality Street leftovers . . .'

'And no booze.'

'Well *exactly*. No bloody booze at *all* – not even so much as a *drop*. God – it tells you everything you really never wanted to know about the silly little man, doesn't it? Hm? I mean – not even a bottle of Scotch in the bottom drawer, or anything. I looked – believe me, I looked. It was just full of things like, oh – *hairspray* and, Christ – *bronzing* gel! Do you think he's mad? Do you? It wouldn't surprise me. I mean *Jesus*, Stacy – what sort of a person wants to spend his whole life on some big boat organizing all these crappy shows and parties?'

'He cried. Did you see? When he saw Nobby like that, he just burst into tears. What do you think will happen to him?'

'Don't much *mind*, do I? I just wish they hadn't carted him off so bloody quickly, that's all. I was well up for busting his jaw.'

'I would've done it for you. Oh yes – didn't tell you: I fixed that horrible American kid for you, you know. Earl.'

'Fixed him? What do you mean you *fixed* him, Stacy?'

Stacy smiled, shrugging it away.

'Oh, you know – usual. Dumped a load of syrup all over him and covered him in feathers. Don't remember quite what made me think of it. He didn't *like* it, I have to say . . .'

'Oh God I so much wish you *had*, Stacy! You're quite right – he was horrible. Very.'

'But I *did*. Mum – I mean it. I really did. I just got so bloody *annoyed*. Hurting you like that . . .'

'What, you – ? You mean you – ?'

'Yup. Tate & Lyle's Golden Syrup. About a ton of it. And a pillow's worth of feathers. I would've taken a photo to show you, but I thought from the noises he was making it was maybe time to go.'

Jennifer's eyes were glittering, as she beheld this daughter of hers.

'You really *are*, aren't you?'

'What,' laughed Stacy. 'Really am what? Quite something? Dark horse? Nutcase? What?'

Jennifer smiled and shook her head.

'My *daughter*,' she said. And then they both laughed.

'Love you, Mum . . .' said Stacy, softly. And Jennifer had to look away.

'I can't quite believe we've done these things . . .' she said.

Stacy sniffed, and seemed to agree. 'It's this ship.'

Jennifer nodded, fairly idly. 'Gorgeous day . . .'

'Summer in New York City! It's really warm now, isn't it? I can't wait to get there. They say about an hour, now. Luggage comes off first, apparently. Makes sense. Anyway – looks like it's going to be all hot and sunny and things for Auntie Min's oh-so-special day, doesn't it?'

Jennifer nodded. 'I do so care for Min, the silly bitch. Do you think *you'll* ever get hitched, Stacy? Please say not.'

'Oh not *again*, Mum! I just don't *know*, do I? Shouldn't think so. Who would have me?'

'Plenty. You're my *daughter*, aren't you?'

'Exactly. That's the bloody trouble.'

'But you can still you know – have *children*, and everything . . . I mean *I* did, didn't I? Have you.'

'Do you ever think about him?'

'Who? Your father? What's to think about? Hardly knew

him – as I've told you. Wish I had more to say. He just . . . came and went, really. I *might* have pursued him – I might have done. But as you know I was married at the time, and . . .'

Stacy smiled her smile (it's OK, Mum: I'm totally cool with it).

'Listen,' she said. 'I promised I'd go up and see poor old Aggie before we, you know – get off, and everything.'

Jennifer gazed at the distance. 'Couldn't believe it,' she said quite gently, 'when he just *died*, like that. Felt so weird.'

'I've never seen anyone dead before. Really creepy. Poor Aggie. He was just everything to her, you know. Her whole life.'

'I know. I don't for a second *understand* it . . . but yes. I know. He was. Well – OK, then, let's go up and see her.'

'Oh – *you* don't have to come, Mum.'

'I don't mind. Feel I should, in some ghastly sort of way. Can't explain.'

They found her sitting in the Captain's cabin, as Stacy had been told she'd be – silent, and apparently composed.

'Ah *greetings* to you both,' said Captain Scar, as Jennifer and Stacy were ushered in to the room. 'Yes well look – I'll leave you all to, um . . . look, Mrs erm – *Aggie*, who's here to *see* you. Yes? Well I'll just . . . if you'll excuse me. One or two things to . . .'

Yes, he thought, with a fair deal of bitterness, as he made his escape and left them all to it. One or two things to *see* to, haven't I? Oh yes. Very much so. And not just the *usual* end-of-crossing paraphernalia, oh dear me no. I've got to write a report for the New York Police Department, haven't I? Yes I have. Oh yes – and also, I have to prepare a statement for the, Christ – *Press*. About the, as one of them put it to me, three-on-the-floor sex romps in the Emperor Suite, yes. And the suicide. And of course the *kidnapping* – yes let's not forget that too. Not to mention the subsequent and very public *death*. And somehow the bastards have got hold of all the *other* ones – the thirteen who died before (that'll be that fucking vicar again, shooting his mouth off: I've told and told him . . .). Yes but look you *get* that, I tried with them. Upwards of sixteen hundred passengers, after all: people *die*, yes? This is known. Not at that rate, they don't, said the *Times* sod. Yes but *Christ*, I was going: the youngest of them was seventy-nine – it's like a floating old folks' home, this ship. And then one of the bitches comes in with Ah – no *births*, though, And I said No, you can't have births because there's a *policy* about heavily pregnant women. We don't let them on board. See? Yes? Nah – they all just *looked* at me.

Anyway – think that's all. Sums it up, pretty sure. Mm. Excellent. Quite perfect. *Right*, then – let's face the music (though I'm not, as you know, very much of a dancing man: no Fred Astaire, I have to say). And me? The future? Well – once this little lot hits the breakfast tables of every living soul in the whole bloody universe, I really wouldn't care to hazard a *guess*, would you? Suffice it to say, it isn't looking rosy.

⚓

'Oh *God*, Aggie . . .' Stacy had managed to say. 'What can I *say* . . .?'

Aggie shook her head, very slowly – and then, to Stacy's immense surprise, she began to talk very fast and with great animation – a flurry of urgency, as if at any given moment, she could well be gagged forever.

'It was maybe meant. Heart, you know. Didn't have his pills. Anyway. He died in the place he most loved, after all. Everyone's been, oh – terribly *kind* – they have arranged for an undertaker in New York to, um – *see* to him. Cremation. And then they say I can take another, one more . . . one last voyage and let him go. Release him. Set him free. Send him down to Davy Jones's Locker. To be at peace. That's the final resting place for people who die at sea, you know. If you're

a sailor, or something, and you die on *land*, of course –
well then you go to Fiddler's *Green*, which sounds a *terribly*
naughty place: all rum and tobacco and dubious ladies.
Some people think, you know, that Davy Jones was a
Welshman, but there is another school of thought altogether
that has the name down as a corruption of Duffy Jonah –
duffy, you see, being the, um – *negro*, I'm pretty sure, word
for *ghost*, yes – and Jonah, of course . . . well, I expect you
know – that extraordinarily unfortunate person in the Bible.
Yes.'

And then she stopped dead and looked back down. All
her fingers were engaged in a terrible brawl, wholly beyond
her powers of intervention. Her lips, Stacy could see, were
trembling, now. Stacy glanced across to Jennifer, who raised
at her a single eyebrow: what can you do?

'Yes . . .' resumed Aggie, in so very small, now, and
tremulous a voice. 'Davy Jones's Locker . . .' She looked up
– and stared at both Jennifer and Stacy, each in turn: her
eyes were beseeching them both to *see*.

'It is a *nautical* term . . . you know . . .?'

And as Jennifer and Stacy solemnly nodded, Aggie suddenly did so too.

'Nobby was my guiding light. It's going to be so *odd*,' she
said, 'sailing on without him . . .'

⚓

Maybe just now would be quite a good moment, thought
Trish. Now that Nicole is busy checking again all their hand
luggage and fussing around those children of hers. David is
just a little apart – just so slightly distant and gazing,
thinking about . . . I've never really known what it is David
thinks about, actually.

'David,' she said.

David turned and nodded his agreement to that. Just like
he nodded when they presented him with his on-board

expense sheet: nineteen hundred dollars, odd. How is this possible? Nineteen hundred dollars. God Almighty – this free trip has cost me dear.

'So. Trish. New York, then. I hear you're, um – staying.'

'For now I am, yes. Do you mind? You don't *really* mind, do you, David? I think it's maybe best.'

David glanced away to the other end of the ballroom, or wherever it was they were all just standing and sitting around, waiting for the off. It all seemed somehow rather, I don't know – *stupid*, now. All these vast and carpeted spaces, with no discernible function.

'Maybe it is,' he said. 'Dwight will take good care of you, anyway. More than I ever could. Which isn't saying much.'

'I don't know what you must be thinking of me. I don't *like* him, or anything. You do know that, do you, David? But you see the *situation* . . .'

'Oh I do, I do. You'll get to like him, I daresay. He's very likeable, actually. Very.'

'He goes mad if I even so much as mention your *name*. Not *shouting*, or anything – he just goes all red and sort of simmers . . . Not because of *me*, is it?'

'Fraid not, Trish, no. It's not because of you.'

'Oh look – Nicole is coming over, now. Did you notice? I called her Nicole. I don't seem to *mind* that she's your bloody wife any more. Is that awful?'

'I don't know, Trish. I honestly just don't know.'

'Well look – very quickly: goodbye, David. I mean – I'm sure I don't mean goodbye for *ever*, or anything. Nothing's for keeps, is it?'

David sighed. 'No,' he said. 'Nothing.'

'*Well*, you two!' Nicole was hailing them. 'We're finally *here*. All *terribly* exciting. Do you feel all right now, Pat?'

'I feel fine. Totally fine. It seems impossible, now, how ill I was feeling.'

'Oh *God* . . .' deplored Nicole, quite suddenly – her attention distracted. 'Marianne! Where are you – ? Don't wander *off*, heaven's sake. They'll be calling us soon, won't they? Hm?'

'I won't be long,' said Marianne. 'It's so stuffy in here. I'm just going out on deck. Bit of air.'

'Well all *right* . . .' agreed Nicole, quite doubtfully. 'But don't let's for heaven's sake have to come and *find* you . . .'

'Two minutes,' smiled Marianne.

Yes, she thought: two minutes ought to do it. Just to look again at the deserted and sunlit wastes of this massive great hulk, and somehow come to terms with having lived here for a week. That, and other things.

She wandered past the big green baize-topped table. The jigsaw wasn't finished. I think, thought Marianne, that as soon as people realized there were all those pieces missing, their hearts just somehow were no longer there. She heaved open the great heavy door leading out on to the deck – sucked in her breath in readiness for the roaring blast of wind and cold, but there was none of that, now. The sun was warm – the white paintwork quite blinding. Where before there had been only the boundless sea, there now loomed the impossible pop-up immediacy of New York City – the tallest of the buildings seemingly mirrored and blazing with reflected sunlight. Marianne walked her usual route, to the very stern. A Union Jack now fluttered brightly from the jutting-out pole – there had been no flag before. How odd. And this is odd, too – no churned-up wake, no wave to set one's eye upon and watch with alarm as it fled to the horizon.

'Hello. Please don't be alarmed.'

Marianne hunched low to save her from the worst of this quite jarring collision with a human voice amid all this empty stillness. But even as she turned, real shock was alive now, and coursing through her like a charge. She simply stared.

'I don't . . .' she faltered, 'I can't . . .?'

'I hardly,' said Tom, very softly, 'can believe it myself.'

'Tom. Can I . . . touch you? Are you *real*?'

And then her eyes were blind with clogged-up tears, and she rushed at him and hugged his waist and his arms flew up and away from him in maybe just surprise – and then they slowly came in and down to rest on each of Marianne's shoulders.

'I'm so sorry . . .' he said. 'I really *did* mean to, you know. There was no question that I wouldn't. I just got so . . . scared. My intention, I think, was to realize what I already deep inside felt myself to be: cast adrift, you see? Had I not met you, I know I would have done it. In the end, I was scared . . . not of *dying*, no – just scared of losing even *more* . . .'

'Tom . . .' moaned Marianne, the whole of her in turmoil. And then she pulled back from him and dashed away from her face what hot tears she could. 'But why didn't you . . .? Where *were* you? They looked *everywhere*, and I – !'

'Here,' said Tom, simpering nearly like an imbecile, one finger pointing skyward.

Marianne thought she might go mad with confusion. She bit her lip and stamped her foot down.

'I don't . . . *understand* . . .!'

'The lifeboat. This one right above us. One hundred and thirty-nine persons – remember? Well, even just for me, it was far from being any sort of a *picnic*, I do assure you. The storm was the worst. Dying would have been preferable to that, but I simply couldn't move, by that time. I prayed – I prayed and I thought of you. I was so very *cold*, Marianne . . .'

'Oh . . . *Tom* . . .'

'My diet consisted mainly of my Mary's macaroons. The very last batch she made for me. As your intuition might have told you, I'm not really much of an eater. One more thing I should like you to know. Do you recall the woman? The woman I approached from behind? Who I said to you reminded me of someone? She didn't. Didn't remind me of anyone at all. I *touch* women in this way quite habitually. I am surprised you witnessed just the one encounter. It's the only way I know how to . . . bridge the distance.'

Marianne just stared at him, unblinkingly.

Tom sighed. 'At least, now, Mary is at peace . . .'

'And you, Tom? What about you?'

'Ah. Me. I am enriched by having known you, Marianne. Thank you. You saved my soul.'

'Tom . . . I can't tell you how I *feel*. I'm just so – . Where are you staying? Can I see you in New York? We have to *talk*.'

'Alas. Not staying. That was never the plan, obviously. No – I'll take the first flight back. This is my address in England. Maybe you might . . . like to write?'

'Oh Tom,' said Marianne. 'Oh *Tom* . . .'

⚓

'Oh *here* she is!' declared Nicole. 'It's all right, Rollo – she's here now. Oh God at last – where have you *been*, Marianne? Two *minutes*, you said – we've all been waiting around like *lemons*. Come on – we're going. Now is everyone sure they've *got* everything, yes?' I thought, you know, of saying something to *Anthony*, that dear Captain . . . but I couldn't think *what* and so I didn't, in the end. Probably best for all concerned. He anyway seems terribly preoccupied: not, I am sure, anything to do with me, alas. Anyway. 'Oh David *do* snap out of it, can't you? You're meant to be on *holiday*.'

'Mm? Oh yes. No no – I'm fine,' David assured her. 'Well, Marianne – all right? Not too bad?'

'All *right*. Daddy. I'm all *right*.'

And goodness, you know, she really did seem to mean it. Marvellous, isn't it, David was musing now: the way the young can just spring back, like that. Seemed suicidal, what – day ago? Maybe it's just that they don't really feel things as deeply as we do. Possible? Could be that. Couldn't really tell you.

A selected list of titles available from

Faber and Faber Ltd

In case of difficulty in purchasing any Faber title through normal channels, books can be purchased from:

Bookpost, PO Box 29, Douglas, Isle of Man, IM99 1BQ

Credit cards accepted. Please telephone 01624 836000, fax 01624 837033
Internet www.bookpost.co.uk or email bookshop@enterprise.net for details.

They were shuffling down the covered gangway – each of them handed back, now, their laminated ID cards (I won't at all, Nicole assured them, be sorry to see the back of *that* little horror) and now they emerged into what seemed to be a colossal and clatteringly active aircraft hangar, piled high with avenues of cases and trunks and crates, what was left of the floorspace swarming with busy busy people.

'We're *P*,' said Nicole. 'Red label, *P* – anyone see it?'

'Down the other end, pretty sure,' said Rollo – squinting in the direction.

'Would be,' grunted David. 'So, Rollo – looking forward?'

'Yes I *am*, actually, Dad. You remember Jilly?'

'Jilly? Oh yes – Jilly. Bargirl. Ah I see. Oh well good luck to you. Won't be seeing much of *you*, then, will we?'

Yes, my dear son – yes: bloody good luck to you. God how I envy you. God I do. There's that woman over there, look. Jennifer. Mm. Never did get to speak to her again. She suddenly vanished. But that's the sort of woman, you know, I should really be with – she'd be so good for me, Jennifer would: just my speed. If she could stand me. Oh Christ – who in hell am I kidding? Even if I had her, how long would it take? Hey? Before I somehow got round to finding a way to fuck it all up. God, my guts are *killing* me . . . that doctor of mine, he's in for a hell of a *probe*, isn't he? Which will, of course, cost me. Because these things *do*, you know (yes they do: these things, and others).

'Hey! Nicole! Over here, girl!'

'*Charlene!*' Nicole was shrieking. And they fell into each other's arms, David could not help but notice, quite as if (a) they had last encountered maybe forty-six years back, and (b) they actually *liked* one another, or something of that nature.

'We're waiting for a, like – *truck*? Twenny-four cases paddery, I got here. Dwight says to me, whadduryou? Opening up a *store*? Whaddurwe, he's going – Bergdorf

Goodman already? Hey – you'll never guess. What lil gal you reckon won the jackpot *sweep*?'

Nicole felt sick as she tried to look thrilled.

'*You* did? Oh how *marvellous*, Charlene!'

'Yup. A tad over two thousand bucks. Good, huh? Dwight says to me Great – howsabout maybe you hand it over? I told him to get outta here.'

Dwight was just standing there, David could not help but observe, in front of those two sulky kids of his (one of whom I briefly cherished). He has stiffened as my eye just momentarily alighted upon him. But he, Christ – just barely held the gaze, and very nearly nodded. I now must close my eyes and set to following Nicole in quest of our baggage. So long, Dwight. If I cherished anyone at all, it just had to be you. Bye, old buddy.

'David!' snapped Nicole. 'What's wrong? Why have you got your eyes closed? Very *strange*, all that – did you hear? Just the day before *yesterday*, Charlene couldn't wait to get us all over to their apartment – Park Avenue, I think she said. Somewhere. Anyway now it's all *off*, apparently, because none of them will be *there*, she says. Maybe going home to Vietnam. But don't you think all that's rather *strange*? A bit *off*? God – now we're on dry land, my legs have all gone to jelly . . . David? What's wrong? Why have you got your eyes closed? You're not *ill*, are you? Not on this day of *all* days?'

'No no,' he assured her. 'I'm fine. Really.'

No no, don't worry, I won't spoil it for you, Nicole – not on *this* day of all days. There is, after all, quite a lot more to come, isn't there, of this Trip of a Lifetime: I haven't forgotten. God, it's so very *warm*, you know. Another perfect summer's day on Terra Firma – and in the Land of the Free. But I'm still locked up . . . and I feel so all at sea . . .

I think I need a drink.